I0635491

HOMESICK

WHAT OTHERS SAY ABOUT DAVE PRATT AND *THE HOME TEAM* SERIES

Written from Dave's deep knowledge of tactical operations and martial arts, and with a Northwest flair mixed in, *The Home Team* grabs you from the start and surprises you at the end. As Dave's former pastor, it was thrilling to read a story of authentic faith lived out in gripping circumstances. A great read that is both tightly written and timely.

Rev. Brian Wiele

www.bluespigot.org

The Home Team is a wonderful story that weaves Dave Pratt's life experience as a Tae Kwan Do master, Christian, and retired army officer. It is a reminder that God's will, love, and guidance are everywhere. Dave brings together his military experience, lifelong journey in martial arts, and his commitment to God and blends it into an action-packed, compelling story of human nature, conflict, faith, and self-discovery. It has the power to touch the heart and to awaken consciousness. It is a story well-worth reading and contains a message we can all relate to.

Grand Master Richard Na

Master Na's Black Belt Academy

Dave Pratt is a master story teller making this well-crafted book fun to read and hard to put down. It grabs you from the beginning and holds you till the end. It is full of life, surprises, twists, and turns. He takes us along with the Home Team as they confront the very present scourge of human trafficking and smuggling. Dave's life experiences as a martial arts master and military officer brings an authenticity to the action scenes that put you right there in the middle with the team. Each move they make is written from personal experience and knowledge, which really brings it to life. Dave takes you to real places that you can see and feel. Dave's deep Christian faith is evident as he shows us how believers live their faith in this broken world in the midst of challenging circumstances. Can God really change lives in the real world? If He can, whose life will he change? *Home Team 2* is a fitting and fascinating sequel to the first book in the *Home Team* series. What a joy to be able to read a timely, well written, action book written from a Christian perspective. It is a fun book to read that everyone in the family can enjoy. It could also be a springboard to family discussion of serious questions.

Robert Samuelson
Retired Pastor and Dave's brother in Christ

HOMESICK

DAVE PRATT

Ambassador International
GREENVILLE, SOUTH CAROLINA & BELFAST, NORTHERN IRELAND

www.ambassador-international.com

HOMESICK

©2025 by Dave Pratt
All rights reserved

ISBN: 978-1-64960-601-3
eISBN: 978-1-64960-652-5

Cover Design by Hannah Linder Designs
Interior Typesetting by Dentelle Design
Edited by Valerie Coffman

Scripture quotations from THE HOLY BIBLE, NEW INTERNATIONAL VERSION®, NIV® Copyright © 1973, 1978, 1984, 2011 by Biblica, Inc.® Used by permission. All rights reserved worldwide.

No part of this publication may be reproduced, distributed, or transmitted in any form or by any means, including photocopying, recording, or other electronic or mechanical methods, without the prior written permission of the publisher, except in the case of brief quotations embodied in critical reviews and certain other noncommercial uses permitted by copyright law. For permission requests, contact the publisher using the information below.

This is a work of fiction. Names, characters, and incidents are all products of the author's imagination or are used for fictional purposes. Any resemblance to actual events or persons, living or dead, is entirely coincidental. Any mentioned brand names, places, and trademarks remain the property of their respective owners, bear no association with the author or the publisher, and are used for fictional purposes only.

AMBASSADOR INTERNATIONAL
Emerald House
411 University Ridge, Suite B14
Greenville, SC 29601
United States
www.ambassador-international.com

AMBASSADOR BOOKS
The Mount
2 Woodstock Link
Belfast, BT6 8DD
Northern Ireland, United Kingdom
www.ambassadormedia.co.uk

The colophon is a trademark of Ambassador, a Christian publishing company.

For Sam Swan,

who advised a troubled teen to try writing as a way to find peace and express himself.

Thanks, Sam!

ACKNOWLEDGMENTS

Special thanks to my wife for supporting me through the creation of this book. She's a true partner, enduring my long hours of solitude, midnight writing binges, and fretting over so many details wherever and whenever they come to mind.

And thanks, as always, to my "beta readers," Bob, Joan, Rob, and my beloved sister Jan. Their input was, as always, immensely helpful.

Special thanks to Gary S., a highly experienced, skilled psychologist, for his help in understanding and relating Post Traumatic Stress Disorder and the potential use of virtual reality in treating patients. To those who suffer from that condition, I offer my sincere best wishes and prayers. I empathize with you more than you can ever know.

I cannot say enough about the team at Ambassador International. No matter how hard I try to deliver a quality story to them for publication, they always make it so much better. Their patience, understanding, and partnership was both encouraging and motivating as I completed this third release in the *Home Team* series.

Special thanks to Valerie Coffman, an extraordinary editor whose expertise added so much to this story. Quality editors are a true blessing for any writer, and Valerie qualifies as one of the best.

To Jesus Christ, I dedicate it all: my salvation, the stories, the message, and, I hope, the fun you have reading this book. To paraphrase Jeff Gerke, author of *The Art & Craft of Writing Christian Fiction*, there's only one Person we really hope to please when creating a Christian Suspense novel, and it is Him.

CHAPTER 1

Leah McCarthy shivered as the cold from the cinderblock and steel warehouse walls seeped through her tactical black shirt, pants, and body armor as she fought to keep tired, sand-gritty eyes open and focused. This was the eighth deployment in as many weeks, and she was feeling the effects of running on high octane for so long without meaningful rest.

She sat on a grated metal catwalk high above the warehouse floor, one leg tucked beneath her and the other pulled up as a shooting rest for the fiberglass/carbon fiber and epoxy frame of the M4A8E carbine rifle balanced on her knee. The *E* in the rifle's official designation was for "experimental" and accounted for the matte black, bulbous Integrated Target Acquisition and Firing scope, or Taffy, mounted atop the rifle. The first of its kind, the scope allowed her to lock a physical target into the scope's memory. Then, sometime later, all she had to do was settle the scope's sights on the target again and activate the carbine's Taffy interface, and the rifle would fire automatically once the target was centered in the scope's glass. She could override the fire function, of course, but then what fun would that be?

She smiled, fighting her growing fatigue and itchy eyes by walking through the specifications for the new tech provided by the

Home Team's boss. If there was anything that could get her excited, it was new tech; and she was eager to try it in the field today.

Above her, long skylights illuminated the warehouse's two-hundred-foot length with a pale light from the typically overcast Washington State sky outside. Heavy steel beams spanned the building's high ceiling like the ribcage of a giant beast. The air smelled of cardboard dust from the seemingly endless rows of pallet stands stacked three high with boxes and crates that ran the length of the building. In addition to the dust, the air held the acidic tang of fentanyl, methamphetamine, and the other assorted illegal drugs being cut, counted, bottled, and bagged by twenty or so white-jacketed workers busy on the warehouse floor thirty feet below and watched over by a half dozen armed guards.

As Leah scanned the workers through her scope, most appeared to be young and female. They sat on tall stools or stood at three long rows of white folding tables. When the faint sound of their voices reached her, Leah identified Mandarin, Spanish, and a Slavic tongue she couldn't quite place.

She'd been in position for four hours, and it was time to report in. The rest of her team would be in place by now. Leah raised her large-faced black tactical watch to her lips, triggering its embedded microphone, and whispered, "Overwatch Prime, this is Romeo Alpha."

"This is Overwatch Prime. Go Romeo." The response came over the cochlear-like implant behind her left ear, and she recognized the voice at once—Paul Samuelson, listening in from the State Department's Extreme Operations Group's headquarters in a small town in northern Florida.

"Prime," Leah whispered. "I am status two and confirm six heavily armed guards and twenty-plus workers in the space below me."

Status two advised Paul that Leah was in position and ready for action. Status one would have meant she'd arrived on site but was not yet ready for mission execution. Status three meant that she was about to engage her target.

"Roger, Romeo. The rest of your team is onsite and status two, as well. DEA agents are a block off site but ready to move in. Hold until further notice. Prime out."

Leah sighed and tugged at the new Thin Ballistics Vest, Deployable—or thin BVD, as her team liked to call it. The vest chafed her skin under her shirt; and not for the first time, she wondered who would ever think it a clever idea to produce body armor in one-size-fits-all. At five feet one, she'd had to fold the vest double at the sides to make it fit under her shirt, the vest's Kevlar-infused material digging painfully into her slim waist each time she shifted position.

She glanced at her watch: 9:00 a.m. She'd picked the warehouse's office door lock at 5:00 a.m. Now, after four hours of silent, motionless waiting, the operation was finally about to kick off. Or so she hoped.

Then again, these things never start on time, she thought. *Every plan sounds good until either the logistics or the opposition refuse to cooperate.*

As her team's sniper, she spent many long periods alone and quiet; and she found her mind running over frequently trod ground. Today, it was about her team, the Home Team, people who'd effectively constituted her family for the past five years. The team had been going through a lot of changes of late. Sam Anthem was married. And Allen Farrell, the other male operator on the team, might as well be; he'd been with his childhood sweetheart for so long. Their off duty lives were more and more focused their significant others. Jessica Falcone, the other woman on the team, had recently purchased a small horse ranch near their base of operations at Joint Base Lewis-McChord in Washington State. No one saw that coming until she showed up for training one day and sprang it on the team. On top of that, she'd relocated her widowed father from Mexico to live with her at the ranch. Now, her after-hours activities were swallowed by the challenges of her land, horses, and father.

Until these changes in her teammates' lives, they had lived in each other's back pockets, heading out on missions to who-knows-where, defending the innocent and fighting bad guys together. When not deployed inside or outside the U.S. borders, they'd trained endlessly together and hung out during their off hours. No more. Everyone was moving on.

Except for me.

Leah sucked in a deep breath and tamped down the queasy feeling that churned in her gut every time the thought crossed her mind. *Is there something wrong with me?* she wondered. *Everyone but me is . . .*

She shook her head, clearing the thought from her mind. *I'm pathetic. I'm a highly trained sniper and covert operator—one of the best in the armed forces, I've been told. I've been trained to stay in position, frosty, motionless, and undetected for hours or even days at a time. And now, here I am feeling sorry for myself for not lunching with the popular crowd?* She blew out a soft breath. *I have a life, and I'm on a mission. I need to be better than that.*

Leah wrestled her body armor's abrasive edges into a more comfortable position and flipped her thick braid of auburn hair back, over her right shoulder. Today, the Home Team's mission was to capture the workers and the operation's leadership and shut down the drug smuggling operation based out of the new Tumwater, Washington, warehouse. Soon the Drug Enforcement Administration's lead agent would give the high sign; and Jessica, Sam, and Allen would emerge from hiding in the warehouse's tall stacks of pallets packed with boxes and crates and take down the guards, along with well-placed shots from her. Then, her teammates would usher the workers to a safe location outside the building. At the same time, at the far end of the building where the warehouse's three offices were located, two DEA agents would secure the operation's leaders.

Leah grasped her rifle and pressed a darkly tanned cheek against its stock, the coolness of the weapon's carbon composite surface reminding her once again of the warehouse's chill air and the cold seeping into her body. She rolled the rifle over and confirmed the green slash on the bottom of the magazine, indicating it was loaded with the EOG's new non-lethal bullets that could be loaded into a standard rifle or pistol, rather than the old dart guns the team carried in the past. Each high-velocity polymer round contained a tiny dart. Once fired, the friction from the bullet's path through the air softened its polymer shell, which fractured on impact, exposing a tiny dart that injected a fast-acting sedative into the target.

Like the darts the Home Team used in the past, which required carrying a small, pistol-like dart gun, the dart now contained in the bullet's polymer casing was made of a rare hardwood. In addition to a fast-acting sedative, it also contained a tiny magnesium pellet that ignited once the dart injected its load into the target and destroyed the dart. The target was rendered unconscious on contact and left with nothing more than a nasty little bruise and microscopic burn mark from where the dart made contact.

Leah reached down to her beltline and touched the grip of her dart gun. The rest of the team had given them up because the new dart bullets could be loaded into their pistols. They teased Leah because she found a sort of comfort in carrying the old-fashioned black dart gun, just in case.

With any luck, she'd knock down all six guards before her teammates had a chance to get a shot off. Then, twenty minutes later, tops, they'd head back to the headquarters building at Joint Base Lewis-McChord, thirty miles north. Could she do it—take out all six guards on her own? She wasn't sure; but hey, a girl needs a goal in life, and today that was hers.

If everything went according to plan.

Leah glanced at the narrow tablet computer strapped to her left forearm and tapped the icon on its screen to call up a diagram of the warehouse's interior. It appeared a second later, along with green dots representing the locations of Jessica, Allen, Sam, and herself. The two blue dots that should have shown the positions of the two DEA agents at the far end of the warehouse were missing. Should she be worried about that? That thought was cut off by Paul Samuelson's voice over her implant.

"Romeo, this is Prime."

Leah pulled her tactical watch close to her lips, triggered its embedded microphone, and whispered, "This is Romeo. Go ahead, Prime."

"Status report?" Paul said.

"I remain status two," she replied, then added with a smile, "and bored out of my mind."

She heard Paul's soft chuckle, then, "Roger, Romeo. Status three is imminent. Rules of engagement are non-lethal ammo. You're shooting darts, unless things go sideways. As briefed, our goal is to capture as many people involved with this group as possible and hand them over to the DEA for questioning."

Leah let out a long sigh. She respected and appreciated Paul but found herself driven to once again address the appropriateness of having a top-tier team like the Home Team involved in something as mundane as a drug bust. "This is Romeo. I confirm the rules of engagement. But like I said before, why are we even involved in this? This is a routine drug interdiction that the DEA and local law enforcement could handle with their eyes closed. This is so far below the Home Team's pay grade—"

Paul cut her off. "Noted, Romeo, as before. Then it should be a walk in the park. I will relate your concerns to the Secretary of State and let her know of your personal objections to the mission, since she personally committed us to assisting the DEA on this operation. DEA is stretched thin carrying out a nationwide drug interdiction operation. Now, standby for status three once I get the order from the agent in charge."

Leah let out another groan, considering the ramifications of squaring off against the U.S. Secretary of State. "Roger, Prime, but you can hold off on calling the Secretary. I'm all in."

In response, she heard Paul's chuckle over her comms implant once again.

"Overwatch Prime, this is Overwatch Second," came the next call over comms. That was Walter Drake, call sign Golf Zulu—or Grizzley, for short. Walter provided technical overwatch from the Home

Team's headquarters at Joint Base Lewis-McChord and had control of two drones the DEA had launched, which hovered five hundred feet above the warehouse.

"This is Prime, Grizzley," Paul replied. "Any sign of the drug operation's leaders from the air?"

"Negative, Prime," Walter replied." Nothing to report so far... Oh, wait, one!"

"Roger, Second," Paul replied.

"This is Second," Walter said a beat later. "I have one drone positioned above the far end of the warehouse from the Home Team's position. I've activated its Light Detection and Ranging Technology, configured to detect ambient air particles given off by large groups of people. The data suggests a dozen or so people positioned within a central office."

"Roger, Second," Paul replied. "I'll inform our DEA liaison. Break for Home Team actual," Paul said, switching his focus from Walter to Leah and the rest of her team. "An update from DEA: the local police are in position a mile from the warehouse, standing by to take custody of captives."

Paul's announcement was answered by two clicks from each of the Home Team members, with Leah acknowledging the update last.

Paul came on the line a heartbeat later. "This is Prime. Stand by. Mission start is imminent. All team members report."

"This is Mike Tango," Sam replied. "Status two and ready."

"This is Fox Tango," Allen added. "Status two."

"This is Charlie Papa, also status two," Jessica added.

Leah smiled as she triggered the microphone in her watch and whispered, "This is Romeo Alpha. Status two and still bored."

"Roger all," was Paul's short reply. "Stand by."

Despite all the years she'd been doing this sort of work, Leah felt her heart begin to pound in her ears as the time for acting approached. She tapped her right index finger slowly, deliberately against her chest—an old sniper tool for regulating the heartbeat and breathing—and felt a sense of calm overtake her.

Walter was next to chime in. "This is Second. I have four individuals arriving in two small sedans at the far end of the warehouse. Visual is available now on the team's tablets."

Leah glanced at her arm-tablet computer, touching a new icon that appeared on its narrow, elongated screen. A visual image of two cars pulling up to the warehouse appeared in the tablet's dim light. What looked like four people in heavy jackets climbed out and entered the warehouse through a side door. All wore hoods pulled tightly around their heads.

"This is Prime," Paul added. "The DEA agents are moving in to intercept the new arrivals. You are status three. Engage!"

Three sets of two clicks followed Paul's announcement. Leah raised her watch to her lips and whispered, "This is Romeo. Going hot."

Leah drew a bead on a guard standing to the left of the workers sorting pills on the tables at ground level. "And it's sleepy time." She pressed a small rubber-coated button on the side of her rifle with her right index finger to activate the Taffy scope's integrated target memory. As the scope's crosshairs centered on the guard's chest, the suppressed carbine rifle coughed softly and spat the first polymer dart bullet. She smiled as the dart struck home below the guard's chin. He dropped to the floor before he realized he'd been hit.

She lined up the crosshairs on the next guard to the right. The weapon's targeting system validated the target, a soft green light highlighting the guard on the scope's small viewing glass. The rifle coughed again. That man dropped to the floor as she lined up on a third guard. Unfortunately, that man jerked his head to the right as Leah's second target crumpled to the floor. Her third dart struck that man low on the cheekbone instead of the more vulnerable flesh of his neck. He managed a single staggering step before he, too, dropped to the floor, his weapon clattering on the concrete beside him.

As Leah brought her sites to one of the three remaining guards and her rifle coughed the shot, her target bellowed, "Take cover!" and dove for a stack of boxes near one of the sorting tables. The dart whizzed by her target within inches of his head.

So much for the plan going perfectly.

Sam barked over comms, using his abbreviated call sign, the joining of the letters M and T into a single word, "This is Empty. Moving in."

"Fox is following," Allen said.

Jessica simply clicked her microphone twice in response. She would not be left behind.

Leah scanned the warehouse floor and saw Allen step from the cover of the tall stands of pallets on the opposite side of the table-lined workspace. In his black tactical uniform and face mask, his smooth, almost floating gait with his M4A carbine at eye level, Allen reminded her of a modern-day television ninja.

A few yards to Allen's right, Sam emerged looking much the same as he yelled, "Federal Agents! Weapons down! Everyone on the ground!"

Jessica moved into view from directly below Leah, on the opposite side of the workspace from Sam and Allen, similar in appearance, except for a long ebony ponytail that trailed down the back of her black tactical shirt. The barrel of her carbine swept left and right as she closed on the workspace, the workers, and the remaining three guards. *"Policia! Todos abajo!* Then, she said the same in Mandarin, *"Jǐngchá! Dàjiā xiàlái!" Police! Everyone down!*

The white-jacketed workers dove for the floor and beneath their worktables. The three remaining guards opened fire in that same instant, rifles cracking and bullets flying wild as they found cover behind boxes and tables.

Apparently not yet discovered by the guards, Leah drew a bead on a guard lining up a shot at Jessica's back. "Cap," she whispered, using Jessica's abbreviated call sign. "Tango at your six. Taking the shot."

Jessica spun in place as Leah placed a female guard in her scope's crosshairs and her rifle gently bucked against her shoulder. In that same instant, the woman behind Jessica opened with a three-round burst from less than twenty feet. Two of the woman's rounds went high and wide as Leah's shot slammed a dart into the woman's shoulder. The guard's third took Jessica in her left side. Jessica spun with the impact of the guard's bullet, turning full circle with her carbine at eye level. As Leah watched, Jessica's rifle bucked gently in her hands once and then again. Jessica's first dart took the female guard high in the chest, within an inch of where Leah's own dart struck. The second one struck under her chin. A triple dose of sleep-inducing narcotic coursing through her system, the woman's eyes closed on impact; and she crumpled to the floor, her assault rifle clutched to her chest.

Leah scanned left, knowing two guards remained to be accounted for. She found one sprinting for one of the warehouse's side doors, then saw Sam and Allen turn and fire in unison. The man's steps faltered as both dart bullets smacked into the cinder block wall on either side of him with a loud thwack as he reached for the door's push-bar. The man stopped and dropped to his knees, throwing his rifle aside and raising his hands high.

"This one knows the drill," Leah heard Allen mumble over comms.

As Allen moved forward to secure the man, Sam pivoted and scanned the warehouse over the sights of his M4 carbine. "This is Empty," he said over comms. "Anyone see that last tango?"

"This is Cap," Jessica replied. "He's using a stack of boxes near the wall at the end of the warehouse for cover, directly beneath Romeo, near where I entered this dance. Romeo should be able to handle him."

Leah looked down through the open grating of the metal catwalk at the man directly below, creeping on silent feet toward the warehouse door Leah used to enter the building hours earlier.

She clicked her microphone twice, letting her team know she had spotted the man. He was so close, anything she might whisper would surely be heard. She gently eased her dart gun from its holster at her hip, glad she hadn't given up on the small pistol like her teammates. She aimed the dart gun's barrel down, through the spacing in the catwalk's metal grating, at the base of the man's neck as he passed beneath her. She pulled the trigger, and the dart spit out with a quiet pfft sound as the little pistol jumped softly in her hand. The dart struck the base of the man's neck. He dropped a moment later, his aged AK47 assault rifle clattering to the concrete floor beside him.

Leah raised her watch to her lips, "This is Romeo. Tango is down. And I might add for all of you who make fun of me still carrying my little dart gun, that's what I just . . . " Her words were followed by the crack of six shots from the far end of the warehouse.

"This is Empty," Sam said over comms. "Shots fired from the other end of the warehouse."

Leah, still on her feet, slung her rifle across her back. "This is Romeo. The catwalk I'm on runs the length of the building. I'm on my way."

"Roger, Romeo," Sam replied. "Will join you at floor level. Cap and Fox, stay with the workers."

"This is Prime. That's where the DEA agents should be," Paul said.

Leah sprinted the length of the catwalk, her soft-soled boots pounding the metal grating. She groaned inwardly as she ran, an all too familiar, acid-like flush of anxiety filling her gut. She'd seen so much death, so many good agents and enemies injured and killed. It came with the job, she knew, but lately . . .

Leah let out a long breath and slowed as the stacks of pallets below the catwalk thinned, to be replaced by a small open space fronting three first-floor office doors equally spaced across the end of the warehouse. Her rifle still slung across her back, she drew her 9mm Beretta from the drop-holster at her thigh, then crept slowly forward to where she had a clear view of the space and the two bodies lying crumpled on the warehouse floor.

"This is Romeo. Two men down. Holding position until Empty arrives."

Beyond an open side door leading out of the warehouse, Leah heard two car engines roar to life. She swung her pistol in that direction, but whoever that was had disappeared. A second later, she heard tires screeching on the pavement outside.

"This is Romeo," she said. "Two vehicles just left the area."

"This is Overwatch Second," Walter added. "I confirm Romeo's observation from the overhead drone's camera. Will track to ID the vehicles and the people in them."

"Roger Second," Paul replied. "Alerting the medics and DEA. ETA for the ambulances is two minutes."

"This is Empty," Sam said. "I'm approaching the office area now."

Leah saw Sam pause and peer around the corner of a box-laden stack of pallets, then heard him say over comms, "I confirm two men down. Gray suits. Both unmoving. I see no sign of any remaining tangos."

"This is Second," Walter chimed in. "The drone captured images of four people in two vehicles departing the area. No facial views. Also captured images of ten people running from the warehouse, scattering in all directions out a back door leading from what appears to be the center of three offices. No chance of tracking that last group. There's too many, but they appear to be unarmed civilians."

Sam stood and entered the open space in front of the office doors as Leah covered him from above. He cautiously peered into each of the three offices, then raised his watch to his lips and said, "All clear."

Leah found a narrow metal ladder leading down from the catwalk to the floor below. She holstered her pistol and half climbed/half slid down the ladder's rails to the warehouse floor. She redrew her pistol as her feet touched down, then covered Sam once again as he bent over the two still forms.

Sam raised his eyes to meet hers, shaking his head. He ran his hands through the dead men's pockets, finding several small leather folders. He examined both and rose to his feet, then said over comms, "Prime, this is Empty. I confirm two DEA agents down. Both are deceased."

"Confirmed," Paul replied, his tone subdued. "I will alert the DEA."

Leah caught movement from the corner of her eye as Paul ended his transmission; she spun and brought her pistol to bear on a small, dark shape that stepped through the shadowed opening of the middle of the three dark office doors. To Sam, she whispered, "I thought you cleared those rooms."

"I did," he said but then stopped as the form took shape in the office doorway.

"Freeze!" Leah yelled. "Stop where you are and raise your hands away from your sides."

The dim light from the overhead skylights provided just enough illumination for Leah to confirm it was a young girl about Leah's size, holding one hand at shoulder level, the other gripping a large, dark bag. The girl's shoulders drooped, her pale face gazing down at her feet in fear. "Please don't shoot." The voice was soft and cracked with each word.

Something about that voice and the girl's shape in the dim light dug at Leah's memory. She felt her knees go weak as her vision clouded and she was transported to a time and place eight years earlier. She gasped as the image, the smells, the sounds overwhelmed her senses.

Leah felt her knees almost give out as she crouched lower into a tactical firing position, her pistol at eye level, aimed at center of mass of the shadowed form before her. Only it wasn't a warehouse doorway any longer. It was the ragged opening of an ancient stone hut in Syria's barren landscape.

An AH-64 Apache helicopter pilot and his front-seat gunner huddled inside, and she was the only person standing between them and a squad of robed terrorists closing on their position.

She was a brand-new lieutenant leading her first pilot-rescue mission as a member of the Air Force's Special Warfare Pilot Rescue team. The other two members of her team had been blown a mile off course by a wind shear when they'd dropped in from fifteen thousand feet. She was alone as the squad of armed men opened fire, and Leah dove through the open doorway of the crumbling building. Bullets pinged off the rock and blew razor-edged chips of ancient mortar in all directions. Two bullets whizzed by so close, they sounded like angry hornets before they smacked into the hut's back wall.

She landed hard on the packed dirt floor, rolled, and, regaining her feet in a crouch, spun to face the doorway. Cloaked by the dim light of the desert's fading crimson sunset, she counted six shadowy silhouettes in traditional pale desert robes, heads covered by more of the same material. All carried assault rifles, although it was hard to identify the make and model from that distance. A seventh attacker followed several yards behind the first group.

One of the men behind her in the hut started to say something, but Leah cut him off with a raised hand. Then, dropping to a prone position at the edge of the doorway, Leah took the first attacker on the right with a single shot to the chest. Another fell a second later with a bullet to the neck.

The remaining four attackers dropped to the ground out of sight, and Leah was once again thankful for the point-and-shoot talent she seemed to be born with—her superpower, her mom used to say after she'd won yet another marksmanship contest as a member of her high school's marksmanship team.

As if on signal, the four remaining attackers rose once again and charged with a shrill yell. They rushed the hut from less than twenty yards away. Leah felt the nausea rise in her gut as she realized it was her and a half clip of bullets between the attackers and the wounded pilot and gunner.

"Looks dark, boys," she whispered. "I've got a half clip left. The rest were damaged when I landed on a pile of large rocks."

"Thank you for coming, just the same," one of the men replied.

Leah exhaled a long breath, then focused on each attacker as they charged, letting years of athletic memory take over. One shot per man, swinging right to left, two shots missing, but all four attackers dropping to the ground, wounded or dead as her pistol locked open, empty.

She holstered her pistol as the seventh person, the one trailing behind the first six shooters approached with dragging steps, rifle hanging loosely from one hand.

"What now?" the pilot asked.

Leah climbed to her feet, knowing her only option was to charge the last attacker and try to take him bare-handed. She wasn't optimistic about her chances, considering he carried a loaded rifle; but it was all she had. "It's in God's hands now," she whispered as she stepped into the hut's open doorway.

Leah staggered a step to her right as her vision cleared and a gentle hand settled on her shoulder. "You okay?" Sam asked. "Seems like we lost you there for a minute."

She blew out a long low breath and stood up from her crouch, holstering her pistol. "How long?"

"Only a second or two, but it seemed like you were somewhere else."

"It was strange, for sure," she replied.

Sam bent close to Leah's ear, his free hand gently gripping her shoulder. "Flashback?"

Leah nodded, not taking her eyes off the girl. "Yeah—and not the first time, but never during an op until now. We can discuss it later. Let's take care of this first. You cover me as I approach the girl and see what we have here."

Sam nodded. "No worries. I've got your back."

"Please don't shoot me," the small, cracking voice repeated from the shadowed doorway.

Leah calmed her breathing and the pounding of her heart once more and managed to make a small smile. "That's the last thing we want to do. Now, please step into the light so we can see you and know you're not someone who wants to hurt us."

The girl took two hesitant steps forward, enough to put her into the dim light cast by the warehouse's skylights. She looked fifteen or sixteen years old, with short, sandy blonde hair streaked with bright red highlights. Her face was narrow with high cheek bones. Wide-set, pale blue eyes flanked a slim nose. Her faded blue jeans were carefully torn at the knees. A red, yellow, and purple tie-died sweatshirt hung stylishly off one fair-skinned shoulder; and a black plastic bag hung from her left hand. Leah recognized the clothing as upscale, the jeans alone probably worth more than Leah's favorite going-out ensemble.

Like I ever go out, Leah thought.

"Thank you," Leah said as the girl stopped hesitantly a yard away. "What's your name?"

"Becca," the girl said.

Leah took a step toward Becca, her pistol holstered but knowing Sam had her covered. "What's in the bag?"

"Gaming gear," Becca said. "The people who brought us here left it behind when they ran for it. I doubt they'll be back for it."

"You said *us?*" Leah asked.

The girl nodded. "There were eleven of us here, aside from the four sponsors. That's what the people who ran the place called themselves.

The other ten split out the back door when the shooting started." She tossed a thumb over her shoulder to indicate the center office behind her. "I hid in there, under a table. That's why your friend didn't see me."

"Smart move," Leah replied, then lifted her watch to her lips. "I left my microphone open. Did you get all that, Prime?"

Walter responded instead. "This is Overwatch Second. Her story matches what we captured on the drone videos when the shooting started."

"This is Prime," Paul said once Walter finished. "She may be our best witness when it comes to the people running that place. Turn her over to the DEA."

"Roger all, Prime," Leah replied.

Sam gestured to the bag Becca clutched in her hand. "How about you set the bag on the ground and take a step back?"

"But it's mine," Becca protested, her eyes flashing. When Leah and Sam didn't immediately respond, she seemed to reconsider and let the bag drop from her fingers. The contents clanked as it hit the concrete floor. "They left it behind. It should be mine to keep."

"Who are *they*?" Leah asked.

"The four sponsors, like I said."

"Why didn't you run like the rest of your group?" Leah asked.

"They weren't my group. I didn't know any of them, and I didn't have anywhere else to go," Becca replied. "The others had been commuting to this place each day from their homes. They probably went there. Sometimes, the sponsors picked them up and then dropped them off at their homes after we'd done our time on the games. But I've been sleeping here. I doubt they even knew or cared."

Leah took another step toward Becca. She gestured to the bodies of the agents. "What about the people who brought you here? Were they the ones who shot these men?"

Becca shuffled her feet, glanced at the bodies, and then quickly glanced away. Her voice cracked softly once again when she replied, "Maybe. Probably. I didn't see that happen, but I heard gunshots."

Leah moved closer and reached out a hand to lay it gently on the girls' shoulder. "So, why exactly did the sponsors bring you here?"

Becca seemed to relax when she met Leah's eyes. "We were supposed to test some new video games using the equipment in the bag. I've been here two weeks. Some of the others were here longer. At least one had been coming here for the last six months."

"Video games?" Sam asked, stepping closer to where Leah and Becca stood as the distant sound of sirens called through the still-open side door to the warehouse.

Becca took a step back as Sam approached. "But you say the games weren't very good?" Leah asked as she glanced meaningfully to Sam, who got the message and retreated a step.

Becca nodded. "I've played better."

"I'm going to look in your bag. All right?"

Becca's expression shifted from frightened to determined; but then as she glanced at Sam with the rifle in his hands, she replied in a more tentative tone, "Okay. But it's just VR gear for the video games."

"Virtual reality games?" Leah asked as she lifted the edge of the bag to examine its contents. "That's pretty high tech."

Becca snorted. "I've seen better; but it was something to do, and they fed us."

The contents of the bag clanked, metal on metal, as Leah opened it. Her eyes narrowed as she reached inside and pulled out what looked like an oversized set of goggles. She held it up for Sam to see. "Virtual reality headset." She turned the headset over in her hands and found a small, embossed label on the underside of the headset. Her eyes narrowed. "United States Space Force. Serial number is AVR15-X."

Sam nodded. "We found some Space Force gear when we cracked down on the Chinese company during the human trafficking mission a few months ago. As I recall, the X in the serial number stands for 'experimental.' That suggests this device is some sort of prototype. So what's it doing here?"

Leah set the headset on the floor at her feet, then dumped the rest of the bag's contents next to it. One of the items in the pile of five additional items was a small black box with cables and cords extending from it. "This looks like the control box that drives the VR headset," Leah said.

Becca nodded. "And the CDs in the bag are copies of the video games we were playing."

Leah nodded as she picked up three CDs in transparent plastic cases. "The CDs also have the Space Force labels and the AVR15-X serial number."

"We can assume they contain the code for the program this equipment was developed to run," Sam added.

Leah nodded. "A fair assessment."

Sam raised his tactical watch to his lips. "Overwatch Prime, this is Empty."

"This is Prime. Go ahead, Empty," Paul replied.

"We found a young lady hiding in one of the offices. She has a bag of technology that may have been stolen from the U.S. Space Force. It looks like some sort of experimental virtual reality equipment."

"Secure the equipment," Paul replied.

Leah cast a glance at Becca, who had heard only Sam's words since Paul's reply came over the team's implants. Leah simply shook her head once in reply to Becca's questioning glance.

Jessica chimed in then. "Prime, this is Cap. The theft of equipment from U.S. Space Command may well constitute a threat to national security. Rather than hand the girl off to the DEA, I'd suggest we take her with us and question her from that perspective. It's supportable under the law, but I do suggest we contact her parents and let them know."

Paul's sigh was clear over comms. "This is Prime. I concur. Take the girl with you back to Joint Base Lewis-McChord. I'll alert the DEA about her status. See if you can get her parents' names and contact information before you go. Send it to me, and I'll reach out to them. And I want one of you to take personal responsibility for her until we've assessed her value to our investigation."

"This is Cap," Leah heard Jessica reply. "I'll take care of the girl. Leah's due to head out on vacation."

"Roger, Cap," Paul said after a short pause. "Don't let her out of your sight. The last thing we want is to remove this girl from her home environment and then lose her in the crowd. Now, you all get moving before you're overwhelmed by the local police. It would be nice if you could protect your anonymity, for once. Overwatch Prime out."

Sam stepped over to Leah and whispered, "We'll talk later about the flashback. I experienced something like that a while ago. But if it were to happen again during a mission . . . ."

Lean nodded. "I get it. Paul will bench me with good cause if I can't figure things out."

Sam smiled. "You're set to start your vacation tomorrow, anyway, aren't you?"

Leah nodded. "And it seems I need one about now. I'll dial in the group's psychologist from my sister's house once I get to Tennessee."

"We'll all be praying for you," Sam replied as Leah reloaded the VR equipment back into the plastic bag and handed it to Becca.

"Here. You can carry it," she said. "We're going to take you on a short road trip."

"Road trip?" Becca asked.

Leah nodded. "Yep. And we're leaving now."

"Cool. Will I get fed?" Becca asked. "And where're we headed?"

"You're not the least bit worried?" Leah said.

Becca shook her head. "Like I said, I've got nowhere else to be."

"Do you have any folks we need to call?"

Becca shook her head, hefting the bag of equipment to lay across her shoulder. "Nope. No folks."

To Leah, Becca's response didn't sound like any sort of diversion or lie but rather like she was repeating the answer to a question she'd been asked too many times before.

"No family at all?" Leah asked again.

Becca pulled a small wallet from her back pocket with her free hand. As they headed for the warehouse door, she fumbled out a

Wisconsin driver's license. She handed it to Leah. "It's at the top right of the driver's license."

Leah examined the license and read the words in the top right corner of the small, embossed card. "You're an emancipated minor?"

Becca nodded. "For the past year. So you don't need to call anyone at all. I can officially speak for myself."

"One moment," Leah replied. She raised her watch to her lips and triggered its microphone. "Overwatch Second, this is Romeo Alpha."

Walter's reply was immediate. "This is Second. Go ahead Romeo."

"I'd like you to run a check on a Wisconsin driver's license."

"Roger, Romeo. Give it to me," Walter said.

Leah rattled off the driver's license number, then spelled out Becca's full name as it was printed on the driver's license. "Rebecca Preston. I need you to confirm her as an emancipated minor."

"Roger, Romeo," Walter replied. "Stand by."

Walter was back a minute later. "I can confirm Rebecca Preston is sixteen years old and an emancipated minor by court order. She's legit."

"Roger, Second," Leah said. "Romeo, out."

She turned back to Becca. "Okay. Let's get going. We need to be out of here in the next few minutes."

"I do have one question before we go," Becca said as they turned together and headed for the nearest door leading from the warehouse.

Leah nodded. "Go for it."

"Who exactly are you? And why are you so anxious to leave before the cops arrive?"

Leah paused midstride and turned to face her. "That's two questions."

Becca's tone was droll, almost sarcastic when she said, "So humor me."

"Fine," Leah replied. "First, we're a covert operations group working for the federal government. Second, the word 'covert' means we don't want to be confronted directly by the local authorities. Keeping our identity as secret as possible is part of the job. The DEA knows someone was here helping them today but not exactly who."

"Where are we headed, then?"

"Joint Base Lewis-McChord, a bit north of here," Leah replied. "That's our base of operations."

"So you're army or air force?"

A long, black Chevy Suburban pulled up next to the warehouse as they stepped through a narrow steel door and into the daylight. Leah paused, turning back to Becca. "Neither, and that is going to have to be good enough for now."

Becca smiled as she turned to follow. "Cool. I'm hanging with super spies."

Allen and Jessica joined them as they approached the Suburban.

"Super spies?" Allen said. "Maybe me, but her?" he asked, pointing a black-gloved finger toward Leah. "I seriously doubt it."

Becca flashed Allen a wide grin.

"More like a family of super spies," Leah replied. "With one defective brother."

Jessica laughed and pointed Becca to the cramped bench seat at the back of the SUV. "Kids in back."

Becca groaned.

Once Becca was secure in the vehicle, Allen, Leah, Jessica, and Sam stripped off their tactical gear and loaded it in the vehicle's rear cargo area; and they joined Becca in the SUV. A dark-suited man with an emotionless expression and reflective wrap-around sunglasses sat in the driver's seat. He kept his eyes forward as the team climbed in, Jessica riding shotgun. Sam and Allen took the middle bench seat. Leah joined Becca at the far back.

Becca elbowed Leah once she was belted in. "The back seat's not just for the kids, I see. Tiny spies sit in the back, too."

Leah worked hard to conceal the grin that tickled the corners of her mouth. "So it would seem."

As they pulled away from the warehouse and made their way north onto Interstate 5, Becca tapped Leah on the shoulder. "Isn't this a little cliché? Dark vehicle, tinted windows, mysterious driver?"

Jessica turned in her seat and said with a wide smile lighting her deep brown eyes, "I like this girl. She reminds me of someone else I know. Opinionated. Sarcastic. Full of spit and vinegar. And tiny."

"Exactly," Sam added.

Allen turned in his seat to cast a glance back at Leah. "It seems so obvious. You sure you two aren't related?"

Becca smiled and said, "Why, thank you."

Once again, Leah found it hard to hold back the smile, but she saw it, too. Sarcastic. Quick witted. Much too similar, but Becca would be Jessica's problem for the time being. In one more day, Leah would be back home in Tennessee on a much overdue month-long vacation. There, she had plans for nothing more than long humid evenings on her sister's back porch and maybe to hike one or more of the state's many national and state parks—and not to forget, at least one session with the group psych to figure out why she was having flashbacks.

Right, she thought. Rest and relaxation. Exactly what she needed.

CHAPTER 2

The next day was a typical chilly late December day in Middle Tennessee as Leah stepped from her rental Toyota Rav4 SUV in the parking lot of a Tullahoma strip mall with a Kroger supermarket as its centerpiece. She sucked in a deep breath of the crisp air, rolling her shoulders as she plotted her quick visit to and through the supermarket, disliking shopping in the first place and, as such, treating most such trips like a tactical operation. After the double set of wide glass automatic entry doors, she would take a hard right for flowers and something from the bakery for her sister, brother-in-law, and niece.

The long drive from Nashville's international airport had flown by as she headed south toward the little community of Hillsboro. Her sister lived in that community of less than nine hundred people; but they'd grown up in Tullahoma, where her mother had been a sheriff's deputy for so many years, until . . . She let the beginnings of that dark memory drift back into the past where it belonged. For now, she just wanted to soak in the feeling of being home, back where her roots sank deep into the Tennessee clay.

She swung her thick braid of red-bronze hair over her left shoulder, then absently reached for the Beretta 9mm pistol at the small of her back, momentarily confused when she didn't find it there. Of course!

She'd locked her gun in the center console in the SUV. Why would she need a weapon for a grocery store visit? She was on vacation.

Leah let out a long deep breath, forcing knotted shoulder muscles to relax and happier thoughts back into her mind. Tonight, she'd be sharing dinner with her sister's family. It'd been too long since she'd seen any of them.

Back to the Kroger mission: acquire a quart of 2 percent low-fat milk and a loaf of French bread requested by Rachael Mae. The flowers were Leah's idea, recalling how her sister loved anything yellow. Daisies, maybe.

The store's first set of double-wide glass entry doors slid aside revealing a line of shopping carts and crates of melons strategically placed to draw the eye. She carefully edged her way around an elderly woman moving slowly toward the shopping carts and for the second set of automatic glass doors. She paused there, as she stepped up behind a young man and his two little girls.

The youngest of the two—with a tiny cherub face, rosy cheeks and bright green eyes framed by a thick mop of curly red hair—stopped halfway through the door and turned to Leah. "Hi! You have hair just like mine!" she said, looking up expectantly.

Leah smiled and squatted down to meet the little girl eye-to-eye. "Why yes, I do. And hello to you, too."

"We're going to buy doughnuts and a card for my mama," the girl said, as if it was the most important mission in the world.

Leah's face involuntarily split into a wide smile as she glanced over her shoulder to ensure she and her new friend weren't blocking anyone else from entering the store. "That sounds very exciting and very important."

The little redhead giggled. "Oh, it is. This is the first time my daddy has taken me and my sister to the store without Mama."

The girl's next words were cut off when her brown-haired father, thirtyish, in worn jeans and a green flannel shirt reached out a hand to the little girl. "Come on, Samantha. Don't bother the nice lady."

"But she's like me. She has red hair, and she's tiny."

The man picked Samantha up and hugged her close. He turned to Leah. "Sorry about that."

Leah laughed. "She's not wrong. I am closer to her size than most people I know."

The man chuckled. "Yeah. Sammy pretty much calls it like she feels it. But I do hope she wasn't too much of a bother."

Leah leaned in and tapped the tip of her finger lightly against Samantha's button nose. Sammy laughed and crinkled her nose in response. "And don't you ever worry about talking to me," Leah said. "You could never be a bother."

Samantha's father raised an eyebrow, suggesting Leah might not be totally correct about that last count. Samantha giggled and gave Leah a tiny but exuberant thumbs up.

The man walked off with Samantha in his arms and another slightly larger version in tow behind him. Leah lost sight of them as they disappeared down the right side of the store toward the produce area with its counters full of brightly colored vegetables, strategically placed stacks of fruit, and the bakery beyond.

Leah paused before moving deeper into the store, getting her bearings. It was bigger than she remembered. Of course, it had been almost twenty years since she'd been in this store. Her parents' old house wasn't far, and she remembered coming here many times over the years before she left to attend the university and ultimately join the air force and its Special Warfare Group.

She felt a gentle nudge against the back of her arm and found a white-haired woman with stooped posture standing close behind her, supported by a silver aluminum walker. "Pardon me, miss, but would you mind if I step around you?" the woman asked in a soft voice.

Leah stepped aside, smiling as the woman passed, then followed her into the store. She wandered left toward the checkout counters lining the front of the store, spotting a display of flowers there. She'd only made it a few steps before the cracks of gunfire split the air. Every sense in her body went on alert, and she dropped to a crouch in front of a checkout counter where groceries lined up on a long conveyor belt.

The shots seemed to come from the right side of the store. She did a quick scan in that direction, and it didn't take long to find the shooter. He stood with his back to her at the entrance of an aisle running down the left side of the produce section, facing toward the back of the store. He was dressed in dark jeans and a black hoodie and holding some sort of black assault rifle tightly against his right side. The rifle's barrel was aimed down the store's long aisle of shelves stocked with health foods and protein supplements. The man pulled the trigger three times in rapid succession, the sound cracking sharp against Leah's ears. The store erupted with screams and pounding feet as people fled the scene.

Still squatting low, Leah pivoted to find the elderly woman she'd passed on the way in, when three more shots split the air, this time from a different direction: the far-left side of the store.

There are two shooters! Leah peered over the top of the checkout counter toward the opposite side of the store but couldn't identify the source of the gunfire.

Keeping low, Leah made her way back to where the elderly woman with the walker stood frozen in place, her shoulders shaking. Leah rose and gently, firmly took the woman by the arm, turned her toward the store's front doors, and gave her a light nudge in that direction. "Keep moving, no matter what. The police are bound to be here soon. They will help you."

To her relief, the woman nodded and began moving at once.

The second shooter, far to her left across the store, fired three more shots. More screams of fear and pain, more people stampeding past her position on their way out through the store's front doors. Holding her ground against the rush of panicked patrons, Leah shoved her way against the tide of people, toward the first shooter. She needed to do something before more people were hurt or killed, and she couldn't tackle both shooters at one time. Her hand flashed to the small of her back once more, where her Beretta should have been. Nothing. She blew out a long breath. She didn't have time to run to her rental car and retrieve the piece. How she wished the rest of her team was there with her. Together, they'd have the problem resolved in minutes. She had to do something now.

Staying below the level of the checkout counters lining the front of the store, Leah moved swiftly in a crouched run toward the shooter in the health food aisle. Unarmed, her only hope was to take the man by surprise. With the sound of the gunfire covering her approach, Leah doubted the man would see her coming, unless he turned her way.

She kept her eyes glued to the man's back as the sound of gunfire echoed again and again from the far side of the store from the second shooter and then the man before her as he triggered his rifle. More screams. More cries of pain rent the air as she closed the distance to the man, her mind registering that the second shooter was firing in controlled three-round bursts, followed by more screams. She needed to dispatch this first guy quickly and locate the second before more people died.

Leah slid around the end of the line of checkout counters in a crouch, then rose, turned hard right, and headed straight for the man. He was walking slowly, almost casually down the aisle now, triggering his rifle into the rows of bottled juices and boxes of health food, turning his head back the way he'd come, in Leah's direction.

Arms pumping, Leah was within twenty feet when she saw him turn and slide to a stop behind a ten-foot-long counter stocked with blueberries, strawberries, and an exotic fruit. She held her breath, willing the man not to see her, then glanced to her right to see the father she'd met at the front door. Cradled on his knees lay little Samantha, unmoving, with a crimson puddle forming at his feet. Samantha's older sister lay on the floor at his feet in another pool of blood, also unmoving.

Leah felt her stomach began to churn. The little girl—so full of life a few minutes ago, so vivacious, so bold in her innocent way—now lay still in her father's lap. Unfamiliar tears stung the corners of Leah's eyes; she swiped at them with the sleeve of her shirt. *How could this happen?* And for the first time in her life, she asked herself, *How could God let this happen?* She had to stop this madness, now!

Heedless of where the shooter might be looking, Leah jumped from behind the berry counter to find the first shooter a few more yards down the aisle. He appeared focused on two store workers running toward the back of the store. Beyond him, two others lay with their backs against the long aisle's neat rows of boxes and bottles, moaning and bleeding from multiple wounds.

She tucked her head, eyes glaring at the man's back, fists clenched, and the unfamiliar sense of hot rage burning in her mind. Legs churning, she covered the last few yards to the man in seconds, sucking in a deep, centering lung-full of air, then blowing it out hard as she leaped for the man's back. Her mind consumed by anger and the image of little Samantha, Leah's athletic memory took over; and she crashed into the man from behind, then scaled his back like a rock climber up a sheer wall. Both hands gripping the man's shoulders, she clamped her legs tight around his waist. Inhaling deep into her abdomen, she shot her left arm up high above the shooter's head, then slammed her elbow down onto the back of his neck, vertebrae cracking audibly under the impact.

As the man staggered under the impact of Leah's strike, she snaked her right hand and arm around the shooter's right side, under his armpit, then forward to grasp the metal service handle atop his rifle. Her breath coming in great gasps, Leah smiled grimly as she recalled her mother's words from so long ago: "It's like you have the heart, lungs, and muscles of a six-foot woman packed onto a five-one frame." Well, she'd need all that and more to do what was needed here, today.

The man seemed to reclaim his feet and shook hard from side to side, attempting to unseat Leah from his back. Leah clung to the man with all her strength, refusing to surrender her grip on him and the rifle she grasped with her right hand. She jerked hard on the rifle, tugging its barrel upward, as a small flame flared from it and a bullet cracked upward into the store's ceiling.

One for the good guys, Leah thought as the shooter paused his shaking to stare down at his weapon in surprise, as though it had triggered the shot on its own. Still gripping the rifle with her right hand, Leah took advantage of the man's sudden stillness, shooting her left arm up, relying on her legs to keep her atop the man's back. As she clamped down even harder on the man's waist, she brought her left elbow crashing down onto his neck once more. Again, the slightest sound of bone crunching. The man stiffened with the impact this time, so Leah raised up her arm and brought her elbow down again, this time striking the point where the man's neck vertebrae connected with the skull.

It was the third blow that cracked several vertebrae at the base of the man's skull. How much she'd hurt him, she could only guess; but she felt his body quake as he started to go down. The rifle came free from the shooter's hand as his grip faltered. She tugged it free and tossed it aside as she pushed off the man's back as he toppled forward, face-first, stretching out onto the store's cold tile floor. She knew he wasn't dead by any stretch of imagination; but he was out of the fight, and that was enough.

Leah retrieved the rifle, which she discovered to be a civilian version of the AK47 assault rifle used by military organizations, police, and criminals for decades. Rather than leaving the loaded weapon where it was, she quickly dropped the magazine from the well, pulled the pin that cracked the rifle open like a clam shell, then pulled a second pin that separated the rifle into two disconnected parts. Those parts she tossed to the side of the aisle.

With the crack of shots sounding in rapid succession from across the store, Leah wrapped one hand in the downed shooter's sweatshirt hood and dragged him to the vegetable display where the father sat with Samantha in his lap. "Secure him with some twine, a belt, or anything you can find. I've got to—"

More shots sounded, followed by more screams from the opposite side of the store. Sammy's father cut off her words with a raised hand and nodded toward the sound of the shooting. Leah took his meaning, spun, and raced back to the front of the store and down the long row of checkout counters once again, this time in the opposite direction.

As she ran, she saw groups of people huddling down several of the aisles. Each time she passed one, she waved an arm toward the front of the store and yelled, "The one by the produce is down. Go! Get out. Now!"

There was no way to know if they took her advice; she was moving too fast.

Seconds later, Leah had passed past the open ends of six aisles, abandoning subtlety and stealth in favor of speed. As she neared the second to last aisle on her right, she slowed and said a silent prayer that the second shooter would be advancing toward the back of the store rather than toward the front, so she could take him from his blind side. From long experience, she knew aggressors of any kind tended to advance, always advance, and seldom reversed direction until their mission was complete or their way was blocked.

Leah slowed only enough to turn the corner of that aisle and saw the second shooter a third of the way toward the back of the store. As she edged around the corner of the aisle, she noticed this one appeared to be a woman. Regardless, Leah continued her sprint toward the shooter, her mind unconsciously registering the woman's relaxed posture and the short-barreled MP5 submachine gun hanging loosely at her side. The posture suggested a trained professional rather than an off-the-street crazy with a rifle.

Those thoughts registered in the back of Leah's mind as she launched herself at the woman's back, just as the woman swung her MP5 machine gun up to grasp the front grip with her left hand. It was the calm fluid motion of someone used to handling weapons and prepared to use it. In this case, the target appeared to be a woman and two young men in work aprons huddled halfway down the aisle.

Just as the woman pulled the submachine gun's trigger, Leah crashed into the shooter's back. Leah's goal was to stun the woman with a body blow and then, as with the first shooter, climb her back and take control of her weapon. But this time, as Leah crashed into the shooter's back, the woman flexed her knees, dropped low at the waist, and twisted her hips to the right as two bullets cracked and her submachine gun flashed. The bullets went wide of their target as the shooter's classic judo throw sent Leah tumbling over the woman's hip and shoulder.

Leah relaxed and let her body move into the throw, arcing over the woman's back. At the peak of the arc, Leah twisted 180 degrees. She came down on the balls of her feet, facing the female shooter from only a few feet away.

As her feet touched down, the woman swung the barrel of her weapon toward Leah's chest. Leah slapped the open palm of her right hand against the weapon, knocking it aside as flame blossomed from its barrel once, then again, the sound deafening and the bullets shredding the long rows of personal hygiene items stocking the aisle's shelves.

Ignoring the ringing in her ears, Leah lunged forward, both hands grasping the submachine gun's hot barrel. Her grip on the weapon firm, Leah twisted at the waist, intending to use her weight and momentum to leverage the weapon from the shooter's grip. The female shooter countered Leah's move by stepping around Leah, then jerked back suddenly, tugging the weapon to her chest.

Still clutching the MP5's barrel, Leah changed direction and pulled herself into the woman, crushing their arms together as they wrestled for control of the MP5. For a moment, the battle came to a standstill, two strong women battling for their lives against another trained operator. Then, without conscious thought guiding her, Leah released her grip on the weapon with her left hand and shoved the woman back a step. Then, with her right hand still grasping the weapon's barrel, she shoved the MP5 and the woman's arms high and to the left. The shooter staggered back a step, losing her balance for the briefest of seconds; and Leah took advantage. She lunged forward a step, looped her balled left fist down, then up in a powerful uppercut to smash into the point of the woman's jaw.

The female shooter's eyes lost focus as Leah's punch connected, her grip on her weapon faltering. Leah twisted the MP5 away, raised it high and around, and smashed the weapon's stock into the side of the woman's head. She expected the shooter to go down, but the woman just stepped back and shook her head once. Leah used that instant to punch the magazine release on the MP5, drop the magazine, and toss the submachine gun aside. She couldn't risk using it to take the woman down, given the chance of stray bullets harming a person located somewhere in the store.

Their eyes met in that moment, the female shooter's dark, dead, and empty. A grim smile spread across the woman's face as her hand swept to her side and pulled a long-bladed hunting knife from a sheath on her belt—not the tactical kind Leah and the other members of the Home Team carried but a six-inch blade like a hunter might use to skin her prey.

Leah dropped her stance low, feet shoulder-width, both hands forward at the waist in guard position just as the shooter lunged, the gleaming blade slashing across Leah's mid-section from left to right. Leah jumped back in time to avoid the slash that would have opened her stomach and killed her. Instead, the tip of the knife carved a thin line of red across Leah's shirt, belly high.

As the woman's knife completed its arc from left to right, she grinned and lunged forward, thrusting her knife straight forward, at Leah's chest. The pain of the wound across her abdomen shocked Leah, seeming to awaken her from the cloud of anger that had driven her to that point. Her vision cleared in that instant; and the calm, deliberate tier-one operator returned as Leah swept her right hand across to counter the thrust, smacking the blade aside with her palm, and captured the woman's wrist in both hands. Then, using the shooter's forward motion against her, Leah pulled the woman into her and shoved the shooter's arm high and above both their heads. As the woman's arm and knife went up, Leah ducked under the arm and spun around to emerge at the woman's right side. With a mighty tug, Leah brought the woman's arm, with the knife now pointed down, slicing deep into the shooter's thigh.

The shooter shrieked as Leah released her hold on the woman's wrist and spun further to smash the point of her right elbow into the woman's temple. The shooter groaned softly, eyes rolling up, and then collapsed to the ground with blood pulsing from the wound in her leg.

Leah squatted next to the female shooter's still form and checked the woman's neck for a pulse. Nothing. The knife must have hit an artery, or maybe it was the temple strike. Or both. She frowned. *So much for my vacation.*

Leah's limbs felt weak as she stepped away from the dead shooter's body, the adrenaline already subsiding. She'd already been exhausted after too many long weeks of deployments without pause. And now this. She checked her watch. Less than four minutes had passed since she'd entered the store. The police and other first responders would arrive in minutes, and she needed to leave. In her line of business, being in the public eye or taken in by the police for questioning was never a good thing, no matter what the good intentions or the outcome.

She located the shooter's MP5 and retrieved it, then stripped it as she had the AK47. She wondered about her body's response, not remembering ever breathing this hard during any past mission. Always the cool, collected member of her team no matter the circumstances, what she felt now was totally foreign. She ignored her labored breathing, grabbing the woman's corpse by the collar and dragging it to the front of the store. She dropped it behind a checkout stand, not far from where the father, the prostate forms of his daughters, and the still unconscious first shooter remained. He met her eyes and nodded, then silently mouthed, "Thanks."

Leah felt her limbs sag even further as she took in the motionless forms of the two little girls, then glanced back into the store to see the dead and wounded scattered about; so many people senselessly gunned down by the shooters. *Why? Why did this happen? Why, God?* she cried in her mind.

When no answer came immediately, Leah turned on her heel and headed for the store's front doors. She paused there before leaving, turning back toward the man and his daughters. The store was eerily quiet as she called out, feeling the tears flowing freely from her eyes, "When the police get here, just tell them what happened. I am so, so, sorry."

The father looked up, shrugged as tears streaked down his cheeks, but offered nothing in reply.

Leah felt a spasm shake her frame; and something wrenched at her gut as she stepped from the store, the flashing lights of the first police cars casting blue and red streaks across her tear-clouded vision as they wheeled into the store's wide parking lot. A few moments later, she was in her rental SUV, wiping her eyes and heading for her sister's house twenty-five miles north with the acrid smell of gunfire, the echoing cries of the wounded, and the image of the two little girls crowding her mind.

———————

Across the Kroger parking lot, near a row of trees flanking an Applebee's restaurant, two men sat in a small, pale blue compact car. The person in the driver's seat was in his early thirties, with thick dark hair and eyes, deeply tanned skin, and the narrow features of his homeland. A laptop computer was balanced on his lap between his small protruding belly and the car's steering wheel. In the passenger seat next to him sat an older version of the man with gray just touching his temples and, as his wife had said just that morning, giving him a decidedly distinguished look. He held a small set of binoculars aimed at the front of the grocery store and the people pouring out through the store's double glass doors.

He nodded at the flow of people from the store. "Panicking like rats from a sinking ship, as anticipated." He turned to the man in the driver's seat and gestured toward the laptop with a hand. "You were successful in capturing the footage from the food market's internal security cameras?"

The younger man nodded. "The last thirty minutes of activity in the store from each of its six cameras. I am bringing up the images now." He turned the laptop's fourteen-inch screen so they could both see the three videos aligned across it. The younger man pointed to one of the videos. "There!" he said. "You can see the recruit and the seed shooter."

They watched in silence as the male and female active shooters positioned themselves facing down two long shopping aisles on opposite sides of the grocery store, then lifted their weapons and began firing.

"Excellent," the older man muttered. "The recruit performed admirably. As did the trained operative acquired from the local cell in Nashville. I've seen enough for now. You may shut down the computer."

"Wait, Master," the younger man said. "I believe what happens next may be important."

The older man humored his underling and continued to watch the laptop's screen as a tiny woman sprang into view, landed atop the back of the male active shooter, and quickly took him to the ground. "Who is that?"

The younger man shook his head. "No way to know. I will run the woman's image through facial recognition, but that will have to wait until we get back to the store."

"Yes, of course," the older man said. "But let's watch and see what that woman does next. She is not an average store customer."

In the next instant, the tiny woman disappeared from one view and emerged in the other. In that view, it took longer for the tiny woman to neutralize their trained operative. The struggle was brief; and at one time, it seemed as if their seed shooter might prevail. In the next instant, their trained operative was on the ground, the tiny woman squatting next to her still body.

"Most interesting," the older man said, then waved a dismissive hand toward the laptop. "But it has little relevance in the long run. The recruit and the trained operative we seeded into the operation created the desired level of fear, panic, and emotional pain. The small town of Tullahoma, Tennessee, will spend months collecting itself from what happened today."

"But, Master, we lost the seed shooter. She was one of our best agents."

The older man shrugged. He loved his protégé for the service he'd provided their country during the past ten years, but the man could be so dense. "The seed shooter was obviously not good enough to survive being attacked by one tiny woman, so we're better off without her. Besides, the goal was to run a pilot test for our greater effort, and we did that. The outcome was most acceptable."

"What about the woman who attacked our people?" the younger man asked, snapping his laptop closed and placing it on the car's rear seat.

"I'm not overly concerned. Any more people like her could be a problem, but her actions seem more coincidental than planned. If you discover anything interesting about her when you run her face through the system, let me know. Otherwise, we can dismiss her as a brave, if inconvenient, intrusion during our successful proof of concept. Keep in mind, as you do your research, she is not important when it comes to our grand plan."

"It will be glorious," the younger man replied.

"Yes," said the older man. "Yes, it will."

CHAPTER 3

Leah navigated a winding route to her sister's house up Interstate 24, along several small state highways to the east, and then one two-lane country road that extended arrow-straight for at least ten miles with a clear view of anyone who might follow her. Everyone had a cell phone with a video camera these days, and there was no way to know if her actions at the grocery store were captured on one of those phones and whether the person who took the video might feel inclined to follow her for an exclusive they could sell to some internet news outlet. As her boss was so fond of saying lately, she and her teammates on the Home Team were covert operators; and as much as possible, he'd like to keep the covert part in place.

Forty minutes later, Leah eased her SUV into her sister's driveway in front of a traditional Southern two-story red brick, complete with white shutters. Winding gardens ran down the sides of the drive and along the concrete path leading to the front door of the home, which sat in the center of an enclave of two dozen comparable homes. Tall, conical evergreen arborvitae flanked the front door, towering over a simple, three-step front porch with a dark, wooden door.

Leah's final steps to that front door faltered as an unbidden image flashed through her mind. This time, it was a snapshot of the two little girls lying at their father's feet. She stifled a gasp as the mental photo morphed into a moving image, complete with screaming people, gunfire, and the smell of gunpowder as though she was at the grocery store once more.

Another attack.

Leah reached both hands for the rough, cool feel of the porch wall, filled her lungs with a deep, grounding breath, then pushed the air deeper, to fill her abdomen. She held the breath for a count of five, then released it slowly, counting to nine as she emptied her lungs and abdomen of the cleansing breath. She repeated the process. And in the second breath, the images from the store, the sounds, and the smells faded; and Leah felt the strength return to her legs.

Intellectually, Leah knew it was hard for anyone in her business to avoid some degree of Post-Traumatic Stress Disorder, or PTSD. You simply saw too much death to get away unscathed. She just never planned on it overcoming her. In fact, for the past two years, she'd been careful to have a conversation with the Extreme Operations Group's consulting psychologist after each major deployment.

She recalled the advice her psychologist had offered her during their last session when the topic of PTSD came up. "Grab onto something solid, like a wall, a tree, or the steering wheel of your car," Dr. Malcome had said. "Then do your martial arts breathing exercise: inhale nine seconds, filling your lungs and then abdomen. Hold the breath for five seconds, then exhale for nine seconds, emptying the lungs first and then the abdomen. Hold for another five seconds and repeat. These two actions will ground you, getting your feet back under you figuratively and literally."

Halfway into the breathing routine, her vision cleared; and the sounds and smells of the store faded, just in time for the house's door to fly open and a tiny red-haired tornado to crash into Leah's legs.

"Annie Mae!" Leah heard her sister call, as Rachael Mae came into view behind her young daughter. "At least, give Auntie Leah a chance to get in the house before you attack her."

A tall, slender five-ten with a flowing mop of wavy, flaming red hair, thirty-two-year-old Rachael Mae had always been exactly who Leah wanted to be when growing up: beautiful, smart, loving, settled, and tall. She looked exactly like that as she stood in her home's doorway.

Little arms wrapped around Leah's legs, and a head pressed against Leah's stomach. Annie Mae was a six-year-old mini version of her mom, with a wild mop of tightly curled red hair framing a small, oval face with wide, blue eyes and a sparkling, impish smile.

Leah blew out a long breath as she rubbed the back of Annie Mae's head, glad for the distraction, then staggered back a step, feeling her head spin as another even more vivid image washed the faces of Leah's sister and niece from her vision.

She had been sixteen and Rachael Mae eighteen. Their mother, on a rare day off from her duties as a twenty-year Coffee County deputy sheriff, volunteered to take a group of foster kids to the Little Duck River Greenway and Sports Park near downtown Manchester. It was a beautiful day with pale, wispy clouds floating across a deep blue sky that lit up the park's wide, crowded playground / sports park with baseball diamonds, tennis courts, soccer field, and a shaded, wooded trail that wandered for several miles along a picturesque creek.

Leah and Rachael Mae were supposed to help with the kids but were delayed: Leah with rifle team practice at the high school and Rachael Mae with an Honors Society meeting. They arrived late and together in Rachael Mae's rusty Dodge quarter-ton pickup as a gray van pulled into the park's small parking lot nearby. Before Leah and Rachael Mae climbed out of the pickup, four people in dark clothes stepped from the van. Leah noticed the weapons at once.

"Hey," Leah said, keeping her voice low. "Don't turn to look; but three men and one woman just stepped out of that van, and they're carrying weapons."

Their father and mother had trained them both from a very young age to be aware of their surroundings, knowing that her occupation as a deputy and his as a military counter-intelligence officer might one day place the family at risk. Their father had died five years earlier during a military deployment, but their mom had continued their training in several forms of martial arts, numerous weapons, and situational awareness.

"They're headed for the park," Rachael Mae said. "Mom's down there."

"You call 911," Leah replied. "I'll text Mom."

Leah sent the text, spotting her mother, who, at six feet tall, stood head and shoulders over the kids and parents gathered under one of the park's long, covered picnic areas. Across the distance, Leah watched her mom fish out her old flip-phone, snap it open, and read the text.

Her mom texted back immediately. I see them. Create a distraction. I'll get the kids headed down to the creek path and toward the city. Be careful.

On it, *Leah texted back.*

"The police are on the way," Rachael Mae said as she disconnected her call.

"Mom wants a diversion. You take the left side of the park. I'll go right. On five, we make some noise."

Rachael Mae nodded, her elegant young face settling into a calm, determined expression. They bumped fists and stepped from the car, leaving its doors ajar to avoid the noise of them closing.

Leah sprinted left, counting to five as she headed toward the west boundary of the park and its expansive playground with swings, wooden forts, jungle gyms, and a bordering line of tall evergreen trees. She dropped behind a red plastic slide descending from a brown wooden play fort and, on the count of five, cupped her hands to her mouth and yelled, "Freeze! It's the police!

From the opposite side of the park, Rachael Mae yelled, "You're surrounded! Put down your weapons."

The four assailants spun in place, two toward Rachael Mae and two toward Leah. Splinters flew in all directions as the tall wooden fort was hammered by a barrage of automatic weapon fire.

As Leah huddled behind the wooden structure, her cell phone vibrated with a text from Rachael Mae. R u safe?

Leah tapped in a quick response. All good, but this won't last. We need to do more!

Leah glanced around the base of the wooden fort, seeing her mother direct children and parents toward the creek-side path and away from the park. In the distance, sirens sounded as the Manchester Police Department responded to Rachael Mae's 911 call.

Leah felt her stomach clench as the weapons fire paused, then began again, this time with more intensity. She glanced around the edge of her protective cover to see the four attackers redirect their fire toward her mother and the few children and parents remaining with her in the covered picnic area. Her mom had turned a heavy wood and steel picnic table on its side to provide cover. As Leah watched, her mother stuck her service revolver

over the top of the table's edge and fired several shots high in the attackers'
direction. Leah grimaced, realizing her mom couldn't aim at the shooters
directly, for fear of hitting her and Rachael Mae. Her mom was trapped by
both her attackers and her daughters' positions as they tried to help.

A few seconds later, her mother bent low around the side of the
overturned picnic table and threw three rapid-fire shots at them. One
attacker went down, a blood red mist exploding from his back. In response,
the remaining three attackers dropped to the ground in prone firing
positions and hammered the picnic table with bullet after bullet, sending
splinters flying in all directions. Leah heard a scream as a parent near her
mom was hit and crumpled to the ground.

Leah texted Rachael Mae once more. We need to move now. Mom's
good, but she doesn't have much time left unless we do something.

Right, Rachael Mae replied. Let's charge 'em. Their attention's on
Mom.

Go now! Leah replied, pocketing her phone just as her mother rose
from behind the overturned picnic table for a shot. But before she could
trigger her service revolver, Leah saw her jerk once, then again as puffs
of dust rose from the front of her thick uniform shirt, then dropped back
behind the overturned picnic table.

Leah screamed and charged the prone attackers, all five-feet-one of her
strong, athletic frame charging with mindless anger and rage. Her mother
was down. She had to stop all this and get to her mother.

The ear-splitting crack of the weapons fire covered the crunching of
her steps on the playground's beauty bark path. Panic and rage drove her
forward; no thought of the danger; only saving her mother.

The three remaining attackers rose as Leah closed the distance, side-
by-side with weapons raised. A female shooter stood closest to Leah, her

rifle trained on the covered picnic area, dressed in dark coveralls with a black mask over her face. A similarly dressed tall, muscular man stood closest to Rachael Mae's approach from the opposite side, with his weapon also aimed at the picnic area. Another man, much like the first, stood between them.

As Leah closed, the female shooter seemed to sense Leah's approach and glanced her way. Through the slits in her facemask, the woman's eyes went wide as she focused on Leah and swung her matte black assault rifle toward Leah and jerked on the trigger. The woman cursed as her rifle failed to fire, its chambering slide open and the rifle empty.

In that same instant, Leah lowered her shoulder and crashed into the woman, the impact of Leah's strong, compact body knocking the woman two steps to the right and into the gunman next to her. That man staggered a step, his stubby-barreled Uzi jerking skyward as three bullets cracked harmlessly overhead.

The female shooter recovered in a moment, tossing her rifle aside and grabbing Leah by the shoulders. She shoved Leah with both hands, sending her back a step as the woman swept one hand down to retrieve her rifle and the other to a cargo pocket on her right leg. She came up with a fresh magazine and her rifle in the same movement, slapped the magazine into the weapon's well, and pulled back the charging handle.

Leah took advantage of the split second of time the woman needed to slide the magazine into place and closed the distance between them. As she did, Leah planted her right foot firmly on the ground, spun ninety degrees to the right, chambered her left foot to her side, and shot the heel of her foot beneath the woman's rifle and into the woman's ribs.

The female gunperson grunted from the impact of the kick, as Leah's weight came down on her left foot. Not pausing, Leah spun to the left and swung her right foot in an arc from right to left, smacking the side of her foot into the female shooter's weapon, hoping to knock the rifle away.

But the woman retained her grip on her weapon, stepped back, and whipped it into line with Leah's chest, as Leah's right foot landed from the kick. But Leah wasn't done yet. Continuing her clockwise spin left, she spun full circle on the ball of her right foot and snapped the heel of her left foot head-high into the side of the woman's face. Leah felt bones shatter in the woman's jaw and cheekbone as the woman's eyes rolled and she spun slowly to the ground, her rifle dropping to the grass beside her.

All of that consumed precious seconds; and as her attacker fell, Leah saw Rachael Mae go to the ground astride the back of the furthest male attacker. She'd locked her legs around the man's chest, her left arm locked around the man's right arm at a painful angle above his head, her other arm wrapped around the man's throat. Leah smiled grimly as her sister squeezed the man's neck, compressing several critical nerve bundles and an artery. In another minute, the man would be unconscious.

The remaining male shooter regained his footing after being knocked to the side by the woman Leah had just downed. He turned slowly, deliberately to face Leah, six feet away, his assault rifle steady in his hands and well out of Leah's reach. "Nice try, little girl. You're skilled, but not nearly enough. First you, then I'll finish your little friend."

Leah closed her eyes for only a second as she whispered, "If now's the time, Lord, Your will be done. But if not, please help me."

Two loud cracks split the air; and the attacker facing her jerked once, then again. His weapon dropped from numb hands to the grass at his feet as the man's face went slack, his glaring eyes dimmed, and he crumpled to the ground.

Leah followed the sound of the shots to a house two hundred yards away, on a low hill overlooking the park. She caught the glint of sunlight *on a rifle barrel at the railing of the house's long covered porch. And then it was gone.*

"Thanks, Lord," Leah whispered as she checked on Rachael Mae, who was climbing to her feet from her unconscious attacker. They both turned and sprinted for the covered picnic area where she'd seen her mother fall.

Leah felt the touch of a small hand on her arm and opened her eyes to find Rachael Mae standing next to her, on the first step leading to the house's front door. "Are you all right?"

Leah nodded slowly, drawing in a deep breath and levering herself upright from the brick wall. "I think so," she replied. Then, after a second, she added, "But I'm not sure."

Leah glanced down to find Annie Mae's arms wrapped around her waist. Leah laid a soft hand atop her niece's tight red curls. "Definitely better now," she said, her eyes meeting Rachael Mae's strained expression with a wan smile.

"Please be okay," Annie Mae said in a soft, small voice.

Leah squatted down and wrapped her arms around Annie Mae's tiny shoulders. "I'm okay now. One of your amazing hugs is exactly what I needed."

Leah took Annie Mae's tiny hand in hers and let herself be led up the steps, past the heavy wooden front door and into the house. The beauty of the place seemed to ease all the tension from her, with its light coffee-colored walls, natural hickory window and door trim, and the two-story tall entry with its simple, elegant crystal chandelier. Gray slate with mocha-colored streaks surfaced the entryway floor and led to a great room with a long, wide combination family room, kitchen, and bay window eating nook. Cheerful curtains in navy blue framed wide windows looking out over a half-acre yard of green, carefully manicured grass and boxwood shrubs lining a black rail fence. The calm and peace of the place felt like exactly what Leah needed right then.

Annie Mae led Leah to a chair at a small round table in the room's bay window. Leah took the proffered chair and let out a long sigh. "You have the touch, sister," she said. "I love this place. I feel my RPM ramping down, already."

"That's a good thing," Rachael Mae replied. "You had me worried out there on the front porch."

Annie Mae climbed into Leah's lap and wrapped her tiny arms around Leah again in a rib-crunching hug. Leah cupped her niece's face in her hands and tilted the little girl's face up. "And when, exactly, did you get so big and strong?"

Annie Mae giggled, then leaned back and raised her slender arms to show tiny biceps.

"She's been doing all sorts of exercises since she heard you were coming," Rachael Mae said. "Every night, she prays she'll grow up to be just like you."

Leah felt a lump form in her throat. Annie Mae noticed the expression and once again stared deep into Leah's eyes. "You're sad, Auntie Leah."

Leah nodded. "A little, but I'm so much better now here with you."

"Mama says that's my job," Annie Mae replied. "To make people smile."

Leah's smile came easier this time as she met Annie Mae's gaze and drew the little girl into a warm hug. "Well, you're doing a great job."

Rachael Mae stepped over to Leah's chair, gently lifted Annie Mae from Leah's lap, and settled her on the floor. "Why don't you go outside and play while your aunt and I catch up? It's big people talk, and I bet Sunny's been missing you and needs water in his bowl."

Annie Mae stood up straighter, all tiny shoulders. "I can do that," she replied. "I'll play with him, so he doesn't get sad like Auntie Leah."

When Annie Mae was gone, Rachael Mae took a seat across from Leah and reached out both hands to take Leah's in her own. Her narrow, angular brows bunched together, her eyes taking on a darker, worried expression. "You've had a busy day. We saw you on the news. You've got blood splatter on your jeans and a thin line of blood across your blouse. Is that a knife wound?"

Leah swallowed hard to force down her emotions as the image of the little girls at the store flashed through her mind once more. "It's just a scratch. But I bought this blouse and these jeans just for this trip. Now they're ruined."

Rachael Mae forced a chuckle. "I bet they were nice choices at the time. The pale blue of the blouse sets off your natural tan and auburn hair and brings out our family's blue eyes. As for the jeans, you fill those out just fine; but blood does nothing for them. How about I dress that wound and you get a change of clothes?"

Leah frowned. "If you can bring me your first aid kit, I can handle the repairs to my stomach."

Rachael Mae laughed. "Nonsense. I'll get your suitcase from your car, but I will definitely be dressing that wound."

Leah rolled her eyes as Rachael Mae turned and headed for the front door.

Five minutes later, with Leah's suitcase upstairs in the guest room, Rachael Mae returned with a small tube of antibiotics and a narrow sheet of paper with a line of adhesive butterfly strips. As Leah lifted her blouse, Rachael Mae dabbed on ointment, pulled the edges of the thin knife slice together, and butterflied the skin into place.

When that was done, she got them both a steaming mug of hot coffee, returned to her chair, and said, "Like I said, we saw you on the news. They showed a video of you taking out the two shooters at the Kroger in Tullahoma."

When Leah groaned, Rachael Mae cut her off with a raised hand. "For anyone who didn't know you, it might be hard to identify you from the angles of the cameras. But I recognized you the moment I saw the video."

"It just happened. I was in the wrong place at the wrong time."

Rachael Mae snorted her disagreement. "Never apologize for what you did in that store. You were exactly the right person in the right place at the right time. I can't imagine the number of lives you saved."

Leah sighed. "It appeared on the news, on television?"

Rachael Mae nodded. "Nothing that clearly showed your face. You did an excellent job keeping your chin down and your face away from the store's security cameras. But it's all over the local stations. Some kid recorded it on his phone."

"Not good," Leah replied. "For a host of reasons."

"Forget about the video," Rachael Mae countered. "And thank God for having you there when He did. Someone must stand up to people like the two in the store. Mom raised us and trained us to help others just like you did."

"And trust in God to deliver us," Leah added. "But so many died. Some little girls . . . "

"That's hard," Rachael Mae said. "It's so hard to see the little ones suffer."

"This time, particularly tough," Leah said.

"Does that have something to do with what happened at the front door? You were practically catatonic."

Leah avoided Rachael Mae's eyes as she inhaled her coffee's rich aroma. She took a long drink from the oversized ceramic mug, wondering how much to say and how much she needed to say something but couldn't.

She brought her eyes back to meet Rachael Mae's gaze, seeing her sister's concerned look and remembering how they'd shared every thought when they were young. How many times had the EOG's psychologist suggested she find someone inside the EOG to talk to, to share her worries and anxieties with?

"Every operative has someone," he'd said. "Someone to lean on when things were particularly tough, to help them through." He'd suggested Leah find someone like that. So while her teammates were so busy building their new lives, why not Rachael Mae?

Leah felt the warmth of the coffee play down her throat. She took in a small breath, then said, "I see a lot of death in my job."

"As an analyst for the Secret Service, but . . . " Rachael Mae paused when she saw the sudden shift in Leah's expression. Her face softened as she added, "I see. You're not really an analyst, are you?"

Leah nodded. "And I don't work for the Secret Service."

This time, Rachael Mae nodded. "There were times when I wondered about that. You're on the road a lot for a desk jockey working out of D.C."

"I don't work in Washington, D.C, either."

"Okay," Rachael Mae said, her eyes narrowing as she leaned back in her chair. "Spill it."

"I'm part of a covert operations group that reports to the U.S. Secretary of State. It's called the Extreme Operations Group. I'm with one of EOG's tactical teams, the Home Team. We work below the radar on missions within the U.S. and around the globe when someone threatens the safety and security of the U.S. and the solution needs to be handled out of the limelight."

"Like the Central Intelligence Agency or Federal Bureau of Investigation?" Rachael Mae said.

"Kind of," Leah replied. "But the CIA is forbidden from working cases inside our country. The FBI has similar restrictions internationally. We don't have those boundaries. We go where we're needed. I can't tell you where we've been or what we've done. That's highly classified. But I can tell you our work is for the good of the U.S. and its people—and sometimes people in other countries."

"So, you're a spy," Rachael Mae said, her smile going wide.

Leah nodded. "Kind of, I suppose. Specifically, I'm my team's sniper. As a result, I've seen my share of death. All of us on the team feel any loss of life is a horrible thing. Then again, the people we come up against are generally trying to kill us or someone else. Normally, I'd feel good about doing what I did there, but this time . . . The death of those little girls? It makes me wonder why God could have let that happen."

Rachael Mae let her gaze drift from Leah to her daughter, playing in the yard beyond the bay windows. "That's the question on the mind of many of us in today's world, but I sense there's more. What else is going on?"

Leah drew in a deep breath. "Right. I've been having flashbacks. Like on the front porch. That one was about the day we lost Mom in the park. It felt like I was living the whole thing over again. I had another during a recent mission, about my first Air Force pilot rescue mission. There've been two others, as well."

Rachael Mae leaned back in her chair, glancing through the bay window to the backyard, where Annie Mae was covered in dirt from head to toe, rolling around on the ground with Sunny, the horse-sized white and brown long-haired dog. Without looking back to Leah, Rachael Mae said, "That must have been scary."

"They all were," Leah said.

"Well, please hear me out when I say this."

"Okay . . . " Leah replied, dragging out the word.

Rachael Mae's expression became intense as they stared into each other's eyes. "First and foremost, the things you did to stop those shooters this morning would have made our mother proud. And what you're worried about concerning God's intent when those little girls suffered . . . I believe that's all a part of God's plan to strengthen your belief in Him and to help you trust and glorify Him. It's like Job, in the Bible. God sometimes lets us suffer through hard times to confirm our faith and become stronger in our beliefs. I believe that to the depths of my soul."

When Leah opened her mouth to reply, Rachael Mae raised a hand to cut her off. She nodded toward the backyard, where Annie Mae and Sunny played. "My little red-headed tornado is safer today because of what you did at the store. Some day in the future, when she learns what you did, how you saved so many people's lives, I'm sure she'll be as proud of her Auntie Leah as I am today."

"But the little girls . . . "

"Did you personally check their pulse before you left?" Rachael Mae asked.

"I didn't have time. But their father . . . "

"Then you don't really know if they died or not. I watched a video clip on the news. No one said anything about two little girls dying. There were reports of other deaths, but not those. But the point remains: there's no telling how many more would have died if you hadn't done what you did. Again, as Mom would have said, some people call it courage . . . ,"

"The rest of us call it faith and preparation," Leah said, completing one of their mother's favorite sayings.

"That's right. It was a blessing that we had parents who trained us and taught us how to handle ourselves in a crisis. And that's what we did in the park the day we lost Mom; we handled a crisis. Yes, Mom died, but God put us there to save the others who didn't die that day. God always has a plan. We must trust that He has a plan for each of us, no matter how hard that can be to bear sometimes."

Leah nodded. "Yeah. There's that, I suppose."

"Well, suppose that and more, little sis," Rachael Mae said. "And if being part of the Home Team is your calling, then I'm glad you found that position. And with the flashbacks, maybe that's God telling you that you need to take a break from it now and then, away from the intensity, away from the death and struggle. Have you seen a psychologist? Your group must have one for people who do what you do for a living."

Leah smiled. "The break from it all is why I'm here with you. And I plan to call the shrink in the morning."

Rachael Mae nodded toward where Annie Mae and Sunny rolled around on the grass in the backyard. "Then I'm glad you're here. And so is she," Rachael Mae said, pointing to her little girl. "You see the look on Annie Mae's face? That's real joy, and we all need some of that from time to time."

"Believe in Him. Trust Him. Have faith in Him. Find joy in him," Leah recited.

"Another one of Mom's famous sayings," Rachael Mae said. "So, do you?"

Leah nodded. "I haven't lost my faith in God. Not at all. But seeing those little girls lying there, I've never felt such loss, such rage. I didn't know what to do with those emotions. On the team, we're cold as ice when we're in the field and the pressure is high. All of us were chosen for our ability to be like that under fire. I'm not used to anything less than the calm, calculated feeling that comes from relying on my skills and working with people like my teammates."

Rachael May chuckled. "'Staying frosty,' as Mom used to say?"

Leah nodded. "Yep. She said a lot of stuff like that."

"Maybe it's not so much the possible death of those little girls that has you down,"

"Now, my big sister's a shrink?"

Rachael Mae gave Leah her best are-you-crazy look. "Not hardly. But I wonder if those little girls might signify something missing from your life or something you're afraid of losing."

"Missing from my life?" Leah held up her hands as if in self-defense. "We've been down this path too many times before, sister-of-mine. I don't need a husband or kids to feel fulfilled. I have my faith, you and your family, my work, and my team. That's more than enough."

Rachael Mae chuckled. "Having a family doesn't mean you give up everything. It just means you have the chance to serve more people, people who love you and are personally involved and interested in your life. Having Karl and Annie Mae certainly hasn't taken anything away from my life. I haven't told you yet, but I earned my seventh-degree black belt in Taekwondo last month. How's that for a full-time mom and professional out doing things?"

Leah's mouth dropped. "You made seventh-degree? While I'm still only a sixth-degree? Fine, but I refuse to call you Grand Master Rachael Mae."

Rachael Mae's face split into a broad smug grin. "You will if you want to work out with me at the dojang while you're here."

Leah returned the grin, crossing her arms over her chest. "Remember, I'm a master, too. Only sixth degree like you used to be, but I'm still a master."

"A baby master," Rachael Mae replied through a bright grin.

They both laughed. "But I do get what you're saying. And I do trust that God has a reason for everything, even as much as it feels like He may have messed this one up."

"If not that, are you worried about losing something from your life right now?" Rachael Mae said.

Leah blew out a long breath. "Not sure, but it could be partly what's happening with my team right now. They're all moving on with their lives: marriage, property, responsibilities."

"Normal adult things . . . " Rachael Mae offered. "And they're not with you as much as they might have been in the past?"

"Right," Leah said. "I know it's silly, but it leaves me feeling hollow when I think about it."

"I wish I could help you beyond what you already know," Rachael Mae said. "In both cases, I guess you'll just have to wait until He lays things out for you. And He will."

Rachael Mae's expression changed in the next instant, a conspiratorial glint brightening her eyes. "And now, beyond the trauma of the day, I know this guy . . ."

Leah groaned. Once again, it was an old conversation. "Thanks, but no thanks," Leah replied.

"But he's tall, good looking, intelligent, and so strong. I'm not going to give up easily on this one," Rachael Mae replied. "You two are made for each other."

Leah chuckled, deciding the best strategy would be deflecting the conversation. "Thanks, but now that my face has been on television, I'm going to avoid anything public for a time. No meeting Mr. Right until things settle down, if ever. I'm supposed to be a covert operator, and the video on the news didn't help with that. I'm sure a sketch of me will be out to the media before long, and that will only make things even worse."

Rachael Mae's next words were interrupted as Leah's tactical watch vibrated. She glanced at it. A message spread across the dark screen in tiny white letters: *Call the Director.* "I'm going to have to take this," she said, rising from her chair.

"Spy stuff?" Rachael Mae asked, her grin giving away her weak attempt at a joke.

Leah gave Rachael Mae a knowing glance, then fished her cell phone from the back pocket of her jeans. As she stepped out of the kitchen and into the foyer near the front door, she pressed a key on her phone to connect the call to Paul Samuelson's office. "This is Romeo Alpha."

"This is Overwatch Prime," Paul replied. "Shift to secure communications."

"Roger," Leah replied. She shut down the cell phone and raised her watch to her lips, activating its embedded microphone. "Overwatch Prime, this is Romeo Alpha standing by."

"It's just you and me on this call, Leah. We can dispense with the communications protocol," Director Samuelson replied.

"Yes, sir," Leah replied.

She could hear the strain in Paul's voice as the first words came out. "Let me get right to the point. Our goal is for you to be on vacation, not become a television personality."

"You saw the news," Leah started. "How much trouble am I in?"

"It made national news a half hour ago. Truth is, you did us all proud. I'm not the only one who thinks it's time people like those two shooters should think twice about attacking innocents. You did your part delivering that message."

"But . . . " Leah countered.

"It's not good to have one of my best operatives on national TV, but I'm doing my best to soften the blow," Paul replied. "Our sources at the highest levels of law enforcement and the media have been advised that your anonymity is a national security concern. All have agreed to delete any artist's renderings of you before they're released and to suppress the videos. The Secretary of State herself made some of those calls. You're in the clear as much as you can ever be after something like that."

"Thank you, sir. So I can continue my vacation?"

"Yes, of course, but the Secretary has taken an active interest in the increased frequency of active shooters across the country and overseas. Is there anything from the encounter at the store you can report that might help us understand what we're up against?"

"Actually, there is," Leah said. "The second shooter I took down, the woman, was no off-the-street crazy. She was a trained fighter. She carried herself and handled her weapons like a seasoned professional."

"And the other shooter?" Paul asked.

"He was more like what you'd expect of a person who'd pick up a gun and act on impulse. He was practically defenseless when I took him down. But the woman . . . "

"That is interesting," Paul replied. "I talked with Dr. Malcome, the group psychologist. He advised me that active shooters have several common characteristics, but being a trained fighter is not on that list. Would you be willing to invest a little of your vacation time consulting with local law enforcement and passing along anything they discover about the shooters? I will, in turn, pass the information along to Dr. Malcome, so he can add it to the file he's developing for the Secretary of State. You do have your Secret Service cover-credentials with you?"

"Of course," Leah replied, her thoughts beginning to spin around the mystery of a trained operator as an active shooter: trained operator versus unstable, impulse-driven active shooter. They did seem contradictory terms. Then again, she'd seen government operators go off the rails and strike out in the past. It was rare, but it had happened within the Extreme Operations Group's ranks not that long ago. "I'm happy to help out."

"That's great," Paul said. "And since you are officially involved in a sanctioned mission, the EOG will be happy to cover the full cost of your time in Tennessee."

"Very kind, sir," Leah said, feeling somehow uplifted about being drafted to investigate the events at the grocery store, like maybe she'd have a chance for some closure. She wasn't a detective by any stretch of the imagination; but if she could uncover information useful in forestalling future attacks like that, it might help. It wouldn't bring Samantha and her sister back, but it would be something.

CHAPTER 4

Thirty miles north of Rachael Mae's home, in the city of Murfreesboro, Tennessee, two men sat at a worn maple desk at the back of a small video game store. Play It Again Video was a modest, glass-fronted shop in a well-kept but aging strip mall off Memorial Drive, a major route through the growing metropolis forty minutes south of Nashville. The store's shelves were lined with carefully sorted video games, both old and new, for ancient systems like Commodore 64, Atari, Nintendo, and Sega. For gamers favoring bleeding edge games, one side of the store was dedicated to the latest and greatest tabletop gaming and virtual reality games. A special, soundproof booth was available in one corner of the store for trying out virtual reality offerings, which sometimes encouraged loud and active participation by the store's customers. The store was a favored destination for young and old gamers across the Murfreesboro and Nashville cosmopolitan area.

The store's manager leaned back in his chair, the heels of his freshly polished tan penny loafers resting on the worn wooden desktop. In his late twenties, his skin was a rich nut brown, as were his eyes. Lanky, he was immaculately dressed in tailored brown slacks, a soft yellow open-collared shirt, and a tan herringbone blazer. His black hair was carefully parted in the middle with thick waves flowing down the sides of his face to his jacket collar.

"Who knew recycling used video games could be so lucrative, Haider," he said. He purposely kept his gaze directed away from the man standing to the left of the desk. Haider wore a dark green tracksuit with white double stripes down his legs and arms. Stocky but very fit, his massive arm and leg muscles strained the fabric of his track suit, rippling beneath the polyester material as he shifted his weight from foot to foot. Sweat dripped down his dark, deeply lined face and into glaring, coal-dark eyes. He wiped the sting of his post-workout sweat from his eyes with an impatient swipe of a thick-fingered hand. "Didn't you see the news, Steven?"

"Of course, I did," Steven replied. "Remember, I was there with The Hatchet when it went down."

Haider swung around to stand directly in front of the desk, fists on hips. He frowned, then swung a huge paw that connected with Steven's soft leather shoes, knocking them off the desktop and spinning Steven in his chair. "Then you know the operation was a bust. And why are you talking about this pathetic excuse of a store and not focusing on our mission when it might be failing?"

In a single, swift motion, Steven was out of his chair and around the desk with a long-bladed knife in his hand, the gleaming, razor-edged steel springing to within an inch of Haider's throat. "Because the store is interesting, as opposed to waiting for almost ten years for a mission to finally get going—long, boring years, I might add." He withdrew the knife and stepped back, waving it from side to side. "And I don't think I would miss you at all if you were to disappear suddenly."

In an equally smooth, sudden flash of movement, Haider stepped forward and shot out the palm of his left hand, connecting hard with Steven's chest in a thump that sent the man and his knife back two steps. As Steven regained his footing, Haider stepped into him, his right hand reaching out to grasp the hand with the knife. He twisted Steven's hand and deftly removed the knife from his grasp.

"I can do this all day," Haider said. "You pull your puny little blade, and I'll take it away every time. We've done it so many times, perhaps it is I who would benefit if you were to suddenly disappear. I remind you that I am skilled with numerous weapons and forms of martial arts. You are skilled at . . . literally nothing useful."

Steven blanched. "I have skills," he stammered.

Haider sneered and tossed the knife aside to clatter against the wall behind the desk. "Yes, you do, and those were important when we started, when we needed your technical knowledge. But our plans are nearly complete, and your value to our cause has certainly diminished—if The Hatchet doesn't pull the plug on the whole thing after today."

"That's not true, and our master knows it; and he's not going to pull the plug on anything. And in addition to those other duties, I have maximized the return on the investment our leaders made in this shop, which has provided important funding for most of the last decade."

Haider shrugged and stepped back over to the left side of the desk, dismissing Steven to return to his chair with a wave of a hand. "That much, I cannot deny. But what happens if and when we begin the actual operation and you are called on to sacrifice your life for our cause? What will you do with your fancy clothes, alcohol-drenched parties, and this store then?"

As Steven framed his answer to the question, he was silenced by Haider stepping away from the desk and down the store's narrow center aisle to the front door. There, he bolted the lock on the door and flipped the *open* sign over to read *closed*. He turned back to face Steven. "You're sure he's coming today?"

Steven nodded and glanced at a large, gold-faced watch on his left wrist. "Any second, in fact. His note said we are to review the proof of concept that took place in Tullahoma and, based on that, decide if we're ready to move forward."

"But it failed . . . " Haider started.

Steven dropped back into the antique, wood-backed desk chair and leaned forward to steeple his hands on the desktop. "I'm not sure he will agree."

The rest of their debate was cut off by a light knocking from the back of the store.

Steven's face brightened. "He is here," he said as he climbed to his feet and disappeared down a small aisle behind tall wooden shelves at the back of the store.

He was back a few seconds later with their boss, a distinguished-looking man in a two-piece tailored gray suit, white shirt, and blue tie. The man's face was darkly tanned, angular, with high cheekbones and an oversized, hooked blade of a nose; and he had coal-black hair with gray streaks at the temples. Steven shivered as he glanced into the man's eyes. It was like looking into dark flames. This was the man who ran not just their Tennessee operation but also controlled a nationwide effort to destroy the United States from within. This was the man whose own team referred to him as The Hatchet, and he didn't mind a bit.

The Hatchet stepped around the desk and lowered himself into Steven's chair. "I see your store continues to be well-organized. And the back room? The gaming room where you take the recruits?"

"Well set up and well-utilized," Steven replied, pulling a chair over from against the wall to sit across the desk from his superior. "We have six solid recruits engaged here daily. I can give you a tour, if you like."

The Hatchet shook his head. "Perhaps later. Right now, we talk about the Tullahoma pilot test."

"How bad was it?" Haider started. "I saw on the news that the recruit we assigned to the task and our own agent were—"

The Hatchet raised a hand to cut off Haider's next words. "The experiment was an enormous success, and you both are to be rewarded for helping to make it so. You, Steven, for acquiring the technology and programming the subjects. You, Haider, for identifying, training, and positioning our seed shooter."

"But . . . " Haider started but was cut off again when The Hatchet smiled as though tolerating two small children incapable of understanding the most basic of points.

"Yes, their efforts were interrupted before they could kill the larger numbers of people we projected." The Hatchet paused, then added to Steven, "What were the final numbers?"

Haider raised a tentative hand. "I monitored the first-responder radio transmissions. The police reported ten dead and seven injured, at least one of those critically."

The Hatchet nodded. "That supports the point that our pilot test succeeded even more, proving the concept of our upcoming operation. We are ready."

"But the woman who interfered—she was able to stop our subjects with what seemed such a small effort. And like you said, we'd hoped for more . . . " Haider said.

The Hatchet waved off the comment once again. "It's not the body count that matters. It's the fact that our shooters infiltrated the store, killed and injured numerous people there, and created panic and fear that right now, at this very moment, is rippling through that community. Law enforcement in the area has been turned upside down trying to figure out what happened. The people living in that city are, without a doubt, suitably terrified. Those were our goals, and those goals were achieved."

Steven's expression became thoughtful. "The reprogramming, the behavior modification routine?"

"I had observers in the store and watching from nearby. From all we can tell, the programming worked as anticipated," The Hatchet replied. "The recruit performed without hesitation. The seed shooter added depth to the horror and fear in that store. I have already talked to the Chairman about our operation. He wants two more demonstrations in two larger cities but is optimistic about our readiness to kick off phase one. And once we do that and follow with the second phase of our efforts, the impact on this corrupted, filthy country will be profound."

"Sixty sites across the country?" Haider asked. "As planned?"

The Hatchet's face went still. "Yes, and when that happens, the core of this heinous democracy will be shattered from within. The United States is weaker now than at any point in its history. When we act, we will tear it apart from the inside out."

"And purge the world of this country's blasphemous, gluttonous ways," Steven added.

Haider rolled his eyes at Steven's comments, purposely eyeing the man from his head to his toes in his expensive clothes.

The Hatchet looked at Steven, ignoring Haider, his eyes more alive than before. "Yes. All of that. And as for both of you; when our work is done, if you have not already been martyred and delivered to paradise, there will be a place for both of you in the new order that follows the fall of this nation."

Haider's face brightened. "New order?"

"Yes," replied The Hatchet. "A world led by people we've placed high in the government. People who see what we do as an opportunity for their own rise to power, who will do our bidding."

"How soon to you think we might begin?" Steven asked, his tone a notch higher with excitement than his usual, arrogant inflection.

"Soon, my brother. Very soon," The Hatchet replied.

CHAPTER 5

The next morning, after seeing Annie Mae off to preschool and Rachael Mae off to her job in nearby Manchester, Leah placed her call to Dr. Malcome, the Extreme Operations Group's consulting psychologist. As a matter of course, Dr. Malcome interviewed the EOG's team members every three months or after particularly difficult missions. The slender, fair-skinned man with sandy brown hair, high cheekbones, and striking blue eyes gave Leah a cheerful wave as his face appeared on her tablet computer's screen.

"Hey, Doc," Leah said.

"Hey yourself, Romeo," he replied, his lopsided grin going wider.

She started to protest, but he cut her off with a raised hand. "I know. I know. You hate the call sign. Not right for a woman, you always say. If I was a Freudian, I'd suggest latent tendencies of some kind; but you are perhaps one of the most stable, well-grounded operators in the group, so I won't do that."

"Thank you so much for that."

They both laughed, then Malcome said, "I wasn't expecting a call from you until after your vacation. What's going on?"

Leah paused, worried about how to express her concerns. Even a psychologist might think the whole flashback thing was strange. He might even pull her off duty if he thought it was bad enough.

She scrubbed her face with the palm of her hand as she considered, then thought the best approach with the shrink was the same one she generally took in life: the direct one.

"I'm seeing things, Doc."

Malcome frowned. "Pink elephants or something more specific?"

"Funny," she replied. "But I'm serious. Before my last mission, I experienced several vivid flashbacks: one from my youth when two bullies tried to steal a picture frame from me that I'd made for a picture I had of my father. The second, from the day when I watched the soldiers carry his flag-draped casket off the C-130. Both flashbacks were so stark, so real, I thought I was living through them again. I've had two others since then. One happened at the end of the mission my team just completed, the second when I arrived at my sister's home to start my vacation yesterday."

"I see," Malcome said. "I'm glad you called. First, let me tell you that what you've experienced is not uncommon for people in your profession, where you see a lot of violence, bloodshed, and death, no matter how righteous the cause. But that's not intended to diminish the seriousness of it all."

"Does that mean my operational status could be pulled?" Leah asked.

Malcome nodded, a frown creasing his brow. "It could, but I think it's too soon to jump to that conclusion. What this sounds like is a symptom of Post-Traumatic Stress Disorder."

"But most of my flashbacks were from my childhood, well before I entered the military, well before I saw any combat."

"An unresolved traumatic event experienced in combat can result in PTSD, but many people enter the military who have traumatic events in childhood that stimulate PTSD symptoms. In fact, anyone can experience PTSD because of sexual or physical assault, abuse, devastating loss, or other trauma. It can be cumulative, resulting in complex PTSD. And symptoms can include flashbacks, emotional numbing and distancing, avoidance of trauma memory, irritability, being easily startled."

"How do I get past this?"

"It might take a little work; but there's a lot of help available for people through Evidenced Based Therapy such as Eye Movement Desensitization and Reprocessing, Cognitive Processing Therapy, Prolonged Exposure Therapy, and other strategies that fall within the Standard of Care. The good news is that 30 percent of people with PTSD fully recover, while another 40 percent get better with treatment. In some cases, people may receive enough support and are able to cope well enough with the impact of the traumatic event that they don't require treatment at all. But before we talk about what you might benefit from, fill me in on a few things. First, how was the issue between you and the two bullies who wanted your picture frame resolved?"

"They were large girls and assumed that because of my small size, I'd be a pushover."

"I gather it did not end well for them?" Malcome asked.

"A shoulder wrenched out of socket for one and a broken nose and swollen knee for the other. I was suspended for a week, even though the principal acknowledged I was defending myself."

"And your mother? I assume your father wasn't in the picture by that time."

"She was disappointed but supportive. She and my father, when he was alive, taught us the best way to avoid a fight was not to be there. I'd failed in that respect. I should have run rather than stood my ground."

"Not sure I agree, but I get the point," Malcome replied. "What about the time when you watched your dad's body being returned to the States?"

"He had a video prepared for us in case he was killed on deployment. My mom, my sister, and I watched it immediately after his funeral. In the video, Dad advised us that he loved us more than life itself and to always remember he died defending his country and the rights of the less fortunate. He told us to be brave and not mourn him, to celebrate the life God provided him, the love he had for us, and to carry on his commitment to God, family, and fighting the good fight."

"And how did you feel after that?"

"Proud," Leah said. The word came without thinking. "I felt strong and, just as he suggested, didn't mourn his loss but determined that I would enter the military and carry on his mission."

"A noble cause," Malcome said.

Leah said nothing in response; and as the silence lingered, Malcome asked. "What about the other flashbacks? I assume one was about your mother's death, and the other involved one of your Air Force Special Operations missions?"

"You know about those things?"

"I've read your file. When you came onboard with the EOG, you were asked to reveal events like those."

"Of course," Leah said. "One was about the day we lost our mother, when four gunmen trapped her and a large number of parents and children in the city park because of a case she broke as a deputy sheriff."

"Didn't you and your sister play a role in stopping that attack?"

Leah nodded, feeling mist form across her vision. "We did, but our mother was killed in the process."

"I read the news reports about how you and your sister, with the help of an anonymous marksman, saved more than thirty lives that day. Your mother was a career law enforcement officer. As an LEO, don't you think she would have been proud of your actions even though she was lost?"

Leah swallowed hard, then nodded. "That's pretty much what she said when I held her as she died."

Malcome nodded. "What about the flashback that brought up your air force mission?"

Leah let out a long, deep sigh. This call was turning out to be way more challenging than she had anticipated. For her whole life, she'd been the quiet, happy one wherever she went. On the Home Team, she was the one who kept spirits high and used humor to keep the rest of the team focused. And now here she was, pouring out her soul and visiting unwelcome memories. The direct approach? Right.

"It was a pilot rescue mission in Syria."

"A mean place, for sure," Malcome said.

"Without a doubt," Leah said. "I was solo. The rest of my team was blown off target by a sheer wind when we came in from fifteen thousand feet. It was me, two wounded copter-jockeys, and seven attackers facing us. I managed to take down six of the attackers before running out of good ammo. The rest of my ammo got beat up when I landed during that sheer wind. A single attacker was left, and it was only me between the two men and the final assault; and they weren't in any condition to fight. That enemy soldier turned out to be a woman with a rusty AK47. Even so, I figured I was toast; and my only option was to charge her and hope I could take her out of the picture so the pilot and his gunner could escape."

"You thought you were going to die."

She nodded again. "I did."

"But you're here now. You survived," Malcome said.

"I am, and I did," Leah said. "That female shooter—she stopped in her tracks as I charged out of the rock hut I'd been using for cover. She looked at me with a combination of disgust and weariness and tossed the assault rifle aside before I got to her. Then she just turned on her heel and disappeared into the desert."

"Again, you survived. How did you feel right then, in that moment?"

"I didn't feel anything. I gathered up those two men, and we hightailed it to our extraction point. Six hours later, we were at a U.S. base; and I was making my way to the mess tent. And I didn't lose a bit of sleep over any of it at the time. In fact, I could say that about all the events in those flashbacks."

Malcome nodded. "PTSD symptoms often manifest well after the events a person experiences. Is there anything more recent that may have played a role in stimulating your reaction today?"

"Not so much," Leah replied. "We found a young girl who seemed to stimulate the flashback about the Syria operation. I had just arrived at my sister's house last night when the one involving my mother's death occurred."

Malcome paused as he appeared to jot some notes on a tablet off-screen. When he met Leah's eyes directly once again, he smiled. "I have some good news for you."

"I could use some."

"You're not all that weird."

"Weird? Is that a psychological term?"

Malcome chuckled. "You'd be surprised. But the truth is what you're experiencing may be complex PTSD, or even simple PTSD. It doesn't help that you're exhausted by the intense operation tempo of your team, about which I talked to Director Samuelson. Your mission-fatigue isn't responsible for the PTSD, per se, but may have cracked opened the door to the symptoms of PTSD, such as the flashbacks. But I need to emphasize that fatigue, alone, isn't causing the symptoms. It's only making you become more vulnerable.

"The psych profile we built for you when you signed on with the EOG suggests you're a strong, self-sufficient person by nature. That leads me to theorize that you are not deep into PTSD so much as you're simply exhausted. All of us, when we are fatigued, experience mind-wanderings, even waking dreams. If we listen to our bodies during those times, we take a break and rest up; and our mind recalibrates back to normal function and perhaps holds off what might be seen as PTSD symptoms. But let me ask you this: is there anything else going on in your life that might be adding to this situation?"

Leah recalled her thoughts about Sam, Allen, and Jessica, and how their lives seemed to be moving on and leaving her behind. She explained the situation to Dr. Malcome.

"There you go," Malcome replied. "I'll bet when the op tempo got tough in the past, the four of you would get together and blow off steam. You would exercise together, train together, maybe simply hang out and talk."

Lean frowned, then said, "That's about how it went in the past. Now, not so much. They're all busy with their new lives."

Malcome made a show of lifting his legal tablet and setting it aside. "Then here's my prescription for you for now: get some rest during your vacation; and after that, find something or someone outside your job to provide you with some of what you're missing from your team. It can be a person but doesn't have to be. It can be an activity, a passion, something that might refresh you and balance your life."

"You want me to 'get a life,'" Leah replied, her tone dry, flat.

"In a nutshell, yes. But I also want to continue our sessions on a regular basis. PTSD is not something to take lightly. It can get worse if a person doesn't or isn't able to get support. I don't want you in that category. You got that?"

"Yes, sir," Leah said, offering him a mock salute. "I will rest and figure out something to occupy my mind in a positive way. Not sure what that might be, beyond chasing bad guys, but I'll give it a shot. And I'll stay in touch. If I do that, does that mean I remain on operational status?"

Malcome shook his head. "Nope. Not at all. You are absolutely deactivated until the flashback situation is resolved. No one needs you to have another flashback at a critical moment during a mission. Too many people depend on you to allow that to happen. There's a person in your area who is one of the nation's leaders in PTSD therapy. His office is in Nashville, and he's under contract with numerous law enforcement agencies. I'll text you his number and call ahead to see if I can get you in to see him. I'd like him to assess your situation and help determine the best course of action to get you back out there kicking down doors."

"I'm not a door-kicker," Leah said, smiling, an inkling of hope entering her mind and lightening her heart. "I'm a sniper."

Malcome smiled again. "Then my goal is to get you back into deep, dark places, spying on people from lofty heights and shooting at them as soon as possible."

"That'll do," Leah said. "And thanks. I feel better just talking about it."

"That's what I'm here for, Romeo," Malcome said.

Leah groaned as he disconnected the video call. "I need to get that call sign changed."

CHAPTER 6

The day outside was cool and clear as Leah ended her call with the EOG psychologist and headed for the Starbucks coffee shop a few minutes from Rachael's house. She had made a call to the Coffee County Sheriff's Office and introduced herself as a Secret Service agent. Tullahoma, it turned out, was watched over by two different counties, with half the city watched over by the Coffee County Sheriff's Office and the other half by Franklin County. After long years of cooperation, the two counties nominally agreed to which would take the investigative lead when incidents like this one occurred on the line dividing the two. In this case, she'd learned that Coffee had the lead in the active shooter investigation. With an investigator from that office on the line, she'd asked to review the evidence the sheriff's office had regarding the active shooter incident in Tullahoma.

She was pleased when an investigator from Coffee County agreed to meet to discuss the case. He'd suggested Starbucks and laughed when she asked which one. "The only one for ten miles," he'd replied. She'd forgotten that coffee shops were not a cultural tradition in Tennessee like they were in Washington State. The one where they were meeting turned out to be the only coffee shop for miles in any direction.

She parked in the coffee shop's small lot and made her way into the store, noting the place was packed with a diverse mix of mid-morning crowd: an elderly couple in sweatpants, a young man and woman in business attire, several others in anything from jeans and t-shirts to overalls. At the dozen small tables in the place, people sat with laptops open, cell phones active, and in quiet conversation.

As she scanned the shop, her operator's mind instinctively sizing up each person as a potential threat, one man seemed totally out of place. Even sitting, he was an imposing presence. She gauged him conservatively at six-three and 230 pounds, dressed in a blue flannel shirt with the sleeves rolled up over forearms knotted with thick muscle and a thick neck and broad, tanned face beneath close-cropped dark hair. He appeared to be studying a cell phone that looked oddly tiny in his massive hands.

He has small-town cop written all over him, she concluded.

When the barista called her name to pick up her order, Leah made her way through the tables to where the man sat. He glanced up from his cell phone as she approached, then stood and gave her an inquiring look. "Agent McCarthy?"

She reached to the back pocket of her pale blue skinny jeans, brushed aside the long tail of her University of Tennessee football jersey, and retrieved a thin black leather folder. She set it on the table as she lowered herself into the chair opposite his.

He folded his massive frame back onto his small chair and flipped open the folder. When he scooted it back across the table, he gave her an inquiring look. "Have we met before?" he asked. "You seem familiar."

Leah sipped her coffee, relishing its rich, warm flavor, then shook her head. "I don't think so. Now, I showed you mine; how about you show me yours?"

He reached a thick-fingered hand into the front pocket of his flannel shirt and produced a similar credential folder, this one in light brown leather with a gold badge embossed on the front.

Leah took it, admiring the folder's leather tooling. "Fancy," she said as she flipped it open and read the name listed there: Investigator F. George Weise, Coffee County Sheriff's Office.

"My brother gave it to me when I graduated from the police academy," Weise replied, his eyes focused intently on her face. "And I am certain we have met. I don't forget faces."

Leah ignored the comment and the sudden chill that raced down her spine. Had they met before? In her business, the goal was to remain as inconspicuous as possible. She set his credential folder on the table where Weise let it lie as he snapped his fingers, then leaned back in his chair and flashed her a wide grin that sent an odd, warm feeling down her spine. "You're one of the girls in the park! I knew I'd seen your face before."

Leah felt something lurch in the pit of her stomach. "I'm not sure I know . . . " she started, but he cut her off with a subtle wave of his hand.

"That day, long ago, when a deputy and some kids and their parents were attacked in the city park. It was a long time ago and I was only a kid, but I remember the picture in the newspaper the next day. You were one of the two girls who stopped the attack."

Leah's stomach continued to churn, the previous warm sensation gone and the aroma of her coffee no longer inviting. She nodded, dropping her eyes to the tabletop as she said, "Right. Me and my sister."

Weise's smile faded as his eyes searched her face. "I'm sorry I brought it up. You also lost your mother in that battle, didn't you?"

Leah nodded. "My sister, Rachael Mae, and I . . . But it was a long time ago."

Weise lifted a hand from the tabletop as if to reach across the table for her hand, then thought better of it and pulled back his hand. "Again, I'm sorry."

Leah shook her head, then raised her eyes to meet his gaze once again. "It was a long time ago. And it wasn't just me and my sister. There was another person who shot one of the attackers from the house on the hill overlooking the park. I never saw him, but Rachael Mae did. She said he was a big kid, about our age."

Her brows furrowed as she cast Weise a questioning look. "Wait. You would have been about the right age . . . " she started. "You were the one with the rifle, weren't you?"

Weise nodded, whispering, "It's not common knowledge; but yes, that was me. When I heard the shooting in the park, I didn't think. I just grabbed my father's hunting rifle and made it to the back deck in time to see one of the shooters draw down on you. If I'd paused to think, I might not have done it, but all I saw was a girl I recognized from around town about to be gunned down. So I took the shot."

Leah reached her hand across the table to lay it atop his, where his fingers wrapped around his paper coffee cup. She squeezed his hand briefly, then pulled her hand back. "I owe you my life and probably wouldn't be sitting here today if not for you."

Weise shrugged. It was a small, almost shy gesture from the big man. "I didn't get any sleep for a long time after that. When I saw that man lying there after I shot him . . . "

"I get it," Leah replied. "I still have bad dreams about that day." *And other days like it.* "So now you're a cop?"

Weise nodded. "I think I decided to go into law enforcement because of all that. Being a police officer now may serve as some sort of validation for my actions back then."

Leah nodded, reaching up to brush a strand of auburn hair from her eyes, then shrugged her long, thick braid back over her shoulder. "I suppose we have that in common."

"Your mom's picture is on the Wall of Heroes at the office," Weise said.

"Good to know. I guess we'll always share some sort of bond from that day, given our life choices," Leah said, noticing Weise's small grin, his hazel-brown eyes sparkling, and how that warm sensation once again threatened to course through her body. She mentally shook herself. *I don't have time for that sort of thing right now.*

After a beat, she redirected the conversation. "Investigator Weise, how about we dig into the case we came here to discuss?"

Weise smiled, nodded, and then said, "But first, please call me GW."

"It's Leah," she said. "And I do appreciate your willingness to meet with me. I don't plan to take much of your time, but I would like to ask a few questions and look at any evidence your team gathered from the Tullahoma active shooter incident."

GW leaned back in his chair. "When we got the call from on high from both the FBI and Secret Service saying you'd be calling, I figured we'd be wrestling for jurisdiction on this case. It's happened before."

Leah took a sip of her steaming mocha, then set it next to GW's smaller cup. The symbolism of her cup being bigger than his was not lost on GW, who let out a low, soft chuckle.

Leah laughed, then said, "This is not going to be a contest of which agency has the bigger stick. I assure you, I'm simply in the area visiting relatives; and my boss asked me to investigate what happened. Why he's taken the interest, I don't know, except for the increasing frequency of these mass shootings across the country. My only goal is to look at what you have, report back to my boss, then get out of your hair and return to my much-needed vacation."

The corners of GW's wide, thin-lipped mouth quirked upward at the corners. "Well, you're direct, at least. And I'm certainly glad to hear it. I'll be happy to not only show you what we've found but also keep you in the loop regarding our investigation, as much as you're interested."

Leah forced a tight smile in return. "That would be great. I know it's early in your investigation, but have you found anything out of the ordinary so far?"

GW nodded, then laid a small envelope on the table between them, along with a pair of disposable black gloves. "Aside from the weapons and ammunition and a knife one of the perps used on the person who broke up the attack, this is the only unique item we've found."

Leah unconsciously pressed her hand against her stomach where the knife wound still stung, then accepted the gloves and snapped them into place with the ease of long practice. GW's thick eyebrows arched once more. "You've done this before," he said.

"Once or twice," Leah replied.

"Point taken," GW said as Leah opened the flap on the manila envelope and shook out a single, dark blue strap to land on the tabletop. She picked it up and examined the words printed in pale gold letters on the strap: United States Space Force R&D. Arnold AFB.

"Space Force?" she asked softly.

"It was in the pocket of one of the perps."

"The man or the woman?" Leah asked. "The male shooter seemed young, perhaps the sort who might collect something like this."

"How could you know there was a male and female shooter? We haven't released any information that specific," GW said.

Leah shrugged, keeping her eyes on the strap. "My boss said something about that, I'm sure."

She pulled out her cell phone and snapped a picture of the band. "Looks like something used to hold goggles or one of those headlamps in place."

"My thought as well," GW said.

"I'll send the image to my boss. He has access to just about every military database and may be able to help us identify it."

"Perfect," GW replied. "While he's doing that, why don't you and I head out to Arnold Air Force base? Space Force has a research and development facility there. Maybe they'll know something. It's a fifteen-minute drive from here, and I still have contacts from when I worked there."

Leah snapped her eyes up to meet his gaze. "You're past military?"

GW nodded. "Air Force Criminal Investigations. I was at Arnold when I ended my enlistment."

Leah smiled. She still held her rank as an air force captain. The Extreme Operations Group recruited from all branches of the service for their covert operatives, effectively borrowing people like Leah under an interservice resource sharing agreement. Her teammates on the Home Team—Jessica, Allen, and Sam—still held their military ranks as well. "I bleed blue, too," Leah said.

"Stationed where?" he asked.

"MacDill Air Force Base when I separated," she replied. "Pilot rescue and special weapons expert, so I got around a bit. And thank you for your service."

"Right back at you!" GW replied.

Leah returned the strap to the envelope, pulled off the gloves, and set them aside. "Perhaps we could head out to Arnold tomorrow, if your trip can wait. I've got a meeting with the Tullahoma PD in an hour. I need to get going."

GW rose from his chair, rising like a giant above the tiny table they'd shared. He held out his hand. When she took it, his fingers dwarfing her own small hand, she found his grip surprisingly gentle, yet firm.

"I'll look forward to it," GW said as Leah picked up her coffee, turned and headed out the door.

CHAPTER 7

An hour and a half later, Leah was back in her rental sport utility vehicle, leaving the Tullahoma Police Department and heading back to her sister's house. The sky overhead was darkening as an armada of heavy gray clouds rushed across the sky from east to west. The air felt cool but humid, hinting vaguely at rain. You could never be certain about Tennessee weather, she knew—clear one moment, then cloudy, stormy with lightning and thunder, then clear again an hour later.

Nothing came of her discussions with the Tullahoma Police Department's detective, although she was assured the case was a priority and more information would be forthcoming. The detective had been candid during the discussion, but the coolness of his attitude suggested he wasn't pleased to have a federal agent asking about his case. She understood that some agents working at the federal level treated local law enforcement officers like second rate cops, but she saw no sense in it. Their goals should be the same at all levels of government: to serve and protect.

Her route took her past the Tullahoma Dairy Queen, the same one she'd frequented with friends during high school. Sitting in her vehicle in the DQ's parking lot with a small chocolate soft ice cream cone in one hand, she dialed her boss with the other on her vehicle's hands-free device. Paul Samuelson picked up on the second ring.

"Romeo Alpha," she said. "Reporting in."

"How are you doing, Leah?" Paul replied.

"Fine, given the circumstances. With Dr. Malcome pulling my duty status, I appreciate you trusting me to check out the situation at this end for you. I met with a sheriff's office investigator and the local PD. I didn't get much, but I do have an interesting photo of what might be a head-strap. I sent you the snapshot earlier. It may be nothing. The perp could have purchased it as part of a headlamp setup at a military surplus store."

"Possible," Paul replied. "I'm looking at the image now. Just below the logo, I see some additional very faint characters. I've enlarged the image, but it lost some clarity when you sent it to me. Can you look at it on your phone?"

"On it," Leah replied, setting the ice cream cone aside and bringing up the image of the strap on her cell phone's small screen. She enlarged the image, focusing on the row of letters spelling out United States Space Force and Arnold AFB. There, just below those letters, was a line of even smaller characters she hadn't noticed before. "I can't believe I missed this."

She enlarged the image to its maximum size on her cell phone's small screen, then keyed the edit function and filtered out some of the photo's fuzziness. She squinted to make out what the letters spelled out. "It's hard to make out, but it looks like AV815-X."

"The military has a logistics database that lists property reported missing from all six of the uniformed services. I'll see if I can find anything there."

"Roger that," Leah replied, as the sound of computer keys being pounded came over the line.

"I think I've found it," Paul said a moment later. "Could the third character be an R instead of an 8?"

Leah leaned into the picture, her nose almost touching the screen. "It could be an R. Hard to know for sure."

"Well, if it's an R, the situation just got a lot more interesting," Paul replied.

"What does that mean?"

"Several sets of experimental virtual reality equipment have been reported missing from the Space Force's research and development shop at Arnold Air Force Base. Could that strap be something like a person would use to hold a set of goggles in place, like ski goggles or a virtual reality headset?"

Leah examined the picture once again. "That sounds like a possibility," she replied. "But the piece Investigator Weise had was maybe six inches long. That would be a bit short."

"Looking at the image from my end, it looks like one end of the strap is frayed. That suggests the piece of strap could have been part of a larger one. I'm going to go with that and take a dive into the Defense Advanced Research Projects Agency database and see what I can find. Hang on."

As she waited, her mind wandered back over the past five years with the Home Team. Those had been great times, doing important work and sharing it with people, with friends just as committed to their work as she was. She wondered if Sam, Jessica, and Allen missed her while she was gone, then shook the thought off. They were a team. Even as everyone's lives were heading down different paths at the personal level, she knew she'd always share a unique bond with her teammates. They'd been through too much for any of them to set that aside. Even so, she felt a wave of melancholy flow through her mind, then shoved it aside as her thoughts were interrupted by Paul's exclamation from the other end of the call.

"Bingo," he said. "Four sets of experimental virtual reality equipment were reported missing from the Space Force's research and development facility at Arnold Air Force Base a year ago. It says the equipment was the fourteenth iteration of gear developed for remote piloting of drones and spacecraft. Since then, there have been four additional generations of prototype VR equipment, with losses reported for the newer equipment, as well. I think our guess about the strap being part of the VR goggles that were developed for the project was a good one. The strap must have belonged to one of the missing sets of equipment. It was officially reported lost on a standard Reports of Survey document, which was closed out without substantial findings and logged into the U.S. Space Command property management database. But wait a second. I've expanded my search as we talked. Those weren't the only sets of VR gear to go missing from the Space Force. I'm seeing dozens of Reports of Survey for even older generations of the equipment."

"They just wrote off classified equipment like that?" Leah asked.

"It's not supposed to happen that way," Paul replied. "But losses of equipment from military bases is more common than you'd think. With the military criminal investigators busy with terrorists potentially stealing important items like missile guidance systems, biologicals, chemicals, and next-generation weapons, it's easy to see how something as innocuous as outdated VR equipment wasn't a priority at the time."

"So, what's an active shooter doing with a piece of that equipment?" Leah mumbled.

"The question of the hour," Paul replied.

Leah scrubbed the palm of her hand across her eyes, then retrieved her ice cream cone and took a large bite of the soft, rapidly melting dessert. "I see where this is headed," she groaned. "I'm supposed to be on vacation."

"I get it, and I am sorry about that," Paul replied. "But I think we need to follow up on this. It may be nothing, but it's too odd a situation to let lie. The local law enforcement folks won't have access to the U.S. Space Force like you do with your Secret Service credentials. Why don't you head out to Arnold Air Force Base and see what you can find? I'll have the Secretary contact the joint chief's office and have word passed down to ensure you get access."

"If anything is going on out there, the higher ups calling them would be like waving a red flag. The bad guys would run for the hills the moment they saw me coming. The investigator I met with this morning says he has connections on the base and suggested we go there. No need for the brass to step in."

"That sounds fine. Get on it as soon as you can. That equipment was part of a classified program, so we need to treat this like a potential threat to national security. If someone were to reverse-engineer the equipment, they might be able to do some real damage once the new system is launched."

"I'll set up a trip."

"Fine," Paul said, then let out a low chuckle.

Leah didn't need him to explain the soft laugh. "Don't worry. I'll be my most diplomatic when I talk to the people out there. I can use Investigator Weise as a buffer if anything comes up."

"Good strategy," Paul replied. "Keep me posted on what you find.

"Yes, sir," she started, but the call had already been disconnected.

CHAPTER 8

S itting in his office after coffee with Leah, GW recalled how he'd been working for the sheriff's office for the past ten years, ever since graduating from the Tennessee Law Enforcement Training Academy; and they'd been good years. Originally hoping to be hired as a Tennessee State Trooper, GW made friends at the academy with a woman intending to apply at the Coffee County Sheriff's Office, which supported a small county located forty miles south of Nashville. Her description of the work, quality of life, and the small-town feel of the county's cities struck a chord with him. It awakened his own desire to support communities like Tullahoma and Manchester, where he grew up, and still have the chance to investigate challenging cases like he'd done as a staff sergeant assigned to the Air Force Office of Special Investigations. With his background and abundance of commendations for his work in the air force, the Coffee County sheriff hired him the day he had submitted his application. After five years in a patrol car, he'd made investigator and now could not be happier in any other role.

GW knew he'd found his place in the world. He loved working with the people in the county, with their diversity of interests and issues. Every day gave rise to something new, so he was never bored. It might be something as simple as a kid making off with his friend's bicycle or as complex as the politically driven drug-smuggling murder case he had cracked a few months ago. It has only been during the last two weeks that the pace slackened enough that he'd considered taking a couple of days off, fishing some of Tennessee's abundant lakes and rivers. Then the Tullahoma active shooter incident happened, and the fishing vacation got put on the shelf.

He'd already received photographs of the two active shooters and their background files from the Tullahoma PD as well as a call from the Franklin County Sheriff's Office asking to share whatever information any of the three offices discovered.

After his meeting with Leah, GW decided to once again review the videos taken by the grocery store's security cameras that he'd received the evening before. He ran the videos back for a second time as he sipped from a rapidly cooling cup of coffee. As in the previous viewing, his eyes drifted to the woman caught tackling and disarming the two shooters: her auburn hair, diminutive stature, and incredible close-quarters combat skills.

He frowned as he froze the frame where the woman climbed the back of the male shooter, then advanced it frame by frame until he finally got a decent facial view for an identification. It was only a side view of her profile; but there was no mistaking the pixie-like face with the small, pointed chin and upturned nose, the wide, deep-set eyes and trim athletic figure. It was the same woman he'd had coffee with earlier that morning: Agent Leah McCarthy. He was certain of it.

GW lifted his *Best Uncle in the World* coffee mug in salute. "Here's to you, Secret Service Agent Leah McCarthy."

His thoughts drifted from Leah to his blue-eyed, dark-haired, six-year-old niece, who'd given him the coffee mug. What if she'd been in that store with his sister-in-law or brother? Any other hour of the day, it could have been them. Then where would he be? His only family gone. "And that's why I became a cop," he muttered. "To prevent exactly that. Yep! Here's to you, Agent McCarthy," he said again.

His family? Beyond his brother's wife and kid, he had none to speak of. His parents had divorced when he was sixteen, right after the attack in the park. His father had died from cancer shortly after that; and his mother was somewhere in the wind, with no contact for over a decade. He'd grown up without the benefit of close relationships other than those he made during football season in high school and his brief tenure in the military. And frankly, he didn't feel the need for any. He had his work; his tiny house on the edge of the city of Manchester; an abundance of parks with woods, hills, and streams to explore and fish; and his brother's family. Exactly how he liked it.

"Hey, GW! Good morning!" GW glanced over his shoulder to see his boss, Sheriff William "Buster" Bryant, step up to the door of GW's small office. The sheriff leaned through the door and glanced meaningfully at the image frozen on GW's laptop computer. "I see you still have that video, even though the feds told us to surrender all copies."

"For national security purposes?" GW droned. "How many times have we heard that? And yes, I kept a copy."

"Good man," Sheriff Bryant replied. "Can't say I wouldn't have done the same thing. What did you find?"

GW ran the video again as the sheriff leaned into the cubicle for a better view of the laptop's small screen. The sheriff let out a low whistle once the videos ran their course. "Whew! The woman took those shooters down like she'd been born to it. And while the male active shooter crumpled quickly under the attack, the female shooter also moved like a pro, producing that knife out of nowhere."

"Yep," GW said. "The Good Samaritan responded to the knife with a speed and sureness I've seldom seen. Whatever skills the female active shooter may have had, they weren't enough for the woman who took her down."

"In any event," the sheriff said. "Pass that information along to the Tullahoma PD and keep doing what you're doing. Let me know if you come up with anything else."

The sheriff turned away to head back toward his office but paused mid-step to glance back at GW. "And if you find the woman who intervened at the supermarket, I'd suggest you keep your distance. She's lethal in her own right and, based on what I saw in that video, pretty enough to steal your heart." He turned and headed through the open bay that served as briefing room and a collaboration space for the office's deputies and investigators and down a side hallway toward his office.

"Ha, ha," GW said as he waved a hand in the sheriff's direction, not yet ready to reveal his suspicion that the Secret Service agent he'd met earlier in the day might well be that Good Samaritan. He turned back to the video, feeling something turn over in a weird way in the pit of his gut as he watched Leah take down the shooters and remembered the liquid depth in her eyes during their meeting that morning and the lopsided smile that curved up on one side when she'd focused on the clue he'd provided.

If you only knew, Sheriff. If you only knew.

GW rose from his stiff-backed office chair, glancing across his desktop with its tall stacks of case files and a low wall of aged pictures of his parents, his brother and wife and little Lindsey and made his way to the coffee bar at the edge of the open bay. Another ten offices littered the periphery of the area with more than half vacant, attesting to the difficulty the sheriff's office and just about every law enforcement agency in the state experienced in recruiting lately.

Fresh coffee in hand, GW let out a long sigh as he eased his massive frame back into his desk chair. It creaked under his weight as he keyed his laptop to run the video one more time and sipped the scalding dark brew.

There! he thought, as he watched the female active shooter duck under Leah's first attempt to take her down. The female shooter simply shrugged and sent Leah over her shoulder; a classic hapkido move. He'd studied hapkido, which emphasized joint locks and leveraging an opponent's own energy against them, for six months in Seoul, South Korea. He'd been part of a US-Korean airman exchange program. The unit he trained with was the SOD-K, or Special Operations Detachment–Korea. That was some of the toughest training he'd ever been through. Twelve hours a day, but he loved every minute it and learned a great deal about empty-hand martial arts and how much a person could accomplish when working within a highly motivated team.

"So you aren't just some off-the-street whack-job," GW mumbled as he focused on the female active shooter. He froze the frame when he had a good view of the female shooter's face, captured it, and packaged it in an email to a friend at the Federal Bureau of Investigation's field office in Tullahoma. "Let's see what the Department of Justice's facial recognition program can find out about you," he mumbled aloud.

He knew one of the agents there, had worked with the man on an interstate human trafficking case. They'd closed that case together and became fast friends because of their shared no-nonsense approach and willingness to go the extra mile to deliver justice. The response to the email flashed on his screen a second later. "It will take a day or so. Talk to you soon."

GW sent back a quick thanks and offer of lunch the following week, which went unanswered. No problem with that. He was lucky his friend was willing to support his request at all, given how busy the FBI was of late. And lunch would be a small price to pay if something came through that shed some light on why the shooting went down in the quiet city of Tullahoma, Tennessee.

Coffee County didn't have a history of active shooter incidents within the county's boundaries. Like most law enforcement officers, GW read his share of articles and profiles about active shooters but had little background on them. As he considered that, he recalled the sheriff's office recently contracted with a clinical psychologist with a background in both criminal justice and criminal psychology. Maybe he'd have something that could help.

GW called up the video teleconferencing application on his laptop, punched in his security ID and then the psychologist's number. A few seconds later, the image of a long-faced, dark-skinned man with short-cut, thick black hair and deep brown eyes appeared onscreen. "Dr. Muhammad," GW said. "I'm George Weise, an investigator out of the Coffee County Sheriff's Office. I was hoping you might have a moment to discuss an active shooter incident that took place here recently."

The man glanced down, perhaps validating GW's identity against a list of approved client organizations and their membership. "Ah, yes. Investigator George Weise, of the Coffee County Sheriff's Department. I don't often get calls from your area. And I do have a few minutes, but only a few. How can I help you?"

"Thank you for taking my call. As you may have seen in the news, we had an active shooter incident in our county yesterday—two shooters. I'll be working on the investigation from our end. I've read many of your articles about active shooters and have some specific questions about this situation."

Muhammad nodded, then muted his microphone and turned his head to call out to someone not visible on his screen. A second later, he was back online. "Please accept my apology for the interruption. Things are busy here at my clinic. We're involved in some significant research . . . "

GW raised a hand. "If this isn't a good time after all . . . "

Muhammad waved off the comment. "No, I'm paid to support you, and you are entitled to my help. Never too busy for my friends in law enforcement." The man's smile seemed forced, but that could have been because of the hectic activities at his clinic. "Before I address your specific question, let me make sure you and I are operating from the same baseline of information about active shooters."

Not waiting for GW's response, Muhammad tapped some keys on a keyboard out of view. A moment later, GW's laptop's screen split into two views: one with the psychologist's face and another with a document entitled *Common Characteristics of Potential Active Shooters.*

"What you're seeing onscreen is the latest information available from law enforcement and those of us who study and treat violent criminals, like active shooters. It's a list of characteristics identified for people who could become active shooters. Understand that someone with these characteristics does not always become an active shooter. Environmental and even genetic factors contribute to that evolution."

GW nodded. "I'm with you so far. A person with the characteristics does not always become an active shooter but has the potential to be one."

"Correct," Muhammad replied. "Not surprisingly, the first item on the list is anger issues. Active shooters have been found to have demonstrated frequent outbursts of anger or uncontrolled rage prior to acting."

"That almost seems obvious," GW said.

"True, but it is often hard for the people closest to one of these individuals to admit their relative or loved one has anger issues, even when they become physically violent."

"Like in domestic disputes, where the victim, often a spouse, is physically abused yet refuses to believe their partner has a problem."

"Exactly," Muhammad said. "Second is impulsivity. Active shooters tend to lack self-control. In their anger, as in a perceived need for revenge, they seldom look at the long-term consequences of their actions. That should not be misinterpreted as lacking the ability to deliberately plan their acts of vengeance. They are often quite adept at developing, rehearsing, and executing plans in considerable detail. However, while you and I might decide against a plan that could hurt others, they experience no such restraint, which also suggests that active shooters are seldom capable of empathy. Those who survive and are captured after the event seldom see any problem with what they've done, no matter the extent of the damage.

"The next characteristic is a sense of isolation. They generally have difficulty relating to others and are often withdrawn before the event.

That can either represent an extreme shift in behavior or a long-term tendency that some might misinterpret as simple introversion. The difference between these people and common introverts is that they deal with so many internal demons, such as extreme depression and anxiety. Emotional distress drives their days, despite what else might be going on in their lives."

"With all this information, it seems like we should be able to identify active shooters in advance, before they act," GW said.

Muhammad nodded. "Fortunately, many of the people demonstrating these characteristics are identified when they present in a clinical setting. For the others who don't seek help, it's almost impossible to sort them out of the general population. And there are yet more characteristics to be aware of."

"Please continue," GW prompted, as Dr. Muhammad once again muted his screen, turned his head away, and shouted a command at someone nearby. He seemed to let out a long breath before carrying on.

"Yes. Of course. Other characteristics of potential active shooters include excessive risk-taking, intentionally or unintentionally revealing a desire to commit violence to a third party, and a dramatic change in work performance that is often combined with overt threats or confrontations on the job and in social situations. Drug and alcohol abuse is common in these cases, to quell the individual's demons, along with retreating into violent media content like movies and, of late, video games."

"That's a long list," GW said.

Muhammad nodded again. "On average, an active shooter is likely to display four or five of the characteristics on the list over time. Recognizing the signs and getting them help can divert them from violence toward others. The challenge is that when people do show the warning signs, those closest to them don't want to admit their friend, spouse, or sibling could ever do anything so terrible. Even when an active shooter takes lives, those closest to them often deny their potential for violence."

"Our eternal hopefulness," GW added.

"Correct," Muhammad said. "In truth, there are probably more potential violent actors out there than we can count. But recognizing these signs and getting help for the individual can contribute to preventing violence and ensuring public safety. As I alluded to earlier in our discussion, few of these people will take up a weapon and attack others, although there is currently an alarming trend in that regard."

GW's cell phone vibrated from atop the chipped wood surface of his workspace desk. He glanced at the number: a 360 prefix. He didn't know anyone with that sort of number. Then again, Leah was visiting from another area code, and it could be her. And they needed to talk about her role in stopping the active shooters at the store.

Something deep in his gut fluttered. The sensation surprised him as he reached for the phone. "Thank you for taking the time to talk with me, Dr. Muhammad. I have another call coming in. I hope I can call on you if I have any additional questions."

Muhammad nodded. "It was my pleasure. And I apologize for the interruptions. We have a major project underway that is about to kick off. In any event, I wish you luck in your investigation."

Once Muhammad's image faded from the laptop's screen, GW accepted the incoming call. "Investigator Weise."

"Good morning." It was Leah. Her voice sounded soft, relaxed—much more so than during their time at the coffee shop. The image of her delicate, pixie-like face flickered across his thoughts; her thick, red-bronze hair, startling blue eyes, and how she'd moved like a cat in that video. There was that stirring in his gut again—an odd, unfamiliar, but not unpleasant sensation. He could almost feel the endearing, lopsided smile tug at the corner of Leah's lips as she spoke. "It's Agent McCarthy."

"It's nice to hear from you. What can I do for you?" GW asked, then mentally kicked himself for his stilted, formal response.

"I received some information about that strap you showed me at the coffee shop, and I'd like to take you up on the visit to the Space Force Research and Development shop at Arnold Air Force Base. The other day, you indicated you might have some contacts out there."

"I thought you were done with this once you passed on your report to your boss," GW replied.

"Me, too," Leah said, her voice soft but her words clipped, precise and her tone all business. "But you know how bosses can be. With the potential link of this missing equipment to the U.S. Space Force, he wants me to dig a little deeper. Probably just means a lot of forms I'll have to fill out after the interview."

GW chuckled. "I totally get it. If there's anything we law enforcement officers live for, it's paperwork—and I'd be happy to head out there with you."

"Yeah, right," Leah replied. "How about Starbucks again? We can grab some coffee for the trip. My credentials will get us on base, so we can use my rental. Half an hour?"

"Sounds great," GW replied. "I haven't been out to the base in a while. It's a pretty drive."

"See you in thirty," Leah replied and disconnected the call.

GW glanced up to see the sheriff once again standing at the door to his office, this time with a thick sheaf of paperwork in one hand. "Someone mention paperwork?" The stocky, fifty-something man had an odd smile on his face as he studied GW's expression.

"What?" GW demanded.

"You're smiling. I haven't seen you smile like that in . . . well, never. Whoever you were talking to sure made that craggy, weather-worn face of yours light up."

"You been hitting the narcotics in the evidence locker again, sir?" GW said.

The sheriff grimaced. "Very funny, GW. I just like it when the morale of my team takes a sudden turn upward."

"Yes, sir," was all GW could muster. He'd long been the punchline in the continuing office joke about people who work too much and socialize not at all. Then again, his arrest record and the number of cases closed each month should speak for themselves.

"I'm headed to the air force base with the Secret Service agent I interviewed yesterday. Her boss has some sort of interest in the shooters. I showed her a scrap of elastic band the Tullahoma PD found on the male shooter, which I borrowed for our own investigation. It had a label on it, linking the scrap of material to a Space Force R&D office at Arnold Air Force Base."

The sheriff nodded, his smile returning. "Is she cute?" When GW didn't reply, the sheriff added, "You go right ahead and do your detecting with her. But be sure to keep your mind on the case."

"Funny, sir," GW replied, deciding to keep his suspicions about Leah's involvement with the active shooters to himself for the time being. He glanced at his watch, then closed his laptop and checked the holster at his hip for the new .40 caliber Glock 23. As always when he checked to ensure his weapon was holstered, he said a silent prayer that he wouldn't need it that day. "I'm headed out," he called across the room.

The sheriff, heading toward a short hallway that led to his office, gave GW a wave over his shoulder. "I'll see you when I see you, Investigator. Be safe out there."

CHAPTER 9

Leah arrived at Starbucks twenty minutes early, waiting in her SUV with her coffee. She held her cell phone in one hand and the coffee in the other, staring at the number Dr. Malcome had sent her for the psychologist in Nashville. She'd thought of calling that number before heading to Starbucks but found herself hesitant to do so. It was as if calling was admitting she was mentally deficient or something. Intellectually, she knew that wasn't true; but she'd always thought of herself as one of the tough people, capable of dealing with anything that came her way. And now she was calling a psychologist for what may be PTSD?

Calling Dr. Malcome had been easier. As an employee, Malcome was a member of the EOG family. In a past life, the man had been a captain in the infantry. He got what it was like to be under fire, and she'd talked with him countless times after difficult missions. But calling a total stranger?

Leah sucked in another of what seemed like way too many long, anxiety-laden deep breaths, then set her coffee cup aside and punched in the number. The call was answered on the first ring.

"This is Dr. Muhammad." The voice was male, with a slight accent and the ring of intensity it its inflection.

"My name is Leah McCarthy. I'm with the state department," she said. "I was referred to you by Dr. William Malcome. He may have sent you a note or called you about seeing me."

"Ah, yes. I got a voicemail from Will. I've known him for years. A good, solid practitioner. And I do have a contract with state to see its employees."

"He suggested I make an appointment to see you regarding PTSD symptoms I might be experiencing."

"Yes, of course," Muhammad said. "I'd be happy to help you. Unfortunately, my calendar is booked for the next two weeks. Perhaps we can schedule a time later, after that?"

At first, Leah mentally cheered. She wouldn't have to meet the man anytime soon, and perhaps she could figure things out on her own. Then, there was something about the man's tone, like he was distracted and wanted to get back to something more important but trying overly hard not to be perceived that way. "No problem," Leah said. "I can always talk with Dr. Malcome and see if he knows someone else."

"No, no, there's no need for that. I'm happy to help." Muhammad said again. "I see your number displayed on my phone, and I've jotted it down. How about if I give you a call next week, once I've had a chance to clear my calendar a bit?"

"Of course. Thanks," she said and disconnected the call.

Once off the call, Leah glanced at her narrow-screen forearm tablet, balanced on her lap. Its screen displayed the image of the piece of head strap. She keyed a button on the side of her black, large-faced tactical watch and raised it to her lips. "Oversight Prime, this is Romeo Alpha."

The response was immediate. She recognized the director's voice at once. "This is Oversight Prime. Go ahead."

"Yes, sir," Leah replied. "I'm visiting the Space Force R&D shop today with an investigator from the local sheriff's office."

"That sounds fine. If all goes well, you can hand the case off to the sheriff's office and get back to your vacation—after you've filed your report, of course."

Leah's phone beeped. It was the phone's tracking app, letting her know GW's car was approaching. "I need to go, sir. The deputy is about to arrive."

"Let me guess: you tagged his vehicle?"

"I did," Leah said. "When we met earlier, I made sure I left the coffee shop before him and stuck a nano-tracker on his right front fender. He seems like a great guy; but after what we went through with internal traitors during the missions in Mexico and closer to home, I don't figure on taking any chances with anyone. Did you happen to run a background on him?"

"Of course," Paul replied. "His name's George Weise, but you already know that. Goes by GW. His record's spotless. He was with the Air Force Office of Special Investigations before he left the military to enter Tennessee's police academy. His record in the military and after are spotless. Turns out you both grew up in Tullahoma."

"He told me that. He was the shooter who took down the fourth attacker in the park when my mom was killed," Leah replied, then filled Paul in on what GW had told her about that day.

"He sounds like a good person to know, then and now," Paul replied. "I called up the classified version of his military records jacket. He received the Silver Star for Valor and a Purple Heart from a deployment to Afghanistan. He was there on an investigation at a joint army-air force base when a company of Army Rangers were ambushed not far from the base. When a rescue mission was put together to evacuate the Rangers, the door-gunner for the army Blackhawk helicopter was unavailable. Rather than not send the bird out for the Rangers, your investigator volunteered, climbed aboard, and filled the job.

"The Blackhawk went in hot and took fire almost immediately. Weise manned the fifty-caliber door gun and accounted for numerous enemy soldiers. He took a bullet to his left arm—a through and through wound—but kept firing. If that's not enough, he left the chopper when it landed and personally carried numerous wounded to the attack helicopter for evacuation. When the chopper was full and could carry no more, Weise stayed behind to defend the remaining Rangers with whatever weapons he could find. The report says he and two Rangers accounted for thirty dead enemy soldiers, including two Weise killed hand-to-hand. By the time Medevac choppers arrived, the battle was over. Weise helped load up the remaining dead and wounded and made it out on another Blackhawk gunship called in to cover the Medevac. Your investigator is an actual hero."

"Wow!" was all Leah could say.

"My response, exactly," Paul said. "The Medal of Honor takes years to be awarded and find its way to a soldier, but it seems one's headed his way. I understand the President of the United States just signed off on it."

"He doesn't know about the MOH?"

"I expect that's true for the moment," Paul said. "But it's hard to keep the news about heroes down for long."

"I suppose," Leah replied. "And you'd never know all that to talk with him."

"I've met a few MOH recipients. Humility is a common ingredient."

"I'll keep that in mind," Leah said. "About Dr. Malcome pulling my duty status . . . "

Paul cut her off. "I didn't mention this the first time we talked about that, but the truth is only I can do that. He can make a recommendation, which he did, and which I chose to support at the time. My thought was you might benefit from a rest. I choose now to reverse that decision. You're one of the best operatives I've got, and I believe in you. I understand PTSD better than most people and feel that with the support of others and advice from people like Dr. Malcome, you can remain the positive, hard-charging covert operator you've always been."

Leah felt a lump form in her throat. Paul had praised her work and the Home Team but never expressed his support for her directly.

"Thank you, sir," was all she could muster.

"Don't mention it," Paul said. "Just promise me you'll work with Malcome for as long as it takes to work through the issues."

"Of course," Leah said. "And thank you, sir," she started to say, but the call had already been terminated.

Right then, GW pulled into the parking spot next to hers. When he stepped from his car and glanced her way, she raised her cup, letting him know she was already set. As he nodded and headed inside, she watched in her side-view mirror with new appreciation. The big man moved with an easy, loose gate, much like the martial artists she trained with.

GW was at the passenger side door of her SUV minutes later, a huge paper cup of steaming coffee in one hand. He pulled the door open and slid into the passenger seat. "You still up for driving?"

Leah nodded. "I see you got the largest cup of coffee they make."

"It takes a lot of coffee to fill me up," he replied as he slipped into the seat next to her. "And this stuff is manna to me. If it wasn't for the cream I put in it, I probably wouldn't get any nutrition at all."

Leah chuckled as she backed out of the parking spot, then drove the short distance to the interstate leading east toward Arnold Air Force Base. "I bet guys as big as you consume massive quantities of food."

"Shows how little you know about the life of an investigator. I'm lucky if I get anything to eat at all between rising in the morning and the end of a late night at the office or on a case."

"Sounds familiar," Leah said. "How about we grab some lunch later? I thought we'd stop by the Tullahoma PD office when we're done at the base. You must know a good burger spot where we can go once we've finished there."

"Absolutely!" GW replied. "There's only one place: Jiffy Burger in Manchester. It's a generational favorite, and I can't get enough of their burgers. The best fries and corn dogs you'll ever eat, but you need extra napkins for one of their burgers."

"Sounds perfect," Leah replied. "A big, messy burger is one of the things I like best."

The rest of the trip to the air force base went quietly, passing tall evergreens and oak trees lining the four-lane interstate. They took the exit to the base only a few miles after entering the interstate, moving onto a well-maintained access road with thirty-foot, manicured shoulders along both sides of a long ribbon of fresh two-lane asphalt. Beyond the carefully groomed shoulders of the road were dense stands of thirty and forty-foot tall, long-needled pines and winter-bare oak trees. Occasionally, they passed open, charred patches of scrub fields that stretched into the distance, showing signs of the frequent controlled burns the government used to reduce the fire danger in the area.

After four miles, Leah and GW approached Gate 2 to the air force base, used primarily by staff and delivery trucks. Leah's Secret Service credentials and GW's badge eased their way through a security gate manned by contract security personnel and got them directions to the Space Force R&D facility. Five minutes later, they pulled up to yet another security gate, this time at the entrance of the R&D facility's parking lot. Their credentials were checked at the gate; and after the guard made a quick call, they were informed that Dr. Alfred Jones would be meeting them at the building's entrance.

Dr. Jones turned out to be a short, pudgy, fair-skinned man. He stood at the front door of the two-story, rectangular red brick building as they stepped from Leah's rental SUV. The building behind him was nondescript, like so many military buildings, a huge red brick box with no adornment beyond the highly polished metal front door and tall, narrow, polarized windows that spanned the front of the two-story building's façade.

Dr. Jones met Leah and GW at the front door, not bothering to extend his hand in greeting when they approached. A small breeze pushed the man's thin, wispy comb-over across his face to reveal a shiny bald pate, his pale blue eyes squinting as he sized them up, despite the building's shaded entry.

"You must be the Secret Service agent and investigator the guard said were visiting. I received no advance notice of your arrival," Jones said, offering Leah a disapproving look as his eyes cast down her diminutive posture, from her thick auburn hair to the loose blouse hanging over pale denim skinny jeans and her Adidas indoor soccer shoes.

Leah ignored the man's derisive, inappropriate inspection, her gaze locked on the man's eyes. "I'm Agent McCarthy, and this is Investigator Weise."

When Dr. Jones cast his glance toward GW, his expression changed dramatically, for the first time appraising GW's imposing physical stature. The man's response to GW's size made Leah smile, a reaction she made no attempt to hide. Accustomed to people dismissing her because of her diminutive size, she knew GW's heavy frame might be just what they needed to put Dr. Jones off guard.

A few minutes later, Leah and GW were ensconced in comfortable leather wingback chairs arranged in front of Dr. Jones's broad mahogany desk. Leah got right to the point of the visit. "Dr. Jones, there was an incident in Tullahoma several days ago. Two active shooters killed and wounded a lot of people in a grocery store. One of the shooters was carrying a piece of elastic strap we've traced to your operation."

GW fished the small envelope from his pocket, opened the flap, and leaned forward to dump the bit of strap on the doctor's desktop. The man stared at it for the briefest of moments, then dismissed the evidence as inconsequential. "Straps like that are common and could have come from anywhere."

Leah leaned forward to pick up the strap and display the letters printed on the edge of it. "If you will examine it closely, you'll see the words U.S. Space Force Arnold Air Force Base in gold lettering. You'll also find some very faint numbers below those letters. Perhaps you could take a look at that and let us know what you think."

Jones let out a long, resigned sigh and took the strap from her hand. Under his breath, he recited the faint, tiny characters beneath the Space Force logo as his complexion went even paler, "AVR15-X."

"And those characters you just recited?" GW asked.

"They're from a project we've been working on here for several years, but it's highly classified."

Leah leaned forward in her chair, laying her open credentials folder on the desktop. "I guarantee you, I have adequate clearance to hear about your project."

Jones examined the credentials folder, then nodded toward GW. "What about him?"

"He's law enforcement, and he's with me. He carries what we refer to as an emergent, situational clearance well above your own," Leah replied. "Now, would you like to tell us about the project and this strap, or am I going to have to arrest you for complicity in the misappropriation of classified government property?"

Jones's shoulders drooped slightly as he sat back in his high-back brown leather chair. "The strap is from a virtual reality headset. The headset was part of a VR system designed for remote pilots of space vehicles, drones, and intelligent intercontinental missiles. The project has been ongoing for many years. The model number on the strap was from one of the earlier versions of the hardware, which has been superseded by at least four later models."

"VR and VR headsets have been used for years by all branches of the service. What makes this gear so special?" Leah asked.

"It's the processing power we've developed for the systems that drive the headsets," Jones replied. "The system has the capacity for retinal projection of data for the user, including the relative speed, trajectory, and realistic, first-person image of the piloted device's forward-looking and surrounding environment. The system also monitors and records the pilot's eye dilation, facial capillary fill, body temperature, respiration, heart rate, and other performance-revealing biometrics, to ensure the pilot is working at peak efficiency and effectiveness."

The idea of an automated device so integrating with her mind and body made Leah shudder. "A bit invasive, isn't it?"

Jones sniffed. "Some might think so, but we hope to integrate artificial intelligence within the system's software to further partner with the system's pilots and increase the speed of decision-making."

"This is very interesting, doctor, but how would an active shooter in Tullahoma get their hands on that strap?" GW asked, easing his huge bulk forward in his chair as he closed the psychological and physical distance between him and Jones, putting subtle pressure on the man.

Jones rocked back into the cushions of his chair. "I'm sure I have no idea."

To emphasize his need to cooperate even more, Leah reached to the small of her back and drew her 9mm Beretta. She laid it carefully on the edge of Jones's highly polished mahogany desk. "Dr. Jones, we need your assistance. Believe me when I say I have the authority to have you arrested or have you removed from your position in this facility if you don't work with us. As the director of this facility, you have ultimate accountability for the resources used by your staff; and that includes the equipment like the VR headset this strap belongs to."

"Well, I . . . " Jones stammered.

GW glared at the man from beneath thick eyebrows on his broad, weathered face. "I'd listen to what she says, Dr. Jones. I can tell you the woman has no tolerance for the level of arrogance you're currently displaying."

When Jones didn't respond immediately, GW said, "How about we take a different sort of approach to this? During my air force days, property accountability was a big deal. All equipment had to be accounted for in the organization's property book, which is the master record of all that an operation has purchased, developed, discarded, and so on. Is the AVR15-X system that strap is from accounted for in those records for this facility?"

"We follow all property accountability regulations to a *T*," Jones replied.

Leah caught his eye, smiled, and made a show of returning her pistol to the holster at the small of her back. "Well, then, if you can simply confirm that you have that equipment accounted for, we can be out of your hair in a jiffy."

"One moment," Jones replied, a bead of sweat forming on his forehead as he opened a laptop computer and tapped its keys. A few seconds later, he said. "I have access to those records here. I'm sure I will be able to show you that all our equipment has been properly accounted for."

"Please, take all the time you need," GW said, then emphasized his next words with a sharp, harsh tone. "A lot is resting on what you find."

Leah found it difficult to hide the smirk tugging at her lips as GW put pressure on the man. It seemed she and GW had the same style when dealing with suspects: to the point, with little deflecting from the main point, keeping the pressure on until they gave you what you needed.

Jones offered a weak smile as he raised his eyes from the laptop to meet GW's gaze. "That version of the equipment has been superseded by four later generations."

"You already said that, and the AVR15-X equipment that was no longer needed?" Leah asked. "Is it still on hand?"

Leah cast a sidelong glance at GW, who returned it with a nod. "The equipment is missing, isn't it, Dr. Jones?" GW said.

"Not missing, no," Jones replied. "It was reported lost from inventory a little under one year ago."

"Lost?" Leah asked.

Jones shifted his gaze to Leah. "As I said, it was lost. We filled out the Report of Survey documents as required by policy. An internal investigation was conducted, as required by policy. The equipment was not recovered; and since that version of the equipment was deemed obsolete, the Report of Survey was signed off by the appropriate authority and the property records adjusted."

"And that authority was?" Leah prodded.

Jones sat up taller in his chair, although his haughty expression gave way to a more humble, hopeful resignation. "That would be me, as the senior Department of Defense official on site."

"Thank you, Dr. Jones," Leah replied. She leaned forward as she started to rise from her chair, but GW laid a warm, strong hand on her arm. She relaxed back in her chair.

"Dr. Jones, exactly how many sets of the VR equipment were reported as lost over the past two years?" GW's tone was flat, devoid of inflection.

This time, when Jones didn't immediately respond, GW rose and leaned over Jones' desk, his intimidating size dwarfing the smaller man. "I repeat, Dr. Jones, how many sets of the equipment went missing?"

Jones glanced at the laptop's screen once more, then replied in a much less confident voice, "A total of thirty-five sets of equipment.

That includes both more recent versions and some that preceded the ones you asked about."

"And the value of that equipment?" GW continued.

"Roughly $15 million, although that is difficult to confirm given the prototype nature of all the previous versions, and the fact they have little remaining value to the program."

"Thank you, Dr. Jones," GW said as he took his weight off Jones' desk and tossed Jones one of his business cards. "My cell number's on that, in case you think of anything else."

With that, Leah rose and led the way to the door. As she reached for the door handle, she turned back as Jones gently closed his laptop computer. She growled, "Stay close, Dr. Jones. We will have more questions for you."

"Of . . . of course," he replied.

———————— *//////////* ————————

Once the office door closed behind them, Jones retrieved a burner cell phone from his desk drawer and keyed in a number from memory. The call was answered on the second ring.

"Yes?"

"This is Jones," he replied.

"Why are you calling me? Our business was concluded months ago," the voice replied.

"But two people just left my office," Jones replied. "One from the Secret Service and another from the county sheriff's office."

"And?" the voice prodded.

"They demanded information about the equipment. A strap from a VR headset was found in the pocket of someone who shot up a grocery store in Tullahoma."

"That is unfortunate," the voice replied. "How long ago did they leave your office?"

"Just a few moments ago—less than five minutes."

"Do you know what they're driving?"

Jones moved over to his office window, which looked down on the small parking lot in front of the R&D building. "They're just pulling out of the parking lot. They're driving a blue SUV. Looks like a Toyota. Very new. Might be a rental."

"Thank you, Dr. Jones. And you needn't worry. I will make sure there are no repercussions at your end. Do you have the phone number for the people who visited you?"

"I do. The investigator's number. He left a business card."

"Good. Wait ten minutes and then call the investigator. Tell him you've found additional information that may be of interest to them."

"I have already told them all I can without implicating myself or you directly," Jones replied.

"And well done, I'm sure. But why don't you print out some of the property accountability documents you showed me when we completed our transaction, the ones you said would satisfy the bureaucrats you work for at the Pentagon. Suggest they return to your office to pick those documents up. I'm sure they'll appreciate the extra help, and it will be a great service to me as I deal with those people and their unfortunate curiosity."

"I don't see the relevance," Jones started. "And they might use the information on the Reports of Survey against me."

"Just do it, Jones," the man said, the words coming out clipped, harsh. "Trust me when I say I will take care of this issue. I guarantee by the end of this day, any worries you might have right now will be like nothing."

Jones let out a long breath. "I appreciate that. I will do as you suggest."

"Good, and after they leave your office the second time, go back to your work as if nothing has happened."

"Will do," Jones replied. "And thank you."

"Believe me, it is nothing," the voice replied.

———— *///////////* ————

Sitting in the back seat of his chauffeured Hummer and headed west on Interstate 24 toward Nashville, Dr. Albert Muhammad, AKA The Hatchet, considered the information Jones had just provided. He frowned, then dialed Haider's number, the hired muscle he'd met with the previous day at the used video game store.

"Yes, master. How can I serve you?" Haider said as he accepted the call.

The Hatchet explained the situation at Jones's office, then said, "Where are you currently?"

"Steven and I are in Manchester, not far from the food store where the shooting occurred. We are posing as reporters, gathering information for the after-action report you asked us to complete for the operation."

"Excellent," The Hatchet replied. "You have your weapons with you?"

"Of course, sir. Always ready."

He knew Haider to be an excellent, well-trained covert operator, while his partner Steven was an information technologist and pretentious. He and Steven had been useful in the early days of their project, recruiting candidates, providing security, and handling the money the video game store brought in; but now, that value was diminishing by the day. Perhaps he could put them to good use one last time before it was time to tie up loose ends.

"I'm glad to hear that," The Hatchet replied. "I need help with a problem that's just come up. It involves a local investigator and a federal agent who may get in our way."

"Of course! Where can we find these people?" Haider replied, sounding truly excited for the first time since The Hatchet had met the man.

"They will be leaving Arnold Air Force Base in the next thirty minutes. I believe the road leading from there to the interstate on the west and the city where we conducted our pilot test to the east, is long, narrow, and infrequently traveled."

Haider chuckled with no humor in the tone. "I know that road well. There are several excellent locations along it for staging an ambush. We will resolve this problem for you."

"Good man," The Hatchet replied. He recited the description of Leah's SUV and disconnected the call.

"Problem resolved," The Hatchet murmured, setting the burner phone aside and settling back into the Hummer's thick seat cushions. "One problem solved, one to go."

He picked up the burner phone once more and entered another number from memory. The woman at the other end picked up on the first ring. "Yes?"

"I need a problem handled," he said.

"The name?" she asked, her voice almost a purr, but with a gravelly undertone.

"Dr. Albert Jones. He works for—"

"I know who he is. When?"

"Today, as soon as possible," The Hatchet replied. "Your usual fee?"

"I'm in the area. It will be done," the woman's voice replied.

"Thank—" The Hatchet started, but the line was already dead. He thought of calling her back, chastising her for treating her benefactor so rudely, but knew from experience he would not get through. The cell phone she'd used to answer his call was no doubt already broken into pieces and disposed of. By the end of the day, he would receive a brief encrypted email, confirming the job was done and providing another number for the next time he needed her services.

The Hatchet smiled, relishing the power he wielded by ending three lives with two simple calls—the same power he would use to bring the United States to its knees.

CHAPTER 10

Steven and Haider pulled off Interstate 24 at exit 117, east of Manchester, Tennessee and headed toward Arnold Air Force Base. They turned right, heading west off the exit and down a two-lane road used primarily by the people working at the base. It was mid-afternoon, and they saw no other vehicles during the fifteen-minute drive past the base's main gate and Gate 2. The speed limit was fifty-five, but Haider stepped on the gas of their late model Ford Ranger pickup, hitting seventy down a long straight stretch to make sure they'd be in position before their quarry arrived.

In the passenger seat, Steven hung onto the suicide handle mounted above the passenger side window, his knuckles white as the tall trees that lined the road whipped by. Two assault rifles and two Colt semi-automatic pistols lay at his feet. In his lap, he held a long, green tube-like device. Haider had explained earlier that it was an M72 Light Anti-tank Weapon, or LAW. The tube contained a small but lethal rocket that Steven would launch by extending the tube to twice its length, sighting his target, and squeezing a rubber button to launch the rocket.

"You're driving much too fast. You're going to get us arrested," Steven said as Haider accelerated the pickup along the smooth, well-maintained government road with its tall pine trees along the north side and bare stretches of charred fields and scrub on the other. "If we get pulled over and the military police see the weapons, we'll be arrested or worse."

Haider let out a loud laugh. "I have driven this road many times since we acquired the virtual reality equipment from the research scientist. The military police hardly patrol this road at all. When they do, it's during rush hour when staff are coming and going from the base. Most of the base's security officers are civilian contractors who only check identification at the gate and don't conduct regular patrols. The few actual air force military police officers they have do so infrequently.

"Relax. It's not much further to where we'll set up the ambush. It's a mile or so beyond Gate 2, near the turnoff for the base's firing range. From there, we'll be able to see the blue Toyota SUV the agent and the cop are driving from a mile away. We'll wait for them with the hood up, like a vehicle in distress."

When Steven didn't express his support for the idea immediately, Haider continued. "The Hatchet texted me that a second team will be joining us. I've texted him with the location of the ambush, so they can meet us there. The second team will close on our target from behind; and if our timing is good, the SUV will slow, thinking we are a vehicle in distress. When they do, you will destroy them with the LAW rocket, while I finish them with the assault rifles. The trailing team will attack from the rear after the explosion, in case our targets manage to exit their vehicle before being destroyed."

"Who are the people in the trailing vehicle? Can we count on them?" Steven asked.

"More people arranged by The Hatchet. I believe they're from a militant secessionist group willing to do just about anything to get money for their cause."

"Secessionist group?" Steven asked.

Haider laughed. "Believe it or not, there are people in the United States who advocate the destruction of their government like we do, although for different reasons. Our backup team is from a particularly rabid group responsible for several recent armed altercations with local authorities. The Hatchet has them on retainer. From what he told me, they have no idea who we really are, just that we intend to strike a blow against the people they hate the most: the American government."

"The enemy of our enemy is our friend," Steven recited.

"You've been studying," Haider replied.

"Yes, and the more I learn, the more I appreciate The Hatchet for his cunning and knowledge of human nature and his belief that countries like the United States must be destroyed."

They slowed as they passed the main gate to the Air Force base, then accelerated again until they reached the turnoff to the Arnold Air Force Base Rifle Range. Haider eased the pickup onto the right shoulder of the road and turned off the engine. "We will set up here. I'll pop the hood and make it look like we have engine trouble."

Steven stepped out of the truck; the short green missile launch tube clutched in his arms. Remembering Haider's instructions, he grabbed the tube with a hand at each end and jerked it open to double its previous length. Then he flipped up the weapon's small, ladder-like sighting mechanism and held the LAW at shoulder level to get comfortable with its weight and balance. Sighting down the road in the direction from which their victims would come, he said, "I'll hide behind the bed of the pickup. You tell me when you see them coming."

Haider reached inside the pickup's cab and pulled out the two assault rifles, leaning one against the side of the truck and checking the other to ensure its magazine was full. He racked a round into the rifle's chamber, enjoying the sound of the bolt slamming forward with a loud metallic clack. Then he positioned himself at the side of the truck's open hood, just as the speck of a vehicle took shape a mile down the road. "Be ready. I believe they are coming."

"I am as ready as I can be," Steven replied. "The sooner, the better. I am a technologist, not a hired gun. I just want to get this over and get back to my shop."

"You are whatever The Hatchet says you'll be," Haider whispered. "You should feel privileged. How many of our brothers get to make a direct strike on the heart of this cursed country like we do today?"

"You make a good point," Steven replied. "But you are trained to handle this sort of thing. I'm not. You need a computer program created or a network hacked, I'm your guy. But launch a rocket at a moving vehicle?"

"Quiet and get ready. It is a blue Toyota SUV, as described." Haider peered around the side of the pickup's raised hood. "And I see a man and a woman in the front seats. The woman is driving. A woman driving? These people deserve to die."

"Just tell me when," Steven replied, his voice cracking softly. "And I will send this missile down their infidel throats."

"Just try to hit the target, brother," Haider replied. "Do that and you will be doing enough."

CHAPTER 11

When Dr. Jones called GW and explained he had additional information that might be useful for their investigation, Leah did a U-turn near the Gate 2 exit and headed back to the R&D facility. Jones was waiting for them at the red brick building's front doors, as before, this time with a thick folder that he handed to her without so much as a hello or goodbye.

GW waited in the SUV; and when Leah climbed back into the driver's seat, she tossed the file folder to him and said, "Copies of additional Reports of Survey for lost equipment. Not sure why he thought it was so important that we come back to get them or why he didn't provide them when we were here before."

"There's no telling," GW replied, flipping the folder open and rifling through the paperwork inside. "People do things for uncommon reasons, like maybe he was feeling exposed and thought he might lose his job if he isn't seen as fully cooperating with us."

"He was definitely hiding something when we interviewed him," Leah said. She glanced at her watch and frowned. "The trip back onto the base, back to his office, and what it will take to get back on the road to Tullahoma has eaten up a good thirty minutes. I'd hoped to be talking with the Tullahoma PD by now."

They traveled for ten minutes before passing back through Gate 2 and turning west toward Tullahoma. They hadn't traveled far before GW spotted a pickup pulled off to the side of the road. "That pickup has its hood up."

"I see it," Leah said.

"We'd better see if they need help," GW said. "No matter what we're working on right now, I'm still local law enforcement and need to check it out."

Leah slowed the SUV as they approached the pickup. As she did, she glanced in her rearview mirror to see another vehicle behind them, an older model, black Chevy Suburban closing fast. "Something feels wonky about this situation," she said. "No one was behind us when we left the base. Now there's an SUV coming up on us, fast."

GW checked the side mirror. "It's probably nothing. This road is the main one leading from Interstate 24 to the base in one direction and to Tullahoma in the other. It could be anyone. Ease off the gas. The driver of the pickup is waving us down."

"Everyone has a cell phone these days. He's probably already called a tow truck."

"Doesn't matter. Like I said, I'm a local," GW replied. "It's my job to help people in distress wherever I find them, and we can spare the time. You're just the lucky person with me now."

"I'm not sure . . . " Leah started, as a second man popped up on the far side of the pickup, aiming a long, army-green tube their way. A LAW! She'd faced those dozens of times in the field and used them herself.

"They've got a missile," Leah yelled as she jerked the SUV hard right, then left, then right again, trying not to present an easy target.

"A what?" GW said, then clutched at the dashboard as Leah jerked the vehicle from side to side so hard the SUV tilted, its right wheels rocking into the air, then crashing down to the pavement, then repeating the process.

Her eyes locked on the man with the LAW, Leah yelled a warning as a long flair of flame shot from the rear of the LAW's launch tube and a small dark missile rocketed their way. "Get down!"

Leah stomped the accelerator and glanced at GW, who ducked low behind the dash, his pistol in his right hand as the thin black missile whizzed by, within inches of the truck's windshield. A second later, a loud explosion and small ball of flame ignited a stand of already charred trees at the side of the road thirty yards away.

GW sat up as Leah straightened and slowed the SUV, glancing at the vehicle's side mirror. "The Suburban is fifty yards to our rear and pulling to a stop. The doors are open, and people are climbing out."

"This is an ambush," she said. "Someone wants us dead."

She stomped the brakes, tires screaming on the blacktop, and flung the driver-side door open wide when the SUV came to rest. Her Beretta in hand, she leveled it at the pickup as flame erupted from the barrel of a rifle at the front of the vehicle. "You cover the Suburban. I'll focus on the pickup. They may have a second LAW."

Leah ducked behind the SUV's door and glanced over to see GW behind the open passenger door.

"Pickup first," he said as he raised his black, long-barreled pistol to eye level and pulled the trigger three times so quickly it almost sounded like one long, single shot. His first bullet took out the pickup's back right turn light. His second and third shots pounded into the chest of the man holding the now-empty LAW launcher.

The man convulsed twice, then he crumpled out of sight behind the pickup.

"Like you said, they may have another LAW rocket."

"Good shot," Leah started to yell as the firing from the front of the pickup landed two shots into the driver-side door she was using for cover. She lined up her own shot at the man firing from the front of the pickup as a half dozen loud cracks sounded from behind her, followed by the angry buzz of the bullets passing close to her head.

She spun and dove to the ground next to her vehicle's rear tire, lining her pistol's sites on four men advancing on them in a line across the road from the Suburban, side by side, now only thirty yards off. Each carried some sort of rifle and triggered them in rapid succession.

Leah pulled off two quick shots, figuring she'd not hit anyone at that distance but might make them think before coming closer. Neither shot struck home, but two of the attackers dropped to the ground, taking up a prone firing position and cutting loose.

With bullets flying at them from the pickup and now the direction of the Suburban, two of the attackers crouched and ran to opposite sides of the road charging toward Leah and GW, rifles spouting flame and lead. Leah squeezed her trigger twice more as a bullet seared a bloody stripe across her right shoulder, kicking up rock and tar from the road's surface and pinging off the SUV's thin metal body. She had stopped the SUV at a slight angle across the two-lane road, which gave both her and GW a modicum of cover from either the pickup or the Suburban but not both.

"This isn't working for us, and you're going to owe the rental company some serious money if we don't do something quickly," GW called from where he crouched behind the passenger side door.

"Happy to pay if we get out of this. Any ideas?" Leah yelled above the ear-splitting sound of the gunfire. "We can't fight two directions at once forever, and they already have us pinned down in this crossfire."

"And we can't hold out too long, either. Sooner or later, a lucky shot or ricochet will get one of us," GW replied in an equally loud voice. "I say we move on the shooters to our rear. There's four of them and only one guy at the pickup—less to worry about there."

Leah nodded. "You move first while I keep the four shooters' heads down. Then you do the same for me. We fire as we move, going full Whack-a-Mole until we take the shooters out or get taken down ourselves."

"There's a cheerful thought," GW replied. "Okay. I'll go on three. One. Two..." On three, GW sprang to his feet, staying low as he sprinted to the right three steps, then left three steps, then right again, firing his pistol at each turn. The gunmen dropped to prone, like the other two attackers as GW charged them. Leah emptied her pistol's magazine covering his advance, alternating targets between the men on the left, then the right, their rifles momentarily quiet as GW and her combined fire did its job. One of the shooters lying prone in the center of the road jerked twice and rolled onto his back as two of GW's shots took him in the shoulder and then face.

After nine seconds and three weaves, GW dropped to the road, prone, sprawling on the road's asphalt surface and sighting his pistol at the two shooters to the right. As he dropped, Leah pushed off the pavement, her pistol reloaded and firing at the shooters to the left. Like GW, she sprinted three steps left in as many seconds, then right three, then left again as she fired controlled, three-round bursts and emptied her pistol's magazine once more.

Laying on the asphalt, head facing the men from the Suburban, GW fired his pistol again and again as she ran. The remaining shooter on the right screamed as a shot took him in the shoulder, then a second in the neck. The man groaned, rolled to his side, and then went still.

Leah dropped after nine paces, then spun to glance back toward her rental car and the pickup beyond. As she turned, she dropped an empty magazine from the grip of her pistol, pulled a fresh magazine from her back pocket, and jammed the fresh one into place. As she did that, GW called out, "Eyes to your six. The remaining two from the Suburban!"

Leah spun and saw what turned out to be a woman and a man, rifles at shoulder level, on their feet and charging from not more than twenty-five feet away. Instinctively, she swung her pistol up and around as their rifles cracked once, twice, and a third time, their shots going wide. Her pistol bucked in her hand as two slugs buzzed past her head and a third clipped her other shoulder, hot fire slicing through her shirt and her skin.

She steeled herself against the pain of the second flesh wound, feet solid under her, eyes forward and fixed on the attackers as she fired. She saw a puff of dust rise from the front of the female attacker's shirt as her first shot punched through. The woman staggered and fell backward, her rifle falling from her hands to rattle onto the asphalt.

To Leah's right, GW's pistol cracked again and again, so fast and with too many trigger-pulls to count. The remaining attacker from the Suburban jerked once, then twice more before he, too, crumpled to the ground.

The rear threat eliminated, Leah spun back toward the pickup to find it racing into the distance. GW stepped up beside her and gave her a questioning glance. Leah shook her head. "Out of range."

"What about the man you knocked down? The one with the rocket launcher?"

They walked together to where the pickup had been moments before and examined the shoulder of the road. Nothing. "Must've retrieved the body," she said.

Together, they turned back toward the four downed shooters from the Suburban. "Let's see if there's anything here we can use. You check the SUV while I check the bodies . . . " GW started when Leah heard a soft, distinctive click, a sound she'd heard too many times before: a bomb detonator.

She spun toward GW, dropped her shoulder, and crashed into his side as she yelled, "Bomb!"

CHAPTER 12

As he watched the last of the team from the Suburban go down, Haider decided it was time to leave. He slipped around the side of the pickup and hoisted Steven's limp body into the bed of the truck. Then he was back in the driver's seat, speeding the bullet-riddled pickup away, giving thanks he'd parked the truck with its front pointed away from the battle.

Minutes later, Haider glanced at his rearview mirror in time to see a ball of flame blossom into the sky, then dissipate into crackling flames and thick gray smoke. He smiled grimly. "Now, that was a surprise. Maybe they all got blown up."

He glanced to where his cell phone lay on the seat next to him in time to see its screen light up with the words *Dr. Muhammad*. He picked up the phone and accepted the call, then fumbled the phone to his ear with one hand while he punched the truck's accelerator and wrestled with its steering wheel.

"Is it done?" The Hatchet asked. Haider knew the doctor didn't handle defeat well. He also knew from experience that a good lie, based at least in part on fact, was often the best recourse.

"I believe the situation is resolved, yes," Haider said. "There was a massive explosion, a bomb in our backup team's vehicle. Our targets were too close to the vehicle to escape with their lives."

"You didn't inspect their bodies?"

Haider swallowed hard. "No, the explosion was sure to draw attention. I had to leave or be discovered."

The Hatchet paused for several long moments before replying. "The bomb was necessary. We couldn't afford to leave any loose ends. I wish you'd been able to inspect the bodies; but just the same, thank you for your service to our cause."

"Most gracious master," Haider replied, happy his lie seemed to have been accepted.

"What of your partner, Steven?"

"Steven was martyred," Haider replied. "He launched the handheld missile as planned but missed his target. He was killed by the return fire from our targets."

"His body? Did you recover it?"

"I did."

"His death was unfortunate," The Hatchet said. "Be sure his body is not discovered."

"Of course, Dr. Muhammad," Haider replied.

"Once you have disposed of the body, I want you to head to Boston and work with the team there."

"Boston? But our work . . . "

"Can be completed by others," The Hatchet said. "The truth is that by not confirming the deaths of your targets, you may have compromised your identity. Dispose of your vehicle once you have dumped Steven's body. Then make your way to Boston. I will text you a link to airline tickets in your name at the Nashville airport."

"Thank you, Dr. Muhammad. I live to serve."

"Indeed," The Hatchet replied but only to himself as he disconnected the call. He checked the text messages on his phone and found one from the female assassin, providing her new number. He dialed the number. It was answered on the second ring. "Yes?"

"I have another task for you," he said.

"So soon?" she replied, then added, "Of course. I am happy to assist."

"I will send you the target's information as soon as we're off this call."

"Of course," she repeated, and the line went dead.

Steven dead and soon Haider, The Hatchet thought as he gazed out the wide picture window of his top-floor Nashville warehouse office, where he now stood, gazing toward the crowded six-lane interstate to the west. *Then again, if the two people Haider ambushed still live and they discover our dealings with Dr. Jones at the air force base, it could pose a serious problem. A decade of planning might have been for nothing. That simply can't happen.*

CHAPTER 13

A searing wave of heat rolled across Leah's back, singeing her clothing and thick braid as the explosion's pressure wave pressed Leah's face into the asphalt. The sound of the blast hammered her ears, despite her hands covering them. Her back felt like someone used a steam iron on it, hot sweat pasting the thin cotton of her flame-singed blue blouse to her skin.

She waited for the pressure and heat to dissipate, then struggled to her knees and squinted through sandy, crusted eyes to where GW lay a few feet off. As she watched, he unwrapped his hands from around his head and rolled his face toward her, offering a weak smile. When he spoke, his voice was a soft croak, muffled by the ringing in her ears. "You okay?"

Leah nodded as GW struggled to his feet. He reached down a hand and helped her to her feet. "No big deal," she yelled, compensating for the muffled sound from the blast. "I've been blown up before, and it was a small bomb."

GW's brow furrowed. "You Secret Service agents get blown up a lot?"

Leah smiled weakly, then said, "The people involved in this seem determined to send us a message, no matter who we work for."

GW nodded. "You think?"

Leah glanced down at her torn jeans and charred, dirt-stained blouse. "Darn. These were new. I've lost two sets of clothes since I started my vacation."

GW chuckled as his eyes met hers. "You have a strange sense of what a vacation should be. Your clothing is a small enough price to be alive, although that outfit did look good on you."

Leah felt her face warm. "Excuse me?"

GW raised his hands in surrender, and she noticed the color flush his cheeks. She decided it was a good look for the big man. "My apologies," he stuttered. "I don't know why I said that. It was out of line."

Leah chuckled. "So you don't think it looked good on me?"

"Whoa," GW said, taking a step back. "I didn't mean . . . "

Leah smiled. "I'm messing with you, and it's all okay." She paused as her hearing cleared and the sound of sirens screamed in the distance. "Sounds like help is on the way. I can't be here when they arrive."

GW cocked his head to one side. "If you were actually Secret Service, that wouldn't be an issue, so I suspect something more."

Leah shrugged. "I don't exactly work for the Treasury."

GW holstered the pistol he'd kept in his hand through the blast, then folded well-muscled arms tight across his chest. "Do tell."

"You'll just have to trust me," Leah replied, then turned and headed back toward their SUV, hoping it might still work despite all the bullet holes.

"In my business, trust isn't something we hand out easily," GW said. He gave her two steps before he followed, calling ahead as he walked, "We just survived a firefight and an explosion. Don't you think I deserve a little more than 'trust me'?

Leah pulled open the SUV's door, slipped into the driver's seat, and pressed the ignition button. Her eyebrows shot up as the SUV's engine roared to life. She intentionally left the driver's side door open as GW stepped close, then shook her head as their eyes met. Once again, she felt something flip in the pit of her stomach as she saw the concern and caring in the big man's eyes. And something else . . . was that doubt? Doubt about her? For some reason, she found what he thought about her mattered.

"So?" GW asked. "You're just going to leave me here? No explanation, no nothing?"

"I wish it was otherwise," she said, then reconsidered and raised her watch to her lips. "Give me a second." She raised the watch's embedded microphone and said, "Overwatch Prime, this is Romeo Alpha."

The response was instantaneous over her implant. It was Paul, the director. "This is Prime. Go ahead, Romeo."

GW gave her a questioning look. Leah pointed to her left ear and silently mouthed the word, "Implant."

She returned her attention to Paul. "The investigator and I were ambushed a few minutes ago on the access road to the air force base. We're still at the site where it went down. He needs an explanation about who I am, and I need his trust."

"You want to drop your cover with him?" Paul replied.

"Correct."

"Text me his number," Paul replied. "I'll handle it."

Leah disconnected the call, then smiled when GW said, "You have some sort of communications implant? I have friends who work for the Secret Service. They don't have anything like that."

Leah tapped GW's cell phone number into her watch's text app and sent it to Paul.

"Nice watch." GW's voice sounded droll. "Do all Secret Service agents get one of those, too?"

Leah smiled at him, GW towering over as she sat in the SUV. "You'll receive an encrypted text in a few minutes from the people I work for. It should answer your questions. In the meantime, I'm going to leave you here to deal with the local authorities."

"But . . . " GW started.

On impulse, Leah stepped out of the SUV and into GW, her head rising barely to chest level as she wrapped her arms around him and pulled him tight. "I hope I see you soon, under better circumstances."

She stepped back, glancing up to find GW's face a mask of confusion, then relaxed as she saw a vacant sort of smile creep across his lips. "Me, too," he mumbled.

She climbed back into the SUV, threw it into gear, and headed west, leaving GW, the carnage, and the wreckage behind. *Now what was that all about? I hugged the man. I must really be slipping. Do I even have time for this?*

In the back of her mind, a small voice replied, *You're not, and you do.*

CHAPTER 14

Back at Joint Base Lewis-McChord in Washington State, Jessica pulled her silver Ford F-250 crew cab pickup into the small parking lot in front of the team's headquarters building. Rain pounded the truck's windshield as she set the brake and turned to Becca in the truck's passenger seat.

Last night, she'd given the teenager a place to sleep at her ranch, with Jess' father Roberto keeping a wary eye on the girl through the night. It hadn't turned out to be much of a challenge. As soon as they'd entered the small house, Becca disappeared up the house's narrow stairs.

"I guess she'll figure out which room is unoccupied," Jessica said to her father, a short, wire-thin man with thick white hair, a weathered face, and a perpetual smile.

His response was simple, direct. *"No tan diferente a ti cuando tenías su edad, hija,"* he'd replied—*Not so different from you when you were her age, daughter.*

In his middle seventies, Roberto lost his wife two months earlier. That his only daughter requested his help at her new place pleased him. He'd been only too happy when she sponsored his move to the United States and her small ranch. Last night, without being asked, he had stayed up all night to ensure the young teenager didn't pull anything on them.

Now, at eight in the morning, the sixteen-year-old's attitude hadn't changed all that much. She remained silent, sulking, and quite different from the girl who was all too happy to accompany the Home Team north after the warehouse interdiction.

Jessica decided to break the ice with some bad news. "I checked your status as an emancipated minor in Washington State. Turns out that while it may hold water in the state where your driver's license was issued, it doesn't here. I did that after you gave me the impression you were pretty put out about staying with me last night. Up to that point, it seemed like you enjoyed your time with us 'super spies,' as you called us. If that's changed and you no longer feel the desire to cooperate with us, I can reach out to your last set of foster parents and ship you back to them. It didn't take much effort to find out who they were."

Becca turned to face Jessica and replied with a frown. "It's a lot less fun now, especially after you locked me in that house last night with that old man watching. I'd rather hit the road than spend another night in that shabby, little house with you and the old guy."

"You're a juvenile, and you're under our care; so no, that's not happening. And that old guy was my father, who's seen more of life and how tough it can be than you'll ever know."

When Becca didn't reply, Jessica continued. "As I see it, your choices are simple. One, I turn you over to the local police and let them sort out your relationship with the people running that warehouse, the people who were in procession of illegal drugs and stolen government equipment. I don't like your chances with that option—most likely jail time while your situation gets sorted. Option two: I will turn you over to this state's human services office and let them ship you back to your home state and your fosters. I believe you left there for a reason, so I'll let you figure out the implications. And three: you dump the bad attitude and help us understand why you were in possession of what may be highly classified government property. When that's done, you'll be free to go."

Becca dropped her eyes, avoiding Jessica's gaze as she said, "I'll take option three, although it's not much of a choice. And what is this dump we're at—all concrete and steel and huge, like some deserted warehouse from a grade C movie? I thought we were heading to some sort of super spy hangout."

Jessica reached for the door handle and pushed the driver's side door open, casting Becca a wide smile. "Then I have a surprise for you. Let's head inside."

They both jumped from the pickup and ran for the cover of the building's metal awning, Becca slamming the truck door with enough force to make Jessica wince. They met in front of the building's double-wide glass doors, dripping rain from hair and jackets. There, Jessica flipped open the cover of a small, eye-level metal box and positioned her face in front of a black glass lens.

"Facial recognition," she said when Becca gave her a questioning look. "Metal detectors are built into the doors. The exterior walls are two-foot-thick steel-reinforced cinder block infused with a Kevlar-plexiglass foam. The place can take a strike from a small missile."

The facial image scanner chirped; and Jess reached for the door, pulling it open and waving Becca inside. "We set this place up just over a year ago," Jess said. "It's a bit different inside, compared to how it looks out here. Stay close."

"What? Robots will come for me?" Becca asked as she preceded Jessica inside.

Jessica laughed softly. "No, but that might be something we could investigate. Maybe program them to keep tabs on recalcitrant teenagers."

Lights flicked on as they entered, illuminating a massive interior with metal beams spanning the building's thirty-foot-high metal ceiling. Jessica lifted a hand to their right, Becca following her gesture as she spoke. "Offices and a conference room to the right. That's where we'll meet the rest of the team later. In the center is our sixty-by-sixty-foot red and blue checkerboard mat space where we practice self-defense and hand-to-hand tactics. Beyond that and to the center of the building is our weight-training area with assorted exercise equipment. And beyond that, you see the back wall with doors leading to restrooms and locker rooms."

"This is amazing," Becca replied. "I've spent a lot of my life working out—you know, gymnastics, parkour, stuff like that—but I never worked out at a place like this."

"Good to know," Jessica said. "You're free to use any of the space and equipment while you're here, but there's more. You see the two doors on the wall to the left? The one closest to the front of the building is the entrance to our confidence course. The other door leads to our sniper simulator, where Leah spends much of her time."

Becca grinned. "Now, this is what I'm talking about. Super spy stuff."

"You mentioned parkour? Then you're going to like the confidence course. We can simulate just about any weather condition you might encounter anywhere in the world: temp, humidity, air quality, rain, even snow. And we have some of the most demanding obstacles you've ever seen. It's my favorite place in the building, although Leah has the record for the best time. Maybe you'd like to try it?"

"Absolutely," Becca said, finally showing a smile.

"The team will be here in a few minutes," Jessica offered. "In the meantime, there's usually some coffee and pastries in the conference room. What say we head there and grab something to eat?"

When they entered the conference room with its beige walls, long heavy-grained wooden conference table and high-backed leather chairs, Becca headed for an open box of warm doughnuts on a counter against the room's side wall. "The cleanup crew must have come in early and stocked the place," Jessica said as she joined Becca to select a pastry.

The next five minutes passed in silence while Becca sat at the conference room table and devoured three doughnuts and two bottles of water. For her part, Jessica located a small tablet computer lying on the conference room table after finishing her doughnut, then dropped into a chair next to Becca. She opened the tablet's screen and opened a file with the latest information provided by the Drug Enforcement Administration regarding the previous day's bust. "Over one thousand pounds of drugs and twenty thousand rounds of .776 caliber ammunition," Jessica read aloud. "That's enough ammo for a small war."

Jessica held up the tablet and directed Becca's attention to the screen she'd just read. "Things may have just gotten more complicated for you."

"I had nothing to do with any of that," Becca said. "I was just there for the video games."

"We'll see," Jessica replied, keeping her eyes on the tablet's screen.

"I don't think I want to talk with you anymore. Will the tiny woman with the big rifle be here soon?"

"Tiny woman?" Jessica asked.

"About five feet nothing, red hair, and a rifle as long as she is tall."

Jessica laughed. "That's Leah. She's away for a bit. Why do you ask?"

Becca wiped doughnut crumbs on her jeans, then ran her fingers through her short, red-streaked sandy-blonde hair. "I think I'd feel more comfortable talking with her."

"And why is that?" Jessica replied.

"I think she and I have a lot in common."

"Oh?"

"Well, she's small, like me, and I bet people mistake her size for weakness just like they do with me. And I bet she's been pushed around and lost a lot of important things in her life. I know I have."

Jessica set the tablet on the conference room table and spun her chair to face Becca more directly, pushing back a long strand of ebony hair as she did. "You may be right about Leah; but I assure you, you can talk to any of us and trust us to do the right thing."

Becca folded her arms across her chest. "I've heard that one way too often. Look, I appreciate you putting me up last night; but you're confident, strong, pretty, smart, and tall like a model. I bet you've lived comfortably your whole life. You can't possibly understand what I've been through, so I don't see how I could trust you."

Jessica held her response, knowing that her fellow Home Team were a collection of people with very diverse lives. Each had experienced their own trials and successes in life before joining the Extreme Operations Group. None were perfect; then again, it had been a very long time since she'd been sixteen like Becca.

"Well, I can tell you this much: as teammates, we all share pretty much everything. Trust is not a luxury for us; it's a must-have. Our lives are on the line frequently, and we have to feel confident our teammates have our back. We must trust each other, or we cannot carry out our missions. Just like you are going to have to trust one of us if you intend to exercise option three and be on the good side of what went down yesterday at the warehouse."

"Whatever," Becca replied. "I hear you, but I think I'll wait until Leah gets here before I spill my guts to anyone."

"As I said, she's on vacation, so that might take a while."

Becca cocked her head to one side, her mouth a thin line. "I've got nowhere else to be."

Jessica took a long sip from her water bottle as she gathered her thoughts, then said, "I'll see what I can do, but I'm not sure it would be worth Leah flying back here just to talk with you. We're simply not sure if you know anything that would be worth the expense."

Sam and Allen entered the conference room then, cutting off anything else that Becca and Jessica might have said. Both wore faded, relaxed-fit jeans and loose shirts that hung over the pistols holstered at the small of their backs. They both stood five-ten, with well-muscled, wide shoulders and narrow hips. They could have passed for brothers, except for Sam's darker complexion, short-cut black hair, and brown eyes. Allen, on the other hand, had blond hair pulled into a short ponytail, lighter skin, and clear blue eyes. Jessica barely suppressed a chuckle at Becca's dreamy-eyed expression. She leaned over and whispered in Becca's ear, "Down girl. They're twice your age and both accounted for."

Becca turned back to Jessica and whispered, "A teenager can dream, can't she?"

They both chuckled, the easy sound Jessica had been hoping for since she'd taken Becca under her wing.

"Hello," Sam mumbled as he sipped his coffee and dropped into the chair across from Becca. "Anything new at this end?"

"Not so much," Jessica replied with a nod toward Becca. "And our girl's not talking. She wants to be debriefed by Leah and no one else."

"Well, that's unexpected," Allen said. "And Leah's not even all that likeable."

"He's just kidding," Jessica said as Sam slid into the chair next to Allen, then frowned when a loud beep sounded through speakers hidden in the upper corners of the conference room's ceiling.

"Call coming in," Jessica said as she tapped several keys on the tablet computer. Paul Samuelson's image filled the center screen of the conference room's three large screen monitors a moment later. His craggy face and thin gray hair appeared more mussed than usual.

"Good morning, Paul," Sam offered.

"It's approaching noon here in Florida," Paul replied, lifting a chipped white porcelain mug to his lips before continuing. "And it's already been a long day. Leah's working with a local LEO and has confirmed that the AVR15-X equipment in Becca's bag is, in fact, classified equipment belonging to the U.S. Space Force. It was reported missing several years ago. It's virtual reality gear developed by the Space Force for remotely piloting orbital spacecraft, drones, and tactical missiles. The version of the equipment Becca had was an early generation prototype being tested at Arnold Air Force Base in Tennessee."

"See," Becca said. "It's old equipment. Like you'd buy at an army surplus store."

Paul smiled onscreen. "Not true, young lady. The equipment you recovered at the warehouse remains highly classified, despite its age. And it is property of the U.S. government, even in its older version. The gear in your bag possesses capabilities and technology we would not want our enemies to know about."

Becca sank deeper into the thick, leather-covered cushions of her chair. "I knew it was too good to be true."

"Things like that usually are," Paul replied. "A piece of a strap from the same type of equipment was found in the pocket of an active shooter Leah encountered at a grocery store in Tullahoma, Tennessee. Tullahoma isn't far from the Arnold Air Force Base. I understand the gear was produced by ThirdEye.com, a company headquartered in Bellevue, Washington."

"Leah encountered an active shooter?" Allen said.

Paul nodded. "Two of them. She was en route to her sister's house and detoured to Tullahoma, where she grew up, for a trip down memory lane. She stopped in the grocery store there to pick up some things for her sister and interrupted two active shooters at the store."

Sam frowned. "Is she okay?"

Paul nodded. "She's fine. She had no trouble with the shooters and saved a lot of lives."

"I knew she was special," Becca added.

Allen smiled as he directed his reply to Becca. "Seriously, wherever that girl goes, trouble follows. And it's always in reverse proportion to her size." Then, in response to Jessica's answering glare, he smiled and added. "It's a joke, folks. I love Leah, too."

Jessica nodded. "She does seem to have a nose for that sort of thing."

Sam let out a soft laugh. "As they say, small but mighty."

Paul cleared his throat on screen. "As I said, one of the shooters had a piece of elastic strap in a pocket with the words U.S. Space Force, AVR15-X on it."

"The same model number," Jessica said.

"Exactly," Paul replied.

"So the question remains, how did Becca and the shooter come into possession of highly classified gear?" Sam said. "What's the connection?"

"At my direction, Leah and an investigator from the Coffee County sheriff's office talked with the research scientist in charge of the virtual reality guidance system project. He told them numerous sets of the equipment went missing some time ago."

"Then he's a likely suspect," Sam offered.

"So it would seem," Paul replied, the crow's feet at the corners of his eyes becoming more pronounced as he spoke. "He provided copies of Reports of Surveys documenting the losses. I checked on that; and as far as it goes, the paperwork's in order."

"So it's a dead end," Allen said.

"Not sure," Paul replied. "After Leah and the investigator departed the Space Force R&D facility, they were attacked in a well-coordinated ambush attempt. They escaped relatively unscathed, killing four of their attackers. Two remain at large, with one presumed dead."

"A busy day for our tiny sniper," Allen said.

Jessica laughed. "When is it not? That suggests Leah and the investigator stuck their noses where someone didn't want them looking."

Becca waved a small hand toward Paul's image on screen. "Leah is okay?"

Paul smiled, his craggy face splitting into a thin line with a hint of upturn at its corners. "She's fine, Becca, and thank God for that. She and the investigator were able to fight their way out of the ambush but not before one of the ambusher's vehicles exploded. That was a close call, but both are fine."

"Thank God," Allen said.

"Leah isn't getting much of a vacation," Jessica said.

Paul nodded. "I know she was counting on the down time. Regardless, the Secretary of State wants us to dig into the issue. If someone's willing to kill over some missing equipment, we need to know who they are and why they're so interested. The Home Team, including Leah, will take the lead on this."

Sam raised his hand just high enough above the conference room table to get Paul's attention. "That sounds like a job for the Department of Defense's Criminal Investigations Department, rather than us."

Paul shrugged. "With everything going on with Ukraine and the Russians, the Israelis and Hamas, as well as China's interest in the United States' military, DOD CID is tapped out. The secretary's asked us to lend a hand."

Paul turned his onscreen gaze to Becca. "Other than what Leah and her investigator friend have discovered, that leaves us with one additional significant lead. And that's you."

Becca sat up taller in her chair. "I don't know anything about stolen equipment or the ammunition Jessica told me about. And I want to talk with Leah. She's the one I trust."

"Becca seems to feel a sort of kinship with Leah," Jessica explained.

"I'm crushed," Allen said, then smiled as Jessica cast him a warning glance.

"Did Jessica explain who we are and how important our work is?" Paul asked.

Becca shrugged. "She did, a little."

"Then let me expand," Paul replied. "And I'm going to be candid, Becca, because it looks like we need your help on this. The Home Team works for me, and we work for the government. The work we do is of the highest degree of importance. We need your cooperation."

Becca grinned and cast a knowing glance at Jessica. "So you *are* super spies."

Allen coughed into his coffee cup, sputtered, then grinned over the edge of his cup. "I like the sound of that. From now on, I will no longer be referred to as Surfer Dude. From now on, I will be referred to as Super Spy."

Everyone laughed as Jessica said, "Not a chance."

"But I haven't surfed a day in my life," Allen protested.

Becca glanced around the room, her expression lightening amid the humor. "You do look like a surfer I saw once in San Diego."

Allen groaned as everyone laughed again, Paul included.

"What about the connection between Becca's VR equipment and the drug bust?" Sam asked. "It feels like the band found on the shooter Leah took down, Becca's equipment, and the drugs and ammunition taken during that bust might be related."

"Agreed," Paul replied. "Anything you'd like to add about that, Becca?"

"Stolen equipment and ammunition? I don't know about all that, but I do not do drugs. Life's tough enough without that. Some of the other recruits, as they called us, were users, I'm sure. A few would start shaking after a while, and our sponsors would take them away. They'd return a little later, looking more normal."

"Knowing that helps. Anything more you can add?" Paul said.

Becca leaned back in her chair; her arms once again folded across her chest. "I'm not saying anything more unless it's with Leah. I'll talk to her. I trust her."

"Jessica?" Paul asked.

"I've tried, Paul," Jessica replied. "She's a hard-nosed one."

"Fine," he said. "There's enough interest in this situation that it may be beneficial for us to bring Leah back for Becca's debrief. I'll have Leah there in short order."

"Thank you, sir," Jessica said as Paul's image went dark. Then, to Becca, she said, "It looks like we have some time to kill. The rest of us are due for a workout. Want to join us?"

"Absolutely," Becca replied.

Allen rubbed his hands together as he rose from his chair. "That sounds like a challenge."

"You're on, Surfer Dude," Becca replied.

"I like this girl," Allen replied. "Spunky, like someone else I know."

"This is going to be fun," Sam added. "I hope she cleans your clock, brother."

Becca stood from her chair, fists on hips, feet wide. "Oh, I'm up to it. I just hope I don't make an oldster like you feel too bad when I run your legs off."

"Oooohhh," Allen added. "I want to see this."

"The more the merrier," Sam said. "And I have a feeling she might just surprise us."

Becca beamed a smile at Sam that was half-determined and half-misty-eyed.

Jessica glared at Sam. "You're not helping."

CHAPTER 15

Regan Acheron settled the folds of her standard-issue mid-green and tan camouflaged air force duty uniform as she approached the Arnold Air Force Base Gate 1 entrance. Her source at the company that manufactured the uniforms for the military overnighted it to her, complete with slash pocket, embroidered name strip, and air force and unit insignia, to a hastily contracted UPS store postal box in Tullahoma. With her thick, straw-colored hair tucked under a short black wig, dark skin tint, and brown contacts, she looked nothing like her athletic, shapely, green-eyed, fair complexioned blonde self. The uniform, combined with a layer of lightweight padding beneath it, transformed her into an unremarkable junior grade officer anyone on the air force base would discount without notice.

Her forged military identification card and Tennessee driver's license were overnighted by another source and identified her as First Lieutenant Sara Taylor. It was a first-time cover that would stand scrutiny within the Defense Manpower Data Center (DMDC), Defense Finance and Accounting Service, Tennessee Department of Safety, and Homeland Security databases. It was good to have underpaid and unappreciated friends in low places, she'd decided long ago; and she paid them well for their assistance.

The sky overhead was pale blue with intermittent scatterings of fluffy white clouds. The temperature was a comfortable seventy-four degrees as she pulled up next to a security guard at the gate in her rented Toyota Corolla—just another in a long line of daily commuters. The contracted security guard at the gate scanned her military ID without so much as a glance at her, his eyes glued to the handheld bar code reader he passed briefly over the ID. She was through less than a minute later and, ten minutes after that, pulled up at a second security gate, this one guarding the parking lot for the Space Force R&D facility. Once the guard there read the fabricated orders assigning her to the facility, the man offered her a salute and a happy, "Welcome aboard!"

Regan parked in front of the two-story red brick building and mentally reviewed her plan: walk in and present her orders to Jones, assigning her to his operation. He would be surprised, not having received word of her arrival; and when he paused to consider the situation, she'd use that moment to remove him from The Hatchet's playfield. Simple and straightforward. Simple plans worked. Complicated plans often went astray, with too many moving parts and opportunities for things to go sideways.

Sitting in her car a moment longer, she keyed her username and password into a banking app on her cell phone. Signed into the app, she examined her checking account's list of most recent transactions. She smiled when she identified a $50 thousand deposit less than thirty minutes ago.

A nice day's pay, she decided, provided everything went as planned, especially considering her client. She assumed the man was a terrorist or criminal of some kind, but she could not have cared less. She'd given up any loyalty for her country and anyone else when she'd been unceremoniously booted out of the marines after her unit commander made unwanted sexual advances. She'd been a young corporal fresh from her first overseas deployment when it happened. He was a major; and when she complained to the next higher up in her chain of command, he'd encouraged her to reconsider the charges lest she ruin a promising young hero's career.

She refused; and the next day, during a surprise inspection, two noncommissioned officers reportedly found contraband in her enlisted quarters. The contraband was a plant, but that didn't matter when her case was processed swiftly and without mercy. A week later, after five days in the brig, she was given a General Discharge and put out on the street.

That she hadn't received a Dishonorable Discharge—which would have had significant consequences when it came to federal benefits, rights, and the chance for a decent job—didn't impress her. A month later, the major was found dead in his quarters, along with photographs of him with numerous enlisted women in compromising positions. It hadn't been difficult to locate the photos once she'd approached the other women in her unit and explained, anonymously, her intentions.

In fact, Regan seldom questioned the identity of any of her clients. If they could find her through the circuitous chain of contacts and intermediaries she'd set up on the dark web and pay her fee, she figured they were suitable customers. The man she knew as The Hatchet had found her through an intermediary, and he paid his bills on time. It was all she felt she could ask for from anyone; and five years after leaving the marines, she had more money in the bank than she'd ever thought possible.

She glanced again at the set of orders identifying her as a newly assigned administrative aid to the senior civilian at the site, one soon-to-be-deceased Dr. Alfred Jones. Smiling, Regan stepped from her car and made her way into the building. She consulted a directory posted on the wall in the building's lobby and located Jones' office on the second floor, room 201.

She climbed the stairs to the second floor and reached a hand to the small of her back as she pushed open the stairwell door. The smooth polymer grip of the silenced .22 caliber pistol located in a squeeze holster felt comforting as she scanned the hallway for potential witnesses and Dr. Jones' office. Easy to hide and even easier to dispose of, the pistol was a ghost model she'd constructed herself from parts collected from a variety of weapon stores. It bore no serial numbers or other markings that could be traced to her or anyone else if anyone discovered it after she dumped it in the deepest body of water she could find.

Arriving at Jones' office door, she knocked lightly.

"Enter," a high-pitched voice called from inside.

She pushed the door open, then mentally matched the face of the man sitting behind the oversized mahogany desk with the photo she'd been provided. That confirmed, she approached Jones' desk, snapped to rigid attention, and saluted. She dropped into a parade rest position with elbows wide and both hands at the small of her back, one hand on the grip of her small pistol.

Jones appeared pained as he looked up from a stack of paperwork. Eyes narrowed, he growled, "Yes?"

Regan used the hand not holding the pistol to retrieve her orders from a breast pocket and presented them to him. Jones snatched the document from her hand, wrestling with the sharply creased folds in the paper before finally getting the paper open to read the text. During that moment of distraction, Regan drew her pistol, swept it forward to within a few inches of Jones' head, and pulled the trigger. The man's head snapped back as a small red dot appeared in the center of his forehead, a small spattering of blood exiting the back of his head and staining the tall, cushioned back of his brown leather desk chair. Jones' eyes went wide in a moment of surprise before they clouded and lost focus and his head thumped forward onto the pile of papers on his desk.

Then, without a backward glance, Regan turned on her heel and left, closing the office door softly behind her and marching down the stairs and out of the building. A minute later, she was back in her vehicle and keying the location into her cell phone's map app for her next assignment: Nashville Airport and Haider Betterly.

CHAPTER 16

Leah arrived at the Seattle-Tacoma International Airport the next morning, having taken the red eye from Nashville. Allen picked her up in his 2018 forest green Mustang GT Cobra and whisked her south to the Joint Base Lewis-McChord headquarters while they caught up on her adventures in Tennessee.

"You win," he'd said after she walked him through the attempted ambush and the explosion. She neglected to tell him about her discussion with the group's psychologist.

Eventually, the discussion turned to Becca as he sprinted the sports car south on Interstate 5. "She's actually a pretty great kid and a surprising athlete. We ran her through the confidence course. She beat both me and Jessica and almost tied Sam. But she won't talk to any of us. She only wants to talk to you."

"Paul explained that," Leah said as they took the Joint Base Lewis-McChord, Lewis North exit. "And I still don't get it. I only met her for a few minutes at the Tumwater warehouse. No matter. I'll see what I can do."

"Yep, see what you can do," Allen said.

"I assume you heard about the active shooters at the store?" Leah said after a short silence.

Allen nodded. "Saw the video. You did an excellent job. Proud of you, girl."

Leah felt her cheeks flush, remembering the little girls cut down by the shooter. "I did what needed to be done—what any of you would have done."

"Even so. Still proud of you. And the family back at the homestead?"

"Good, as much as I can tell. With everything going on, I saw my sister and niece twice for maybe a couple of hours, and her husband not at all. But they seemed happy."

Allen frowned. "You don't sound like someone who got to visit their family, survived an ambush, and saved countless lives."

"There were two little girls in that store. I didn't act soon enough to save them," Leah replied.

"Ah," Allen said. "Definitely did not know about that. Then again, there's no one better at what we do than you. If there'd been a chance to save the lives of a couple of little girls, you would have done it. You've saved my life more times than I can count."

Leah took a deep breath, then reached an arm across the seat to gently punch Allen's shoulder. "I get all that, but those little girls . . . I've loved and worshipped God since I was little. Even so, it makes me wonder how He can let that sort of thing happen."

Allen let out a long sigh. "The question of a lifetime . . . You recall Sam faced the same thing—that little girl that died in his arms when the roof of a building collapsed beneath him during a mission. He almost resigned the Home Team and probably would have if he hadn't met Consuelo and accepted Christ into his life."

Allen reached out a hand to lay it gently on Leah's shoulder. Leah responded by covering the hand with her own and squeezing it gently.

"You have Mallory in your life, like Sam has Consuelo and his adopted son. Jessica has her ranch, her horses, and her father." She dropped her hand back onto her lap with a resigned sigh.

"Wait a minute!" Allen said as he steered his way to the headquarters building. "You're not just upset about what happened. You're concerned that you're losing us, too, because we haven't been spending time together like we used to."

Leah shrugged, keeping her eyes glued to the windshield as Allen turned his glance her way.

"No, I've heard of this sort of thing," Allen said. "A person goes through some sort of trauma and relates the outcome to something going wrong in their own life, like it's some sort of sign. How you're feeling right now isn't just about the little girls. It's about you feeling left out by the rest of us."

"I'm sorry I brought it up. Really, I could not be happier for all of you. I mean that."

"I have no doubt, but let's factor Jessica into this. What she has isn't really a ranch," Allen said, flashing her a gentle, sidelong grin. "It's only ten acres and rough around the edges. That hardly qualifies."

Leah chuckled, the first real laugh she'd shared since visiting her sister's house days ago. "Right, but don't tell her that. She's really investing herself in that place."

Allen paused again, his expression softening. "Seriously, I'm no psychologist, but maybe those little girls did represent what you think you've lost. They died, and you felt you'd let them down like you're letting us slip from your life."

Leah swallowed hard. "Maybe you should be my psychologist."

Allen rolled his eyes as he turned into the headquarters parking lot. "Oh *yeah*, that'd be *great*. But you really have no control over either of those things. First, based on what you've told me, I'm betting the little girls were wounded before you took on the first shooter. You couldn't have done anything to help them, no matter how much you wanted to. Second, our team is made up of individuals, all making their own decisions about their lives. You have no control over that, either. As you say, it's a normal part of life.

"But all that said, you, me, Sam, and Jessica are a team, Leah, as well as family in our own right, no matter how our lives develop outside the job. That will never change. You have to trust that. We've been through more together than any blood-related family will ever face, and the truth is that I trust each of each of you more than the members of my actual family."

Leah held a hand up in surrender. "In my brain, I know that. It's just . . ."

Allen let out a long, deep sigh, his expression moving from frown to compassion in an easy second as he pulled into a parking spot at the building, shut down the car's engine, and turned in his seat to face Leah. "Different directions in one respect, certainly. But we're still, and always will be, family. We've been through the fire of combat together. Nothing can ever change that; and perhaps more than any other event in life, that creates a connection few people will ever experience or understand. But like you said, evolving into our individual lives is a natural thing. God's path for each of us is bound to take different turns at some point; and so far, I'd say He's done everything He can to keep us together."

They climbed from his car in silence and met at the front of the vehicle. Allen pulled Leah into a crushing hug. "You are now, and always will be, my little sister."

She laughed, stepped back, and punched him hard in the shoulder. "Little? You want to fight and see who comes out on top?"

Allen chuckled, then glanced at his watch and hooked a thumb toward the building's entrance. "Sparring with you would be the highlight of my day any other time, but I think we have some business to attend to. Rain check? You'd best get in there and see what this Becca girl has to offer. And I'd watch that one if I were you. She's small, but she almost beat Sam through the confidence course—and that with the room set for a torrential downpour. She looks like some sort of pixie, but she's strong. Wait! Who does that sound like?"

Leah harrumphed and bent down to place her face near the facial-recognition plate. "Funny man. I still hold the record on that course."

Stepping into the Home Team headquarters building always felt like coming home for Leah. As always, the building greeted her with the faint aromas of cleaning agents and sweat and the clinking sound of metal on metal as the others worked in the weight training area. The muscles in her body seemed to relax in that instant, and she realized how much she'd missed the place during her short time away. When not at her apartment or on a mission, this is where she spent her days. She loved the space and loved the time spent training, planning, and socializing with her teammates. This was the center of her life, right after her faith and family. *Only a few days and homesick already?*

Enjoying the moment, she glanced around to see Sam in the free-weight area, knocking out a rapid series of bench presses on the

Universal Gym. Jessica, tall and slender in her gray sweat suit with her long ebony hair soaked and clinging to her shoulders, was on the pull-up bar, her body moving up and down fluidly, easily, as she pumped out a set of pull-ups that would make an accomplished gym rat jealous. Near Jessica, Becca, with her sandy blonde hair and bright red highlights, sat on the floor, legs extended to both sides in a respectable Chinese split. Leah snorted as she got closer and saw her own name embroidered on the sweatshirt Becca wore.

"'Lo, sister," Jess called out as Leah approached and she dropped from the pullup bar.

Becca paused stretching, her eyes reaching out to Leah, meeting her gaze. Leah felt a slight jolt of recognition run through her as their eyes met, just like at the warehouse. Something about her was so familiar—like looking at a younger version of herself.

"Hope it's all right if I used your sweats," Becca said. "They fit, and I didn't have anything else."

"No problem, and hey back at you, Jess," Leah said, then cast a knowing glance at Becca. "Someone wants to talk to me, I hear."

Becca raised her hand in a shy wave, her sweat-soaked hair clinging to her face like a skull cap.

"Then how about you grab a shower, and we can have that talk?" Leah said.

Becca nodded, snatched a small white towel from the floor next to her, and climbed to her feet. "Back in a few," she said and was gone in an instant.

"Any clue why me?" Leah asked.

"No idea," Jessica replied. "She seems to like the rest of us well enough, but she's held firm that she will talk to you and only you."

Leah shrugged. "I'll give it a try. Any advice on how to proceed? You've been with her for the last couple of days, and you know I don't have a lot of experience with kids."

Jessica laughed. "You're asking me? She seems like a nice enough girl—not overly social but she does seem to enjoy working out. Maybe you should take her somewhere you can do something physical, maybe a long walk somewhere away from here."

"Like the wildlife refuge?" Leah said, referring to the Billy Frank Nisqually Wildlife Refuge ten miles south on I-5 and its four-mile walking trail and boardwalk suspended out over the Nisqually inlet.

"Might be worth a try," Jessica replied.

An hour later, Leah and Becca climbed from Leah's Brown Chevy Equinox in the parking lot at the Billy Frank Jr. Nisqually Wildlife Reserve. Dark gray clouds crowded the sky; and the air smelled of damp grass, dirt, and pine needles. Tall evergreens and oak trees flanked the lot, with an attractive log cabin visitor's center on the lot's north side.

Leah tossed Becca a forest green zip-up storm jacket. "This should keep you snug if the wind and rain cut loose on us."

Becca caught the jacket and shrugged into it, zipping it to her neck. "I lived near here once before when my parents were still around. I never got used to the damp winters."

That was one piece of information they didn't have before, Leah thought. Then, to Becca, she beckoned toward a narrow opening in the trees at the edge of the parking lot. "We'll enter the trail there."

"Where are you from originally?" Leah asked, as they stepped from the asphalt of the parking lot onto a trail of well-packed dirt and then, a few minutes later, onto a long-weathered boardwalk with high, rough wooden railings winding through a thick forest of pines and oaks and past carefully preserved wetlands. Rain began in a slow drizzle through the trees, soaking their hair as they carried on at a slow, wandering pace.

"California. Near Bakersfield," Becca said after a long minute. "It was dry, hot, and not at all like this place."

"When did you leave?" Leah asked several minutes later, as the trees thinned ahead of them and opened to a long gravel road that led to a tall wooden observation tower that marked the entrance to the longer boardwalk extending a mile out over the silver waters of the Nisqually Estuary. The tide was in; and ahead, they could already see flocks of gulls and smaller birds whirling over the calm waters flanking the walkway. Two bald eagles circled slowly above the water, holding close to tall hills covered with evergreen trees and leaf-bare oaks across the inlet. The day's dark clouds seemed lower as they stepped from the gravel road and onto the thick planks of the long boardwalk.

"When I was five, my parents moved to a place north of Seattle, near Bellingham," Becca said, her eyes distant as spoke. She swept a hand in a broad arc to indicate the view of the boardwalk, the water, the hills, and the wildlife. "But we never made it this far south before they passed. I was twelve when that happened." She paused, then added, "This place is beautiful, even with the rain."

"I agree. I come here as often as I can," Leah said. "And as many times as I walk this path, I always see something different: harbor seals, sea lions, cranes, herons hunting their dinner, even some sea otters from time to time.

"And there's this white bird that you'll see once we get further out. Looks like a small seagull. They flock in large numbers, the individual birds hovering above the water until they spot a fish below the surface. Then they drop like a rock headfirst and smash into the water like they're hitting a brick wall. Sometimes, they come up with a fish, but often not."

Becca laughed. "That's got to hurt."

"That's what I think, but they just keep doing it. Seems like a metaphor for my life sometimes."

Becca chuckled softly. "I get that when it comes to my life, but not you. You're strong, competent, and some sort of super spy. I can't imagine you beating your head against anything, ever, and not coming up with a fish."

Leah laughed this time, finding herself liking the girl. "You'd be surprised. I'm just human, like you, doing the best I can. And I don't always get things right."

The rain pattered and slicked the surface of their jackets as they continued their way down the boardwalk, side by side. Leah found herself feeling like she was the older version of the young girl walking beside her.

They walked another quarter mile, past a second observation tower, before Becca broke the silence once more. "Jessica told me you graduated from college and became an air force officer. She said you're tough as nails. I think that's what I want to be."

"Tough as nails or an air force officer?" Leah asked.

Becca shrugged. "Both, maybe. You did it. I think I'd like to do it, too. You know, make something of my life."

"So what's holding you back? You can finish high school and enlist, or you could try for an Air Force ROTC scholarship or academy appointment. You seem smart enough."

"I don't know. Sometimes, it feels like the world doesn't want me to succeed at anything. When my parents died in the car crash, I went to live with my uncle in Minnesota. That was when the insurance settlement left me over a million dollars. Turned out he was more interested in the money than being my guardian. He burned through a lot of money buying cars and gifts for his real kids. A friend found me a lawyer who had him removed as my guardian after a several-month legal battle that ate up more money. After that, I was put into foster care with a couple, who were great. They were the ones who helped me become emancipated. At first, they volunteered to be my legal guardians; but as nice as they were, I'd had enough of that sort of thing. Now, I'm emancipated and get to run my life any way I like."

"And you like that?"

"Sometimes," Becca said, pausing to lean against the rail and stare out over the silver water. Leah pulled up next to her as she continued, "And sometimes not. I look younger than I am because of my size, like you. People don't take me seriously because of that. They write me off as too young to know anything and think they know better what I need. They're not always wrong; but once they realize I have money, it all changes. After years of people wanting my money or ignoring me like I'm not worth the time, I'm not sure I trust anyone anymore. That's why I wanted to talk with you. Your teammates seem cool; but for some reason, it seemed like you might take me seriously, like you might be able to relate."

Leah chuckled, still looking out over the waters on the west side of the estuary. "Believe me when I say I can relate. My mom died when I was sixteen. My sister, Rachael Mae, was eighteen. She put off going to college to take care of me. Even though our parents left us a good deal of money, much like yours did, no one thought my sister was old enough to take care of me. I know how hard she fought to keep us together, despite the naysayers. And there were quite a few."

"So how did you handle it?" Becca asked, her eyes focused on the spot where two seals poked their heads above the water, then rolled over and dove below the silver, rain-dappled surface.

"I think she and I both have always worked twice as hard as anyone else to prove ourselves, back then and now. For her, it was proving that she could offer me a sense of family better than anyone else could. For me, it was then—and still often is—my small size that creates issues. Sometimes, I feel like my life's work is proving that size is not a determining factor.

"But that wasn't all. In school, I studied harder than my friends to get good grades, so no one could say anything about my sister not doing a respectable job raising me. That carried on into college, studying, competing on the University of Tennessee's rifle team and in Taekwondo, the sport my mother trained us both in before we lost her. If my teammates spent an hour at the rifle or pistol range, I spent two. If the members of the Taekwondo club spent an hour at the dojang, I put in one more, as well as road time pounding my running shoes into submission."

Becca laughed. "I love running. It would be great to live where I could do the sort of stuff you did when you were growing up."

"Including finishing high school?" Leah asked.

Becca nodded. "Even that. If I want to get into a good university, high school is important. I did try martial arts a few years back. I lived near a dojo that taught Okinawan Karate. I made it to green belt before my parents died and I went to my uncle's place. And I've seen every Jet Li movie."

"Jet Li," Leah repeated. "Actually, an incredibly talented guy. So why not go after what you want? Go back to school, study martial arts, do all of it. It sounds like money's not a problem."

Becca turned away from the rail and headed back along the boardwalk without responding. Leah caught up with her a moment later as the rain continued to soak their jackets.

They made it to the third and final observation post before Becca spoke again. This tall, open-sided wooden tower looked to the north, where the estuary met Puget Sound. On a sunny day, the majestic lineup of the Olympic Mountains saw-toothed the northern horizon but not today. Today, all they saw was the silver ribbon of water and the gray clouds overhead.

"It's not the money. Since I became emancipated, I just haven't found a place where I fit in. I've visited four states before landing here in Washington, and none of them felt right. The video game thing just sort of showed up when I visited a used video game store a few weeks back. And you know how that worked out."

"Can you tell me a little about that?" Leah said.

"Why not?" Becca replied as they ducked under the cover of the observation post's tall log posts and shingled roof. She rested her chin on folded hands atop the rough wood railing. "I always loved video games," Becca said, her voice hardly a whisper. "They were how I killed time when I was in foster care. My foster parents, as nice as they were, were always busy with work and their three kids; so I had a lot of time on my hands. I got pretty good at them, too. I was at a video game recycling store when I was approached by the owner of the store, suggesting I might like to try out a new VR game."

"Where was the store located?" Leah asked.

"Near Bothell, northeast of Seattle," Becca replied. "The guy at the store arranged for me and a bunch of others to meet at the store early one day and transported us to the warehouse where you found me. The bus was fancy, very plush, and we were given snacks and protein drinks along the way. We were all excited about the new VR games we were going to try. When we arrived at the warehouse, we were each given a virtual reality kit. That's where I got the one you found me with. The VR games turned out to be very cool, very lifelike. I'd never seen anything like it."

"In what way?"

Becca glanced sidelong at Leah and smiled. "I've played a lot of video games and more than one with VR. What I'd seen up to that point was infantile compared to what I experienced at the warehouse. It was beyond 3-D—so lifelike. The dummy weapons they had us use felt real in my hands: kicking, vibrating, and getting warm. And the imagery was amazing. The first day, I blasted aliens from outer space that were so real, I actually felt afraid at one point, when one got close. It was that real.

"My second day there, I was paired with another player online, from some other location. We battled soldiers invading our country. I never learned who my partner was, but he had a lot of good advice as we kicked the invaders out of the good, ol' U.S.A. On the third day, I was on my own, battling criminals and people who looked like anyone you might find along the street. They seemed like normal people in most respects, but it was made clear I had to kill them or be killed by them. That game was frantic and so cool, the most difficult I've ever played. The good guys were impossible to sort out from the bad ones in some of the games, and the sessions ran well into the night. We repeated that session, with different settings and locations, for the rest of my two weeks at the warehouse."

"If you saw them again, would you be able to identify any of the people there with you?"

Becca shook her head, her expression intent on the mist rising above the estuary, as if she might find some answers there. "I didn't interact with any of them; I was totally absorbed by the game. It was so realistic. On that last day, they gave me a set of gloves and a vest with sensors that were linked to the game. When I fired a weapon, I felt it in my hands and through my whole body. They took the vest and gloves back an hour or so before the shooting started."

"They?" Leah asked.

"Our sponsors, the ones who brought us food and energy drinks and reset our games when we needed help. But I didn't notice much about them. I was so into the game . . . "

Becca went silent again as a group of sea lions hauled out of the water and onto a gravel beach not far from where they stood. The huge animals lay at the edge of a gravel spit that extended north from the observation tower.

Leah used the silence to drop onto a wooden bench facing the far waters. She unraveled her thick braid and combed the water from it with her fingers. That done, she dug two protein bars from the pockets of her jacket. She handed one to Becca.

"Hmm. Chocolate and peanut butter," Becca said as she accepted the bar and sat down on the bench next to Leah. "Thanks."

"So it was a pretty sophisticated video game?" Leah said.

After a pause to chew a bit of the bar, Becca said, "It was. And at a different level from anything I'd ever experienced. But when the real shooting started at the warehouse, that all came to a crashing halt. We'd been shut down for a system refresh and were told to return the vests and gloves to our sponsors. They said we'd be closing things down early that day. When we heard the gunfire, I noticed the sponsors were nowhere in sight. The other players disappeared, too. I stayed behind to grab my equipment and hid under the table in the office."

Leah nodded. "How about a very direct question?"

"Don't hold back now," Becca said, her mouth closing around another chunk of the protein bar. "I said I'd answer your questions if they brought you here to talk with me, and I always keep my word."

"Good to know. Did you hear anything about drugs from your sponsors while you were there?"

Again, Becca shook her head. "Not at all. I did overhear one man and a woman discussing something about having plenty of money to finish things. And come to think of it, one of them mentioned being happy the day would end early that day. He said they were told to leave because there would be visitors who shouldn't find them in the warehouse and that there could be trouble."

Leah took the final bite of her protein bar, crumpled the wrapper, and stuffed it in her jacket pocket. She stood; and Becca joined her, both casting their eyes across the water and to the gray sky overhead. "How about if we head back before the rain gets any worse and even the sea lions run for cover? We can grab a burger on the way back to headquarters."

"I'm down with that," Becca said. Then she added, "Thanks for bringing me here. I know your goal was to get as much information out of me as you can, but it felt nice to talk to someone I think I can trust."

Leah laid a gentle hand on Becca's shoulder. "If this was an interrogation, you've made it one of the most pleasant I've ever been involved in. I'll pass what you've shared with me to Director Samuelson and the rest of the team. Unless you have more to tell us, it probably means we'll be letting you go soon."

"Will what I've told you make a difference?"

"I have no way of knowing; but in my line of business, any intelligence tends to be good intelligence, so I'm hopeful."

"What happens to me now that we've talked?"

"I expect you'll be free to go, emancipation and all," Leah said.

"Jessica said as much. Would you know somewhere I could get a room, besides one of the fancy hotels where they look at you sideways when you're sixteen and on your own?"

Leah shrugged, and the next words came spilling from her mouth before she'd had a chance to consider them. "I have a spare room and bed at my place. My apartment is small, but I suppose you can crash there until you find a place of your own."

"So you can keep an eye on me?" Becca added.

Leah grinned. "Maybe a little of that. Someone needs to keep you out of trouble."

"I guess you'd know about that," Becca added.

They both laughed but were cut off by the sound of Leah's cell phone chiming. Leah retrieved it from her jacket pocket and examined the text streaming across its face. *Mission alert.* "We have to go," she said. "Now."

CHAPTER 17

Two hours later, Leah, Sam, Jessica, and Allen were in the Gulfstream G500, headed east for Nashville with Sybil Carmen at the stick. A tall, attractive blonde, Sybil was ex-air force, an Emergency Medical Technician 3, and proficient with most of the weapons the team carried. She was rated to fly anything up to and including a Boeing 737.

The Gulfstream was the smaller of the two personnel transport jets owned by the Extreme Operations Group. This G500 was set up to seat six, with four swivel executive chairs and a small couch that morphed into a well-equipped trauma bed when required. The head, or restroom, was shallower than the standard version of the craft, with a movable rear wall that concealed a weapons cache of M4A7X carbine rifles, ammunition, an assortment of 9mm and .40 caliber handguns and explosives. Below the head and the hidden cache was a trap door that could be dropped to provide a jump point when the team needed to infiltrate a target from high altitude.

Sybil's soft voice, with just a hint of Southern drawl, came over the passenger compartment's speakers as the jet angled into the sky and headed east toward the imposing, snow-covered bulk of Mount Rainier. "We have a nice tail wind and a flight time to Nashville of approximately four hours. Director Samuelson explained we're flying against the clock; so we'll be pushing Mach 0.9, this jet's top end. We'll be flying about 690 miles per hour—or, as we say in the pilot business, very, very fast. I'll turn on the autopilot once we reach our cruising altitude of thirty thousand feet. I'll join you then, to confab with you mighty warriors about your plans for our arrival and today's mission."

"Well, she's in a good mood, anyway," Jessica said, sitting in one of the swivel chairs and leaning over her off-white canvas go-bag. The team was in civilian dress for this operation, as opposed to their standard black tactical cargo pants and utility shirts. Jessica wore well-tailored skinny jeans and an oversized forest-green, button-top blouse that accentuated her deep tan and long, ebony hair. Like the others on the team, her clothing was carefully chosen to be contemporary but loose enough to conceal the .40 caliber Sig Sauer pistol she carried holstered at her back.

"I talked with Sybil before the flight," Jessica added. "Like Leah, she's scheduled for vacation, but something seems to come up each time she tries to take the time off. Once we're done with her, she's booked somewhere warm and tropical. That probably explains the cheerful attitude. She's highly motivated to get us to Nashville and back again in rapid order."

Sitting across the aisle in another of the four plush swivel chairs, Leah rolled her eyes. "No one's explained to her about vacations not being part of our job description."

"Don't be so grumpy, Romeo. Sybil's in a good mood. Why not you?" Allen replied.

Leah punched her fist hard into Allen's shoulder. "Stop calling me Romeo, Surfer Dude. You know I hate that call sign."

"Roger that, Romeo," Allen said as he reached into the canvas bag at his feet and produced a fifteen-round magazine and a Langdon

Tactical Beretta 92 Elite compact 9mm pistol. He twisted his seat around to face her as Leah's second punch slid just past his shoulder. He shot her a toothy grin as he examined the magazine to verify its load of fresh bullets, then slid it into the well at the underside of the pistol's black, checkerboard grip. His longish blond hair was pulled back into a short ponytail that brushed the back of his brown leather bomber jacket. He smoothed the legs of his Wrangler slim-cut jeans over low-heeled cowboy boots and held his pistol up like a showpiece.

"Say what you like, Romeo. I'm in a good mood today, and nothing's going to ruin my mood. Not even you."

"Ah, yes. The life of young love," Sam said, his words drawn out for effect. "I remember those days."

Allen pointed an accusing, black-gloved finger at Sam. "Just because you've already gotten married . . . "

Sam held up both hands in surrender. "Fine. Let's just agree that we've both been blessed."

Allen extended a fist across the aisle between them and Sam bumped it with his own. "Amen to that, brother."

As she listened to the good-natured exchange, Leah found much of the anxiety she'd been facing over the past few months beginning to dissipate. Her breathing seemed to come easier and the deep sighs less frequent. As her shoulders noticeably relaxed, she recognized that this was what she loved about her team: the camaraderie, good humor, and support. Her fingers fumbled with the hem of the loose navy-blue Tennessee football jersey and found her thoughts shift in the easy feel of the situation to GW and what he might be doing right then.

She shook her head to clear it. *What is happening to me? First the flashbacks and now I'm fantasizing about a man I met only a few days ago.*

As if reading Leah's thoughts, Jessica said, "Okay, boys, Leah and I may not be up to our armpits in romantic relationships; but we are a part of this team, and we have a mission to plan. Sam, you have the details provided by Director Samuelson. Why don't you read us in?"

Sam nodded as Sybil stepped from the cockpit and took a seat on the couch at the rear of the passenger compartment. "Wait on that," she said as she keyed a remote control that dropped a small screen on the wall to the right of the cockpit door. Paul Samuelson's image appeared onscreen a second later. "I have news," he said, before any of the team could raise a question.

"We've had two more incidents like the one Leah broke up at the grocery store in Tullahoma, Tennessee: one in Boston at the aquarium and another in Denver in a large grocery store. In both cases, there were two shooters. In the Denver incident, we can confirm one of the shooters was a skilled operator. That is based on the observations of a retired police officer providing security at the grocery store. By a stroke of luck, he was able to take down both shooters shortly after the attack started. The Boston incident did not go as well. A substantial number of people were killed and injured."

"This all has to be related," Sam said.

"Yes, indeed," Paul replied. "We can assume that, I think, with the similarities between the Tullahoma incident and these two."

"You're suggesting it might be a conspiracy?" Allen said.

Paul nodded. "I think it's possible. The FBI is taking that position and the lead on the investigation."

"Is there anything from this you feel we should consider when it comes to the Nashville mission?" Jessica asked.

Paul shrugged and then shook his head. He sipped at his signature chipped porcelain coffee cup, then leaned back in his chair and said, "I can't think what that might be, but I wanted to have the information in hand in case you find anything there that might be related."

"I have something that might be important," Leah said. "I talked with Becca just before we were alerted for this mission. She advised me that her sponsors at the warehouse—the people who transported, fed, and equipped her and the people there with her—may have received advance notice about us taking the Tumwater warehouse. They were advised to wrap things up early that day and not be there when visitors showed up."

"And those visitors were us and the DEA agents," Allen said.

"I believe so," Leah replied.

"Then we have to assume there was a leak about the Tumwater mission. I'll follow up with the DEA about that. And I have one more thing for you all." He angled his view onscreen to focus on Jessica. "Are you aware of a technologist by the name of Harley Maestro?"

Jessica nodded. "Of course. The man's a genius. I read he developed a severe case of Duchenne Muscular Dystrophy when he was young but graduated college at nineteen and opened his own business at twenty-one. He pioneered the use of virtual reality technology for patients bound to their wheelchairs and their beds, enabling them to explore their world and engage others directly, albeit within a virtual environment."

Paul sipped his coffee, then said, "Maestro's company, ThirdEye. com, developed the VR equipment and the programming for the Space Force project at Arnold Air Force Base. I talked to the man myself and appreciate how he's made a difference in the world. In fact, his contract with Space Command contains a clause requiring a significant reduction in cost in exchange for the military using the system's technology to create employment opportunities for Duchenne Muscular Dystrophy victims like him, as well as paralytics and other physically challenged individuals."

"That sounds about right, considering what I've read about him," Jessica said.

"A very rare perspective," Paul replied. "Interesting, without a doubt."

Sam opened his mouth to add something, but the screen had already gone dark. "Am I the only one he does that to?"

"No," Jessica, Leah, Sybil, and Allen replied in unison.

They all laughed as Sam pulled his forearm tablet computer from his go-bag. He strapped it to his arm and activated the screen, calling up the mission brief Paul had provided him earlier. "You've all got this information on your tablets, but to summarize: another drug operation has been identified near Nashville, Tennessee. It's an electronics warehouse just off Interstate 24, west of the city. The building is owned by the Retread IT Corporation, a business that acquires, imports, buys, and refurbishes used electronics for resale. The warehouse isn't more than twenty minutes from the Nashville airport, where we'll be landing. The president of Retread IT is Alvin Michael."

"Any background available about the man?" Allen asked.

Sam shook his head. "The man's a mystery. No record of him anywhere before the year 2014. He just showed up on the business scene with a lot of capital and more than a little skill in building relationships within Nashville's business sector."

"We should assume Alvin Michael is deep into the drug trade," Leah mumbled.

"Without a doubt," Sam replied. "We'll connect with EOG's Omega Team at an outlet mall not far from the warehouse. Omega was constituted to replace the Alpha Dog team after that one was betrayed by one of our own in Central America just over a year ago. They're headquartered out of Fort Knox, Kentucky, with responsibility for missions in Southeastern U.S., the Aegean Sea, and Eastern Europe. They've been fully active as a team for the past six months."

"So new! Are they any good?" Leah asked.

Sam nodded. "Seems so. They just finished a mission in Ukraine. Weapons were being smuggled to Russian loyalists by the Russian mob. Omega located one of the shipments, destroyed it, and then traced the shipment back to Saint Petersburg. Working with the CIA, they infiltrated that city and took down the Russian oligarch running the operation and disassembled his network from the inside out. One of their team members is some sort of public relations genius and created such a stir on social media in the surrounding NATO and non-NATO countries that the Russian government hasn't made a peep about the disappearance of its oligarch or his network."

"Impressive," Allen said.

"I know the PR guy," Jessica said. "I recruited him for Paul from the army's Special Operations Command. He's not only good with words; but he's also a force to be reckoned with, wielding any sort of weapon or in close-quarters combat. And he speaks with a pretty cool Jamaican accent."

"Then we should be in good company," Leah said.

"The plan is to rendezvous with Omega Team, then move on the warehouse in sync," Sam continued. "Omega Team will approach and enter the building from the east, through two loading bay doors that face away from the interstate. We'll come in from the west, through another set of loading-dock doors. Our entrance is on the interstate side of the building but is protected from view by a stand of evergreen trees at the edge of the warehouse's parking lot. A copy of the building's floorplan is available on your tablets and will display the locations of the Omega Team and each of us once we enter the warehouse. Omega will appear on the floorplans in real-time in blue. We will be green. They don't use implants for comms but use standard tactical headsets. We'll use our primary tactical frequency. Paul will be Overwatch Prime from Florida. Walter will be Overwatch Second, as always, from our building at Joint Base Lewis-McChord. Walter will have satellite coverage provided by the Defense Intelligence Agency, National Security Agency, and anyone else who owns a bird hovering overhead, as well as control over several DEA drones."

"Will I be setting up a sniper hide?" Leah asked.

Sam shook his head. "Not this time. Our orders are to crash this party with no opportunity for advanced knowledge by the people working there. The FBI has a Ground Observation Team on site, which reports as many as twenty tangos in the building at any time. Many of those will be well-armed and show evidence of being disciplined fighters."

"That's a lot more resistance than we faced at the Tumwater warehouse, and we had more time to plan and set up," Leah said.

Jessica nodded. "But we have more people this time, with Omega Team."

"Correct," Sam added. "And according to Paul's sources, the place may be center-of-mass for what the DEA feels is a larger corporate endeavor."

"And if it is another drug processing point, we should expect a large number of noncombatants," Allen said.

Sam nodded. "That's a good assumption."

Leah felt the anxiety rising in her gut at the mention of the civilians in the building. "We should confirm that in advance," Leah demanded, the images of the two little girls at the store flashing across her mind. "We can't go charging in without some idea of the potential for harming innocents!"

Everyone turned in Leah's direction. Jessica reached a gentle hand across the distance between their seats and rested it on Leah's arm. Leah smacked it away. "We can't afford any civilian casualties."

Jessica ignored the slap and laid her hand on Leah's arm once more. "You're not alone in that desire, sister," she said. "We've all seen our share of innocent deaths and injuries. You can count on all of us to protect those who need our help, no matter what the cost. It has always been our way and will remain so."

Leah felt the churning in her gut abate a bit at Jessica's words, her cheeks reddening as she realized the scope of her outburst. She cast her glance around the group to meet each of their eyes in turn. "I'm sorry guys. You're right, Jess. I know each of us will do all we can to do this right."

Sam drew Leah's gaze and met hers with understanding eyes. "We can do this, Romeo. There's no group better at what we do—and at doing the right thing. You know the One Who guides us will direct our actions, as He always does at times like this. So have faith, Romeo, in both Him and us."

Leah nodded, feeling a smile tug at the corners of her lips. "Yeah, but I still hate that call sign."

They all laughed, and Jessica squeezed Leah's arm.

Sybil glanced at her watch. "Wheels down in two and a half hours, boys and girls. You'll have a Nissan Armada for your use when we land. It will be gassed and waiting near the private hanger where I'll park the jet out of sight until you're ready to head home. We're borrowing the Armada from the U.S. Marshal's Service, so try to return it in one piece. It's powerful, armored, and has bullet-proof glass all around. Now, try to get some sleep. This is going to be a long day for all of us."

———————————

The Hatchet sat in his second-floor office at his Nashville warehouse, facing a wide window overlooking the building's interior. On the warehouse floor below him, twenty-five people in white lab jackets sorted and packaged pills, powders, and marijuana at folding tables. Fifteen men and five women surrounded the workspace, each armed with older model Heckler and Koch MP5s and a few assorted assault rifles. After what happened in the Tumwater, Washington warehouse, he was taking no chances. He'd barely gotten his leadership team out of that place in time to save them, although he'd lost a lot of product. That his armed guards were taken, he'd anticipated. Each had been paid enough to ensure their silence, along with threats against their families and friends should they inform the authorities about the operation in any way. It wasn't a fool-proof plan, he knew, but they were literally only days away from executing their master plan. After that, the loss of a few guards, workers, and drugs would matter little.

His cell phone buzzed, announcing an incoming call. He examined the caller ID on the screen. It was the Chairman, and he sat up straight in his chair as he pressed the button to accept the call. He'd only heard from the man directly on three occasions in the past: when he was brought into the United States and his psychiatric practice and research was financed, when he'd received the funding to set up the drug operation as a means for financing his operations, and five years ago when the singleton active shooter operation was given the green light.

"Yes, sir," The Hatchet said as he accepted the call.

"Dr. Muhammad. You are ready?"

The man was direct, Muhammad thought. Best to be the same, understanding the breadth and depth of the power this man held. "We are. Each target has been identified. The singleton shooters have been recruited and trained. The seed shooters are standing by and are some of our best operatives, prepared to martyr themselves for our cause."

"What about the debacle at the Tumwater, Washington, warehouse?"

Muhammad cleared his throat softly. "A minor setback. We lost only drugs and some recruits who were, candidly speaking, too green to be of value. I received a heads up about the mission several hours before it occurred. I was able to get my leadership team out of the warehouse before the federal agents entered the place. The guards captured there were freelancers, hired out of Seattle. They only knew about the drugs; nothing about the rest of our plans. The recruits who escaped knew only that they were testing a pre-market virtual reality video game."

The Chairman paused for several long heartbeats before replying, then said, "So, you remain confident of the security around the larger operation? You literally have only days before it is scheduled to kick off."

"The three pilot efforts in Tennessee, Denver, and Boston were successes. We experienced some resistance in Tennessee and Denver, but I write those off to coincidence. What are the odds of Good Samaritans being at our target locations, with the skill needed to stop what we plan to do? In short, I remain totally confident in our plans and the people involved in them."

"Good," the Chairman said. "If all goes well, you will have accomplished something I've waited a lifetime to see. You'll realize a level of vengeance greater than I could have ever dreamed."

"It is for Allah," Muhammad replied."

The Chairman paused and, by the shift in his tone, seemed to collect himself. "Yes, of course. On another note, when all is said and done, I'll expect you and the leaders of your team to disappear for an indefinite period. Return to your home country, if you like. Or go somewhere else. It matters not at all to me or the others on the council where you go, as long as you remain accessible. We see great promise in your work and may want to leverage your skills again in the future."

The praise took Muhammad by surprise. "I am honored, sir."

"You have earned my respect, Dr. Muhammad—or should I say *The Hatchet?*"

Muhammad frowned as the line went dead. The Chairman's use of the team's nickname for him suggested the man had ears inside Muhammad's operation. He'd have to proceed with extreme caution, lest the extra money he'd collected from the arms sales he'd been running through his warehouse come to notice. Otherwise, those funds might be good only for shipping his dead body back to his country.

His cell phone chimed. He answered it, and the voice at the other end waited no time to speak. "It's your Nashville warehouse this time. You have five, maybe six hours before they hit you."

"Thank you, sir," Muhammad started, but the voice on the phone cut off his next words.

"There must be no DEA agent deaths this time."

The Hatchet frowned. "Those two agents found my people entering the building. They saw their faces and recognized several of them. They had to die."

"We agreed there would be none of that."

Muhammad blew out a long breath. Tell him what he wanted to hear. In another week, all would be done. "I will personally ensure none of your agents are harmed this time."

Once the call was disconnected, Muhammad dialed the number for his warehouse supervisor. When the man answered, Muhammad said, "Please send my three visitors to my office immediately. We need to finish our meetings. And be prepared to evacuate yourself. In five or six hours, we may receive visitors. Make sure you pay each of the security guards a hefty bonus and let them know that none of the visitors are to leave the warehouse alive."

CHAPTER 18

Leah, Sam, Allen, and Jessica rendezvoused with the Omega Team in the parking lot of one of Nashville's newest outlet malls. The location sat conveniently across Interstate 24 from the Retread IT warehouse, which was their target. The teams gathered in the space between their vehicles, a large gray Nissan sport utility vehicle for the Home Team, and a midnight blue Ford F250 crew cab pickup for Omega Team.

The membership of Omega, for all its newness within the Extreme Operations Group's structure, surprised Leah. While Sam, Allen, Jessica, and Leah could have done justice during an Olympic trial in any number of sports, Omega looked more like a cluster of average men and women from the suburbs. She estimated the two women and three men on the team all stood five eight or less and, from outward appearances, were the sorts you'd see during rush hour in any city, not making an armed assault on a strongly defended criminal facility. They seemed thicker in their middles than a highly skilled covert operator ought to be and generally a lot more physically average than expected. All had what she might label bland facial features—not attractive or unattractive, simply average.

Mark, a lightly tanned, mustached man dressed in gray slacks and a long-tailed, short-sleeved business shirt, stepped forward when the Home Team exited their vehicle. With thin brown hair fringing a noticeable bald spot atop a round face with pale blue eyes, Mark approached Leah with his hand outstretched. Leah shook the hand, expecting a soft, pasty grip, but was surprised at the strength she found there.

"Mark Bashall, Omega One," he said, a pleasant smile brightening his face. "I'm the team's weapons expert and sniper. I understand you're my counterpart on the Home Team."

The guy's approach was so friendly and open, Leah's smile was genuine as she returned his grip. "So you're the one who keeps your team out of trouble?"

Mark chuckled. "What would they do without us? I know you by reputation, and I'd love to get a look at your M24 American rifle."

Leah felt her mood lighten with the man's interest in her favorite weapon. "Sure, when this is all done. I've fitted it for either a sixteen or twenty-two-inch barrel. Also modified the chamber to handle both standard and non-lethal rounds and increased the number of turns in the barrel, increasing the rifle's accuracy by 15 percent."

"Additional turns, huh," Mark started but was cut off as a matronly looking woman lay a gentle hand on his shoulder. "Don't get him started, or we'll never get this op going," she said.

Leah guessed the woman was a few years older than herself, with short brown hair and a fair complexion. She wore a floral blouse that hung shapelessly to her hips, over plain brown slacks that made her appear more like someone's mother than a covert operator. "I'm Jerrie, Omega Two. I'm the team's tactical lead. Sorry to interrupt, since I'm sure you two weapons geeks would love to dig deeper into your weapons; but we do need to get going."

Jerrie's words took Leah by surprise. In contrast to her appearance, Jerrie's voice was strong, with a steely edge. When Leah met the woman's dark gaze, she realized that no matter how Jerrie might appear on the outside, her inside was hard steel and all strength. The woman projected an aura that spoke to Leah: this was a woman to have at your back.

"Of course," Leah replied.

Jerrie gestured to the remaining three members of Omega Team. One was a Jamaican named Rascal Smith, call sign Omega Three. He was the PR man Jessica knew from her past and recommended for the team. He had a wide smile, skin the color of darkest night, and eyes that lit brightly. He projected a genuine interest as he shook each Home Team member's hand. "I am so pleased to meet you," he said as he took Leah's hand. "I'm the team's close quarters fighting expert."

"And this is Oscar, or Omega Four," Jerrie said, nodding toward a squat man with a ruddy complexion and thick black hair that hung to his shoulders.

By now, Leah knew better than to mistake the man's blocky appearance for a laggard physicality. As he stepped forward to shake each of the Home Team's hands, Oscar moved with the smooth, fluid grace of a cat.

"I blow things up," Oscar said, grinning mischievously as he lifted a hand in Allen's direction.

Allen chuckled in response. "A man after my own heart."

"Someone needs to know how to keep these clowns safe," Oscar replied.

The remaining woman on the Omega Team was a thin, edgy character, standing maybe an inch over Leah's own five one and wore a perpetual frown.

"And this is Tiffany, Omega Five," Jerrie said. "She's our tech and politics expert, although she's also a mixed martial artist, who can hold her own with just about any weapon in the inventory."

Leah glanced to Jessica nearby. "Someone you can talk to."

"Tiffany!" Jessica said, stepping around Leah to grab the small woman in a crushing embrace.

Tiffany's sulking expression brightened at the sound of Jessica's voice. "Jessica? Is it really you?"

Jessica released the woman out to arm's length. "How long's it been?"

"Five or six years, at least," Tiffany replied. "I remember our last bout like it was yesterday—the Army Mixed Martial Arts Championships in Falls Church, Virginia."

Jessica laughed. "We fought to a draw," she said, turning to Sam, Allen, and Leah. "The old codgers running the tournament didn't know what to do with us. All three judges scored us a draw and made us fight another two rounds to break the tie. We fought the additional time, but it still came out a draw."

"Those were very long rounds," Tiffany replied. "I don't think I've ever been so exhausted."

"But we parted as co-champions," Jessica said.

"And as friends," Tiffany added. "I still feel the effects of that throw you put on me. What a move!"

"Okay, girls," Jerrie said, stepping up to them. It was becoming rapidly obvious who kept Omega Team on track. "Let's confirm our roles and get on our way to the target. Director Samuelson wants us in and out in short order."

Sam stepped up to stand beside Jerrie. Until then, he'd been at the back of the group. "The Department of Defense has special interest in this one. Homeland Security wants to know how this shakes out, as well."

"It's the VR equipment, right?" Jerrie said. "As I understand it, you all identified classified military equipment being stolen from the government. DOD and Homeland want to know if we find any of that when we take down this warehouse."

"That's correct," Sam said. "As for the mission, we will enter the building in sync. Home Team will neutralize as many guards as possible in the first few moments. Omega will enter the building from the opposite side of the warehouse, with the same goal. We know there's a large number of tangos in there, so we need to be fast and accurate and ensure we neutralize them as rapidly as possible. We also understand there's a substantial number of noncombatants in the building. Once the guards are down, we will isolate and relocate the noncombatants as soon as possible."

"And the leaders of that operation," Jerrie added. "We want to take them alive if possible. Everyone have their arm-tablets on and synced?"

Everyone nodded before Jessica continued. "Coming in from opposite sides of the building creates an opportunity for friendly fire casualties, so let's be extra careful. Comms are on tactical channel one. Overwatch is out of Florida, with Paul Samuelson. Overwatch Second is Walter, call sign Golf Zulu or Grizzley, out at Joint Base Lewis-McChord. Walter will have operational control over several drones. Both are armed with nano-tracers; so if anyone departs the area, Walter will tag the vehicle or, if he has a shot, the person making their escape."

"Then we're ready," Sam said. "Let's do a final comm check and saddle up."

Jessica lifted her watch to her lips, activating the device's embedded microphone. "Overwatch Prime, this is Charlie Papa. Comm check."

"Cap, this is Overwatch Prime. You are Lima Charlie," Paul said, indicating her call was received loud and clear.

"Roger, Prime," Jessica replied. "Overwatch Second?"

Walter replied a moment later. "This is Overwatch Second. Lima Charlie here, as well. I confirm the drones are in the air courtesy of our buddies at the FBI, hovering well out of sight at a thousand feet."

"Roger, Second," Jessica said. "Omega One, Two, Three, Four, and Five?"

"Cap, this is Omega One," Mark replied over his tactical headset. "Also Lima Charlie."

Jerrie, Rascal, Oscar, and Tiffany repeated the report in sequence, followed by Sam, Allen, and Leah.

"This is Prime," Paul Samuelson said a moment later. "You are status three and authorized to approach the building. God speed."

"Roger Prime. Executing now," Sam said. Then, to the rest of the Home Team and Omega Team, he said, "Let's saddle up."

CHAPTER 19

Before approaching the warehouse, Walter circled the place with the drones and found no exterior guards visible. With that information in hand, Leah and her teammates gathered in an ingress column at the side of the warehouse, with Sam leading, Jessica following him, then Allen and Leah at the rear. Each had a matte-black M4A8E carbine rifle with sound suppressors and short, close quarter barrels at the ready, with Sam's aimed ahead, Jessica's and Allen's to either side, and Leah's focused to their rear. With the stocks folded, the rifles looked more like submachine guns, but they expected tight quarters and needed their weapons configured for that sort of fight. Each of them had one hand on the shoulder of the person ahead.

When the clock ticked down to the agreed upon go-time, Sam raised his fist and pumped it up and down once. At the back of the column, Leah silently squeezed Allen's shoulder, indicating her readiness. Allen repeated the signal to Jessica, who did the same to Sam. In the next instant, they were moving, pausing at a narrow warehouse personnel door that Sam swung wide and then charging in with a shuffling, tactical crouch.

As she entered the building, the image of the two downed little girls at the grocery store flashed across Leah's mind. She frowned and fought the image from her mind, focusing on the view to either side of the door they'd just passed through. Allen cast a glance over his shoulder, sensing her stride falter. She nodded a silent response and chastised herself for the lack of mental discipline. For good measure, she whispered a soft prayer as she scanned the warehouse to either side, seeking targets. "Lord, give me strength."

Ahead of her, she heard Allen whisper, "Now and always, sister," as they continued into the warehouse.

Moving on silent feet, the team fanned out, Jessica to the right, Sam straight ahead, Allen left, and Leah backing in with eyes to the rear. Bright lighting illuminated the warehouse from long skylights that ran the length of the massive building. Six long rows of pallets stacked three-high and loaded with cardboard and wooden boxes ran its length, much like the Tumwater building. To their right, above the building's south wall, she saw a single, second-story window with a soft glow backlighting the space.

"This is Romeo," she whispered. "We may have people in a second-floor office."

"This is Cap. Our forward position is clear to the pallet stands," Jessica said. "No workers or tangos in sight."

"This is Omega One," Mark said over comms. "We've entered the building and remain undetected. A dozen or more armed tangos are positioned against the walls of an open work area to our right, obscured by the pallet stands between us and them. Could be as many as twenty. All are fighting-age males and females carrying automatic weapons."

"This is Empty," Sam replied. "Roger, Omega One. Fox, peel off and verify the status of the office upstairs. Romeo, move out with Fox. Cap, turn north and flank the work area at the other end of the warehouse, opposite Omega Team's position. I'll be at your back."

"Fox," Allen replied. "On it."

"Romeo. Moving with Fox," Leah said.

Allen and Leah moved silently side-by-side to the stairway door leading up to the second-floor office. As they approached the door to the stairs leading to the office, they encountered two additional first-floor offices. A quick scan of the spaces revealed evidence of recent occupancy, but the offices were unoccupied.

"This is Romeo," Leah whispered. "Two first-floor offices are clear. Fox and I are moving upstairs."

"Overwatch Prime. Roger, Romeo," Paul replied.

Allen took position behind Leah at the door to the stairs, then squeezed her shoulder. Leah reached for the door's handle and drew it open, cringing as its hinges screeched softly, then climbed the stairs two at a time. The butterfly strips across her torso stretched and stung as she moved, as did the flesh wounds on each shoulder.

A reminder, she told herself. *Be ready for anything.*

She paused at the top of the stairs at another door leading into the office and held up three fingers. She lowered them one at a time. On three, Leah kicked open the door and charged inside, Allen at her back. Her carbine at eye level, she scanned the room to her left, knowing Allen was doing the same to the right, both trigger-ready.

Her side of the room was empty, devoid of anything more than descending dust motes lit by the room's dim lamps and the illumination from the warehouse beyond the room's large window. She felt Allen's touch on her arm and spun his direction on the balls of her feet, her rifle remaining at eye level, ready to engage. That's when she saw fifteen people of diverse ages, clothing, and appearance pressing themselves against the back wall of the room with their hands raised in front of their faces. Half the group held VR headsets like the ones Becca'd had when they found her. The other half quaked with eyes wide.

"Please don't shoot," a petite young girl with tangled blonde hair pleaded, her eyes full of tears.

With Leah covering him, Allen lowered the barrel of his rifle and stepped toward the girl. "We have no desire to hurt you." He raised his eyes to take in the entire group. "Please step away from the person next to you, creating an arm's length of space between you, and raise your hands."

The members of the group spread apart, so Allen could see between and what might lay behind them. When they were in position and seeing nothing more than the people there, he approached each one in turn. He had all of them spin slowly in place to show they were unarmed, with him occasionally lifting the hem of a shirt or jacket to be sure. The cursory search was completed in less than two minutes.

"Overwatch Prime, this is Fox," Allen whispered over comms. "We have fifteen non-combatants in the second-floor office. No armed tangos. Appears to be a group of scared gamers like the one we experienced in Tumwater."

"Roger, Fox," Paul replied. "Secure the people, then move out to support the mission. All else, hold position until Fox and Romeo join you on the warehouse floor."

"This is Omega One," Mark replied. "Roger all for Omega One."

"Empty. Roger, Prime," Leah heard Sam say over comms.

"Roger, Prime," Allen replied, stepping over to where Leah covered him and setting his rifle at her side.

Allen retrieved a thick bunch of zip ties from his back pants pocket and held them up for the noncombatants to see. "Please take a seat on the floor and get as comfortable as you can. I'm going to zip tie your wrists and ankles so you don't get any ideas about running. There could be gunfire soon, and I wouldn't want any of you to get hurt."

The blonde teenager whimpered but was the first to drop to the floor with her back against the office wall.

"Thank you," Allen said as approached her, kneeled, and zip-tied her wrists and ankles. "I'm sure it won't be for long."

Minutes later, with Leah covering him as he did the chore, all the people in the office were secure. Allen gave Leah a thumbs up, then raised his watch to his lips and said, "Prime, this is Fox. The second-floor office is secure. Moving to the warehouse floor."

"Omega One," Mark said over comms. "We remain undetected and have fanned out around the east and north sides of the work area. Around a sixty-by-sixty-foot work area, at least a dozen guards are visible, with more likely positioned in the pallet stands. Confirm when you are in position, and we will take the lead on the central body of tangos and draw any we can out of hiding. Suggest Home Team remain out of sight and take on the tangos that show up once we've initiated contact."

"Romeo. Roger all and watch the civilians," Leah added, as she and Allen exited the stairway and headed for the other end of the warehouse and their position with Sam and Jessica.

"Omega Two," Jerrie replied. "None of us are beginners here, Romeo. Get your head in the game."

Jerrie's words stung, and Leah felt her hackles rise. *Who was she, some upstart newbie . . .*

In the next instant, Leah checked her anger. Ever since the grocery store incident, she'd become obsessed with the potential for collateral damage, even though every operator in the Extreme Operations Group was trained to protect the innocent. Jerrie was right; she needed to get her head on straight. She sucked in a deep breath and whispered, "Guide me, Lord."

"He will," came Allen's swift, soft reply as they moved down the stairs and out along the warehouse wall. "Now, we need to move!"

"This is Prime. The Tennessee Bureau of Investigation is on scene. They will take custody of the people you located in the office once the warehouse is secure."

Paul's last word was hardly out of his mouth before a rifle cracked and a bullet smacked into the cinderblock wall next to Leah's head. A firestorm of weapons fire followed in the next moment.

CHAPTER 20

"Overwatch Prime, this is Empty," Sam said over comms. "Cap and I and Omega Team are taking fire from a dozen armed guards. They were ready for us. Omega Team is retrograding to a row of heavy wooden boxes at the northeast corner of the building. Cap and I are secure for the moment behind a pallet stand near the west wall. We have approximately two dozen noncombatants on the floor between us and Omega."

"This is Prime. Do what you can to protect yourselves and the civilians. I will call TBI in to back you up."

Leah felt a surge of adrenaline, then a sudden sense of calm, as always happened when she was under fire and came up with a plan. "Break. Break. This is Romeo," she whispered over comms.

"This is Prime. Go ahead, Romeo," Paul replied.

"We know there are more guards, so Fox and I will find covered position and hold until they reveal themselves, while Omega Team, Empty and Cap hold off the force that's in view."

"Roger, Romeo. You are clear to proceed," Paul said.

Leah slung her carbine across her back and drew her Beretta from the small of her back. His face a grim mask, Allen matched Leah stride for stride, moving with his carbine and she with her pistol at eye level, scanning forward and side to side. The crack of the opposition's weapons and soft *sputt* of Omega and Home Team's suppressed weapons grew louder as they jogged silently down the warehouse's central aisle, between tall rows of yellow metal pallet stands stacked three levels high.

"This is Empty," Sam whispered over comms as they closed the distance. "There's a tall stack of pallet stands four pallets high with wooden crates that should provide good cover. It's immediately south of where Cap and I are pinned down. Another stack flanks the east side of the warehouse, to the right and above where Omega is positioned."

"Roger all," Leah replied, holstering her pistol as they approached the first set of pallet risers Sam described. She turned to Allen, lifting a finger toward the top of the tall pallet stand, and gave him a thumbs up. He nodded, slung his carbine across his back, and pulled himself up to the first pallet in the tall riser. A minute later, he was scrambling over the top of the uppermost stack of boxes and settling in. A moment after that, Leah found the stack of pallets overlooking Omega's position and did the same.

Leah stretched out, prone on the boxes as the firefight continued below her, the air thick with the gray fog of spent cordite. Mark came over comms a second later. "This is Omega One. Omega Three is down. Shoulder wound. Non-critical, but he's going to need help."

"This is Prime. Roger, Omega One," Paul replied. "Medical help is standing by."

"Omega One, again. What's the ETA on TBI?"

"This is Prime," Paul replied. "Remains five minutes and holding. Bureaucratic clearance is lagging."

"Roger, but that may be too late."

"This is Prime," Paul replied. "Stand by. Romeo? Fox? Status?"

Allen's voice came next as he whispered. "I'm in position above the fight. Clear field of fire. I believe I'm undetected."

"This is Romeo," Leah whispered into her watch's microphone. "In position. Opening fire on my mark."

"This is Fox. Roger, Romeo. On your mark," Allen said.

Leah unslung her carbine and lined up her first shot—one of the center tangos in a group advancing on Omega's position in a slow, creeping crouch, weapons up and trained on the boxes and crates shielding Omega. Her first target acquired, Leah scanned left and right, choosing her next four shots. Any more shots than that and she knew from experience her targets would scatter to find cover. But if she could take down four in her first round and Allen did the same, the situation in the warehouse would have improved significantly, and it should draw the remaining shooters from hiding. *If* . . . How she wished she had her trusty M24 sniper rifle.

As she scanned, she saw the noncombatant workers crouched beneath their worktables, many whimpering audibly in fear. Her stomach churned at the sight, the memory of the little girls in the store and the two shooters' victims huddled on the floor of the store's aisles. Leah blew out a long breath and forced the image from her mind, steadying her weapon's sights on her first target. "Mark!"

As one, Allen and Leah opened fire. The thwack, thwack, thwack of suppressed rifle fire sounded from her right as Allen fired, even as her carbine thumped softly against her shoulder. Her first target's head jerked, his baseball hat flying off to reveal a bald head and the impact of the shot. The man crumpled out of sight. Then, as fast as she could trigger her rifle, Leah found her second target, fired, and moved onto the next. Each shot went true as her second, third, and fourth targets dropped from sight.

Leah didn't bother glancing to where Allen lay atop the next stack of pallets. She knew, as much as he was not the team's sniper, his abilities with a rifle were exceptional. Sure enough, a second later, his voice came over comms. "This is Fox. Confirm four tangos down."

Leah smiled. "Romeo. Ditto here."

She smiled as the weapons-fire from the remaining tangos below her position withered, then stopped. The momentary, sudden silence in the warehouse seemed surreal, hollow, empty, as it always felt at the end of an intense firefight. Only she knew this one wasn't done, by a long shot.

As she scanned the area below her, a guard previously hidden in a stack of boxes lifted her head, eyes scanning the area above to identify Leah's position. Leah triggered the shot. The woman's head jerked to the side, and she dropped to the floor behind the boxes.

"Fox, this is Empty." Sam's words were sharp, to the point. "Two tangos splitting off from the main group, headed your way."

"Roger, Empty," Allen replied. "Relocating now."

"This is Cap," Jessica added. "I confirm two more down, taken by Omega. That leaves an even dozen tangos somewhere in this place."

As Jessica spoke, the firing resumed with deadly concentration, bullets careening toward the Omega team's position and ricocheting with loud thwacks and pings off the cinderblock and steel warehouse walls. Leah covered her head and ears as the haze of gun smoke cast an even thicker gray fog over the workspace below, sharp shafts of sunlight slicing through to illuminate the long folding tables and the white-coated workers huddling beneath them. Then, as quickly as the shooting started, it stopped once again and Leah raised her head to scan the area once more. As before, the sudden eerie silence felt heavy and oppressive.

"This is Omega Two," Jerrie said. "We need another plan. The quiet suggests they're regrouping."

"This is Omega Five." Leah recognized Tiffany's voice, the member of the Omega Team who'd known Jessica during her mixed martial arts days. "I see a cluster of heads forming up opposite our position. We're about to be stormed by the remaining tangos. My guess is there'll be twelve or thirteen. Their reserves have been committed."

"Roger, all," Paul said, his voice barely a whisper over comms. "Suggest Omega use covering fire to move to new positions, create space between each of you, and spread your fields of fire. Can you do that from your current position?"

"This is Omega Two," Jerrie replied. "Omega Three and I will provide covering fire while the rest move to new locations, but we need to go now."

"Go. Go. Go!" Paul said.

Suppressed gunfire and flame lit the area from Jerrie's position, with the wounded Rascal joining in. While Leah couldn't see where the rest of Omega Team moved, the shooting stopped once again as Jerrie came back online. "Omega two. Our team has successfully redeployed. Now, we need a plan."

"This is Omega One. The tangos plan to storm our position. I suggest we let them get close before we open fire," Mark said. "If Home Team can close on them from the flank, we should be able to resolve this quickly."

"This is Empty. Roger all," Sam said. "Fox and Romeo, redeploy to join us on the floor, opposite our position, across the workspace. Once the guards begin their advance on Omega, we will trap them in a crossfire."

Sam's response was confirmed by Jessica, Allen, and then Leah with a double click of their microphones.

"Take prisoners, if you can," Paul said. "Godspeed. Overwatch Prime out."

CHAPTER 21

Leah hurried down from her perch on the high pallet without being observed and made her way down a short aisle of pallet stands, to the counterattack. As she crept forward on silent feet, her carbine clutched in her hands, she caught a glance of Allen, one row over and paralleling her path.

She heard a noise behind her and to her left and ducked behind a pile of unstacked empty boxes in time to see a tall, muscular man in black shirt and cargo pants turn into the aisle she'd just left. The man moved slowly, with a sound-dampening heel-toe movement, the snub-nosed barrel of his MP5 submachine gun leading the way. Leah held her breath as he paused within several feet of her position, close enough she could have reached through the boxes and touched him. If she tried to warn her teammates, the man would hear her. She held her breath as she listened to the man's smooth, rhythmic breathing. Then, after several seconds when Leah thought her heart might beat out of her chest, the man took two tentative steps forward, paused, and then moved forward at a slow, deliberate pace.

Leah remained frozen in place until the man was well down the aisle, turned right, and moved out of sight. Then she eased from behind the pile of boxes and slung her rifle across her back. Carefully, silently, she followed the man's path until he was once more in view.

When she spotted him, he held a small radio to his lips. In a low, gravelly voice, she heard him say, "In position to flank the target."

As he continued, Leah used the sound of the man's voice to cover her soft footsteps as she approached him from behind. She'd planned to climb his back and attack his head and neck like she'd done at the grocery store; but before she got close enough, some sixth sense alerted the man, and he spun to face her. She had just enough time to close to within arm's reach and swing the butt of the weapon into the side of the man's head. He staggered back but didn't go down. Leah followed him, closed to arm's length again, and smashed the barrel of her rifle into the man's neck, just below the chin. He staggered back again, one hand rising to clutch at his crushed windpipe, the other still clutching his MP5. Leah pursued him again, stepping close as the man gasped and glared at her through dark, hate-filled eyes and raised his MP5.

Leah swung her M4 carbine in a wide arc that connected with the man's weapon, smashing it aside. The submachine gun spun from his grasp as his knees began to tremble and he continued to struggle for breath.

Leah reversed the direction of her pivot, arcing her M4 carbine into the weakening man's temple. His knees gave way and he slumped to the ground as he drew his MP5 protectively to his chest and his eyes closed around a painful frown. Leah pulled two thick flexi-cuffs from her back pocket and secured the man's wrists and feet, then tore off a piece of his shirt and stuffed it into his mouth.

Leah stepped over the downed guard's unconscious form and jogged ahead to the edge of the open workspace, hoping to catch up with Allen in the parallel aisle. She pulled up behind a stack of pallets laden with heavy wooden boxes, glancing left in time to see a hint of blue flash into position one aisle over. It was Allen's dark blue football jersey. She fixed her gaze across the workspace, catching a glimpse of two figures there: Sam and Jessica crouched within two tall pallet stands, concealed behind stacks of boxes.

The warehouse was silent now, and Leah watched as seven guards quietly emerged from cover, dropped around the workspace, and moved low and swift to join the remaining guards there, using several overturned worktables for cover. After a moment of whispered words unintelligible from Leah's position, they rose as the guards formed into two loosely configured semi-circular lines with six shooters in the front line and five to the rear, rifles collectively pointing in the direction of Omega's cover. The lines were staggered and spaced so that the shooters in the back could fire forward without fear of wounding anyone ahead of them.

They began moving forward with deliberate steps, each operator with their weapon at eye level. All at once, the first line of guards opened fire, emptying their magazines as their rifles spouted flame and lead. The first line paused to drop their empty magazines and reload as the next line of shooters began firing, blazing flame and death from their rifles. The sound was deafening as they advanced on Omega Team's position like a line of British troops might have advanced during the Revolutionary War. As they progressed and continued firing in alternating lines, the boxes behind which Omega Team huddled shredded, sending splinters of wood and cardboard in every direction.

Worried that the guards would break through Omega's shield of boxes any moment, Leah smiled grimly as she heard Jerrie whisper over comms, "Wait for it. Wait for it . . . "

When the second line of tangos advanced within fifteen feet of Omega Team's position and paused to reload, and the first line stepped up to fire, Jerrie cried out over comms, "Now!"

In the pause as the warehouse guards reloaded, the five members of Omega Team rose as one and sprayed bullets in a one hundred twenty-degree arc in front of their position. Leah and her teammates stepped out from hiding at that same moment, triggering carefully targeted shots in three round bursts to knock down guard after guard. Less than twenty seconds later, all the warehouse guards lay wounded or dead on the cold concrete warehouse floor.

The air above the workspace's white tables was dank and gray and smelled even more of cordite as the Home Team steadied in place to cover the area, in case any additional guards showed themselves, rifles remaining up as they scanned the area, heads on a swivel. Omega Team's five members came forward as well, Jerrie pausing next to the table closest to her to offer a hand to a lab-coated worker who'd remained hidden under the table until then. Leah did the same for a person under a table near her; and with Allen and Mark keeping watch, the rest of Omega and Home Team rounded up the workers, reassuring them and herding them to a spot near the door where the Home Team had made its entry only twenty minutes before but which felt like such a long time ago.

Leah found herself oddly rooted in place as she handed off a worker to Jessica, not far from where two motionless warehouse guards sprawled in unnatural positions on the warehouse's concrete floor. She'd seen this image before. *When was that? Two months ago? Six months ago? In Mexico? Or was it that time in Germany? Why did she feel like her feet were anchored in concrete?*

Jerrie stepped up next to Leah. "We're done here, Romeo," she said, her M4 hanging in one hand at her side, her other hand sprinkled with blood from a scratch that traced a path beneath a tear in the side of her flowered blouse.

Leah jerked around to face Jerrie and was met by the same comforting maternal expression she'd seen at the pre-operation rendezvous. "But, but . . ." Leah replied. "All the shooters? All those noncombatants?"

"The bad guys are down. The workers are safe," Jerrie said, laying a comforting hand on Leah's arm. "The noncombatants are being zip-tied and will be turned over to the Tennessee Bureau of Investigation in a few minutes."

Just then, a young girl ran from the tight knot of workers Jess was herding toward the door and threw her arms around Leah's waist. "*Xiexie*," the girl cried, tears streaking down her face. "*Ni Jiule Wo.*"

Jerrie smiled as she untangled the girl from Leah and handed her off to a man who'd just entered the warehouse, wearing a windbreaker with the letters TBI across the front of his dark baseball hat. "In case you're wondering, that means *thank you* and *you saved me*, in Mandarin."

Leah shook her head to clear the rest of the fog that seemed to have formed there but was rapidly clearing. Thanks to Jerrie. "I speak the language," Leah said.

"I should have guessed," Jerrie replied with a small smile, removing her hand from Leah's arm.

"The tangos? All down?"

"Yes, thanks to our coordinated counterattack," Jerrie said. "Overall, I think Omega Team and Home Team did a pretty great job working together to get the job done. I noticed you accounted for more than your share."

"And you?" Leah asked.

Jerrie shrugged in a wordless response.

Mark, Omega One, smiled as he stepped close and caught Leah's glance. "Don't let her fool you. She's always counting, ever since one of us told her she looked more suited to be someone's mama than a covert operator."

"Don't listen to the man," Jerrie replied. "My goal is non-lethal force, like all of us in the Extreme Operations Group; but sometimes, a girl has to do what a girl has to do."

Leah sucked in a deep breath, then chuckled as Director Samuelson's voice came over comms. "This is Prime. Nice job, people," Paul said over comms. "As you've already seen, no doubt, the Tennessee Bureau of Investigation is on site and ready to take possession of the surviving tangos and noncombatants. Homeland Security Investigations will be taking custody of the crowd Allen and Leah found in the office. They have a warrant to search the place. Exfil immediately so they can get started. Romeo will remain on location to review what Homeland and TBI find in the warehouse. Once that's done, Romeo, please tie in the investigator from Coffee County. We may be able to leverage his relationship with the local Homeland, FBI, and TBI agents and officers to learn what they find."

"This is Romeo," Leah replied. "Roger, Director. I'll need some wheels."

"Your sister's husband is right outside, waiting for you," Paul replied.

Karl is Homeland? "Wait . . . What?" Leah asked.

Paul cut her off. "Your sister's husband has worked undercover for Homeland Security Investigations for several years, investigating criminal organizations with foreign ties working out of the Southeast. He'll be your link with HSI."

Leah laughed softly and wondered briefly if Rachael Mae knew her husband was an undercover agent, then checked herself. Of course, she would know. No one could keep a secret from that woman, Leah knew from them growing up together. No wonder Rachael Mae wasn't all that surprised when Leah revealed her work with EOG. She chuckled under her breath, again, then said, "Roger all, Prime."

"This is Overwatch Second," Walter chimed in. "I've finished processing the information captured by the drones. We have good images of several people leaving the warehouse and departing in two sedans immediately before the firefight started."

"Just like in Tumwater," Leah mumbled, forgetting communications protocol for the moment. "They knew we were coming."

"Exactly," Walter replied. "And it might well be some of the same crowd."

"Nice job, Second," Paul said. "Forward the images and I'll pass them to the FBI, Homeland, and the TBI. The rest of you pack up and exfil to your home stations. Get some rest if you can. I have a feeling this is going to get bigger before we figure out what's going on."

CHAPTER 22

An hour earlier, as Omega Team and the Home Team approached the warehouse, The Hatchet once again found himself making a hasty escape from his place of business, along with the three men who served as his regional coordinators for the project. The goal of today's meeting was to tie off any remaining threads before they launched the first phase of the decade-old plan for bringing the United States to its knees. He'd had a secret door installed in the back wall of his second-floor office, along with a roll-down emergency ladder, just for this sort of contingency; but it rankled him to have to use it. He'd barely had time to round up the recruits being conditioned at the warehouse and sequester them in his office before he'd had to run.

As they slipped out through the door and dropped down the ladder, he bristled at the thought of all the work he'd put into organizing the warehouse and that its contents would be lost. Of course, he'd had more than enough advance notice this time to organize his departure, along with his regional managers; but the Nashville warehouse had served for years as a highly profitable storage site and mission-central for his group's planning effort. Many of his longest-term recruits had been conditioned here. It had become a matter of pride for him to steal equipment from the federal government and purchase comparable items off the open market and then use it to bring about his plans. It felt like stealing a weapon from a person and then using it to shape their own demise: irony and the sweet taste of vengeance, in one sweep.

With a physical shake of his head, The Hatchet forced the thoughts from his mind. He was, after all, the leader of one of the most far-reaching, potentially most effective terrorist operations in history. What happened to the warehouse and its contents after today would not affect his plans at all. It had served its purpose.

Today was the last meeting between him and his three counterparts from the Western, Northeast and Central regions of the U.S. before the phase one attack. The goal was to ensure everyone's individual portions of the plans were well-coordinated and in sync. Each of the three clinical psychologists leading the regions had been carefully groomed for their roles, all three serving as consulting psychologists within multiple sectors of law enforcement and government. They'd managed enough discussion to provide confidence that they were ready to move forward when he'd received word of the government's impending attack on his building.

Now, as The Hatchet and the three psychologists reached their two nondescript, gray sedans, The Hatchet raised a hand and drew them close. "This is our last time together before we kick off the attack. Even with our relatively hasty departure from this place, I feel confident our schedule remains in place. We will strike in three days. Is there anything one of you wishes to discuss before we head out?"

"Master, we must leave now! The warehouse will be taken in moments," Dr. Mahmad Sylvester replied. He was a short, rotund, pasty man The Hatchet had never respected. The man had taken advantage of the privileged life he'd led as a noted professional in his field as they planned this operation over the past decade. Life in the United States had softened him, but The Hatchet humored him, regardless. He was one of the world's leading experts in the application of virtual reality tools for treating clinically challenging patients.

The second of the three men stepped closer to The Hatchet, his intense dark eyes fixing The Hatchet's gaze. This was Dr. Carlos Vantage, his regional leader out of Seattle. Compared with Sylvester, this man was a warrior who never misplaced his origins and his cause. The Hatchet could see the fire in the man's eyes as he whispered, "As Dr. Sylvester stated, we are ready. And we will succeed. The profiles of those we've trained and those we have chosen from our own ranks speak to the success of our plans. Our plan is bold, innovative, and we will strike the very heart of this godless country."

The Hatchet placed a hand atop Vantage's shoulder and squeezed it warmly. "You are true to our cause," he said, then turned to the third man in the group, Dr. Raul Farley. Over the past decade, Farley had leveraged his professional credentials, both forged and real, to acquire a position at an army medical center in San Antonio, Texas. The resulting access to federal files had proved invaluable as they brought their plans to fruition. "And you, Raul. You are the key to the success of our plan. But tell me, does your assessment of our plan suggest we will have the coverage we need to achieve our goals?"

The tall, thin, athletic man, whom The Hatchet also held in high regard due his spartan lifestyle and continued commitment to the death of infidels everywhere, nodded his head. "I ran the statistics yesterday, and I anticipate 40 percent of our subjects, at most, will fail to follow through at their assigned targets. As we all know, we cannot guarantee full compliance of anyone when we ask them to take a life, no matter how we prepare and program them. That said, the remaining 60 percent should be more than enough to realize our goals."

"Very good," The Hatchet said, stepping aside so he could face all three men directly. "We have selected our recruits carefully. We found them, groomed them, shaped their behaviors, and motivated them deep within their psyches. If 60 percent of our recruits behave as anticipated, we will strike a major blow against this accursed country. You three have made it possible through your dedication and brilliant efforts. The Chairman will be pleased.

"Now, return to your offices and dismiss your staffs. Ensure there are no loose ends."

Vantage frowned. "Must we have all of them killed?"

The Hatchet nodded. "I know how hard it will be, with some of them working with you for almost ten years; but it must be done. There can be no witnesses to our roles in what is about to take place. If you cannot do what needs to be done, I have several resources available to assist you. You will need to pay them from your own accounts."

"You will do the same thing?" Raul asked.

"I have already terminated two of my key resources in the area. They were expendable from the beginning but served their purpose."

"You are a hard man, Master, but your command will be carried out," Vantage said.

"Good," The Hatchet said. "Then let's be off."

The three men nodded, Dr. Vantage breaking the brief silence that followed The Hatchet's words as he glanced at his watch. "With all due respect, Master, I suggest we make our escape now. We cannot carry out our grand plan if we are taken captive, and you must be the one to turn the switch."

"Of course," The Hatchet replied. "Let's get moving."

———————

From the trees at the edge of the parking lot, Steven watched and listened to the discussion and realized it was The Hatchet's plan to have him killed all along. He'd arrived at the warehouse only moments earlier, after he was awakened by fat drops from a downpour not far from the ambush site. With blood leaking from the wounds in the upper left corner of his chest and his side, he'd limped his way into Tullahoma, to an urgent care facility at the edge of town. A disastrous hunting accident, he'd explained to the medical technician on duty alone at the clinic. Then, with a large roll of cash, he'd convinced the young man to clean, stitch, and bandage the through-and-through wounds and sell him some clothes.

An hour later, recharged with two pints of blood expanders, Steven felt half human: clean, wearing the extra clothing the medical technician kept at the clinic, and on his way to Nashville in a taxi. He reached out to Haider on a cell phone he purchased from a quick shop store next door to the clinic. A recording announced that Haider's line was no longer in service. Feeling alone and in some pain from his wounds, the taxi driver dropped Steven several blocks from the warehouse ninety minutes later.

He'd planned to enter the warehouse and seek help directly from The Hatchet—or, as the man preferred to be called, Dr. Muhammad. But he'd just made it to the trees when The Hatchet and three other men emerged from the warehouse down a roll-out metal ladder from the second-floor office.

It seemed an odd departure, so Steven remained in the trees, unseen, as the four men made their way across the building's small parking lot and then paused beside two gray cars. He listened carefully as he caught what sounded like the last words of a very intense discussion less than ten yards from where he crouched, hidden by the thick branches of the trees. It was about the plan The Hatchet so often referred to during their times together. They were about to kick it off. Only three days. And the plan had been, all along, for Haider and Steven to be assassinated.

He sucked in a breath. Deep in his heart, he felt proud to have been part of such a complex endeavor, spanning almost a decade of planning and several years of conditioning subjects—or recruits, as Muhammad liked to call them. But being gunned down or knifed by the man who'd led him during the planning and the work with the recruits was not what he signed up for.

Perhaps he should reach out to The Hatchet, he thought, as the two gray sedans drove past his hiding spot and disappeared down a partially hidden gravel drive to the parking lot of another large building next door. Maybe this was all just a big misunderstanding. *No*, he thought. The truth was, he liked his life in the United States, even as much as he had planned to be part of its demise. But what to do?

In answer to his question, two men and two women pulled up to the warehouse in a heavy-looking SUV. They were dressed casually, but all held some sort of assault rifle. After a brief pause at the warehouse's door, the four entered the building via a gray steel access door, followed in short order by long bursts of gunfire; yelling; screaming; more gunfire; and eventually, after what seemed an eternity, an unsettling, ethereal silence.

Shortly after that, several cars with the Tennessee Bureau of Investigation logo on the doors and an ambulance pulled up to the warehouse, and that gave him an idea. He was not married to The Hatchet or his plans. Perhaps he could leverage what he knew about those plans to surrender and barter an opportunity to be free from The Hatchet and remain in the United States. He'd heard of the U.S. Marshall's Office Witness Protection Program. Maybe he could get into that program and start a new life somewhere well away from all the shooting.

Steven watched from cover as two more vehicles pulled up to the warehouse, this time smaller sport utility vehicles with the Tennessee Bureau of Investigation logo on their sides. Two armed officers in windbreakers with TBI printed across their backs emerged from each vehicle. As they did, Steven rose from his hiding place on shaky legs, arms raised in the universal sign of surrender, and approached the officers.

The officers took notice of him instantly. "On the ground, face down," one yelled. "Hands behind your back."

Steven complied. A moment later, his wrists were secured with thick, sharp-edged strips of plastic. His wounds screamed as the officers jerked him to his feet, but he could not have been happier. He could feel his new life starting already.

CHAPTER 23

His three district managers well on their way home, The Hatchet relaxed in the rear seat of his extended Ford Expedition. The fact that he'd just escaped from his warehouse didn't faze him a bit. In fact, the advance warning was a testament to his advance planning. His source at the DEA was an operations manager who monitored DEA field operations across the country. During a session with the man as the DEA's contract psychologist, the man revealed things that he felt Dr. Muhammad would hold in confidence but which would be life-altering, should anyone ever find out about them. Dr. Muhammad, in his role as The Hatchet, advised the man that he would be happy to keep the DEA employee's confidence, provided certain conditions were met. The man had no recourse but to comply; and from that day on, when the government agency planned an operation that might impact The Hatchet's plans, the DEA officer advised him accordingly. Sometimes, that occurred only hours before the operation, as with the Tumwater warehouse. Other times, like today, the notice was received many hours in advance, allowing for a more deliberate departure.

The Hatchet picked up his cell phone and texted his on-call assassin. He provided the DEA officer's name, home address, and work address and acknowledged the usual fee. No need to talk over the phone. It was a simple assignment. A moment later, he received her response: *Of course.*

Ten years of planning coming to fruition in only a few days, he thought. It seemed such a short time ago, when he, a freshly graduated PhD psychologist had arrived in the U.S. He'd received an appointment to conduct behavioral modification research at the U.S. Army Research Institute for the Behavioral and Social Sciences, recommended by a powerful U.S. senator. He'd never questioned the nature of the senator's relationship with his people. It was enough that the relationship had placed him on a fast track to realizing his country's goals.

Once at USA RIBSS, the young Dr. Albert Muhammad had slid into his research duties like a seal into water. It didn't hurt his chances for success that several articles appeared in noteworthy psychological journals about using behavior modification to treat Post Traumatic Stress Disorder, with him listed as a major contributor. With the army's rising emphasis on treating PTSD, the Institute had been all too happy to leverage his expertise. It was never revealed, of course, that he'd played no part in any of the research documented in those articles.

Within a year, he co-authored an important paper on the use of virtual-reality-based behavior modification techniques and PTSD. The paper documented how he and another psychologist leveraged the Deese-Roediger-McDermott (DRM) false memory paradigm to achieve positive results with PTSD patients. At its most basic form, the DRM paradigm suggested that systematic gist-based false memory errors, or replacement memories, could be inserted into the active memory of an individual when done in the right clinical setting, with the right tools, guided by a trained professional. For example, if a combat veteran experienced PTSD symptoms during recurring flashbacks or dreams of a traumatic combat experience, a trained clinician might, through hypnosis and deep meditation, walk the patient through the traumatic experience and replace the traumatic scenes with positive imagery.

If the traumatic dream sequences included a devastating ambush within a jungle or forest setting, for example, the clinician might recreate the memory, step-by-step, and substitute more positive imagery in place of the jungle setting. The substitute imagery might replace a tree line infested with deadly snipers with a pastoral home setting or a pacific meadow or lake. The approach was not considered a panacea but showed enough promise that it was snapped up by the Department of Veteran's Affairs when the articles went public.

Once virtual reality technology was added to the equation, the time required to reconstruct the traumatic setting and insert the false, more positive imagery was vastly reduced; and patient outcomes improved substantially.

It wasn't long before Dr. Muhammad found himself a celebrity, invited to speak at conferences and consult with private and government treatment facilities. In short order, his ideas were in high demand with the military, law enforcement, and across the medical profession.

It was about then that he received a call from the people who had originally sent him to the United States and orchestrated his meteoric rise. "It is time for you to use your skills to help your country and your faith," the man who called himself the Chairman said. "We want you to develop a training program for singleton active shooters, people carefully screened for their potential to act out against those they perceive as oppressors, who can be used to strike at the soft belly of the American people in a nationwide, synchronized assault."

He'd agreed at once. It was a chance to serve his homeland and leverage his knowledge in the field of virtual reality-based psychotherapy. And the project came with a virtually unlimited budget. And now, an older, seasoned version of Dr. Albert Muhammad, AKA The Hatchet, who never left his love of his homeland behind, nor his intense desire to bring the United States to its knees, was about to accomplish his country's goals.

Several weeks after he received the call, a series of lucrative grants were funneled to him through charitable organizations within and outside the U.S. borders. There was more than enough money for him to leave the Institute and start his own research lab. He'd no more than signed the lease on the building for his new facility when Dr. Vantage, Dr. Sylvester, and Dr. Farley had arrived on his doorstep. All were first generation immigrants positioned in the United States by the same people who'd sent him. The rest was, as they say, history. Or it would be, soon.

The Hatchet's musing was interrupted by the subtle vibration of his cell phone. He recognized the number at once. "This is Dr. Muhammad," he said.

"Report." The voice was short, the words clipped, the tone like a young man not fully matured by his years. It was not the sort of tone one would use to address a world-class expert in any field, but that didn't bother The Hatchet one bit. This man, the Chairman, supported his plans, shared his goals, and kept the money flowing. He was to be revered and respected.

"We are ready," Muhammad replied.

"My observers report your warehouse operation in Nashville was attacked by government agents."

"That is true," Muhammad said. The Chairman had eyes everywhere, and he'd learned long ago to be candid and truthful with the man. "That is true, but we had advance knowledge of the attack. I left orders and bonuses with the security team to ensure there would be no survivors. The attack occurred well after my final coordination meeting with my regional associates, and we all escaped. Based on my discussions with them, I can confirm our readiness, in spite of the loss of the warehouse."

"You feel confident the operation has not been compromised?"

Muhammad felt a chill run up his spine but ignored it. "I do. All the necessary pieces are in place. The singleton active shooters have been programmed using VR technology and the latest behavioral modification techniques. We anticipate 60 percent or more of our subjects will successfully carry out their assignments. The 40 percent most likely to not follow through will be paired with a trained operative, who we identify as a seed shooter, who are each anxious to martyr themselves for our cause."

The line was silent for several long seconds before the Chairman replied, "You should feel proud of your team's accomplishment. The ten years you've spent away from the comfort of family and the beauty of your home country—it will have been well worth your sacrifice when our plans come to fruition."

"And phase two? Is that in place?" Muhammad asked.

"The Council has positioned resources necessary to implement phase two of our plan immediately following the success of your active shooters. Our agents have been prepositioned in large cities across the country. The day after your operation decimates the country's law enforcement, government, healthcare systems, media, and the general population is reeling from their losses, we will execute phase two. Thousands more will perish, making phase one's toll small by comparison. Institutions of healing, faith, commerce, and law will be destroyed, crippling the country's ability to function and bringing its government down."

"It will be glorious," Muhammad said.

"And that will not be the end of it. We have partnerships with others who hate America. We will do our part; and in four days, when the beginning of the end commences for the United States of America, our partners from around the globe will execute their own plans."

Muhammad felt his heart stir, his thoughts brighten. *It will be glorious, and I will be the tip of the spear!*

"There is one more way you can serve the Council, if you are willing," the Chairman said, his voice grave.

Muhammad felt his excitement rise even higher. "Yes. Of course. Whatever you need."

"Two of your facilities have been raided by unknown government operators, who seem focused on disrupting our plans. I am uncertain how much they know of our phase one and two operations, but we cannot take a chance that they might know enough to get in our way."

"I am aware, through my sources, that the Drug Enforcement Administration has been targeting our warehouse operations," Muhammad said. "And they may have support from other government agencies."

"The Council feels we should send a message to those who have taken an interest in your operations. I need you to locate the source of those attacks and eliminate the people involved. We have the video recordings from your security cameras at the Washington and

Tennessee warehouses. At both facilities, two male and two female agents were involved. Our allies in China have run the images through their facial recognition programs. We don't yet have names for the faces in those images, but I want you to find them and send a very clear message to the people they work for."

"I believe I can do that," Muhammad replied. "The doors at the warehouses were all coated with a nano-level tracking compound—a sticky film that rubs off on the hands touching doorknobs and lever. If those agents touched any of that, we should be able to track them."

"Good," the Chairman said. "I look forward to the success of what is to begin in three days, as well as hearing about this additional undertaking."

"Thank you," Muhammad started, but the call was already disconnected.

He shifted his phone to text messaging and sent a quick note to the anonymous female assassin who had served him so well over the past few years. Her familiar voice came over the line a second later. "Yes?"

"I have some work for you. I will double your usual rate."

CHAPTER 24

Becca woke early the morning after Leah's departure, lingering in the comfort of the small double bed in the extra room of Leah's apartment. Before leaving, Leah gave Becca a key, a knowing look, and one condition for sharing the apartment: a man by the name of Pastor Jim Carson would call. Becca would meet with the pastor at a coffee shop in nearby Lacey, Washington, and have a talk. That's all Leah asked for: just a talk. Becca agreed; and in return for talking with the man, she had a place to stay for as long as she needed, rent-free.

The rent-free part had her wondering. Ever since her parents had left her the insurance money—and it was a lot of money—everyone she met seemed to focus where this young woman acquired her means. But Leah? Not at all. She seemed interested in nothing more than giving Becca a place to be. So Becca had agreed to meet Pastor Carson.

She climbed out of bed and brewed a cup of coffee using Leah's espresso machine, savoring the aroma and considering her situation. At first, she'd tried to be upbeat about being taken by the members of the group called the Home Team but still felt like some sort of prisoner. Then, after she'd spent the night at Jessica's place—and despite her intention not to get close to them—she'd found herself softening and reconsidering her situation. It'd been a long time since she'd been with anyone she might remotely consider a family. The four members of the Home Team seemed about as close to being one as any group of friends could be, no matter what they did for a living. They'd even trusted her with the location of their secret hangout. At least, she thought it was supposed to be a secret.

She frowned as she sipped the steaming espresso. They'd demanded so little of her in exchange for what she knew about the warehouse where they'd found her, and that was something she wasn't used to. So she'd decided to talk with the man. What harm could it do? He was a pastor, after all, a man of God.

Before she could explore that thought further, her cell phone vibrated. The text on the screen announced, *Jim Carson. Leah's friend. The Fog and Fern in an hour?*

Becca checked the keys Leah had provided and found one for her Subaru, right next to the apartment key. She whistled a few happy notes, tossed the keys into the air, and snatched them with her left hand, then tapped her reply into her cell phone: *Will do.*

An hour later, Becca parked Leah's SUV in The Fog and Fern coffee shop's small parking lot, across a tree-lined avenue and a community college's sprawling, modern campus. The atmosphere created by the shop's garden-colored walls released a long, deep breath that rose up from the pit of her stomach. She felt her shoulders relax as she admired the place and the coffee shop's vibe sank in. Floor-to-ceiling windows lined two of the shop's walls, admitting streaks of late morning sunlight across a dozen dark, two and four-person tables scattered around a broad open area. A combination pastry counter and barista station dominated one side of the shop, with doors leading into what Becca imagined was a kitchen and storage area. Two young women stood at a counter offering fresh pastries, surrounded by the rich aroma of fresh-ground coffee.

She spotted Carson in a moment at a table next to a wall papered with a green, brown, and tan farm scene. He lifted a hand in her direction and nodded toward two cups of coffee in tall paper cups on his table and the empty chair across from him.

As Becca approached, Carson's dark-skinned face split into a wide smile, weather-crafted lines and creases highlighting his bright expression. When Leah had mentioned him before, Becca had imagined a man in a black tunic and reverse white collar; but instead, he wore faded jeans and a blue Seattle Seahawks football jersey. The jersey hung over shoulders that strained the seams of the garment but hung loose at his waist. Gray touched the temples of Carson's short-cropped, tightly curled black hair. Becca found the man's smile infectious and felt a grin involuntarily tugging at the corners of her lips as she took the offered chair.

Carson reached a hand three times the size of her own across the table. As Becca took it, she flinched involuntarily, expecting to have her fingers crushed. Instead, his grip was warm, firm, but gentle.

"Good morning," he said as she picked up her cup and inhaled the rich aroma of coffee and sweet chocolate.

"Ah," she said. "A mocha. How'd you know?"

He shrugged. "Simple. The Bible says I'm supposed to love my neighbor as myself.[1] I love a mocha, so that means you get one, too."

"Pastor humor?"

Carson shrugged again. "A weak attempt, at best."

---

1   Mark 12:30-31.

She took a sip and set the coffee aside, leaning back in her chair and crossing her arms over her chest. "Leah said you'd be calling, Pastor Carson."

Carson nodded. "Please call me Jim."

Becca nodded, and he took it as a sign to continue. "She called me and explained your circumstances. I was interested to learn you're an emancipated minor, living on your own at such a young age."

Becca nodded. "Circumstances dictated that after my parents died and I was left money others felt should be used for their own purposes."

Carson frowned. "That sort of greed happens all too often. I assume you're talking about some sort of foster care situation that went badly."

Becca unfolded her arms and sipped her mocha, then said, "My foster parents were fine. It was my uncle who was the problem."

"Unfortunately, I'm all too familiar with the plusses and minuses of growing up without a family. Leah lost her parents at about the same point in her life, as did Sam. I grew up in the foster care system until I graduated from high school and enlisted in the army. I stayed with three families. Two were great, but one put me on the street when I refused to do something for them. They ended up in jail after I reported them to the people at the foster care office."

"You were in the army? You haven't always been a pastor?"

Carson chuckled. "Before I was called, I spent five years in the army and another twenty with the Central Intelligence Agency. It was something meaningful for me to do during a time I now recognize was about me trying to make sense of the world. At that point, I was pretty much a wreck. That's when God came tapping on my door, and I found my calling."

"So you regretted your work with the army and the CIA?"

"Not for a second," Carson said. "The work I did for both groups made a difference in the world, without a doubt. But no matter how solid a person feels about what they're called on to do, things can build up on them. In my case, it was Post Traumatic Stress Disorder. PTSD doesn't just happen when bombs go off or someone shoots at you. The symptoms can manifest from an accumulation of things, like the loss of a close friend or parent or the work nurses and doctors do day in and day out. In my case, it was cumulative. For me, a close friend who worked for the agency suggested I talk to God about it. I thought he was crazy at first but then figured I had nothing to lose. So I tried it."

Becca frowned. "And God replied?"

Carson nodded, his smile softer now. "He did. In droves. As clearly as I am sitting here with you right now, He guided me to the help I needed, which included faith in Him."

Becca forced a smile. She'd heard the story too many times before from born-again people who lived anything but what she would call a Christian life. "A voice from above? Right?"

She regretted her tone as soon as the words left her lips. She started to apologize, but Carson cut off her words with a nod. "Pretty close. I remember being exhausted by what I'd been through on an agency mission. Until that day, I'd never lost a minute of sleep over what I'd been called on to do. I believed in what I did, in the righteousness of our missions. But a lot of people died on that mission, including several friends. That hit me hard, mentally and emotionally. I remember sitting in my apartment alone afterwards, with tears running down my cheeks. I sure wasn't feeling like the stereotypical fearless covert operative at that point. I flipped on the television as a distraction and chose a random station. And there, on that screen, was the son of Billy Graham, the famous evangelist, offering the Lord's comfort to all who would accept Jesus as their Savior."

She started to say something, but Carson again lifted a hand. "But that wasn't enough for me. I'd seen too many religious people on television hawking their faith for donations that went to huge, palace-like facilities and personal privilege. But I remembered what my friend suggested, so I listened to Graham talk. When he said I could have a friend for life through God's Son, Jesus Christ, I felt like he was talking directly to me, like someone was washing me clean from the inside out with warm, refreshing water. The emotions and pain sloughed off me like old dirt under a shower.

"How we find God is different for each person, so I called that friend of mine. We spent an hour on the phone, with him telling me about how he'd found Jesus and how it changed his life. He was still with the agency, still a covert operator kicking down doors and taking on the bad guys; but he told me how it made him a better, more intentional operator. Right then, right there on the phone with my friend, I accepted Jesus Christ as my Savior. Several weeks later, I retired from the agency. A month later, I enrolled in seminary."

Becca let out a long breath. Something about Carson's story sent a chill, a sort of tingling sensation from the top of her head to the tips of her fingers and toes. It was a pleasant sensation; and it seemed like her vision cleared, her hearing became more acute, and the weight of the past few years of her life lifted from her shoulders.

Carson gave her a curious glance. "You're feeling it, aren't you?"

Becca shrugged. "Maybe. Possibly. Yes. But I've heard all this before. But what happens next? When we're done with our coffee, I step out the door of this shop and into the real world. Then it's all about what people want from you, not about who you are."

Carson's gentle smile returned. "That doesn't have to happen. Faith, like happiness, is a choice. God's love and joy can travel with you out the door of this coffee shop and wherever you go, if you choose for that to happen. It worked for me, and it's part of the lives of every member of the Home Team."

"Leah, Jessica, Sam, and Allen are Christian? But they carry weapons and shoot at people."

"Without a doubt, but they fight for a righteous cause. Their boss, Paul Samuelson, would never ask them to take on a mission that wasn't consistent with their faith."

Super spy believers in Jesus Christ? It was hard to reconcile what she felt they must be called to do with any sort of spiritual faith. On the other hand, she'd connected with each of them once she'd gotten to know them, and the same was happening now with Pastor Carson. Maybe there was something in all this Jesus stuff.

Carson seemed to sense her thoughts and said, "I'm not here to convert you, no matter what you may have felt after hearing my story. Ultimately, that's between you and God. I'm simply here because Leah asked me to look in on you."

Becca took a deep breath. "Yep. Sounds like her, like the mother or older sister I never had. And I have to say, if this Christian stuff is good enough for her, it may be good enough for me."

Carson leaned back in his chair; his kind eyes locked on hers. "Okay, so talk to me."

Becca took a long pull from her coffee cup, then felt the words start tumbling out, surprising herself as she unloaded the complicated, painful years of her life, up to the point where she met Leah and the Home Team at the Tumwater warehouse. "I was pretty much homeless when I met the people from the warehouse in Tumwater. I slept in a friend's car for several nights, not because I couldn't afford a room but because a person my age gets a lot of uncomfortable questions when we try to book a room at a hotel on our own. Will your parents be staying with you? Are you sure you're able to pay? Is there someone we can call for you?"

"Uncomfortable, indeed," Carson said.

She nodded. "I wandered into a video game store called Retread IT in downtown Olympia. The shopkeeper approached me to see if they could be of assistance. I explained I was only killing time, since I had nowhere else to be right then. Before long, I had a cup of coffee in my hands; and we were sitting at his desk at the back of the office, talking about my life. I realize now that he was much more than a store attendant; he asked some serious questions. Had I experienced frequent outbursts of anger, impulsiveness, problems relating to others at a personal level, depression, or anxiety? Did I find myself taking excessive risks? Did I ever threaten those who disagreed with me, make threats against anyone, abuse drugs or find myself drawn to violent media like movies or video games?"

"He sounds more like a psychologist than a store attendant," Carson said.

"Exactly," Becca said. "But at the time, I'd experienced most of those things at one time or another, although drugs and violence have always been off the table for me. Talking about it back then felt like just what I needed. Afterward, he suggested several new virtual reality video games that I might like to try, ones he'd found helped him ease those same feelings. So I signed up.

"That afternoon, I was driven to the warehouse in Tumwater where Leah and the Home Team found me. I stayed there for days, playing online VR video games around the clock. If I tried to rest between sessions, I would be encouraged to continue, that the benefits of the program would be lost if I did not. They fed me and provided energy drinks to keep me going and a cot to sleep on when I couldn't take it anymore. There were at least ten others there with me, all doing the same thing: trying out virtual reality video games.

"I noticed early on that the attitudes of the others playing the games started to change as the days went on. I couldn't relate to what seemed to be happening to them at the time because I didn't feel all that different from my experiences with the games. Sure, I was running around in those games, using weapons nearly as big as me to gun down aliens from outer space in one game, then fighting human armies in another. But I knew it was all fake, just games, even when the targets became people dressed like you and me and not necessarily carrying weapons. I found that last part hard to relate to. Who wants to gun down innocent, unarmed civilians, even if they're not real? But it seemed like the others really got into it. When I expressed my concern to our minders, I was advised that I needed to play harder, try harder if I was going to release whatever it was inside me that was responsible for my depression, outbursts, anger, anxiety, and so on."

"Sounds like they were trying to shape your behavior more toward violence than help you resolve any negative feelings," Carson said.

"That's where I'd landed just before Leah and the Home Team showed up. The other gamers seemed to get angrier and more antisocial by the hour. Some suggested they might do the stuff in the games if they had the chance, that they knew people who deserved to die for what they'd done to them and their families in the past. I didn't want anything to do with any of that."

"It's a lot to digest," Carson replied.

"I'd decided to leave just about the time the shooting started at the warehouse," Becca said. "In fact, I'd already bagged up my VR equipment, thinking I might keep it for myself, when we heard the shooting and the rest of the gamers made a run for it. The people supervising us were already gone by that point. I was just a bit slower than the rest and ducked for cover when I heard all the shooting."

"We're all glad you made it through that safely. As I understand it, the equipment you had in your possession was the first evidence anyone had that something more than drugs was involved where you were staying," Carson said. "And thanks for talking me through your life and all that.

"I do a good deal of counseling and have read about the use of virtual reality in therapy. I understand enough about human psychology to worry that the same technology used to treat mental illness and things like PTSD can be turned to more nefarious purposes. With what you've described about being recruited and the escalation of violence in the games, how they morphed the game's targets, it sounds like those people were grooming candidates to commit acts of aggression."

Becca blew the steam off her mocha, then took a sip and said, "Like terrorists?"

"Hard to say," Carson replied. "Studies have shown that active shooters, for example, demonstrate some of the characteristics the shopkeeper asked you about."

"I could never be one of those," Becca said.

"I agree, and not everyone with those characteristics will ever become an active shooter or terrorist. Regardless, what you've told me about your experience at the warehouse may be important. Would you mind if I shared the information with the Home Team and Director Samuelson?"

Becca's forehead furrowed. "I figured that was the whole point of this discussion."

Carson chuckled softly. "I'm a pastor, not an interrogator; and I take the confidence people place in me when we talk very seriously. I would not share anything you've told me today with anyone without your permission."

Becca rocked back in her chair, arms once again crossed over her chest. She met Pastor Carson's gaze for what seemed like a long time before replying, then said, "I believe you. And there's one more piece of information I might share."

Carson nodded for her to continue.

"When I was using the bathroom at the warehouse, two of our minders passed by the restroom door. I overheard one of them say that they were waiting for a call from a doctor named Muhammad and that something important was going to happen in the next few days. That's all I got, but maybe it's something."

Carson smiled warmly. "It may well be. If it's okay with you, I'll pass that along to the team right away."

She smiled in response. This man was so different from so many of the people she'd encountered during her time with her uncle, her brief stint in foster care, and since her emancipation. There was no hint of insincerity in anything he said. He'd revealed his own background, told her his story, and revealed his own vulnerability. She decided then and there, she would trust this man.

"Please do," she said finally. "But on one condition."

"And that is?" Carson said.

"That you talk to me about this faith thing that you, Leah, and the others seem to think is so important."

Carson's dark eyes lit brighter than before. "Of course. We can meet at my church office or this coffee shop whenever you like. Although right now, I need to make a call. I think Paul Samuelson and the Home Team will find your information to be of immense value."

Becca lifted her coffee cup in toast as Pastor Carson pulled a cell phone from the front pocket of his jeans. He punched a number in from memory. "Paul. It's Jim," he said. "I've got some information for you . . ."

CHAPTER 25

By the time Leah and her brother-in-law pulled into the home he shared with Leah's sister, the day was getting late. A dark sky blanketed with brilliant stars loomed overhead, with the shadows of heavy winter clouds drifting from horizon to horizon. Leah lingered in the passenger seat of Karl's gray Toyota Rav4 after they pulled into the driveway, still wrestling with the idea that Karl was an operative, like her. The idea of her sister's life being so different from her own, so normal, had become a sort of idyllic image in Leah's mind of what life should be like. That image did not include Homeland Security and undercover work by her sister's husband.

She snapped out of her thoughts when the passenger side door swung open and Karl waved her from her seat. "My sister married such a gentleman," she said as she climbed from the car.

He chuckled as they turned and headed for the front door. "Not so much. I can smell the pot roast all the way out here, and I am ravenous."

Leah's stomach growled, and they both laughed. It had been a very long time since she'd had a sit-down dinner with anyone other than her teammates, and those were generally meals scarfed in the back of a jet or vehicle during a hasty deployment. And those sudden-notice deployments had been occurring more and more frequently of late. As they entered the house, she wondered if the EOG psychologist, Dr.

Malcome, might well be right when he suggested some of what she was experiencing might be related to simple fatigue. Perhaps one of her sister's amazing meals and a good night's sleep might be just what she needed to start her journey back.

They found Rachael Mae in the kitchen, the rich aroma of slow-cooked roast beef, potatoes, carrots, and biscuits filling the air. Rachael Mae leaned against the edge of the white granite kitchen counter with her arms folded across her chest as they dropped their jackets and headed for the table. Annie Mae stood next to her mom in very much the same position, the same knowing look in her eyes as she duplicated her mother's posture. Leah found it difficult to hold back the soft chuckle that leaked from her lips at the image of her sister and her mini twin.

"So, now you know," Rachael Mae said, her face sporting a lopsided smile. "My husband is not a normal businessman."

"He's a spy," Annie Mae announced proudly.

"Shush, little one," Rachael Mae said, placing her hand gently atop Annie Mae's red curls.

"But he is," Annie Mae protested.

Karl stepped over and planted a peck on his wife's cheek, then hoisted Annie Mae into his arms. "And you're not supposed to talk about that with other people."

"But Auntie Leah's not *other people*."

Karl smoothed Annie Mae's hair with a gentle hand. "Fair enough."

"So Karl works for Homeland Security Investigations," Leah said. "My team's worked with that organization countless times in the past. Why keep it from me? I have the highest-level clearance a person can have."

Karl nodded as Annie Mae snuggled into his shoulder. "We didn't know that at the time. And my experience is, it's best not to discuss my work with anyone, unless there's a specific need. Your work for the Secret Service—"

"Ahem," Rachael Mae interjected, lifting a hand in Leah's direction. "Tit for tat: Leah doesn't work for the Secret Service."

"Auntie Leah's a spy, too!" Annie Mae added, her smile wide across her tiny, cheerful face.

Karl nodded. "Homeland Security Investigations has tracked weapons sales to the location you and your people hit today, not just the drugs the DEA is focused on. I've been in that warehouse many times undercover as a prospective buyer, first for video games, then virtual reality gear, and ultimately some highly classified artificial intelligence technology. When I arrived onsite today and saw what was going down, I called my boss at HSI. She hooked me up with your boss at State, and he read me into your operation."

"My boss?" Leah said.

Karl nodded again. "Paul Samuelson. He filled me in with the details of your mission and who you work for."

Leah sighed. "A day full of revelations."

"For all of us," Rachael Mae added.

"So you'll want to head back with me in the morning to check what's been inventoried in the warehouse?" Karl asked. "I'm anxious to meet this Investigator Weise that Paul Samuelson told me about. It seems the man you two visited at Arnold Air Force Base was found dead in his office recently. We have security camera footage of a female air force captain entering his office, who was most likely the person who pulled the trigger. We also located footage of her driving onto and off the base but have been unable to identify her. I suspect a high-priced assassin, contracted for the job."

Leah shrugged. "Sort of ties right into the ambush after we left his office."

"Ambush?" Rachael Mae repeated. "Seriously?"

Leah shrugged. "I'm fine, but something big has to be going on to warrant that sort of effort by the people involved in all this."

Karl nodded. "No doubt, but how about we dispense with all the spook-talk and dig into the dinner your sister's prepared? I'm starving."

Leah was about to agree when her cell phone vibrated in the back pocket of her jeans. She retrieved the phone and examined the name displayed on the screen. It was Sam. "I need to take this."

She stepped from the kitchen and into the foyer. "Hey, Sam."

"Right back at you," he replied. "Sorry to bother you; but after we left the warehouse, agents from the Tennessee Bureau of Investigation snagged a guy hanging out in the trees at the edge of the warehouse parking lot. He had bullet holes through his chest and side and a story to tell. Once the TBI questioned him at the scene, they contacted Paul and turned him over to us."

"He's associated with the people who ran that operation?" Leah replied.

"Roger that," Sam said. "And more. He worked for the owner of the warehouse and was involved in the ambush attempt on you and the investigator. He was wounded during the ambush, and his partner left him for dead in the trees not far from where they attacked you. He made his way to the warehouse, where he learned his past boss planned to kill him in any event."

"We may finally get some answers," Leah said.

"Correct. And in addition to that, Becca provided some information to Pastor Carson that may bear on what's going on. Paul directed us to rendezvous at our Lewis-McChord headquarters to put this all together. He wants you to head back with us and bring the investigator from the Coffee County Sheriff's Office with you. Apparently, the local TBI office thinks a lot of the man, and considering your partnership with him . . . ."

Leah felt her cheeks redden at the mention of GW and was glad Sam couldn't see her reaction. She cleared her throat softly, then said, "I'm sure he'll agree to come, but why take things back to Washington State when the major operation appears to be here in Tennessee?"

"Paul feels this may be much bigger than one location."

"Got it," she replied. "Are you all still here in Tennessee?"

"We are, at the Nashville airport. Sybil has the jet gassed up and ready to go. You get ahold of that investigator—"

"Investigator George Weise," Leah interrupted, the big man's friendly smile flashing across her memory, accompanied by the tingling sensation that ran through her body and was becoming all too familiar.

"Please get you both here as soon as you can. It'll be a snug fit in our little jet, but I expect we'll manage."

Leah disconnected the call and stepped back into the kitchen, where Karl, Rachael Mae, and Annie Mae sat at the little table in the bay window. Rachael Mae looked up, a ladle of gravy in her hand and, when she met Leah's eyes, set the big spoon back into its cradle. "I know that expression. No dinner for you tonight?"

Leah nodded. "Sadly. Could you put together two to-go plates for me and a friend?"

Rachael Mae stood and walked across the kitchen to wrap her arms around her baby sister. "I knew you'd do something great with your life, and that's exactly what you do as part of the Extreme Operations Group. The organization's legendary, despite the secrecy surrounding it."

Leah pushed her sister back to arm's length and stared into her eyes. "And exactly what would you know about that sort of thing?"

"A topic for another day and time," Rachael Mae replied.

"Fine, but I'll hold you to that. Right now, I need to call GW, the investigator I've been working with. If he's willing, he's going back with me and the rest of the team to our base in Washington State."

"I know GW," Karl chimed in. "Works out of Coffee County. Great guy. He has a stellar rep as a law enforcement officer."

"He's the guy I suggested you meet when you first arrived," Rachael Mae said. "I'm glad you found him. But you make your call, and I'll prepare those to-go plates. But not for two. I made enough leftovers for a week. How many of you are there?" Rachael Mae asked.

"The four of us and GW and . . . our pilot." She paused and gave Karl a knowing glance. "Plus one more."

Karl waved a hand in her direction. "Heard about the guy the TBI captured. No worries. If we get a crack at him when you're done with him, it's all good. Send me what you have when you can and I'll pass it up my chain."

Leah nodded. "Will do, although I will defer to my boss on that."

Karl nodded and shrugged. "Of course."

Leah stepped back into the entryway and dialed GW's number. He answered on the first ring. "Hello, ma'am. I've been hoping you'd call. I've missed our little trips around the countryside."

"And the gun battles and ambushes?" she replied.

He chuckled, the sound easy, warm, and even over the cell phone. "Those, not so much. But I did come across some information you might find interesting."

"About Dr. Jones at Arnold Air Force Base?"

"And just how did you hear about that? We just found his body a bit ago," GW replied.

"Word travels fast," she replied. "I need a big favor."

"Shoot," he said.

"By now, you know I don't really work for the Secret Service."

"Your boss sent me a secure text that filled me in. I was impressed by the security I had to work through to get that information: two forms of ID, my badge number. The only thing he didn't require was a valid credit card."

"Good, then I'll get to the point. My team has a jet standing by to take us back to our headquarters in Washington State. A man was captured in an operation earlier today, and he'll be going with us so we can interview him there. We'd like you to come along and lend a hand. You apparently have relationships in law enforcement that my boss feels may help. Any chance you can do that?"

GW laughed again. "What? I get an expense-paid trip to the Pacific Northwest on one of the Secretary of State's corporate jets? Who could turn that down?"

"Thanks," Leah said, then paused and added, "I'm looking forward to seeing you again."

GW paused, then replied, "Can't wait. And ditto about the seeing you again, too."

"I'll pick you up in thirty," Leah said.

"Let me pick you up. I can get us to the airport quicker; my car has sirens and lights."

Leah chuckled. "Sounds exciting."

"I'll be there soon, go-bag in hand."

GW picked her up in twenty minutes rather than thirty; and ninety minutes later, they climbed aboard the EOG's Gulfstream. Sybil met them at the bottom of the stairway, glancing at her watch and the stack of foil-covered plates in Leah's and George's hands. "You made good time. And you brought food."

Leah smiled and hooked a thumb over her shoulder toward GW as she climbed the boarding ramp from the tarmac. "He has lights and sirens, and my sister's an amazing cook."

Sybil chuckled. "Come aboard and I'll get us in the air."

Leah dropped into one of the executive chairs in the front of the jet's passenger compartment and passed the plates around, first to Jessica who occupied the couch at the back of the compartment, then to a thin, dark-complexioned man in a brown herring bone blazer who had bright red zip ties on his wrists. Allen and Sam occupied two of the remaining thickly cushioned executive swivel chairs and gratefully accepted the dinner.

Sam gestured to the two seats across the aisle. "Welcome aboard, and thanks for the grub," Sam said, then nodded to GW. "You must be Investigator Weise. We can shake hands all around, once Sybil has us airborne and we're done eating."

Jessica called forward to Leah, indicating the prisoner. "Leah and Investigator Weise, meet Steven. He says he has the information we need. Turns out his previous boss left him to die along the roadside after he and one of his friends tried to ambush the two of you."

"No hard feelings, I hope," Steven said.

"You tried to blow us up with a rocket," Leah replied. "Hard feelings, indeed."

"I say we take him to thirty thousand feet and shove him out the door," GW added.

Steven's eyes went wide. "No, no," he protested, his voice several octaves higher. "I have information. I can help you."

Sam held up his hands in surrender. "All right, you two. We need Steven." He handed Leah two pages of yellow tablet paper with handwritten notes. "Take a look. It's what we've gotten from him while we waited for you. It appears what we're involved in is much more than a matter of missing government equipment."

Leah scanned the notes, then glanced at GW and back to Sam, the acid rising in her stomach. "It's a full-fledged terrorist plot using active shooters?"

Allen leaned back in his chair and chewed a piece of roast beef, then said, "It's about as evil as you can get."

Leah spun in her chair and called through the jet's open cockpit door. "We need to get going, Sybil. This paper says we only have a couple of days to stop this from happening."

"Roger that," Sybil replied through the passenger compartment's overhead speakers. "But I just got a message from Paul. We're rerouting to Fort Knox, Kentucky, where we'll rendezvous with the Omega Team. It's a short hop, so get strapped in."

CHAPTER 26

It was coincidence that Regan was in the Nashville area when the call came through from The Hatchet. Normally, after any major job, she relocated, putting distance between her and her victims. It wasn't always necessary; but she felt it a good practice, and it had served her well over the years. In this instance, she'd been headed for the airport to book her own flight.

She'd just turned in her rental car and headed for ticketing when the call came through. With a good photo of the man on her cell phone, she'd spotted Haider at a ticket counter almost at once, booking his flight to Boston. It was a simple thing to purchase her own ticket to an arbitrary city in California, pass through TSA, and catch up with her target at a popular coffee shop. He'd purchased a drink and sat at the single table near the shop. She purchased her own drink and approached the man, asking if it would be okay to share the table.

They talked as they sat and sipped their drinks; and she felt his growing interest, as happened so predictably with the men she met. She knew they found her attractive, but that was just another tool in her toolbox. After only a few minutes, Haider leaned forward to whisper something in her ear. She feigned interest and leaned into him, then pulled him even closer and sank a narrow-bladed knife deep in his chest between the fourth and fifth ribs. She used her close position to the man to block the view from passersby and held him close for several long minutes, her lips covering his to stifle any sound he might make. He was dead within a minute; but she held him long enough to be sure, relaxing only when she felt his body go limp.

After that, Regan gently moved Haider's hands together on the tabletop and lowered his head to rest on them. To any observer, he was either napping or disappointed with how the conversation went with the woman he'd just shared the table with. The knife still in place in his chest slowed down any blood leakage, giving her the time she needed to make her escape. She was well down the airport's long corridor of boarding gates before she heard someone at the coffee shop call out in distress.

She smiled as she walked. *An easy 50K. Sometimes you get lucky.*

Her cell phone vibrated as she headed to the boarding gate for her California flight. It was The Hatchet again. He needed the team that had been hitting his warehouses eliminated. She'd agreed to the assignment at once, since it would be four times her normal rate. That, and taking out groups of people was often simpler than a single hit. A well-placed bomb in a communal meeting place or vehicle often did the trick. There were many options, and the money she'd make on the job would allow her to finally shut down operations for a time and take the vacation she'd been considering for a while.

He texted her a video captured from the Nashville warehouse that showed a tiny woman carrying an M4 carbine meeting a man in plain clothes. As she watched, the two stepped into the vehicle and drove away, the license plate number of the car clear in the image. From there, it had been a simple matter to hook up to the airport's internet and run the license plate past a long-term, well-paid associate at the Tennessee Department of Motor Vehicles. The plate belonged to a man and woman living near Manchester, Tennessee, an hour southeast of the airport.

Regan rented another vehicle from a second rental company at the airport using a different alias and drove to the small enclave of red brick houses where her target lived, parking several blocks away but with a clear view of the dwelling. Using a long-barreled device more like a pellet gun than a rifle, she shot a sticky tracker and microphone, which affixed to the fender of a car parked in the house's driveway. She also sent two sticky transmitters onto the house's front and second-floor windows. The devices were the size of a fly, with a sticky coating that felt much like Playdough. Tiny but powerful, they linked to a nationwide cellular network she'd hacked long ago. Once in place, she could listen to conversations in the house from anywhere in the world, in real-time.

Regan tuned her vehicle's radio to an FM frequency that allowed her to scan the devices and got a hit on the first try. From the microphone on the front window, she heard a woman's voice already deep in a conversation. "Good, then I'll get to the point. My team has a jet standing by to take us back to our headquarters in Washington State. A man was captured in an operation earlier today, and he'll be going with us so we can interview him there. We'd like you to come along and lend a hand. You apparently have relationships in law enforcement that my boss feels may help. Any chance you can do that?"

The voice paused as the person at the other end of the call replied.

Then the woman let out a long sigh that was clearly audible and indicated her desire to work with the person again. The tone of the woman's voice changed: more tentative, almost hesitant. Regan smiled. A romantic interest? Maybe she could use that.

Twenty minutes later, a Coffee County Sheriff's Office Ford Excursion arrived at the house. Regan hunched down in the seat of her car and watched as the tiny woman from the video dashed out of the house and climbed in. As the Excursion drove by her parking spot, Regan shot another sticky-tracker that affixed itself to the Excursion's rear quarter panel. A moment later, the tracking app on her cell phone showed the vehicle turning onto Interstate 24, heading west toward the Nashville airport. It was easy enough to follow them and watch as they entered the Nashville airport through a private gate and parked near a small Gulfstream corporate jet. Leaving her car, Regan climbed the airport fence, crept to the edge of a small aircraft hangar, and shot a sticky microphone and tracker onto the Gulfstream jet's window, then retraced her steps back to her car.

Once back in her rental car, she tuned into the microphone's frequency. She counted six voices, consisting of two women and four men, one named Steven. She made a mental note to reach out to The Hatchet regarding the Steven character, as well as to update her fee to include six rather than four targets. It would be a nice payday.

She watched the Gulfstream lift into the sky and opened another application on her cell phone that used an artificial intelligence program to track aircraft tail numbers and predict likely destinations. After only ten minutes waiting, the AI reported the most likely destination of the jet, given the nature of its occupants and the flight plan filed with the FAA: Louisville, Kentucky, and most likely the Fort Knox, Kentucky, army airfield, not far from the city. The margin of error reported for the prediction was less than 5 percent.

She smiled as she shut down the app, then dialed an associate who had recently retired from the business who owned an airplane located at the nearby Oakley Airport. It was a private strip that saw little activity during the evening. With minimal discussion, he agreed to her fee and said his two-seat Eclipse 500 jet would be ready when she arrived at his place. The trip would take no more than forty minutes, with touchdown at another associate's private landing strip not far from the army base. For a minimal additional fee, she could also borrow the landing strip owner's new F150 pick-up.

She agreed with the arrangements and was on her way without delay. As she drove, she triggered her vehicle's voice-activated texting program and selected The Hatchet's number, then dictated the message. *New intel shows six tangos on an aircraft headed to Kentucky, including a person named Steven. The fee just went up.*

The response was immediate. She keyed her hands-free system, which read the response from The Hatchet. *The additional fee is acceptable. A substantial bonus will be provided with proof of death of the man named Steven.*

She smiled. The Hatchet really wanted this Steven out of the way. She triggered the vehicle's voice-texting function once again and sent the text: *Consider it done.*

Then a curious thought struck her: the Haider hit was obviously one of The Hatchet's employees. Most likely, it was the same for the man named Steven. If The Hatchet was in the process of eliminating trusted employees to protect his back, he might well consider her to be yet another loose end to be snipped. She slapped the palm of her hand hard against the vehicle's steering wheel. That's why she made it a practice of doing no more than one hit for any customer during any calendar year. Do more, and they started thinking they owned you, had a claim on you, and then that you might be a liability. For The Hatchet, that could mean he'd hire someone to come after her. She'd let the abundance of work and the money provided by the man drop her guard.

She smiled grimly as she turned her rental car into the drive of her associate's private airfield. *First the people on the plane and the money that went with it. Then she'd reconsider her relationship with The Hatchet. Loose ends were no good for anyone, least of all her.*

CHAPTER 27

The Home Team, with GW and Steven in tow, arrived at the Omega Team's headquarters at Army Base Fort Knox ninety minutes after takeoff from Nashville. Jerrie met them at their building's high-security entry in a gray sweat suit with a frown and her hair matted atop her head. "Great timing. Director Samuelson just dialed into the conference room, interrupting my workout."

Entering the large warehouse-like facility was déjà vu for Leah. The building had been completed within the past month and constructed as a twin to the Home Team's building at Joint Base Lewis-McChord: the same conference room and office setup to the right of the double entry doors, the same sixty-foot square mat space against the right wall, and an extensive free weight area directly ahead of and beyond the mats. Across the building on the left was the entry to the sniper simulator and indoor firing range, and to the left of that was the door leading to Omega's indoor confidence course. At the far wall across from the entrance was a line of doors to locker rooms, showers, and bathrooms.

Jerrie noticed her roving glance. "You like? Bet it feels a lot like home."

"Eerie," Leah replied. "I keep wondering if I might find a change of clothes and my weapons load-out in one of the locker rooms."

Jerrie laughed. It was a soft sound, and a surprise coming from the matronly woman Leah knew as a tough, efficient, and effective covert operator, despite outward appearances.

"Follow me," Jerrie said and led the way to the conference room. Jerrie nodded toward Steven, hanging close to Jessica with his wrists zip-tied and both Allen and Sam following close on his heels. "What about him?"

"He has information we need," Leah said.

Jerrie cast her a dubious look, her chestnut brown eyes hooded. "He'll know who we all are. We are a covert organization, after all."

Leah laid a friendly hand on Jerrie's shoulder. "You'll understand in a moment, and I hope that's our biggest problem. If we don't get a handle on what's going on soon, there will be bigger issues."

Greetings were passed around as everyone took seats at the room's long conference room table. Sam and Allen took seats on either side of Steven, who was advised to speak only when spoken to. Paul Samuelson, appearing in the center of three large-screen monitors at the far end of the conference room, started the meeting. "I'd planned for Weise and Leah to help inventory the warehouse Omega and Home Team secured. As it turns out, its contents matched the Tumwater, Washington, warehouse almost exactly, right down to the presence of people brought to the facility to play video games using virtual reality technology. Given that, I decided I'd rather have the investigator's expertise here, along with Leah, to help us assess the situation and identify next steps."

"Can you be a little more specific about what was found at the Nashville site?" Leah asked.

Onscreen, Paul nodded. "Forty sets of virtual reality equipment, much like the ones lost from the Space Force's stores at Arnold Air Force Base. Five of those appear to have been taken directly from the Space Force R&D facility. The remainder of the virtual reality setups are knock-offs produced at an unknown location but appear identical to the ones from Space Force. Given all that, I think we can assume what was found in the warehouses, the attempt on Inspector Weise and Leah, the apparent assassination of Dr. Jones at the Space Force R&D facility, and the theft of the VR technology are related."

"And someone wanted to keep Jones quiet about all that," Allen said, running a hand through his shoulder-length blond hair and leaning forward in his chair. "It's not a big leap to think the man was selling the early versions of the equipment to the people involved with the Retread IT warehouse in Nashville and the one in Tumwater and that they killed him after Leah and the investigator showed up."

"And now we have Steven," Jessica said, leaning forward to place her elbows on the conference room table. "Who says he has critical information regarding this case. We interrogated him during the flight, and he's revealed several things about the VR equipment and his involvement with it. And it's ugly.

"Steven holds a master's degree in clinical psychology and was hired to run a Retread IT videogame store in Murfreesboro that sold new and used video games, including some with virtual reality. His job was to identify potential active shooter candidates who came into the store, using a checklist produced by law enforcement and available online. He also communicated with other clinical psychologists in the area to identify additional candidates. He worked for a well-known psychologist based in Nashville, named Albert Muhammad, known as The Hatchet by those who worked for the man."

"I know that list," GW added. "I was briefed by our state's consulting psychologist. There are eleven different criteria. Anyone with four or five of those characteristics is considered a potential candidate to become an active shooter. It's not a lock that they'll pick up a gun, but it's a lead."

"Exactly," Jessica replied. "Steven informed us the plan was to identify individuals with at least seven of those behavioral characteristics and then bring them in to participate in a VR-based behavioral modification program disguised as a video game. The goal of that program was to encourage and empower those people to act on their need for vengeance or retribution against a specific individual, group, or the general population."

Paul nodded on the screen. "I received word from Pastor Carson. For the rest of you, he's the Home Team's unofficial chaplain and a good friend. What he learned about Becca's experience in Tumwater matches what Steven is suggesting. She indicated that many of the people with her at the Tumwater location seemed to change attitudes over time, based on their experience with the VR program, becoming more aggressive, surly, and angry."

Leah felt her pulse quicken. "So they were recruiting active shooters?"

Jessica nodded. "And grooming them. Developing them. Empowering them in the worst way possible."

Onscreen, Paul frowned, then lifted his chipped and stained white porcelain mug and took a sip. His normally weather-worn face seemed even glummer than usual. After a long silent moment, he set the cup aside and returned his eyes to the screen. "Empower, an unfortunate choice of word. And if that isn't bad enough, the agents at the warehouse discovered a large cache of weapons and ammunition: pistols, MP5 submachine guns, assault rifles, and tens of thousands of rounds of ammunition."

"They were arming their recruits as well?" Leah asked, again seeing the image of the little girls shot down at the grocery store in her mind. She set the image aside and glared at Steven. "We've seen evil in our time, but this tops it all."

Steven seemed to shrink into his chair under her wilting gaze.

"Gearing up for war," Sam said, his voice a deep growl. He'd been quiet until then, but Leah knew he'd seen his share of conspiracies where groups of people wanted nothing more than to cause pain, suffering, and chaos.

"Did he provide any information about why they were doing this and the scope of it?" Paul asked.

This time, Sam took up the story, running a thick-fingered hand through his close-cropped black hair. "We have some specifics, although not yet enough to move on. Steven stated that the plan is for active shooters to engage locations across the country. It will be a coordinated attack on soft target locations like schools, hospitals, grocery stores, and other places where people gather. The attack will take place in three days. He was able to identify a half dozen specific targets, including Tampa, Charleston, Washington, D.C., Boston, Chicago, and New York. He said that there are plans that identify a total of sixty targets where the attacks are likely to receive the most press. Those plans were created by four PhD-level psychologists with carefully groomed connections within law enforcement, the Department of Defense, and other state and federal agencies, including his boss, this Muhammad character."

"Any names of the people involved, besides his immediate boss?" GW said.

"Only the man he worked for directly," Sam replied. "Dr. Albert Muhammad." Sam held up a photo of the man and turned it slowly so everyone in the room saw the image.

GW blew out a long breath. "I know that man. He's a psychology consultant for the State of Tennessee. I talked with him a few days ago."

"And that's the name of the psychologist Dr. Malcome, the EOG's psychologist, suggested I see in Nashville," Leah said.

Over the video conferencing system, Leah heard Paul tap the keys on a keyboard. "That name and image is also associated with the State Department, FBI, DEA, and ATF."

Rascal Smith, Omega Team's close-quarters combat expert, spoke next in his musical Jamaican accent. "So we have a coordinated effort to recruit active shooters for a synchronized attack on soft targets across the United States that will take place in three days."

"That about sums it up," Paul said. "And we only know a handful of the cities where it's going to take place."

Steven sat forward in his chair and raised a tentative hand. All eyes turned to him. "There is more I can offer."

Paul frowned, then nodded for Steven to proceed.

Steven smiled tentatively, took a deep breath, and began, "The major targets will not be attacked by the active shooters alone. There will be what are called seed shooters: trained operatives brought into the country and recruited from the ranks of the faithful as martyrs. We anticipated up to 40 percent of the singleton active shooters would not follow through on their targets. It's simply too difficult to shape every person's behavior to take another person's life. Many people won't cross that line, no matter how they're conditioned. The seed shooters will be paired with the singletons perceived as most likely to fail in their mission. The seed shooters will take up the slack for the singletons who don't follow through."

"Even knowing that, we still need to get a handle on the specific cities and targets within those cities," Allen said.

Steven raised his hand again. "I may be able to help with that, as well. I believe my leader thinks I was killed after the ambush near the air force base. If that's true, he may not have bothered to delete my credentials from our team's computer network. If I could have access to a computer and the internet, I might be able to get into that network and locate the details of the attacks."

Leah felt her rage climbing, wanting nothing more than to put her hands around Steven's neck and squeeze as the man pretended to cooperate. "Why exactly should we trust you? You were involved in an attack that already killed innocent people, including two little girls who did nothing but be in the wrong place at the wrong time!"

"The answer to your question is simple," Steven replied, the crease of a smile forming at the corners of his thin, pale lips as a bead of sweat rolled down his forehead. "I want a deal."

"You shot a rocket at Agent McCarthy and me when you ambushed us," GW said, his voice a low, dangerous growl. "I can't imagine why you think you'd deserve anything less than spending the rest of your life in jail."

Leah rose from her chair with a loud slap against the top of the conference room. It sounded like a rifle shot and made Steven jump.

"Your actions killed those little girls. You were complicit in their deaths and many others at the grocery store. I was there. I saw the carnage. There is no way you're walking out of this room with any kind of deal. And if, for some strange reason you do, I will be waiting for you on the other side of that door."

Jerrie, who'd risen quietly from her chair a few moments earlier to retrieve a cup of coffee from the counter at the side of the conference room, padded her way around the conference room table to stand behind Leah. She laid a hand on Leah's shoulder and leaned forward to whisper, "Calm, sister, calm. Here's your coffee. Drink it and remember the number of lives we may save using this man's information."

Leah spun to face her. "I didn't ask for any coffee."

"I know," Jerrie said. "But take it, anyway. And take a breath." She put downward pressure on Leah's shoulder with one hand, easing Leah back into her chair.

"But . . . " Leah started, again, glancing around the room and noticing how everyone's eyes were on her. She felt the wave of anger dissipate under the weight of their gaze, some of the people she cherished and respected more than anyone else in the world, and silently prayed, *What am I doing? God, please help me stop this anger building in me!*

In response to her prayer, Leah felt an immediate calming of her senses, her muscles relaxing and her vision clearing. She blew out yet another long breath, then met Paul Samuelson's gaze onscreen. "I apologize for the outburst, Paul, and to the rest of you. The death of some kids at the store really affected me."

"Understood and appreciated," Paul said, his expression one of concern and empathy that surprised Leah, when he, in fact, had grounds for relieving her on the spot. Paul instead focused his dark, intense gaze on Steven, his eyes pinning the man to the back of his chair. "As Agent McCarthy asked, why should we believe anything you tell us?"

Steven cleared his throat, his voice coming out scratchy and uncertain when he replied. "Because I am highly motivated to gain your trust. I desire to be placed in the U.S. Marshall's Witness Protection Program with a new identity, a new life, and a safe distance from the people I worked for. They wanted to kill me, too, once my value to them was exhausted. Promise me that, and I will tell you everything I know."

It was Jerrie who brought the issue to a head when she said, "We really don't have any choice. We need any information this man might offer. We're dealing with something big here."

"Steven, I have the authority to make that call and get you into that program," Paul said. "But only if the information proves to have value."

Steven glanced at Leah, who kept her eyes carefully averted, no longer trusting herself to hold back her anger. GW, sitting next to her, reached a hand to gently squeeze hers, below the tabletop. His touch sent a welcome wave of warmth through her; and without thinking, she laced their fingers.

GW let a small smile wrinkle the corners of his lips as he glanced her way and whispered, "We've got this. God's got this." Then he leaned back and nodded.

The gesture was over in a moment, but the reassurance she felt from GW and his reminder of God's presence lifted her as she returned her eyes to the team as Steven continued to speak.

"Get me a computer with internet access and I will get you the information you need."

Paul nodded to Jessica. "Jessica, you work with him. Report back as soon as you have something. The rest of you, watch him like a hawk. Any step in any direction other than toward what we need and I'll see that he's thrown into the darkest prison we have for the rest of his life."

The room went silent as Jessica led Steven from the room to a small office located next door. Leah rose to follow, then stopped as her cell phone vibrated. She retrieved it from her pants pocket and examined the text appearing on the phone's small screen. It was Paul. *Talk to Dr. Malcome.*

Leah groaned. Paul wanted her to talk to the Home Team's shrink again. After her rant in the conference room, she wasn't surprised, but having her head examined right now was the last thing she wanted.

As if her boss was reading her mind, a second text message appeared. *That's an order.*

Leah groaned again, then turned to find both Jerrie and GW standing next to her chair, talking softly. Jerrie started to speak, but Leah cut her off with a raised hand. "Thanks, Jerrie. And you, too, GW. I was out of line."

Jerrie nodded, flashing Leah another of her warm, motherly smiles, then turned and made her way out of the conference room. GW remained by Leah's side. "You have friends," he said when Jerrie was out of earshot. "A whole room full of them. And I'd like to be one of them."

Beyond caring what the remaining people in the conference room might think, Leah stepped into GW and pressed her face against his chest, wrapping her arms around his waist. He returned her embrace, his thick arms drawing her closer, his warmth filling something inside she'd not realized was missing.

They stood there for several long minutes, neither speaking until Jessica stuck her head back into the conference room and threw Leah a knowing smile. "Steven is in their system. We have a download. We need to get the director on the line right now."

Sam, lingering near the coffee maker, moved to the head of the table and picked up the small tablet computer that controlled the room's communications system. He tapped a few keys, and Paul Samuelson appeared once again in the center of the room's three large-screen monitors.

Paul looked weary as he stared into the camera. "What have you got?"

Jessica paced up the side of the conference room to stand at the side of the screen, as Jerrie re-entered the room, holding two pages of printer paper in one hand. She lifted it to the screen. "Steven was able to get into his group's network and retrieve the information. It's a coordinated attack on sixty cities across the country by as many singleton active shooters, twenty-four who will be paired with seed shooters—experienced operatives. We have the names of the shooters and the specific targets in each city. And as we already knew, it kicks off in three days."

"Good news," Paul said. "Send me the list. I'll work with the Department of Justice, Homeland, and the FBI to get the word out to each city's police department, along with the names of the shooters and their targets. It's not much time; but perhaps they can pick up the shooters before the attacks begin or, at the least, have officers waiting at the targets."

"I can't be more specific about the seed shooters Steven mentioned," Jessica continued. "The list shows where they'll be, but their names appear in some sort of code."

"Then the locals will need to have people at each site, watching for them," Allen said from where he stood next to the conference room's coffee bar.

Paul nodded on the screen. "There's a lot to get done in three days, but I'll get the information flowing. Stand by for more information as I hear back from the target cities."

Jessica cleared her throat to regain the group's attention. "But that's not the end of it. The active shooters are only phase one of their plans. There's a phase two."

Paul frowned and ran a hand through the wispy gray hair on his scalp. "As if sixty active shooters and assorted seed shooters isn't enough, there's a phase two?"

"Yes, sir," Jessica replied. "We don't have a lot of information about the second attack, but we do know it is scheduled to happen the day after the active shooter attack when the morale of the people and trust for our government is at its lowest."

"What *do* you know about phase two?" Sam asked.

"We have a list of cities and targets, "Jessica said. "What we don't know is how the attacks will be carried out."

Leah felt churning in the pit of her stomach as Jerrie chimed in. "They're counting on our country being devastated by the impact of sixty simultaneous active shooter attacks across the country. Law enforcement will be tied up responding to the active shooters, the casualties, and the panic that follows. If the second attack is substantial at all, it will happen when law enforcement is fully consumed by the aftermath of the active shooter attack. They won't be able to respond effectively to a second attack. People will panic, become fearful, and lose confidence in our government's ability to protect them. Fear will become the rule, not the exception."

Sam nodded as he dropped into the nearest chair. "The police departments around the country can handle a lot more than we may give them credit for. Their SWAT teams and special activities units are highly skilled. We can't lose hope that they'll be able to find and secure the active shooters before the first attack happens and be ready if another follows."

"A good point," Paul replied. "How many targets are in the phase two attack?"

Jessica examined one of the pages Steven printed out in the office. "Six. Seattle, Los Angeles, Denver, Chicago, Boston, and Dallas. It also identifies the specific targets in those cities. In Seattle, the target is the waterfront area where cruise ships dock. Steven explained that the cities chosen for the phase two attack were selected because they're hubs for travel and commerce, yet not so large that the effects of the attack could be downplayed by the media."

Paul took another sip of coffee from his chipped, white coffee mug, then frowned and set it aside. "Awful coffee," he said. "We'll assume the local authorities in each active shooter target area will deal with that threat. We'll focus on phase two. To that end, I'm going to bring six of the EOG's teams in on this, including Home Team and Omega Team. Sam, Leah, Allen, and Jessica will return to Joint Base Lewis-McChord to cover the phase two target in Seattle. Omega Team will handle the Boston target with the same level of support and coordination. Four other teams will be assigned to the remaining cities. Get going now. Get on the ground. Coordinate with the locals, as well. Your priority is the phase two attack. Find out how it's going down and stop it by any means necessary. Within the hour, I will brief the secretary of state and the president, and I guarantee all six teams will have their full support. Now, get moving!"

As the group filed from the conference room, Jerrie caught up with Leah. She took Leah by surprise when she paused between Leah and the building's exit. "A moment?" she asked.

"Of course," Leah replied.

"I just want you to know that a lot of us have been where you are right now," Jerrie said.

Leah started to protest, but Jerrie cut off anything Leah might have said with one of her kind, knowing smiles. "I noticed your concern about the potential impact to noncombatants before the Nashville operation and earlier had a long talk with Paul. He thought I might be able to relate to what you're going through. I've been through it myself."

"You? PTSD?"

Jerrie nodded. "Yep. While I don't have a military background, I worked for a long time as an FBI SWAT team negotiator. My last case involved a small family. Their next-door neighbor, a deranged drug user, took them hostage after breaking into their house to steal some money. He was high on drugs and killed everyone before I could talk him down. My failure to save that family just about killed me. I had flashbacks and relived the scene from that murder again and again for what seemed like a very long time. Nightmares were a normal occurrence. And the depression . . . that was some of the worst of it.

"I took six months' leave of absence from the FBI to deal with it. I found a psychologist to help me deal with the flashbacks, horrible dreams, and depression. She equipped me with tools to combat the PTSD symptoms. My brothers, sisters, husband, and kids rallied around me; and my church embraced me with their love and support. Through that treatment and support, I was able to put the flashbacks and nightmares behind me. I rejoined the FBI's SWAT team and committed my life to ensuring that, as much as I can possibly do, more innocent people don't die on my watch."

"That's a lot more than what I'm up against. I haven't had a flashback for a couple of days, and I've only experienced four of those," Leah said.

"That's good news," Jerrie replied. "I'm no expert about PTSD, except as a person who's been through it and will live with some aspect of it for the rest of my life. But maybe your situation is more reactive than chronic. If it's reactive, maybe it'll pass quickly. Regardless, I have a suggestion for you."

"Okay?"

"When you feel yourself getting down—when you find yourself in a situation where you feel the circumstances might trigger a flashback, anxiety, or depression—try to focus on all the support you have in your life. You have your team. You have your faith. You have that mountain of a man, the investigator, who is obviously interested in you."

"No, we're just—"

"Sister, anyone other than you can see the interest in that man's eyes. Again, regardless, you have your team and, from what your team members tell me, your church and your faith. You also have Paul Samuelson, our director, and his willingness to invest in whatever it takes to keep you going. Focus on those things when times get tight. It will make a huge difference once you realize you're not alone."

Leah shrugged, her eyes drifting across the rest of the Home Team and Omega Team. She saw GW there, too, and wondered at what might come of his feelings for her and hers for him, if Jerrie was right. "Maybe . . . "

"First and foremost, don't forget your faith," Jerrie added. "You've accepted Christ as your Savior. I heard that from Jessica. You were born again; and because of that, He is always with you, whether it's in the thick of battle or in the quiet, hard times when our regrets and the tough memories creep up on us. Remember Job from the Bible. He has a plan for you; and that plan includes Him walking with you through it all, no matter the challenges. We are never alone when we invite Him into our lives."

Leah smiled, then on impulse pulled Jerrie into a long hug. When they released each other, Leah could have sworn there was a tear in the woman's eye; but it was gone a second later. "I think you missed your calling," Leah said. "That was a sermon my pastor would have been proud of."

"Nothing but the truth," Jerrie said. "And if you ever need to talk with someone, I'm here for you."

"Thank you, sister," Leah said.

"Don't mention it. Now, let's go get those bad guys," Jerrie said as she turned and headed for the door.

CHAPTER 28

The following morning, The Hatchet sat in a hotel room near Nashville International Airport and glared at the information on his laptop's screen. The longish night-black hair he'd sported as one of the nation's leading consulting psychologists was gone, his hair now buzz cut and died a pale brown. Dark blue contacts replaced his natural brown eye color, and the sport coat he wore had thin layers of padding cleverly sewn into its lining to flesh out his thin, angular physique.

Onscreen was a spreadsheet showing the sixty phase one cities and the specific targets within each city. The name of the recruit, the singleton active shooter assigned to each target, was also listed. He nodded as he examined the list. It was a good list, full of men and women carefully selected, shaped, and empowered—as much as any person could be—to carry out the attack. His sleep the night before had been short and fitful and left him listless, his mind plagued by a lingering doubt.

Shaped and empowered. He rolled the words around in his mind as though tasting fine wine. *Such appropriate words.*

A message flashed in the upper right corner of this screen: *SR is online. Do you wish to connect with SR?*

SR is online? That's impossible. Steven Roberts is dead. Haider assured him that he'd left Steven's lifeless corpse in the woods a mile inside the air force base's Tullahoma-side boundary.

The Hatchet felt a lump form in the pit of his stomach. Steven must not have died, after all. That incompetent Haider Betterly must not have checked the body close enough, so busy running to save his own skin. And now, the dead man was online, accessing the system.

The Hatchet signed into his system's root program, fingers flying across his keyboard. Moments later, he located Steven's logon history and the files he'd accessed when the alert appeared on The Hatchet's screen. He'd accessed the system's master file, the same file The Hatchet currently had up. No, wait. Not the same one, an earlier version. Steven must have figured the latest version of the file might be in use and hoped by opening the older file to go unnoticed.

The Hatchet pounded in a string of commands on the laptop's keyboard, then rocked back in his seat as the system shut down Steven's access. But a question lingered in The Hatchet's mind: what had Steven downloaded and why?

He examined the file Steven had accessed during his time in the system. It was an older copy, but the changes were insubstantial. He must be working with the government to secure immunity.

The Hatchet felt bile rise in his throat. How could Steven do this? No matter that he'd been left for dead, Steven was a believer. No matter their differences, the cause should come first. In fact, if Steven had approached him directly, The Hatchet would have had no problem receiving Steven back in the fold with open arms, even celebrating his survival. *And then have him killed.*

But Steven hadn't given The Hatchet a chance, no matter how great a lie it would have been. And now their plans might well be compromised. If Steven passed the detailed list of targets, shooters, and timeline to the authorities, they would be prepared for the attack when it happened in two days' time. That left only one option: move up the timeline. Attack tomorrow! Everything is in place, so why not? He would catch the opposition off guard, regardless of what Steven might have provided them.

The Hatchet turned back to his laptop, opened the system's virtual private network, and keyed in the words that would change the world. "The timeline for phase one has changed. Phase one kickoff is tomorrow at noon, Pacific Time."

The response from his three regional directors came seconds later and was unanimous. "Confirmed. All resources standing by."

The response from the artificial intelligence program hosted within his organization's cloud was equally immediate. "Confirmed: phase one accelerated. All traffic to be disseminated immediately."

The Hatchet smiled. From this point on, the first phase of the operation was on remote control. Texts and phone calls would be sent to each of the sixty recruited active shooters by the artificial intelligence system, directing each shooter to initiate their attacks on their assigned target. Driven by the AI program, each message was customized to match the needs of the recruit about to open fire on a soft target across the country. The system was linked to a sophisticated voice synthesizer that mimicked the voice of someone important to the active shooter, someone they'd trust when they were told to go to their target and open fire on the people there. The message would encourage each recruit to act, to target people they'd been conditioned to see as a threat or responsible for some personal failure.

Dr. Muhammad smiled at the thought. Setting up the trigger alerts had been one of the toughest parts of the operation. It wasn't enough for the recruits to be desensitized to the use of violence;

they needed active encouragement from someone close to them to push them over the edge, someone perceived as just as passionate, just as angry as they were. It could be the voice of a parent, sibling, past teacher, or fellow criminal. To that end, the AI program had cloned the recruit's phone, monitored each recruit's phone calls, and captured the voices of those who called the potential active shooter most frequently. In most cases, that turned out to be someone close, someone the recruit relied upon and listened to.

In the few cases where a suitable voice was not identified, a text would be sent from the phone number of someone the recruit recognized as important, someone they looked up to, like a past mentor or even a celebrity. The text was not expected to be as effective a trigger as the voice message but was found during testing to be nearly so. He always felt it amazing how something as impersonal as a few words on a cell phone's screen could assume such power in a person's life, particularly Americans.

The voice messages and texts were prepositioned to go out the day before the attack, which, as of a few minutes ago, was now. If all went according to plan, the calls and texts would stimulate action tomorrow at noon.

The Hatchet shut down the system and closed his laptop. The phase one attack was on autopilot now. Within a few hours, the recruits would receive their special messages, take up the weapons they'd been provided by their sponsors, and change the world.

CHAPTER 29

The first two hours of the four-hour flight from Omega's headquarters at Army Base Fort Knox to Joint Base Lewis-McChord seemed the longest Leah had endured in years. She tried to sleep but failed again and again. Her eyes felt gritty and swollen, like she hadn't had a good night's sleep in years. When she did close her eyes, her mind filled with the images of children in the sights of crazed shooters, DEA agents lying dead, and foreign attackers closing on her position.

Two hours into the flight, she decided to text Dr. Malcome, the EOG psychologist. *I could use a talk. R u available?*

What can I do you for? came his immediate lighthearted response.

She typed her text with thumbs flying across her cell phone's tiny keyboard. *I'm dead on my feet. I went on vacation because the op tempo had been so intense, and I needed a break. That hasn't happened; but for two days, the flashbacks have stopped. Now, it's the memories. I need to get my head together.*

Dr. Malcome: *No flashbacks? That may be the beginning of some good news. What's the difference between the days when you had the flashbacks and now?*

Leah: *I did get a couple of hours sleep. Spent some time with my sister and her family, got ambushed, shot at, blown up, and had coffee with a cute investigator.*

Dr. Malcome's response lagged several seconds before appearing on her cell phone's screen. *Doesn't sound like much of a vacation. The family time was good, although it must have been brief considering the rest. What about that investigator? Anything interesting there?*

She paused, uncertain how much she should reveal about her feelings for GW, then decided she needed to go all in. If she wanted her life back on track, she had to go all in. She tapped in her text: *Enjoying working with him. Admit that I have developed feelings for the guy. It was nice, if you can say that about fighting my way through an ambush with someone as talented, understanding, and strong.*

Dr. Malcome: *Being with your family no doubt helped settle your mind; gave you a mental holiday. The experience with the investigator and your feelings for him may have helped further. Something like a simple, meaningful affiliation with others can help take the pressure off and help with PTSD symptoms. I do wonder why you don't get that same benefit from being with your team. In past sessions, you talked about being close, like family.*

Leah swallowed hard as she responded, again recognizing the need to be all in with Dr. Malcome if she was going to beat this thing. *I avoided mentioning it, but things have changed with the team. The guys are deep into their relationships with Consuelo and Mallory. Jessica has her new ranch to occupy her time. We don't spend as much time together as a group. It feels like I'm losing them. We're just as good working together as we've always been. We just don't spend much off-duty time together anymore.*

Dr. Malcome's reply took several minutes to reach her, then showed up on screen with what seemed a carefully chosen abundance of words: *I think the fatigue you've been feeling may have opened the door for the PTSD symptoms that you might otherwise have successfully held at bay. Mission fatigue is something many of the EOG teams are experiencing.*

The world has become a dangerous place. Your skills and those of your teammates are needed now more than ever and, unfortunately, more often. You may probably feel some anxiety rising from the changing relationships within your team. The good news: what you're experiencing can be dealt with. The prescription for now: get as much rest as you can and keep in mind that you are part of a four-person team of unique, very special individuals. And while they are all top-tier operatives, like you, they are also people with complex, evolving lives. I suggest you talk to them candidly about how you're feeling and see where that takes you as teammates, friends, and a type of family. And finally, embrace your feelings for your sister and her family and the new relationship with the investigator. Families and new relationships can be salves for the soul. And then there's your faith in God.

Leah: *My faith is still intact. I would never abandon that!*

Dr. Malcome: *You are a Christian, and that is an especially important part of your psyche. For Christians, the goal is to find a home in Jesus Christ, a place where you'll never be alone. You do that by accepting Him and surrendering everything to Him. It sounds to me like you haven't done that much recently, that you feel frustrated because things are changing around you and you have no control over it.*

Leah: *I've never considered myself a control freak, but that may be close to the truth. I've lost a lot in my life: my mother, the two little girls at the grocery store, potentially my teammates and, like you said, me feeling unable to stop any of it from happening. That's what's left me wondering why God would let bad things happen to so many good, innocent people.*

Dr. Malcome spent a few minutes replying, then texted back: *As a frame of reference, you might consider Job, from the Bible. When Christians wrestle with the question of why bad things happen to good people, he's a person we often turn to. In Job 1:1, we learn Job was a man who was blameless and upright. He feared God and shunned evil.*[2] *But God allowed Satan to test Job's faith because Satan felt Job would only love God while things were going well. So Job lost his children and his property and ended up destitute and covered in sores. He and his friends kept wondering why God would do that to him, considering how righteous he'd lived his life until then. Job goes through all that but holds on to his faith regardless and, praising God, said, "The Lord gave, and the Lord has taken away; may the name of the LORD be praised."*[3] *Satan failed to break Job, and God returned him to a good, prosperous life. The bottom line is it's not wrong to ask the Lord, "Why am I struggling in life?" or "Why are those around me struggling, even suffering?" Job's trials suggest we hang in there, even when it feels like we've lost everything or we see someone else suffer, like those little girls. Job reminds us that through our faith in Him, we trust that God has a reason for what happens us and to others. It's all under His control, not ours.*

Leah: *That was quite an epistle.*

Dr. Malcome: *Thanks. Seriously, maybe part of what you're going through is, at least in part, because you've forgotten to trust that He has plans for your team, for you, and for the kids at the store. Only He has control over it all, not us. That's the essence of the faith that you've lived your life by. When we forget that, we risk wandering off the path He's laid out for us, losing sight of the home that He made for us, here on earth and in Heaven, with Him. Perhaps the flashbacks subsiding over the past few days are because of your time with your sister's family, with the investigator, and with working with your team on a project. You might consider that it's part of His plan for you for you to recognize the blessings in your life and see even more progress.*

Leah: *And I won't feel so alone, so lost?*

---

2   Job 1:1.
3   Job 1:21.

Dr. Malcome: *That might be. Reach out to Him. Ask Him for the strength you need to deal with the things going on in your life. Surrender it to Him, and I bet you'll find your way back home quicker than you think.*

Leah let out another of the long sighs that seemed to come so frequently, lately. It had been a long time since she'd had a long talk with God. She typed in her response: *Homesick. That sounds right. When my faith is strong, I feel strong, like He's with me, watching over and guiding me. It feels like I'm home, just like you say, no matter where I am or who I'm with. BTW, I didn't realize shrinks could be Christian. Wouldn't Freud object?*

Dr. Malcome: *LOL. Freud provides one perspective. There are many, many others, including those from our shared faith. When I counsel any person, Christian or non-Christian, I have to consider whole person, including their faith. In your instance, we just happen to share the same faith.*

Leah typed in *Thanks, doc.*

Any time, Malcome replied.

Leah set her cell phone on the floor beside her chair, leaned back, and closed her eyes. Silently, she reached out to God. "Please forgive me for not praying sooner, but I need Your help. Please forgive me for my steps off the path You've set before me; for my selfish concerns about the changes in the lives of my friends; for forgetting that while I may not understand it, You have a plan, even for the little girls in the store. Please guide me home to Your love and my feelings for GW . . ."

With those last words, Leah's shoulders shed months of tension; her mind settled and cleared like silt washed away by a clear mountain stream; and she fell into a deep, much-needed sleep.

CHAPTER 30

They landed in Olympia two hours after Leah's text with Dr. Malcome. She awoke as the jet touched down, feeling remarkably refreshed after only two hours sleep. The trip to the headquarters at Joint Base Lewis-McChord was brief, and Becca met them all at the headquarters building's front doors with a coffee carrier with four cups, plus one in her hand. She frowned when she counted six, rather than four, people.

"We'll make do," Leah assured her, taking one of the coffees and leaving GW and Steven empty-handed.

"Director Samuelson is already onscreen," Becca said as she followed them in. "It sounds important."

Leah paused and turned to meet Becca's gaze. "How are you doing?"

Becca shrugged. "I've been using your car, and I'm still at your place; but I spend a lot of my time working out here at the clubhouse. This place is so cool."

Leah smiled at the word "clubhouse." She'd often described the place as exactly that, with its high-tech obstacle course, shooting range, exercise equipment, and martial arts mats. She'd spent some of her best days there with the rest of the team.

"Paul has been waiting onscreen for twenty minutes," Becca said.

"Then I'd better get in there," Leah said, then paused as Becca stepped between her and the way leading into the conference room.

"Can I say something?" Becca asked.

Leah started to step around Becca, then paused once more when she noticed the worried expression in the young girl's eyes. Remembering Malcome's advice about God blessing her with the people in her life, she said, "Of course. What's up?"

"Do you remember when you told me how your sister raised you for the last two years of high school?"

Leah nodded. "Sure . . . "

"I was wondering . . . " Becca said, her eyes drifting down to her feet. "You've got that extra room in your apartment, and I do need a place to stay. Maybe I could stay with you? You could watch out for me like your sister looked out for you. It'd only be a couple of years. I checked with the high school near your place, and they said I could enroll immediately."

Leah frowned. This was the furthest thing from her mind. Leah pushed out a quick breath. "I'm no person to be looking out for anyone. My schedule is nuts. I'm never home, always out on some mission somewhere. And I wouldn't know the first thing about raising a teenage girl."

"But that's the beauty of it," Becca countered, her eyes boring into Leah's with her sincerity, her hope. "You don't need to raise me. I'm emancipated, so you wouldn't have any official responsibility for me. You'd be off the hook for all that, and I can pay rent. I'd go to school and take care of myself when you're gone. But you'd be there when you aren't on the road. Like I said during our walk, I don't always make the best decisions. I could use some help with that, and I could use having someone there for me. I could use having a home. I haven't had that for a long time."

For one of the first times in her life, Leah felt beyond words. She tried to tell Becca no; but the hopeful look in the girl's eyes bored into her heart, and the words simply wouldn't come out.

She was saved when Sam stuck his head out the conference room door and yelled, "Get in here, Romeo. Things are about to get going."

Becca reached out a hand to tug at Leah's sleeve as she turned away. "Can we maybe talk about it when you're done with all this?"

"Yeah, sure," Leah replied, then stepped around Becca and headed for the conference room door.

Leah took her seat at the conference room table, where the rest of the Home Team, GW and Steven were already in their seats. Also at the table was Walter Drake, the only person in the room who could meet GW eye to eye. The two sat side by side, looking for all the world like two huge tactical bookends. In the chair to Walter's right sat the skinny, pale Barry Whitman, the team's technology specialist. Both Walter and Barry were brought into the EOG fold as part of Home Team Two a year ago, when the second covert operations group was activated at Joint Base Lewis-McChord. The rest of Home Team Two's five-person team were currently deployed in training mode at locations around the country and the globe.

Paul Samuelson opened the meeting. "I reached out to a colleague at the Defense Health Agency and came across some information that could be useful, given what we've learned. Stand by."

Paul tapped keys on a keyboard, and the screen to the left of his image came to life with the face of a smiling, ruddy man with a thinning hairline and eyes so blue they appeared white. "This is Dr.

Garnet Speers, a psychology consultant for the State Department and Department of Defense. He works closely with Dr. Malcome, whom some of you talk to on a regular basis. He's a retired army colonel and just finished an additional fifteen-year stint working for the Defense Health Agency. Dr. Speers has deployed around the world to address the needs of wounded soldiers, PTSD victims, detainees, and prisoners of war. I asked him to describe what we're up against with the singleton active shooter attack. Dr. Speers, please take it from here."

"Good morning," Dr. Speers said. His voice was mellow, soft. His words were precise, exacting. "Thank you for inviting me to discuss one of the more interesting cases I've encountered in a very long time. I know time is of the essence, so I'll get right to the point. There's been considerable research into the value of using virtual reality tools in the clinical setting to help patients who present with Post-Traumatic Stress Disorder, depression, excessive anger, certain phobias, and even violent tendencies. The results of clinical trials and associated research suggest virtual reality tools can provide value within a patient's treatment regimen.

"In conjunction with other treatment modes, such as talk therapy, medication, and other protocols, VR scenarios can be constructed to place patients in situations where they can be desensitized to stimuli responsible for the onset of certain symptoms. A PTSD patient, for example, can be walked through a scenario where they confront environmental variables responsible for stimulating their symptoms, such as explosive sounds, the presence of weapons, the presence of a dying or injured person, and so on. Using VR, less threatening scenarios can be substituted to replace the negative stimulus with all else in the virtual reality scenario remaining the same. The idea is that through numerous repetitions, the person undergoing treatment would be desensitized to the loud sounds, presence of weapons, and so on and grow to live a normal, less reactive life."

Jessica raised her hand, and Speers nodded in her direction. "Doctor, how do you see this playing out in the current situation, with VR potentially being used to condition active shooters?"

"That's why I'm here, so let me get to it," he replied. "I have reviewed one of the VR scenarios provided in the programming recovered from the warehouse in Tumwater. What I found there resembled traditional games where players battle space invaders and escalate to human targets. It appears the overall program was intended as an iterative conditioning tool. Successive iterations progressively presented human targets as increasingly evil, as dire threats to the participants, their family, their community, and country. Based on my analysis, after what I believe could take weeks if not months, the program was intended to desensitize subjects toward carrying out violence to the point where they might experience little difficulty attacking and even killing another person."

Sam cleared his throat. "Sir, I find it hard to believe any group of people could be conditioned to kill someone if they had any moral upbringing at all."

The psychologist smiled. "A good observation. In fact, classic research attributed to Dr. Stanley Milgram in the 1960s showed that otherwise good, responsible, moral people can be encouraged by another perceived responsible person, such as a psychologist conducting research, to cause pain to others. In that study, subjects were encouraged to deliver electrical shocks to people sitting on the other side of a partition if that person didn't answer test questions correctly. Sixty-five percent of people administered the painful shocks.[4] Very few people refused. That sort of research has been considered unethical for many years, due to the emotional impact on the person administering the shocks. That said, the results were clear and are cited to this day. So in answer to your question, an otherwise normal person can, in fact, be programmed to commit violence against others. Add to that a pre-existing propensity for violence, lack of empathy, and so on, and virtual reality programming might well be effective as a tool for encouraging select candidates to become an active shooter."

Jessica spoke this time. "Some people declined to deliver the shocks during those experiments?"

"Yes, indeed," Dr. Speers said. "Which suggests you can expect a number of the active shooters programmed for the attack to not pull the trigger, although a large percentage may well do exactly that."

"Which is why the group behind all this has planted what they call seed shooters with some of their recruits, people prepared to follow through with the attacks in addition to, or in place of, the conditioned subjects," GW said.

"Exactly," Speers replied, then glanced at his watch. "That's about all the information I can provide for now. With more time, I am sure I could do a better job profiling the situation; but I hope what I've provided to you helps in some way."

"Any thoughts about the phase two attack?" Jessica asked.

"Actually, yes," Speers replied. "I have seen the target criteria list for Seattle, which suggests the cruise line docks may be the most likely target. I support your supposition that they will attack a high-density

---

4   Kendra Cherry, "Understanding the Milgram Experiment in Psychology," Very Well Mind, Accessed August 2024, https://www.verywellmind.com/the-milgram-obedience-experiment-2795243.

population area like that. The terrorists are likely to want the impact of their attack to be visual, visceral, and highly emotional."

"Like a cruise line terminal with ships loading passengers?" Leah asked.

Speers' eyes went wide but just for a moment. "Exactly. It is only conjecture on my part, of course, but a cruise line terminal should be considered a high-probability target. The fact that the phase one attack involves active shooters and not the terrorist group's leaders personally wielding the weapons suggests a bias toward a hands-off violence. In other words, the people planning the phase one and phase two attacks prefer targeting from a distance over dirtying their own hands. To me, that suggests the use of long-distance weapons."

"Like missiles?" Sam said.

"That seems likely. Add to that, these sorts of terrorists tend to be very results-driven, with large egos. That suggests they will have a backup plan to ensure maximum impact should their initial approach fail."

"Like a suicide bomber?" Allen asked. "We've seen a lot of that in the past."

"I can see you've thought this through," Speers replied. "Yes, suicide bombers are used all too often in attacks of late, people martyring themselves to feed the ego of terrorist leaders' sadistic need to see others suffer, yet still not dirty their own hands."

Dr. Speers glanced at his watch again. "Unfortunately, I have somewhere I need to be. Do you have any additional questions?"

"Thank you, Dr. Speers," Paul said from onscreen. "I appreciate your time and bringing your knowledge to the team. You have confirmed much of what the team discussed prior to your arrival. I believe we can move forward with some confidence based on what you've told us."

"Happy to help," Speers replied, and then his screen went blank.

"Do we have anything more to discuss?" Paul asked once the psychologist was offscreen.

No one spoke.

"Then go get—" Paul was cut off when Steven charged into the room.

"The attack's been changed," Steven said, waving a small piece of paper before him.

"What are you talking about? I thought we had two days to prepare," Sam said.

"No longer," Steven said. "The people I worked for locked me out of their master system but not from their virtual private network. I'm the one who created the VPN. When I did, I inserted a back door and a verbatim communications log, so I could monitor specific communications when needed. I accessed that log just now and found a message from my boss, The Hatchet. He's accelerated the phase one attack to tomorrow. I believe he discovered I'd accessed the system and his plans, and this is his response."

"And that means the phase two attack happens the day after tomorrow," Leah said.

Paul frowned. "Beyond the dates, nothing's changed. GW, you're our coordination point with the Seattle PD. Let them know the schedule's been moved up. The rest of you get to Seattle. Find out how they intend to stage the attack and stop it."

CHAPTER 31

D r. Albert Muhammad settled into the thick cushions of his first-class seat on the red-eye from Indianapolis to Seattle. He'd intended to fly out of Nashville, relying on his well-crafted disguise, then thought better of it, rented a car, and drove the five-and-a-half hours north to Indianapolis. There, he purchased a round-trip ticket to Seattle. He'd learned long ago that one-way tickets were a potential red flag when boarding lists were inspected by federal agents.

His plans depended on his artificial intelligence program prepping the active shooter attacks for 6 p.m. tomorrow, Pacific Time. That should give him ample time to land in Seattle, catch a shuttle to his hotel, and observe the impact of the phase one operation from the sidelines. The phase two plan? He couldn't be certain about how that would go. The Chairman had that covered personally. The hope was that accelerating both plans would at least put their adversaries off guard. He smiled at the thought, looking forward to the outcome of the next two days. It had been a long time coming.

He slept fitfully during the flight. There was simply too much rolling around in his mind. Five hours later, after a relatively smooth flight where the flight attendants mercifully left him undisturbed, he de-planed at Seattle-Tacoma International Airport and headed for the hotel. He had no bags and carried his laptop computer in a blue nylon backpack, so he planned to be out of the airport in a few minutes.

The Hatchet checked his silver Rolex as he made his way down the airport's long N Gate corridor. It was after midnight, and he hoped to catch up on some long-needed sleep at the hotel before watching the impact of the phase one attack on the evening news. Those thoughts were cut off as his cell phone vibrated. He pulled the burner phone he'd purchased at the Indianapolis airport from his pocket and accepted the call. "Yes?"

He recognized the voice at once. It was the female assassin who'd served him so well during recent years. He'd texted her this new number before his departure from Indianapolis. "I have an opportunity," she said. "The group of people you requested I deal with departed the army base at Fort Knox in a private jet. I was able to plant a tag on the jet's fuselage before they took off. That team has long since landed not far from Joint Base Lewis-McChord in Washington State. I plan to go there, enter the base, locate them, and complete our agreement."

"I can help you with that," Muhammad said. "We painted the door handles at the warehouses in Nashville and Tumwater with a substance that contains nano-trackers. It is pervasive and difficult to remove, meaning anyone or anything touching it can be tracked using a VHF, or very high frequency radio receiver, if they are within five miles of the person's location. It is reliable for a week or so. The idea was that we'd be able to track any workers or recruits who left and arrived at the warehouses."

"The team I'm tracking was at your warehouses, so all I need is the frequency?"

"Correct. I will text the frequency immediately," Muhammad said.

"There is one more complication," the assassin said. "We talked previously about there being six people in the group I'm following."

"Yes? I agreed to the extra money."

"I will need the money for that job now, in advance, if I am to complete the assignment."

Muhammad paused, then said, "We've always paid you in full when a job was done."

"That was before you ordered hits on your own people."

"Ah. I see. You think I might have you killed, as well?"

"At this point, Dr. Muhammad, I'd say it's a possibility."

She knows my name! He'd gone to great lengths to keep his identity from her over the years, and she had just let him know she had that information in hand. That meant she could find him, and that was a complication he wasn't prepared for. He felt a bead of sweat form on the bare skin of his upper lip and said, "I will deposit the money in your account immediately."

"Thank you," the assassin said.

"I'm sure you will be as effective as always," Muhammad started, but the connection had already been terminated. *In another two days, the money won't matter, either way,* he decided. *And my clever assassin will have served her purpose.*

As he stepped through the airport's arrival doors and into the cool night air, Dr. Albert Muhammad smiled. "It's all in place," he murmured too softly to be overheard. "In two short days, we will change the course of America's history."

CHAPTER 32

Regan Acheron, The Hatchet's personal assassin and problem-fixer, pulled her compact rental sedan to a stop at the security checkpoint at Joint Base Lewis-McChord's main gate early the following morning. The day was chilly and clear, with a bright sun climbing from the east, beyond Mount Rainier and its accompanying line of mountain peaks. As she approached the base's main gate, she noticed the gate guard dressed in dark jeans, shirt, and tactical vest, with a pistol in a drop-holster at his right thigh. SECURITY was spelled out in bright white letters across his black baseball hat. She presented another forged military identification card for inspection, this time identifying her as a military spouse. He ran a hand-held barcode reader across its back in the same manner as the security officer at Arnold Air Force Base. The device beeped, and he waved Regan through with a mumbled, "Have a nice day, ma'am."

Regan's thin lips broke into a small, shy smile for the sake of the omnipresent security cameras. "You, too, officer."

The guard finally met her eyes when she offered the greeting, nodding his head with the vacant look of someone who sees too many faces in a day to distinguish one from another.

To ensure she blended into the guard's preconceived image of a woman passing through his gate, Regan wore simple, loose jeans and a sleeveless, brightly flowered frock. Her hair was freshly colored chestnut brown, and she wore hazel-brown contacts. Thin pads tucked in both cheeks reshaped her face. If anyone examined the footage from the gate's security cameras, all they would see is another woman in a long line of female workers, spouses, or soldiers coming and going from the base, with nothing out of the ordinary to draw their attention.

She tucked the identification card into the front pocket of her jeans and put the gray four-door Toyota Corolla into drive, lifting a hand to the guard, who ignored the gesture as he waved the next car forward.

As she drove along the base's main thoroughfare, she activated the cell phone's tracker application. She keyed in the frequency provided by Muhammad, and the device picked up the signal an instant later. It was going the opposite direction. She cursed as she saw the signal for her targets moving away from the base, heading north along Interstate 5.

Regan swung into a minimart near the main gate, reversed direction, and headed back out through the security gate. Twenty minutes later, she'd closed to within a few car lengths of two large sport utility vehicles pacing each other nose-to-tail north on the interstate. The two vehicles had settled into the interstate's high occupancy vehicle lane and were cruising at a consistent seventy miles per hour.

She'd just settled in for what might be a long drive, when her cell phone rang. It was a number she'd been provided years ago by the person who'd put her in contact with Dr. Muhammad, which had never been used until this moment. Her directions at the time were to answer any future calls from the number without fail and that doing so would generally equate to a lucrative business deal. She pressed the button on the car's hands-free talk function and accepted the call. "Yes?"

"Ms. Smite," the voice said. "Is this a good time?"

"Of course," she replied. "How can I help you?"

"A few minutes ago, I deposited one hundred thousand dollars into your account. That is a demonstration of my good-faith and only half of what you'll receive if you complete a small task for me."

"What is it you'd like me to do for you?"

"I am texting you a photograph of a man. I want you to make him disappear. But I want you to wait until the day after tomorrow."

Regan sighed inwardly. That would delay her departure from this area. If there was any fallout after taking out the team she was following, sticking around could become problematic. Then again, there was all that money.

"Not today or tomorrow, but the day after that?" Regan repeated. "Do you have the target's location?"

"That is correct, and yes, I do. He is staying at a hotel in Seattle. I will text you the name of the hotel and its address."

Her cell phone chimed, indicating the text had arrived. She propped her knee against the car's steering wheel and opened the text, then downloaded the photograph. "I have it," she said.

"That's a photograph of the man. He uses many aliases, such as The Hatchet, but his actual name is Dr. Albert Muhammad. I believe you have been working for him for some time."

She wasn't about to reveal that she had already secured Muhammad's identity, but the photo would be a definite plus. "I accept the commission," she said.

"Very good," the man said. "You have my complete confidence."

The call disconnected, but the tone of the conversation lingered. There was something about the man's voice, a higher tenor with a slightly erratic inflection. *Was it anxiety, fear, or nerves she sensed in the voice?* In her line of business, it was never good to ignore an observation like that, in case the man had another plan in mind. To ignore that sort of intuition was to end up at the wrong end of someone else's sniper scope.

This time, however, it was worth the risk. Any threat imposed by The Hatchet, aka Dr. Muhammad, would be removed; and she would have two hundred grand more in her account.

CHAPTER 33

Leah, the rest of the Home Team, and GW cruised north on Interstate 5 from Joint Base Lewis-McChord in a pair of jet-black Chevrolet Suburban SUVs. The heavily tinted windows blocked most of the glare from the unseasonably warm December morning, with a deep blue sky overhead and a bright sun climbing beyond Mount Rainier's snow-covered flanks to the east.

Allen drove the lead vehicle as they sprinted up the interstate, bumper to bumper, with Leah riding shotgun and GW in the back. Jessica drove the second Suburban, with Sam in the passenger seat, no doubt coordinating with Walter at Joint Base Lewis-McChord and the Director in Florida. Each vehicle's cargo area held three large duffel bags packed with weapons and ammunition. Also tucked within the pile in the back of her SUV was Leah's silver-sided Pelican Vault Long Case containing her much used, modified M24 sniper rifle.

All members of the Home Team were fully kitted out in tactical gear, including dark cargo pants, shirts, body armor, tactical vest, and slender tablet computers strapped to one forearm. Her attention was on her tablet's small screen as a note from Barry, the team's IT lead at Lewis-McChord popped up. *Details for the waterfront area centered around the cruise ship terminal,* the note said. *Refreshed five minutes ago.*

The detail was amazing, captured by an overhead satellite and showing in high definition the myriad buildings along Alaskan Way, the street lining Seattle's waterfront and passing directly in front of the cruise line passenger terminal. Two massive cruise ships sat side-by-side next to the terminal, with boarding ramps extending across the distance. Across the street from the terminal and running the length of the waterfront area, she confirmed several apartment buildings, one office building, two four-story parking garages, and at least four condo buildings of varying sizes. Further down the street, she noticed the city's giant Ferris wheel and busy pedestrian walking area. On a hill overlooking the waterfront was Seattle proper, with its collection of skyscrapers, apartment buildings, and tall business offices. Even at this early hour, the area was alive with a sea of tourists walking the streets and heading for the cruise line terminal.

"There's too many buildings for us to screen prior to the phase two attack," she mumbled.

Allen cast her a sidelong glance. "It's a big city. But we should be able to narrow things down if we start with the information we received from the psych's profile of the terrorists."

"Give me an example," Leah replied.

"They like to be hands-off and not get their hands dirty. As the psychologist said, that means it's likely they'll use something like a portable rocket launcher," he said.

"Which is what they used when they ambushed Leah and me," GW said from the back seat.

"Correct," Allen said. "If they use a weapon like that, they'll want to be close enough to ensure they hit their target without a lot of difficulty but far enough for an easy escape. Shooting downward from a tall building at a long distance can be problematic, given projectile drop, wind factors, heat off the streets. And then there's the back-blast when a LAW is launched. The place where it's launched would have to handle that backblast without being overly visible to passersby."

"And if there is a suicide bomber in their plan," GW added, "they will want a place to stage that person far enough from the missile to keep the suicide bomber calm and committed to the plan but close enough for easy deployment. Suicide bombers have a long history of losing their courage at the last minute, and a missile blast might cause that. So we can anticipate them positioning the suicide bomber with someone there to make sure they follow through when the time comes."

"That rules out highly populated places, like Pike Place Market and the skyscraper office buildings and apartment complexes above and near the waterfront," Leah said.

A call came over Allen and Leah's comms. This time, GW wore a tactical headset to link him into the conversation. "This is Overwatch Prime." The voice was Paul Samuelson's.

"This is Mike Tango," Sam replied from the other SUV. "Go ahead, Prime."

"I have news," Paul said. "The Seattle PD apprehended the singleton active shooter at the West Seattle store this morning. According to the arresting officers, the man was visiting the store to get the lay of the land before the attack this evening. A plain-clothes Seattle PD officer used the photo on record for the man's driver's license to identify him. The seed shooter was with the man. That person put up a fight and was killed by the police officer. Unfortunately, it appears that the morning news has carried the incident nationally. We are receiving reports from all over the country, indicating similar events. Local law enforcement is on its way to shutting down today's attack altogether."

"Good news, for sure," they heard Sam reply.

"Right," Paul replied. "It's loaded with implications. If the people in charge see that the phase one active shooter attack has crumbled around them, we have to anticipate the phase two attack may be accelerated further, maybe even today."

"This is Cap," Jessica said. "The politics of the terrorist world demand outcomes, no matter the cost in human life, theirs or ours. Failure is not tolerated. The man running this thing will feel pressure to produce some sort of results. As you say, he may well see kicking off the phase two attack today as his only option."

"Then we will assume the phase two will take place today," Paul replied. "Move forward on that premise. Today, you are no longer scouting potential locations for the attack on the cruise line passenger terminal. You are on mission to stop it. Good hunting. Prime out."

"This is Whiskey Golf to Home Team Actual," GW said, using his freshly assigned call sign. "The Seattle Police Department is a top-rate organization. I'm not surprised they shut down the phase-one attack. I know people there and will reach out to them for support for the phase two attack."

"Roger, Golf," Paul replied. "Great idea. There are a lot of buildings around that terminal, along Alaskan Way, and above the site in the city. If we can get their help clearing those, it would be a Godsend."

Leah's eyes remained on the map of the Seattle waterfront displayed on her forearm tablet computer when she said, "Not many of those would be optimal, but I may have found one. It's a parking garage directly across from the terminal. It's four stories high. The top floor would suit a rocket launch through the terminal's front door and at the ships docked nearby."

"This is Empty," Sam said. "What about cover for the target? Is there somewhere you can set up your sniper hide while we check the parking garage?"

"I believe so," Leah said. "It's a five-story condo building across the street and just north of the passenger terminal and the parking garage. I'll have an unobstructed view of the front and north side of the passenger terminal, as well as the street all the way down to the Ferris wheel a quarter mile away."

"This is Fox," Allen said. "Romeo's been pouring over the city map for some time. I think we should follow her lead," Allen said.

"I'd like to have someone else confirm what I think I see. Jessica has a program that can do that on her laptop," Leah replied. "Cap, this is Romeo."

"This is Cap. Go ahead Romeo," Jessica replied from the second vehicle.

"Cap, can you check a condo building across the street and one building north of the cruise line passenger terminal for me? Any information will help."

"Roger, Romeo," Jessica replied. "I've monitored your communications and have loaded both the parking lot and the condo. Give me a second."

As Leah waited for Jessica's reply, she noticed how the traffic slowed as they approached Boeing Field Airport, south of their Seattle exit. An abundance of multi-colored passenger jets sat along the field's runway, awaiting test flights and delivery to the company's customers.

Minutes later, they passed by Seattle's expansive professional football and baseball arenas on the left as Jessica came back online.

"Romeo, this is Cap. I searched the topographical maps of the buildings and their surrounding structures, as well as the city's construction permits system. The condo is currently undergoing renovation. Depending on the stage of the renovation, you may well have the building all to yourself."

"Roger, Cap. And thanks," Leah said.

"This is Empty," Sam said. "I want to agree, again, with Romeo's suggestion that the parking garage seems like the most likely location for the terrorists. Not only would the top floor of the garage be a good launch platform for a LAW attack, with the first three floors open to traffic coming and going no one would suspect that location."

"This is Overwatch Second," Walter said over comms. "I located the website for the company that owns both the condo building and the parking garage. Both buildings have been undergoing renovation for the past two years. The condo renovation is near completion. The parking garage renovation was completed six months ago, including the top floor, even though overhead surveillance suggests that the fourth floor has been closed for line painting. There's no reason for them to be re-lining the parking area after it being renovated twelve months earlier. And get this, Romeo: the condo is not scheduled for work today. The construction company is engaged in labor negotiations."

"This is Empty," Sam said. "Once again, it seems like the parking garage is our best bet."

"This is Prime," Paul added. "Nice work, everyone. GW, please contact the Seattle PD and have them clear the surrounding buildings as much as possible, without alerting the terrorists. For the rest of you, the terminal is going to be a busy place when you get there. Two ships—one from Carnival and one from Disney are docked there for their annual Christmas cruises and are scheduled for departure tomorrow. The ships carry twenty-five hundred passengers apiece and another five hundred crew. If the terrorists launch just one missile, it will be a disaster."

"This is Romeo," Leah replied. "We'll just have to find them before that happens."

"God willing," Paul replied. "God willing."

CHAPTER 34

An hour later, GW stood tucked into the shadowed doorway of a restaurant near Seattle's famous Pike Place Market, a quick two blocks away from the waterfront. The Home Team dropped GW near the popular restaurant on Seattle's Fourth Avenue to meet the Seattle PD, then parked their vehicles at a pay-by-the-hour parking lot not far from where he stood. Sam's voice came over GW's tactical headset as he shifted weight from foot to foot in the chilly air tainted by street bus and commuter exhaust fumes. "Overwatch Prime, this is Mike Tango. We're kitted up and headed for the parking garage."

"This is Prime. Roger, Empty," Paul replied over comms.

GW pulled his cell phone from the pocket of his jeans and dialed the number for the Seattle Police Department's SWAT team leader. When the call connected, he didn't wait for a greeting. "This is Investigator Weise. I'd like to talk with the SWAT team commander, if possible."

"This is Chief Challenge," the woman's voice replied. "What can I do for you?"

GW was surprised to hear the voice of the Seattle Police Department's chief, rather than the SWAT team leader, a past member of the Tennessee Bureau of Investigation's SWAT team. "Ma'am, I'm not sure how much you've been briefed, but we have substantial evidence that the cruise line passenger terminal on the waterfront will be attacked today. Did you get the support request relayed by the Department of Justice?"

Chief of Police Martha Challenge was a recent appointee to lead the Seattle Police Department, an organization decimated during the defunding trend of the past few years. An intelligent, accomplished deputy chief from another large Western city, she'd been chosen for the job because of her tough stand on crime but also because of her keen aptitude for community relations. GW knew she was fighting an uphill battle to fill the SPD's ranks, which had been reduced to bare bones by defunding, a pull-back on police authority, and general dissatisfaction within the ranks. The fact that she might have any resources to offer the EOG's waterfront mission after effectively dealing with the active shooter incident yesterday was a miracle in and of itself.

"I got the priority alert, yes, and the request for support," she replied. "But I've barely got enough officers to patrol our streets, let alone to do a building-by-building search. The Pike Place Market has a big event today, and that means the hotels and restaurants in the city and along the waterfront area will be packed."

"Not to mention a cruise ship terminal that may have several thousand passengers checking in at the same time," GW added. "We feel the terminal will be the terrorists' target. We need your help, ma'am. The threat is credible."

Chief Challenge groaned. "You don't need to tell me that. We just got things relatively settled down in the waterfront after months of problems there, and then there was the active shooter in West Seattle. For two years, the waterfront was practically abandoned by tourists and business people due to the high crime rate. It was just too dangerous. We are now finally seeing a drop in the crime rate and a resurgence in tourism thanks to a police force that is stretched thin but fully committed. If I pull officers out of that area to clear the buildings above the terminal, I will have business owners and the city council all over me. There's simply no way I can support the request."

"But can you afford not to, knowing the threat?" GW asked. "Even back where I work, where we have a small town by comparison, a day never ends without something happening that stretches us thin. But we all signed up to make a difference; and that's what keeps us going, especially when a major threat presents itself."

"You don't need to lecture me about commitment," the chief said, her voice showing her irritation. "We are fully committed to protecting our citizens."

"My apologies, ma'am," GW replied. "I didn't mean to suggest—"

Chief Challenge cut off his next words, her sigh clearly audible over the cellular connection. "No offense is taken. I'm just frustrated. Tell you what: I will divert our Special Weapons and Tactics Team to help you. SWAT's only a handful of men and women compared to your need, but they are the best of our best."

"That's great, ma'am. I expect your SWAT team, with their training, can clear buildings in half the time of the average law enforcement officer. They know what to look for. They know the signs. And your people know the area."

GW heard the chief sigh once more, long and loud. "It's lose-lose for me, but we will support you. If you and the SWAT team find the terrorists and stop the attack, I'm still going to get hit by the same business owners and city council members, since critical resources were diverted to thwart an attack that never happened."

GW gave this some thought, then replied, "Maybe I can help with that. The people I work with prefer to remain in the background. They're some of the best people I've met, but the work they do for the government is work that's best left in the shadows."

"Not illegal . . ." the chief started.

"Never that," GW replied. "In fact, quite the opposite. But how about this? If your SWAT team can pitch in and help clear the buildings to eliminate potential hides and bolt holes for the terrorists and we stop the attack, I will do my best to ensure the Seattle PD gets total credit in a very public way."

"And if it isn't *thwarted*?"

"That simply isn't an option," GW replied.

GW could almost hear the wheels spinning in the chief's mind as she considered. "Okay," she said after a long pause. "I will commit my SWAT team, and members of the regional SWAT force from the surrounding areas and the Port of Seattle. That should give you at least thirty good officers."

GW blew out a sigh of relief. "When can they be on site?"

"I'm scanning my crime response log on our intranet site. It appears we have a clean slate at this moment, especially after so many were deployed to support the West Seattle active shooter hunt. I estimate my own SWAT team can be with you within the hour. The rest will be available as soon as possible, depending on their organization's workload and traffic, which is never good."

"Thank you, ma'am. That'll be a big help," GW replied. "Have them contact me at this number. I will be their single point of coordination. I will provide an in-brief for your team leader as soon as they arrive."

"Sounds good," the chief said. "While you were speaking, I sent the alert to the regional teams in the surrounding municipalities, as well as to my SWAT leader. All appear available and are rallying now and preparing their weapon loadouts."

"That's fast," GW replied.

"We have our problems at the SPD, but our communications technology and commitment to our mission are not them," Chief Challenge replied. "Good hunting."

"Thanks, ma'am," GW said as he disconnected the call.

Seconds later, his cell phone rang. "Weise," he replied.

It was his friend, the SWAT team leader he'd known in Tennessee. "You the guy organizing this hunting party, GW?"

"You've got him. Where can we meet and when?"

When he finished that call, GW placed one over EOG comms. "Overwatch Prime and all stations, this is Golf Whisky."

"This is Prime," Paul replied. "Go Golf."

"This is Golf. We've secured help from SPD. I will meet the SPD SWAT commander in thirty minutes. I estimate they will begin clearing the buildings overlooking the waterfront at that time."

"This is Mike Tango," Sam said over comms. "That's good news. We're set up in an abandoned shop near the entrance to the Pike Place Market on the hill above the waterfront area. There's a stairway down the back of the market to the waterfront parking lot. We'll use that to ingress the area. From there, it's a ten-minute walk to the parking garage, at most. Giving SPD SWAT the time they need to make progress clearing the surrounding buildings, I recommend mission kickoff in two hours."

"This is Overwatch Second," Walter added. "I have visuals of the area from two overhead drones I just launched from Boeing Field. I can pipe those visuals to the SWAT commander if you get me his team's network ID."

"This is Golf. I'll have that info for you as soon as possible. I'm sure they'll appreciate the assist."

"This is Empty," Sam said. "We're continuing with the theory that the terrorists will be using the top floor of a parking garage across from the terminal. We've decided to enter the garage from the stairwells on the northeast and southeast corners at the back side of the building."

"This is Romeo," Leah added. "I'll split off from the team and head for the condo to set up my hide. My ETA is ninety minutes to be in place before the Home Team moves on the garage."

"Roger that, Romeo," Paul said. "And, Romeo, I have officially advised Dr. Malcome that you remain on active-duty status. That is ultimately my call, not his. You are a critical member of this team. You good with that?"

"More than good," Leah replied. "Grateful. I won't let you all down."

"We know you won't, Romeo," Paul said, followed by a series of double clicks from Sam, Jessica, and Allen, their positive affirmations of confidence in Leah.

GW felt a lump form in his throat. He'd known she was special since that first day at Starbucks and rapidly sensed she was much more than a dedicated operator but also a person he wanted in his life, a person with exceptional character and warmth. *Maybe after all this* . . . He forced the thought from his mind. Now was not the time. They had a mission to complete, and lives depended on everyone retaining their focus on stopping the terrorist attack on the passenger terminal.

Paul came online in the next beat. "Please proceed. Report when positioned. Prime out."

CHAPTER 35

Two hours later, Sam, Jessica, and Allen hunkered at the rear of the parking garage, having made their approach down the back stairs from Pikes Place Market to a wide parking lot at the base of the hill overlooking the waterfront. Even in their black tactical gear and weapons harness, no one gave the team a second glance as they made their way north to the parking garage. This was Seattle, with its share of survivalists, odd characters, and people dressing to project some sort of often-unfathomable image. To the people around them, the three operators in tactical gear were just people in the crowd and normal for one of the country's most eclectic cities.

Sam, Allen, and Jessica hunkered at the northeast corner of the concrete-walled parking garage and its gray metal stairway door. Sam and Allen watched their flanks, while Jessica's eyes were glued to the narrow screen of her forearm tablet computer. On that screen appeared an image provided by Walter, whose long-range carrier drones now hovered over their area. The carrier drones had each just released the four micro-drones they'd ferried from Walter's location at Joint Base Lewis-McChord. All eight mini drones were now busily gathering the images that cycled across Jessica's computer screen. Two were specially focused on the parking garage's open fourth floor, with clear images of eight men in blue jeans and gray sweatshirts, armed with assault rifles and several long, green tubes Walter identified as LAW shoulder-launched missiles. The remaining six tiny drones searched openings in the first through third floor parking areas, in case the team's theory about a backup suicide bomber being staged elsewhere in the garage proved correct.

"This is Cap," Jessica whispered. "I confirm images of eight individuals with assault rifles and missile launch tubes clustered at the northwest corner of the parking garage's fourth floor. All are fighting-age males. All eight are huddled and appear to be discussing something. If we hit them now while they're distracted, we can take them before they stage their attack.

This is Fox," Allen said. "Grizzley, do you have any evidence of a suicide bomber?"

"Roger, Fox," Walter replied. "That image just came in and should be available on your arm-tablet. I confirm two people positioned at the southwest corner of the building's first floor. They are stationary and may be your suicide bomber and that person's controller."

Allen turned to Jessica and Sam. "You two take the tangos on the fourth floor. With the element of surprise, you should be able to handle them. As your explosive's expert, I should head for the other two and address the suicide bomber situation."

Sam nodded and said into his watch's microphone, "Prime, this is Empty. We're prepared to move on the tangos. Fox will handle the two on the first floor. Cap and I will take the eight up top. If this goes right, we have a good chance of shutting this thing down before they can launch those rockets."

"This is Romeo," Leah said. "I've reached the base of the condo building and located an unlocked door left open by the contractors renovating the building. Once I've cleared the condo, I'll set up and address any fleeing tangos. ETA another fifteen minutes."

"All Home Team and support," Paul said. "This is Prime. You are authorized to proceed on Romeo's mark, but I want her in position to provide support in case we have any runners."

Paul's comment was followed by four double clicks from the Home Team members' microphones.

Leah glanced at her watch, pulled open the condo's door and listened for noise from anywhere on the first floor. Hearing nothing, she took the stairs to the second floor at a jog, her long rifle case slapping against her thigh with every step. "This is Romeo," she said, her breath matching the even rhythm of her strides. "Almost there."

"Roger, Romeo," Sam said. "We will take the parking lot as soon as you're in position. Golf, did you copy?"

GW's voice came over comms, and Leah felt her heart jump. "This is Golf. Relaying the information to the SWAT team leader now. Good hunting, all."

"Roger, Golf. And thanks for the assist," Sam said. "Empty, out."

CHAPTER 36

When the SWAT team arrived in the team's Mobile TC3, or Tactical Command and Communications Center vehicle, GW relocated to a small Formica counter in the back of its command center. From the outside, the heavily armored black vehicle with the words SPD Operations painted on the outside looked overbearing and ominous, sitting on dual thirty-inch run-flat tires on the back and towering eleven feet above the street. Inside, the back of the truck housed the department's deployable command-and-control workspace, ten feet wide and twelve feet long, with light gray walls reaching a nine-foot ceiling. Soft LED can lights illuminated the space with a narrow walkway separating the two functional sections on either side. The vehicle's interior carried the distinct tang of recycled air from an air purification unit that protected the vehicle's occupants from the effects of gas, smoke, and heat.

They were parked in a lot behind the restaurant off Seattle's popular Fourth Avenue, where GW met them. GW occupied one of two high-backed ergonomic swivel chairs on the left side of the space, sitting near the vehicle's double-wide rear doors. Across from him was a communications desk with multiple computer screens, staffed by a young female officer with a thick, brown ponytail streaming down her back from beneath a black SWAT baseball hat. Her fingers flew across her keyboard with a degree of surety and speed too fast for GW to follow. Her focus and intensity reminded him of Leah and how she approached everything with the same confident manner. He smiled and wondered how Leah was doing, where she was, and if she was safe.

Next to the communications tech sat the mobile center's information technology and intelligence desk, staffed by a dark-haired young male officer. That officer, like the woman at the communications desk next to him, operated numerous computer screens. He looked relaxed and totally at ease as data, graphics, and images from SWAT team members' chest cameras flashed across a screen with a half dozen partitioned views.

The SWAT team commander and GW's past acquaintance, Captain Scott Roberts, sat at the workstation next to GW, facing a single large-screen computer monitor displaying a map of the waterfront area. Colored star icons on the map indicated the location of his team members. GW's position held an identical monitor and keyboard, along with a communications headset. To say the command center was impressive would be an understatement. The Coffee County SWAT team had nothing like this, although the demand for their services in a county of just over sixty thousand souls was not nearly as demanding as a large metropolitan area like Seattle.

The vehicle rocked softly on its heavy-duty suspension as its two-inch thick steel rear doors swung wide as SWAT team members in black jump suits, skull helmets, tactical vests, and an array of special weapons climbed into and out of the space, gathering information from the techs or reporting to their captain. GW swiveled his chair and noticed Captain Roberts glancing at a large tablet computer balanced on his lap, rather than the large screen at his workstation.

Captain Roberts was a lean, fit, fifty-year-old with a kind face framing pale gray eyes that reflected the steel in the man's character.

Captain Roberts noticed GW's glance, checked his watch, and said, "It's forty-five minutes since your call to the chief and the last of the teams have reported in. We have our own SWAT team, along with three others from the surrounding area. They've all got their assignments and are checking the buildings above and flanking the target parking garage. Two teams of eight officers are working from the north and south above the waterfront, with each team divided into two squads of four to cover more ground. A third team will search Pike Place Market and its complex vendor stalls and stairways with the fourth team held in reserve in case backup is required."

GW felt his eyebrows rise. "You got that done in the fifteen minutes you've been here?"

Captain Roberts shrugged. "SWAT teams from around the area train together and support each other regularly. We know each other well and have worked together frequently. We'll get the job done."

"Do you have team member images I can provide to my folks?" GW asked. "They're wired pretty well and have systems that can recognize the good guys if they inadvertently end up in the line of fire."

Captain Roberts swiveled his chair and retrieved a second smaller tablet computer from the work surface behind him. He handed it to GW, then turned to his IT guy. "Mike, send the face and shoulder images of our teams to Investigator Weise."

The technician tossed a "Roger, sir," over his shoulder, then hit a series of keys so fast it was hard to distinguish each tap. Next to him, Captain Roberts noticed GW's surprised expression. "No way I can run a keyboard like that, either. It's the new generation of law enforcement officers. Computers are their lives, almost an extension of their minds and bodies."

"Let's hear an amen for that," GW replied. "What would we do without them?"

"The images should be on the investigator's tablet now," the technician said a few seconds later.

GW scanned the images. He'd been gifted since birth with a talent for retaining facial images and pairing them with names. It wasn't total-recall or eidetic memory; it was simply something he had a knack for. Once he'd scanned all thirty-two images, GW keyed in the access code that connected the tablet with Walter at Joint Base Lewis-McChord. He shipped the images to Walter, who would in turn send them to the Home Team, so they'd have some knowledge of who they were working with. The images were also uploaded to Walter's drones, which possessed rudimentary facial recognition software.

GW removed his SPD headset, donned the one provided by the Home Team, and tapped the earpiece. "Prime, this is Golf," he whispered.

"This is Prime. Go Golf," Paul replied instantly.

"Be advised I just sent the images of the SWAT officers working in the area to Overwatch Second. Thirty-two images total."

"This is Second," Walter replied. "Have the images. Confirm that all team members now have them loaded on their forearm tablets. Also uploaded to the drones. Good to go, Golf."

"Roger all, Second. Golf out." GW replied.

GW settled back into his chair, then with an inspiration, leaned toward the IT tech and said, "Is there any way you can access the security cameras in the area around the passenger terminal, the parking garage, and the condo building next to the garage?"

"Of course," the technician replied. "Authorize the request, Captain?"

Captain Roberts nodded, then said with a grin, "Make it so." He elbowed GW. "I love to say that. I'm a huge fan of *Star Trek* and Captain Picard."

The female technician at the communications desk groaned and cast GW a glance over her shoulder, rolling her eyes. "And we have to live with it."

Captain Roberts chuckled. "Because of recent difficulties in the waterfront area, we have an abundance of cameras there. There are at least a dozen cameras along Alaska Way, the street that runs through the area, from the gift shop at the south end to the condo buildings beyond the passenger terminal."

"Can you give me a visual starting just south of the cruise line terminal, along Alaska Way to the first condo building north of the terminal, and along the east side of the street?"

"I can do that," replied the IT technician. "A composite image of that stretch of road should appear on your SPD screen now. You'll see six views which will rotate from camera to camera every thirty seconds. If you need to switch views or enlarge a single image, just touch that image with your finger."

GW set aside the tablet Captain Roberts gave him a moment ago and glanced at the screen at his workstation's laptop. A half dozen images appeared there in neatly partitioned sectors. As anticipated, the images showed the area was crowded with people walking the waterfront, being dropped off at the cruise ship terminal, and emerging from the parking garages near the location.

"Busy already," GW mumbled.

"Welcome to my world," Captain Roberts said, his eyes once again fixed on the tablet computer in his lap.

GW selected the image of the target parking garage and tapped the screen. The view of the front of the garage expanded to fill the screen. As anticipated, the first three floors of the garage appeared busy with a stream of cars and people coming and going. The building's fourth floor appeared devoid of motion of any kind, even more reason to suspect the terrorists might be located there.

He reduced that image and examined the other five views of the area leading from the passenger terminal to the parking garage and the condo building next door. He zoomed in on the image of the condo, noticing a female SWAT team member approaching the condo building, carrying an assault rifle in her right hand.

GW turned to Captain Roberts. "I thought your teams were clearing the areas above the waterfront. Did you assign an officer to check out one of the condo buildings?"

Captain Roberts called up a display on his workstation laptop and ran a finger down a detailed list of the SWAT team assignments and their current positions. "Nope. What have you got?"

GW gestured to the monitor at his workstation, pointing a thick finger at the female SWAT officer moving up Alaska Way toward the condo. "Here. It looks like a female SWAT team member headed that way, solo."

"I don't have anyone assigned to that area," Captain Roberts replied. "Let me check with my sergeant."

GW zoomed in on the person's face as the officer glanced back over her shoulder. In his mind, he mentally ran through the images provided of the SWAT team members; she matched none of them. He froze the image onscreen and again called over to Captain Roberts. "Call your sergeant if you want, but that face doesn't match any of the SWAT officers you have on the street."

Captain Roberts lifted a small radio to his lips. "Sergeant Wilbert, this is Captain Roberts."

"Wilbert here. What can I do for you, sir?" came a deep-voiced reply. "Did you send one of your team to the condo building we discussed?"

"Negative, sir. We were told to avoid that location, that others would be there. We have no one in that vicinity and no one to spare. Our hands are full clearing the area above the waterfront in the city."

"Thank you, sergeant," Captain Roberts said. Then, to his IT tech, he said, "Give me a count of body-monitors for our team and their locations."

The technician tapped a series of keys on his keyboard. The monitor before him, with the map of the waterfront and search area, blinked with thirty-two flashing green icons. "Everyone's accounted for, sir. Thirty-two LEOs," the tech said, using the abbreviation for Law Enforcement Officer.

"No one up west of the search area, down on Alaska Way, north of the cruise line terminal?" Captain Roberts asked.

"Negative, sir," the technician replied.

"So who is that person?" the captain mumbled. "Did one of the other jurisdictions show up and head there on their own initiative?"

GW shook his head. "No, we have confirmation from each of the teams logging in for this operation."

GW lifted his watch to his lips. "Cap or Empty, this is Golf. Confirm that all team members are positioned at the parking garage, preparing for ingress."

Sam replied in the next second. "This is Empty. Romeo is moving into position at the condo. She should be there now. All else are here at the parking garage, preparing to engage."

GW felt a sinking feeling in the pit of his stomach. The memory of the assassin who'd infiltrated the military base flashed across his mind. Then the report of the man involved in the ambush at Arnold Air Force Base now dead, the assassinated director of the Space Force R&D facility, and the description of the unidentified female officer coming and going from the facility. Could the woman approaching Leah's position be the same woman, disguised as a SWAT team member? GW had long ago given up on coincidences. There had to be a connection; and if so, Leah was right in the middle of it.

He triggered the microphone on his headset. "Empty, this is Golf."

"This is Empty. Go for Golf," Sam replied.

"I think the assassin from the Space Force R&D facility may be onsite and headed for Romeo's position."

Sam paused a beat before replying. "Acknowledged, Golf, but we're about to move on the tangos in the parking garage. Fox is deployed to tackle the suicide bomber. Romeo is monitoring this line and will manage the situation if your suspicions are correct."

GW keyed a message into his tactical watch's text function and sent it to Leah. "Not alone, she won't," he said as he jumped from his chair and charged out the mobile command center's thick back doors, hitting the asphalt at a run.

CHAPTER 37

A moment after GW's message, Sam called into the microphone on his tactical watch, "Romeo, this is Empty. What is your status?"

After five seconds of no response, Sam called again. "Come in, Romeo. Status report?"

Sam and Jessica remained huddled in a small space behind the parking garage's northeast corner stairway door, both with M4A carbine rifles clutched at their chests. The cinderblock walls of the garage were gray and spotted with green, gray, and black algae. "If they actually did remodel this building a year ago, they should have spent more on the outside walls," Jessica whispered, tucking her long braid of ebony hair over her shoulder with one hand.

Sam dropped his watch-hand to his side and said, "I expect we'll find that the owners get their money from a host of different sources, including terrorists, and aren't too worried about the building's aesthetics. What I really want to know is what's happening with Leah. We need her in position to cover us in case any of the tangos make a run for it."

"Roger that," Jessica said.

"This is Fox," Allen said over comms. "I'm on the first floor, ducked behind a pickup. I see two tangos in the southwest corner of the parking garage. One's a frightened looking woman in a thick overcoat. I suspect she's our suicide bomber. The other person is a bearded, thirty-ish man in a windbreaker that does nothing to hide the pistol holstered at his back."

"Roger, Fox," Sam replied. "Waiting for a report from Romeo before we move."

Jessica turned to meet Sam's eyes directly, her expression grave. "She may be having communications issues. We can't wait much longer. We may need to trust that she's in position if we're going to have the element of surprise on our side."

Sam raised his watch to his lips once more. "Prime, this is Empty. Romeo is out of comms, but we need to move now."

"This is Prime," Paul Samuelson replied. "Roger, Empty. Give her another minute, then move on the target."

"Break. Break. This is Overwatch Second," Walter said over comms. "Images from the overhead drone confirm the eight tangos at the northwest corner of the parking garage are gathering next to the wall overlooking the street. They appear animated and ready to take some sort of action. I also confirm Fox's view of the two individuals at the southwest corner of the garage's first floor via one of the mini drones."

"This is Prime. Confirmed, Second," Paul said. "All team members: the tangos appear ready to launch their attack. We can't wait for Romeo. Fox, Empty, and Cap, initiate your assault. We'll have to hope Romeo is in position to support and her comms are just offline."

"Roger that," Sam replied, reaching for the parking garage's stairway door. "We are moving now."

CHAPTER 38

Leah made it to the roof of the condo building with ten minutes to spare before the Home Team was scheduled to kick off their assault of the terrorists in the parking garage. The condo turned out to be a five-story concrete and glass structure. It sat one building north of the terminal and across the street from a dock frequented by small commercial boats offering tours of the Puget Sound and San Juan islands.

On the way in, she'd navigated and cleared all four floors without encountering anyone and wondered why any contractor renovating a high-end building like this would leave it wide open and unsecure. "With the crime rate in this city, you'd think they'd learn, but good for me," she mumbled as she pulled the door open for the building's roof and scanned the area.

Finding no one, Leah made her way to the southwest corner of the roof, the spot that would give her a clear line of sight to the front of the parking garage, the entrance to the cruise line passenger terminal, and the street in between. She smiled as she holstered her pistol and knelt at the waist-high wall at the corner of the building's roof, peering over the edge and down Alaska Way to the cruise ship terminal.

"Now that's what I'm talking about," she murmured. "An absolutely clear line of sight."

Leah set her long, silver rifle case at her feet and flipped the lid open to reveal her M24 sniper rifle. It was an older generation weapon, for sure, but with modifications. The lighter, stronger matte black composite stock and trigger guard were new and made the weapon easier to carry over distances. The new twenty-two-inch barrel with additional rifling increased the number of spins a bullet would make before leaving the barrel, adding accuracy and a more level trajectory. They'd been her ideas, and she was anxious to put her tools to the test.

She affixed a ten-inch aluminum sound suppressor to the front of the rifle's barrel and extended the rifle's bi-pod, settling it on the rooftop's low wall. She snapped the Evander Infinity Scope into place atop the weapon, fired up the scope's heads-up display, laser range finder, wind monitor, and projectile drop function and slapped a fresh eleven-round magazine into place. She was ready.

Once again, she checked her tactical watch and its communications function. She tapped the face of the watch with a thin-gloved finger. Still nothing, and an unbelievably inconvenient time for equipment failure. Her team would be waiting for her to confirm her position and readiness.

She glanced at her forearm tablet computer, thinking that might be a viable alternative to reach her team; but that, too, appeared off-line. Odd, since she'd checked the building's plans on the tablet just before arriving. From experience, she knew things happened to confound the communications equipment all the time. No matter the technology behind it, communications was an imperfect science, with anything from weather to building materials to human error to sabotage throwing a wrench into the best of plans. That said, the one thing she and her team needed to count on, no matter what, was that they would all do their jobs. Right now, that meant she needed to cover the operation going down at the parking garage, communications or no communications.

Leah peered into the rifle's scope, measuring the distance to the front of the parking garage. The scope's heads-up display automatically measured the range to the target and accounted for ambient air humidity, direction and speed of the wind, and the total drop from her position. She mentally locked the numbers into her memory, knowing that the scope would do the same calculations within seconds of her selecting a target when the time came.

She next scanned the street between the parking garage and the passenger terminal, noticing the two massive cruise ships docked side by side along the south side of the building. Beyond the growing crush of people making their way from the area's parking garages to the terminal along Alaska Way, nothing seemed amiss.

She decided to try her watch and tablet one more time. Her forearm tablet computer remained blank, without reception. In frustration, she knocked the edge of her watch against the rooftop's concrete wall. The screen fuzzed, then cleared; and she breathed a sigh of relief as it started working again. About to raise the watch to her lips to speak, she noticed a banner of text scrolling across the watch's small screen. It was from GW. *Your position may be compromised. An unknown female disguised as SWAT is headed your way.*

She raised her watch to her lips. "This is Romeo. I'm in position."

She smiled as Sam's response came over her implant. "This is Empty. Roger, Romeo. You missed the go-call. Moving on the tangos, now."

Eyes still on the street below, Leah was about to reply when she heard the distinctive metallic sound of a bullet being chambered in a pistol, coming from directly behind her. She turned her head to see a blonde, pale woman dressed in black tactical coveralls facing her. The bill of the woman's black baseball hat was pulled low over her eyes; and she held a large caliber semi-automatic pistol in both hands, the barrel aimed at Leah's chest.

CHAPTER 39

Jessica clapped Sam on the shoulder and smiled. "Romeo may be late to the party, but I'm relieved she's there."

Sam pulled the stairway door open and led the way up with Jessica on his heels. They moved silently on soft-soled shoes and reached the door to the fourth floor of the parking garage without encountering another person. Arriving there, Sam paused and tapped a message into the tablet computer on his forearm. *Empty and Cap are at the door on 4.*

A second later, Allen responded with his own text. *Fox. Roger. Ready, here.*

Sam tapped in the next few words, feeling his heart rate drop, his breathing deepening as a decade of special operations training kicked in. *Go! Go!!*

Sam jerked the door to the fourth floor open wide. He and Jessica cleared the door with Sam moving right and Jessica left. They spotted the terrorists instantly, clustered fifteen feet away near the garage's concrete half-wall railing, looking out over Alaska Way. All eight men were dressed in inconspicuous jeans, running shoes, loose sweatshirts, and baseball hats.

With his carbine's stock snug against his shoulder, Sam identified his first target, a man holding an assault rifle who spun at the sound of the stairway door opening. Sam fired twice in rapid succession.

The first bullet took his target in the chest, the second tagging the man in the left shoulder and spinning him around as he fell to the cold, concrete floor.

Feeling rather than seeing Jessica on his left, Sam took only a second to identify his next target. Two of the tangos stood a step away from the half-wall, assault rifles hanging loosely at their sides but rising in their direction. The remaining three terrorists held LAW rocket-launcher tubes, surprise on their faces as Jessica and Sam interrupted some sort of discussion. Sam heard Jessica's rifle crack twice, then twice again. Before he could trigger his shots, the two terrorists with the rifles crumpled to the ground, their rifles clattering onto the concrete floor.

Sam smiled grimly. Taking a life, no matter the circumstances, was a horrible thing; but when the odds were against you and the lives of countless innocent people were on the line, it was good to know someone like Jessica had your back. She would do what was required without hesitation.

Weapons still up, Jessica and Sam advanced on the remaining three terrorists with slow, deliberate steps. All three men pulled small pistols from holsters at their backs. As the first man's pistol came around, Sam squeezed his trigger once. The man flinched as if stung in his right shoulder, then twisted left at the waist as Sam's second bullet took him high in the chest, sending the man sprawling. The man twitched once as Sam kept his aim fixed on the downed terrorist, then lay still.

Sam didn't bother tracking Jessica's next shot. The woman simply never missed. Shifting his aim left, he found a second man, a rocket tube at his feet and pistol aimed dead-center at Sam's chest. The barrel of the man's pistol spouted flame, the sound cracking hard against his ears as Sam squeezed his own trigger. Sam's aim was ruined as the terrorist's bullet slammed into Sam's chest, feeling like someone hit him with a hammer. His shot went high and wide as Sam's body armor absorbed most of the impact. He staggered back a step. Gritting his teeth and planting his feet firmly under him, Sam pulled the trigger once more. Sam's rifle cracked and bucked against his shoulder as the second bullet took the man through the nose but not before he heard a soft grunt from Jessica's direction. As the terrorist staggered back, his pistol dropped from limp hands as he wobbled on his feet, then toppled over backward to lay still on the ground.

Sam spun left, hearing two shots from Jessica's rifle crack through the air and seeing a terrorist on his periphery drop to a crouch, avoiding the bullets. The terrorist raised his pistol and fired. Jessica gasped as the man's shot slammed into her body armor, low on her left side. Knowing Jessica had been hit but not how hard, Sam swung his carbine's barrel toward the man and pulled off three rapid-fire shots. The man jerked left, then right, then right again as Sam's shots put the terrorist down.

"You hit?" Sam yelled.

In response, Jessica pulled off two more shots as the last terrorist ducked low, grabbed his LAW rocket launcher, and made a run for the stairwell door. The man held his pistol over his left shoulder; aiming behind him, he ran and triggered it as fast as he could. Both Sam and Jessica ducked low to avoid being hit by the random shots, then raised their rifles to find the man gone, the thick metal door to the parking garage's stairs clanging shut behind him.

Sam climbed to his feet and was beside Jessica in an instant, where she kneeled, her carbine clutched to her chest.

"You hurt?"

Jessica shrugged. "Four shots to the body armor. Felt like a jack hammer," she said between pained gasps. "Lost my wind. Tried to get him before he made the door, but my aim was off."

"But you're not injured badly?"

"You got hit the same as I did," she replied, her face a wrinkled mask of pain. "You tell me."

Sam chuckled, hearing the frustration in Jessica's voice. "Hurts like crazy. We'll both be bruised and sore for days. But at least we're alive. We need to get after that guy."

He held out a hand to help her to her feet, but Jessica swatted it away and climbed to her feet. "Let's go get him."

Sam raised his watch to his lips. "Prime, this is Empty."

"Go, Empty," Paul replied.

"We dropped seven tangos, but one escaped down the stairwell. Pursuing."

"Pursue, but be advised the crowd is thick on the street, and the sound of the gunfire from your location has panicked them. People are running in all directions to find safety. Tackle the remaining terrorist yourselves only if Romeo is unable to do the job. She can act surgically. You and Cap are likely to panic the crowd even more if you have to fire on him."

Then, to Walter, Paul said, "Second, do you have visual from the drones overhead?"

"Roger, Prime," Walter said. "I have the one tango leaving the building and turning left. Your target is carrying a rocket launcher and winding his way through the thick crowd. It appears he's looking for a clear firing position on the terminal."

Allen came over comms then. "Break. Break. This is Fox. I have secured the suicide bomber at my end. Her controller is down. It turned out the suicide bomber wasn't all that keen on the idea of martyrdom. Her explosive vest is secure."

"This is Cap. Good news, Fox," Jessica mumbled as she led the way to the stairway door and down the parking garage's stairs. "We are in pursuit of the squirter."

"Romeo, this is Prime," Paul said. "We need coverage now! One tango confirmed on the street, with a missile launcher. Empty. Cap. This is Prime. I repeat, Romeo is to take the shot if possible."

"Roger, Prime. Will hold waiting Romeo's action," Sam said, his breath coming in heavy gasps as he and Jessica pounded their way down the stairs, the bruises from the shots he took in his body armor stabbing his ribs like a knife.

"This is Second," Walter replied. "The people on the street are disbursing, and the area in front of the terminal is clearing slightly."

"Not good," Jessica mumbled. "The tango may get his shot away before we reach him. Can you get a visual of Romeo's position? See if she's okay?"

"I can do that, Cap," Walter said. "Redirecting two of the mini drones."

"Not good at all," Sam replied as he slammed through the door to the ground floor and they charged into the street. "We may be too late."

CHAPTER 40

"If that's a microphone on that watch, I suggest you think again." The voice was low-pitched, softly feminine, and coming from behind.

Leah rose and turned slowly to face a woman in black tactical coverall and baseball hat with the letters SWAT embossed across the front. She was petite, nearly eye to eye with Leah, with pale blonde hair and a mouth like a thin-lipped slit. Her face was narrow, with high cheekbones and cold, glass-like pale blue eyes shadowed by the bill of her hat. She held a large, silenced mat-black pistol in both hands, its barrel pointed at Leah's chest.

"Not a problem," Leah replied, dropping her hands to her sides.

"And don't think about drawing the 9mm in that drop holster at your hip. No one is that fast."

Leah frowned. "Who are you?" Leah asked, forcing down the urge to take her chances and rush the woman; but knowing every second she remained alive was another moment when something might happen to change the game, change who had the drop on whom.

"Just a businesswoman," she replied. "Here on a job."

"And I'm the job?"

The woman nodded, her face expressionless, her eyes empty and devoid of emotion. "You and the rest of your team."

It clicked then, in Leah's mind. This was the assassin responsible for at least two deaths: the Space Force R&D director and the man found at the Nashville airport, who'd participated in the ambush. "You're the one who took out the director of the R&D facility?"

The woman nodded; her eyes locked on Leah's. "A simple enough job."

"And you killed the guy they found at the Nashville airport?"

"My client seems to be tying up loose ends for whatever he's up to."

"You mean, you don't know what he's doing? You're just killing people he tells you to kill?"

The blonde woman's face split into the faintest of grins. "It's just business; and no, I am not aware of what he's up to. I don't really care. What I do care about is finishing you and your friends. It's what I do. I don't suppose you'll tell me where they are and make this easy for me?"

Leah snorted. "Not a chance, but I can fill you in about what you're involved with by association."

The woman pushed the baseball hat back on her head and glanced at her watch. She seemed to consider Leah's words, then said, "I've got some time. So, enlighten me. Based on what you tell me, I may well raise his rates."

"Your client has terrorists with shoulder-mounted rockets in a parking garage a block from here, across from the cruise terminal. There's a suicide bomber with them. They're part of a conspiracy to blow up the terminal and the people in it, along with targets in other cities across the country. Thousands of innocent people are going to die here and at five other locations. And that was supposed to be preceded by sixty active shooters hitting soft targets in as many cities across the country. We think the active shooters will be stopped—or have been stopped, for the most part. My friends and I are here to stop the attack on the cruise terminal, which is going down as we speak."

Leah noticed the woman's expression changed subtly, her forehead beneath the baseball hat's brim wrinkle with soft lines. "That is dark, but I'm not part of any of that. I've never killed anyone who didn't deserve it. And regardless, I have my contracts; and I focus on my own business."

"Didn't deserve it? That's a laugh," Leah said. "You are part of it, whether you admit it or not. Your job is to keep me and my team from stopping the attack on the passenger terminal. If you do that, thousands may die; and that will be on you. You'll be just as guilty as the terrorists, and there will be nowhere you can hide after that."

It seemed like the woman was about to speak but then reconsidered. Finally, through clamped teeth, she said, "Just tell me where your team is."

"If I tell you, you'll kill me. I don't tell you, and you kill me. So no, that's not happening."

The woman shrugged. "I can make it quick, or I can make it painful. Your choice."

Leah shrugged. "I've heard that one before, and I'm still here. I know God has my back. You send me from this place, and I'll be home with Him. I've been feeling homesick for Him for too long as it is; so it's a win-win for me, no matter how this goes. What about you? You think He has your back?"

The barrel of the pistol wavered ever so slightly, the woman's expression suggesting Leah's words might have struck home. And that moment of hesitation was all Leah needed. She lunged forward, her hand sweeping to her thigh, drawing and triggering her pistol in one smooth, swift motion. As Leah's pistol bucked in her hands, the assassin took a step back and fired her own pistol.

Leah's bullet pounded into the woman's shoulder, spinning the assassin to the right. In the same instant, the assassin's bullet hammered Leah with a crushing blow to the sternum. The impact knocked Leah back against the roof's low wall as the Kevlar-composite fibers of her Very Thin Ballistic Vest absorbed the impact and spread it across her chest, around her sides and down her back. While the vest saved her life, the impact knocked the air from Leah's lungs and left her gasping.

The assassin shifted her pistol to her left hand, righted herself, and charged, her pistol's sights rising into line with Leah's face. Leaning against the low roof wall, Leah forced her breathing to calm, taking small breaths to counter the effects of the blow to her chest. Her legs wobbly, she planted her feet and stepped forward into the woman's charge.

As the assassin closed, her finger tightening on her pistol's trigger, Leah slapped the assassin's pistol aside with her right hand, then shot a weak left fist toward the woman's face. The assassin ducked the punch, then swung her pistol back up and around, crashing it into the side of Leah's head. Leah rocked to her right under the impact, seeing stars streak across her vision, and dropped back to lean against the knee-wall behind her. That's when she heard over her implant, "Romeo, this is Empty. Seven tangos are down. One's headed for the street. He has a LAW rocket. We need you to take him, now."

Leah held up her hands in surrender as the assassin closed on her once more.

"You ready to talk now?" the woman said.

Leah grimaced at the pain in the side of her head and her sore chest, then pointed to her left ear. "Comms implant. I just heard from my team. One terrorist has escaped and is on the street below us with a LAW. His target is the cruise terminal across the street. The rest of my team took out seven of his friends and is counting on me to take that man down before he sends that missile into a crowd of people. A lot of people are going to die if I don't do that. Look, I can't beat you in this fight, but I need to take them down before..."

Leah felt her head swim as her words trailed off and her vision began to fade. The strike to her head must have been worse than she thought. Through fuzzy vision, Leah watched the blonde assassin holster her pistol, cast Leah a puzzled look, and then shake her head once and blow out a long breath.

"I've failed," Leah mumbled. "They're all going to die. So many people . . . "

Helpless to do anything more than watch through what seemed like a dense fog, Leah heard a soft buzzing sound from behind her and then a voice behind her ear crying out, 'Leah. Leah. Are you there? Please be okay. Leah!'

"Now, I'm hearing voices?" she mumbled as she saw the assassin pick up her M24 sniper rifle, check the rifle's bipod stand, then check for a round in the chamber and lean it back onto the edge of the roof's low wall. "It's already sighted," Leah mumbled, her words slurred, her hand reaching slowly for the small pistol-shaped dart gun on her left side as the woman focused her attention on the rifle.

As Leah watched, the assassin leaned into the rifle's scope as she aimed at the street below the condo. She appeared to search the street through the rifle's scope, then came to rest on a specific spot, let out a soft breath, and pulled the trigger. Without pausing, she pulled back the sniper rifle's bolt, ejecting the spent shell and inserting another into the chamber. She pulled the trigger once more, then swiveled around to face Leah. "There. You don't have to worry . . . " she started, then noticed Leah sitting with the dart gun held in her direction with shaky hands. "A dart?" she asked.

Leah shrugged.

"But I took out the terrorist," the assassin said.

Leah shrugged again and squeezed the dart gun's trigger. A tiny wooden dart struck the assassin in the neck, just under her chin. The woman's eyes crinkled, like she was about to laugh at the irony of being taken down by a simple dart. But before she could form any words, she crumpled to the ground. A moment later, a tiny flare of flame and a puff of smoke replaced the remains of the wooden dart where it penetrated her skin, leaving only a small bruise and a burn mark the size of a pin head.

"Thanks for the help, but you murdered those other people," Leah whispered, her vision still fogged but slowly clearing. "You have to answer for that."

Leah climbed slowly, unsteadily to her feet, then waved at the tiny drone hovering behind her, beyond the roof's wall. She made her way slowly to where the assassin lay and collected the woman's pistol. As she did that, the roof's access door clanged open. Leah turned slowly in that direction to see GW charge through the door, his pistol up, eyes searching for a target.

Their eyes met; and he slowed, casting Leah a knowing smile. "I should have known you'd have this handled."

Leah chuckled. "Not totally."

GW was immediately at her side. "You're hurt?"

Leah gestured toward the side of her head. "She clubbed me pretty good—"

But he cut off her words as he wrapped Leah in his arms. "I don't know what I would have done if you'd been . . . " He paused.

Leah placed a hand against his chest and pushed him back a foot, looking up to meet his eyes. "I'll be fine. Just a little sore. And you would be just fine if anything happened to me."

GW's eyebrows knit together as he glared down at her. "You know what I mean."

She started to protest; but in the next instant, his lips were crushing hers.

At first, Leah was shocked. *Did not see that coming,* she thought, then found herself warming as the kiss lingered, and then, a few minutes later, disappointed as GW gently pulled back.

"Hmm," Leah murmured. "This is not normal covert operator behavior," she said, her gaze once again locked on GW's eyes.

"You're no normal covert operator," GW said, his smile wide, his eyes bright.

She pushed GW back another step, with more force this time. "The rest of the team?"

"All safe. I don't know about the terrorist who got away."

Just then, Jessica called in over comms. "This is Cap. Nice shooting, Romeo. The terrorist is down. No one in the crowd was injured. Most are simply videotaping the scene on their phones. Go figure."

Leah raised her watch to her lips. "This is Romeo. Roger all. Will be ready for exfil in a few."

"This is Prime," Paul said. "What's your status, Romeo?"

"This is Romeo," Leah replied. "I have a tango at my site. I believe she's the assassin who killed Dr. Jones at Arnold Air Force Base. Tagged her with a dart after she knocked me around pretty good. Will cuff her and stand by for assistance."

"Roger, Romeo," Paul replied. "Do you need medical assistance?"

"Negative, Prime," Leah replied, glancing at GW. "I think I've been helped enough to get by."

GW smiled, as Paul said, "Is Golf Whiskey with you?"

"Roger, Prime," Leah said.

"Have Golf stay with the tango. We will have the SPD SWAT team take custody of your prisoner. And nice going capturing her. As per normal, I need you all out of the area as quietly and quickly as possible. Your ride will be waiting at the entrance to the Pike Place Market."

"Roger all," Leah replied. "Romeo, out."

Jessica, Allen, and Sam repeated the "roger all" exfil confirmation.

Leah returned her rifle to its case and slowly headed for the door leading from the roof, leaving GW to cuff the assassin. Halfway there, she turned back and called out, "See you around?"

GW slid thick flexi-cuffs in place on the unconscious woman's wrists and ankles, then glanced up and grinned in reply. "Just try and keep me away."

Leah smiled, raised a weary hand in reply, and headed for the stairs.

CHAPTER 41

With a small backpack his only baggage, The Hatchet stood at the front doors of the Edgewater Hotel, awaiting the shuttle to the airport. The weather had turned unseasonably warm, and he regretted adding the thin padding to his tan blazer and brown slacks as part of his disguise. He could feel trails of sweat creeping down his sides and back as the twenty-passenger van pulled up to the curb and he climbed aboard.

He took a seat halfway toward the back of the van, thinking he might be the only passenger until a thin, older man with a craggy face and wispy brown hair climbed aboard. He was followed by a young, fit-looking woman of diminutive size, with a thick auburn braid running down her back from beneath a Seattle Seahawks cap, wearing stylish brown slacks and a flowered tan and gold blouse that hung loose at the waist. The older man took a seat at the front of the van, next to the driver. The woman moved to the very back as the driver, a tall, muscular man in his early thirties, put the van into gear and pulled away from the hotel.

They hadn't gone far before The Hatchet noticed the van turning toward downtown Seattle, rather than to Interstate 5 and the airport. "Driver? Driver?" The Hatchet called. "Why are you diverting from the route to the airport?"

The older man at the front of the van turned around, raising a large, silver 1911 .45 caliber pistol above the back of his seat. "My name is Paul Samuelson, and our route is no diversion, Dr. Muhammad."

The Hatchet reached for a snub-nosed .38 caliber pistol at his waist, but the tiny woman at the back of the van was on him in a second. One small, inordinately strong hand clamped down on his right arm, while her other arm snaked around his neck, squeezing tight and cutting off his breath.

"Slowly reach across with your left hand and remove the pistol from the holster at your waist. Use your thumb and forefinger," she said in a soft, decidedly feminine voice. "Be very careful and hand it to me gently."

With no other recourse, The Hatchet handed the woman his pistol as directed. When she removed her arm from around his neck, he shrugged and drew in a deep breath. "Who are you? And by what right . . ."

Paul answered his question, his pistol rock steady and pointed at The Hatchet's chest. "I work for the government; and you are under arrest for treason, numerous counts of conspiracy to commit murder, multiple counts of domestic terrorism, and too many other crimes for me to list. I'll leave that to Homeland Security and the Federal Bureau of Investigation once you're in their custody."

"You've made a grievous mistake," The Hatchet said. "I am a renowned psychologist. I work closely with law enforcement across the country."

The tiny woman shifted to the seat directly across the aisle from The Hatchet, also holding a pistol aimed his way. Her startling blue eyes held an intensity The Hatchet found oddly unsettling.

"Renowned, without a doubt," she said. "Do you remember me? I was referred to you for help, but you were too busy. Now, we all know why you were so busy."

"I have no idea what . . . " The Hatchet started but stopped when he considered Paul's expression.

"We captured the assassin who worked for you," Paul said. "In exchange for leniency, she revealed to us a way to track you and your conspirators. Seems like the nano-tracker chemical you treated your warehouse doors with that she used to track my team also rubbed off on you. We used that and the signal it emitted to track you here. A few minutes ago, my friends received an electronic warrant to search your computer files. One of your past employees is cooperating with us. He used a back door into your system to check your files and your email, which led to the identities of your three co-conspirators."

Paul made a show of glancing at the watch on his left hand. "All three should be in custody right about now."

The Hatchet let out a long sigh. First, no reports about any of the active shooter attacks or phase two attacks appeared on the news. Now this. He forced his posture more upright, his chin jutting out as he said, "You may think this is done, but it is not. The people I work for have other plans."

Paul's expression shifted from determined but tired to angry. "No, we used your phone logs and email history to track down the final character in all this. I believe you refer to him as the Chairman: Harley Maestro, the brilliant scientist and owner of ThirdEye.com. Analysts at Homeland Security traced deposits from his company, through fictitious fronts, including charitable organizations and others, to you. If you think he has more plans, I guarantee you that he will be unable to execute them from where he'll be spending the rest of his life."

The van pulled into a parking lot next to the federal building in downtown Seattle a few moments later. A man and a woman in dark suits entered the vehicle, handcuffed The Hatchet, aka Dr. Albert Muhammad, and unceremoniously escorted him out through the van's wide door.

GW turned to Paul and Leah from the van's driver's seat and glanced at the large-faced tactical watch on his wrist. "We have just enough time to make it to Tugboat Annie's Restaurant if we hurry. I've heard so much about the place, and I am starving."

When Paul and Leah gave him a questioning glance, GW shrugged. "This has been a very busy week."

EPILOGUE

Jessica, Allen, Sam, and Becca were waiting when Paul, Leah, and GW climbed the wide steps of a water-side restaurant in Olympia, known as Tugboat Annie's. When Jessica waved them to a long table against the restaurant's far wall, Leah paused, taking in the scene. These were her people, her friends and family. She knew that would continue now, regardless of how their lives might change over time.

Paul stepped around her while GW remained at her side; and she paused to gaze around the place, with its crowded tables and tall windows looking over the silver waters of Puget Sound. The old-world Irish charm of the place warmed Leah's heart as she took in the rich wood trim, canoes and row boats hanging from the ceiling, along with draped fishing nets, posters, maps and other boating paraphernalia and recalled the great times she and the rest of the Home Team spent in this place.

This might not be home in the true sense; but it certainly felt like it with her team, and now GW, and the One Who made anywhere home for those who love and worship Him. And she was one of those people.

And then there was Becca, she thought, as their eyes met from across the room. The girl's expression was hopeful, tentative and worried, all in the same moment. Home was something Becca lacked, as well. That made Leah think about Rachael Mae and growing up together after they had lost their mom. Leah knew what she had to do.

GW wrapped a warm arm around Leah's waist and eased her toward the table. As he did, the wounds across her abdomen and shoulders stung just enough to let her know they hadn't fully healed. She ignored the pain as she reached one arm around GW's waist and hugged him close as they walked.

"Hey, little sister," Allen called as she and GW dropped into chairs, shoulders touching.

Jessica and Sam each raised a weary hand in salute as GW took Leah's hand in his beneath the table. Leah cast GW a quick smile that didn't go unnoticed by Jessica, who gave Leah a teasing elbow in the ribs from the chair next to hers.

"About time," Jessica whispered.

Paul eased onto a chair at the head of the table and raised his hand for silence. "Before we get started on a much needed, much deserved celebratory meal, let me wrap a few things up for you. The Hatchet and his three cronies are in custody. All, I repeat, all of the active shooter attacks were shut down by local police in the sixty target cities. Our teams from the Extreme Operations Group, including you all, stopped all of the phase-two missile attacks."

Allen let out a whoop that was repeated around the table, drawing curious looks from others in the crowded restaurant.

Paul continued once the noise subsided, lifting a glass of ice water in salute. "Your country is grateful. And to you, GW, a special thanks. You could have stayed in Tennessee; but you joined us, traveled across the country, and played a big part in this success. The Secretary of State has already sent a letter to your sheriff commending your actions."

Another round of applause, quieter this time, followed before Paul continued. "And finally, all of you will be taking a much-needed break. Four weeks of paid leave. No discussion."

Paul turned his eyes to Leah, with a quieter voice. "I have some news for you. Those two little girls at the store in Tullahoma?"

"Sir?" Leah replied.

"It was touch and go for several days, but the Coffee County sheriff advised me this morning that they are both expected to recover from their wounds."

"Thank you, Lord. What a gift!" Leah said, her eyes heavenward. Then, she shifted her gaze to Becca. "I'd like to offer you a home with me while you finish school—if you still want that, of course."

Becca jumped from her chair, jogged around the table, and threw her arms around Leah. "Thank you. Thank you. Thank you."

Leah eased Becca back to arm's distance. "There will be rules, of course."

Becca groaned, even as she flashed Leah a bright smile. "Of course. And I will comply to the best of my ability." Becca turned to face the others seated around the table. "I have a home!"

Another round of applause followed as Becca retook her place at the table. "Now, let's eat." Paul said over the noise. "And after that, the Gulfstream is standing by to take Leah and GW back to Tennessee whenever you're ready."

Leah turned to GW. "We'll go together."

"I'd like that," GW replied, then nodded toward Becca.

Leah took his meaning at once and turned to Becca across the table. "How about you? Want to come along? Since you're now a part of the family, I'm sure there'll be a place for you at my sister's home."

Becca nodded as her eyes glistened. "I'd love that. My home is wherever you are."

Leah glanced around the table, then said, "'By wisdom a house is built, and through understanding it is established; through knowledge its rooms are filled with rare and beautiful treasures.'"[5]

"Proverbs 24:3-4," Allen said. "Good choice."

Beside Leah, Jessica leaned close and whispered, "Amen to that, sister. With Him and all of us beside you, you don't ever need to feel homesick again."

THE END

---

5   Proverbs 24: 3-4.

COMING SOON . . .

FINDING HOME

The rain poured down in sheets, soaking through Allen's thin black tactical shirt and cargo pants as he hunkered down on the cold gravel, his back against a low, crumbling concrete retaining wall. The barrier was hardly tall enough to conceal his head and shoulders from the six gunmen in the squat, white stucco building ten yards behind his position. The red tile-roofed house sat in a tiny enclave of similar buildings surrounding a small, cobbled plaza in the tiny town of Tuxpan, Mexico, a few hours east of Puerta Vallarta, a popular tourist destination. Normally occupied by a husband and wife working for a Christian non-governmental organization, or NGO, today, the little house held five hostages and the cartel thugs.

And another bomb.

There is always another bomb, Allen thought.

With knees pulled close to his chest, Allen cradled his short-barreled M4A7B carbine rifle across his lap, his mind a mixture of frustration at being stuck in this rain while the higher-ups in his chain of command debated his team's next move and his bleak thoughts about his own life. Rivulets of cold rain ran down the back of his neck, soaking his undershirt and sinking his mood further into the conflict between doing nothing when so much was at stake and his own need to be away, to create distance from this perilous situation and his own crumbling future. He reached down and wiped the wet gloss off soft-soled desert boots that felt like soggy sponges kept too long under a kitchen faucet.

Are You there, God?

While he knew the answer to the question from a lifetime of faith, current circumstances had led him to wonder. Everything today seemed so wrong.

"Would someone please turn off the faucet?" Allen finally mumbled, trying vainly to raise his own mood with the weak humor. "Enough is enough."

Leah McCarthy sat two feet to his right, crouched down in a similar position, and glanced his way as she wiped the water off her own rifle with a soggy scrap of cloth. The diminutive special operator, team sniper, and tough-as-nails jiu-jitsu master flashed startlingly blue eyes his way as he met her glance. "When the four of us signed onto the Home Team, the EOG never promised sunny weather," she said.

The acronym Leah used referred to their parent organization, the Extreme Operations Group. As part of that organization, Allen, Leah, and their other two teammates constituted the Home Team, a forward operational element that reported to the U.S. Secretary of State. Their role as an elite covert operations team found them deployed around the world and across the U.S. to combat those who threatened their country or its allies.

"Besides, I love this stuff, and so do you. So quit the moaning and groaning I keep hearing from you," Leah added.

Allen let out a long sigh.

As if reading his dark thoughts, Leah wiped a dripping strand of red-bronze hair from her deeply tanned face and tucked it under a black baseball hat worn backward. "Then, again, it would be a bit more convenient if the bad guys hadn't chosen such horrible weather for this operation."

The other two members of the Home Team, Jessica Falcone and Sam Anthem, were ranged further to Leah's right, both sitting in similar positions with their backs to the low plaza wall.

"No one said criminals were smart, Romeo," Sam replied.

Leah's formal call sign was Romeo Alpha. She hated the informal moniker. Allen smiled as Leah growled her usual response to Sam's use of her call sign's abbreviated form. "It is not an appropriate call name for a female operator. I really need to change it."

Sam Anthem, call sign Mike Tango—or Empty for short—chuckled but kept his gaze forward. Allen's virtual twin at five ten, with a finely-tuned athletic stature and highly trained physical abilities, Sam served as the Home Team's unofficial leader and empty hand-fighting expert. Unlike Allen, with his paler complexion and shoulder-length blond hair pulled into a short ponytail at his back, Sam was darker-skinned with short-cropped black hair covered by his own dripping tactical baseball hat, bill forward.

Allen grumbled deep in his throat. He and his teammates were like a family in so many ways—siblings who comforted, teased, cajoled, and relied on each other often for their very lives. Normally, their presence and sarcastic humor comforted him, calmed his thoughts. On most days, he found a form of solace in the challenging, often dangerous missions he and his team were assigned. With so much on the line with each deployment and their success rate as a group, he normally found a deep sense of pride and affiliation with the elite membership of the Home Team. But today? Not so much.

In this instance, their mission was to rescue the U.S. Ambassador to Mexico's daughter and son, along with two other children and their nanny. All five were held in the tiny, red-roofed, stucco building not thirty feet away, with a bomb and a ransom demand due to expire within the hour.

Allen leaned forward, glancing around Leah to where Sam sat, just as Sam raised a large-faced black tactical watch to his lips and spoke into the device's embedded microphone. The words came out clearly across the communications implant each team member had behind their left ear.

"I just received an encrypted text from Director Samuelson," Sam whispered, wiping the water from his face with the back of a dripping gloved hand. "Paul says we need to wait a while more before we take the building. The ambassador wants more time to negotiate with the captors."

"You've got to be kidding," Jessica replied.

Call sign Charlier Papa, or Cap for short, Jessica crouched between Leah and Sam. Tall, angular, and beautiful, Jessica Falcone served as the team's political and technological resource. As the talented, accomplished, mixed martial artist turned to face Sam, water poured down the thick ebony braid that hung down her slender back from beneath her tactical baseball hat.

"During her recon of the house, Leah confirmed the table with the bomb under it, the four kids sitting on the table and the nanny standing close by. She also ID'd the six cartel thugs. She did that hours ago, with the bomb's timer clearly visible and time running out. We don't have long before this situation goes from bad to worse and the hostages die. We need to move on the place now."

Allen felt his tactical watch vibrate on his right wrist. He frowned as he raised it to eye level and wiped the water from its screen. It was a text from Mallory, his fiancée and Drug Enforcement Administration agent, currently completing a DEA-sponsored doctorate at Baylor University in Waco, Texas. He was supposed to be with her there right now. He let out a long breath as the words and his worst fears materialized across the watch's tiny screen.

"Where are you? Of course, you can't tell me. That is three times in two months you have let me down. I carved time out of my research just for us and now this . . . again. When you were headquartered out of Florida and I worked in D.C., before your team's move to Washington State, we at least had our weekends together. Now, it's like we don't exist for each other at all. Your work is important, I know, but this isn't working. Don't bother calling me when you get done with whatever you are doing. We need a break, and I need to think all this—and us—over."

Leah glanced over at him, searching his face with her eyes. "What's that all about? You look like you just lost your best friend," she said.

Allen swallowed as a sharp pain cut through his heart. "We need to finish this, and I need to get out of here, now."

How many times had his life been turned upside down by one priority mission after another somewhere in the world? He never complained, always leaned into the greater need of the team. And now he had just lost the woman he planned to spend the rest of his life with, whom he had known and loved since they were kids.

Allen leaned forward and poked an angry finger in Sam's direction. "We need to finish this. Jessica said it: we should have moved on the house hours ago. If the bosses in D.C. and Florida can't make up their minds, I'll do it for them."

Leah clutched at Allen's arm with small, strong fingers. "Don't do it, man. The bosses have spoken, and the director has never let us down. We need to follow his lead."

"Not this time," Allen replied. "He doesn't have any idea what's on the line for those people in that building—or me—while the talking heads fiddle with their politics."

Sam's voice came over Allen's cochlear implant. "We need to wait, Fox," Sam said, using the familiar form of Allen's own call sign: Foxtrot Tango. "Paul knows what he's doing."

"Nuts to that," Allen growled. "You all stay here, while those kids are put at risk and my life falls apart. I am going in. Then I am gone."

"Hold, Fox," Sam replied, leaning across Jessica as he spoke. "Stay with the plan."

"I'm tired, Empty," Allen replied. "I have had enough of politicians trying to figure out whether they want those kids to live. No kid's dying today if I can prevent it. I'm going in there with or without you all. I am the team's explosive expert. I'm going to take out the thugs in that building, then defuse that bomb and save those kids. And then I'm going home."

Allen saw how Sam drew back against the wall as Allen let the words fly and almost regretted saying them. On a mission years ago, a little girl had died when Sam's mission went sideways. Sam had not been to blame, but Allen knew his teammate carried the pain of her death with him wherever he went.

Even so, Allen's frustration with the politicians was so high, his own anxiety so burning inside his heart, he figured he had little to lose. And those kids had everything to lose. If the EOG director dropped him from the team for saving those kids, he could live with that.

Allen met Sam's glare directly, his expression intense, fierce. Finally, Sam shrugged ever so slightly and raised his watch to his lips. When he spoke into its microphone, he directed the call to the EOG headquarters, where the mission was being monitored by Director Samuelson and his overwatch team. "Overwatch, this is Mike Tango. We are status three and engaging now."

In Home Team parlance, a status of one meant the team was in position. Two meant the team was ready to move. Three meant they were engaging the target. Apparently, they were about to engage as a team. Not just Allen on his own.

Allen nodded grimly as Paul's voice came over his communications implant, his words clipped, to the point. "This is Overwatch. Hold your position as directed."

Allen rubbed at his leg muscles, then gathered his feet beneath him. He smiled again as her heard Sam's reply. "We have a situation on the ground that demands we act now. I repeat, we are status three and moving on the target."

"You have been ordered to hold your position by the ambassador," Paul replied once again.

"We can't do that," Sam replied, gathering his feet beneath him as Leah and Jessica did the same.

Allen would later recall hearing the director's deep sigh as he realized that the Home Team was going to move on the target regardless of anything he might say. After a short pause, Paul replied, "Godspeed."

"Roger that," Sam replied. "Empty, out."

Allen said a soft prayer under his breath. *God, please guide me and my team. I may not be able to do much about my future with the woman I love—I may have doubted Your presence—but those kids need us.*

Allen turned, staying low, then placed one hand atop the low plaza wall and vaulted over. He hit the ground, carbine barrel forward, feet churning the broken concrete and gravel of the weathered plaza floor. He didn't need to glance to either side to know that Sam, Leah, and Jessica were on his heels.

ABOUT THE AUTHOR

David Pratt is a native of most of the U.S. west coast, from Bakersfield, California to Anchorage, Alaska. A retired U.S. Army officer and private sector project manager consultant, he is based in Olympia, Washington, and spends the majority of his time living and wandering the Pacific Northwest with his wife and family. Mr. Pratt has wide and varied publication credits, including magazine articles and short stories in a variety of regional and national magazines and journals, and six fiction and nonfiction books. His guiding light in life is Our Lord Jesus Christ, and his focus is glorifying God in all he does. He considers his wife, family, and friends as some of God's greatest blessings in his life.

For more information about
Dave Pratt
and
Homesick
please visit:

www.daveprattbooks.com
www.facebook.com/DavidPrattBooks

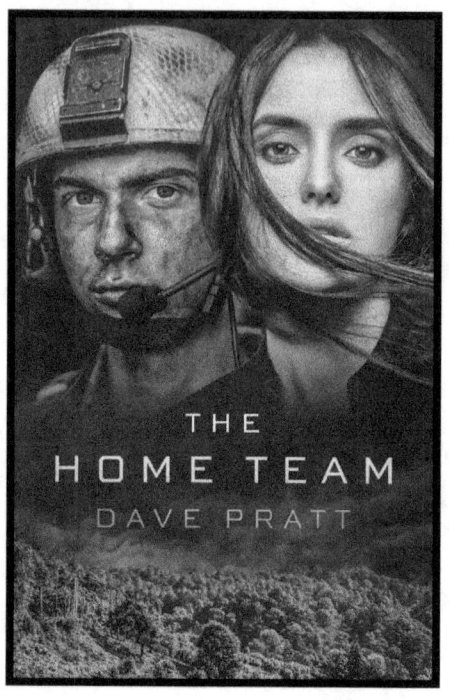

S am Anthem has always been a team player, leading his Home Team on secret missions around the world. When he is forced on a vacation, he is introduced to a former covert ops soldier-turned pastor. But the vacation takes a turn when the Home Team comes under attack. As the team fights to stay alive against an unknown adversary, Sam begins to wonder if there is more to life than just the job. With his life on the line, Sam must decide between the job or his newfound faith and possible love.

After a successful mission for the Home Team, the government is ready to create a Home Team 2 to help thwart human and drug trafficking. But finding recruits who can handle the assignment is not so easy. And the measures that the Lees will take to protect their investments puts everyone on the team at risk. When Washington State Patrol Trooper Ellen "Ell" Evander is reassigned to spend time with the Home Team, motivation to find her kidnapped niece clouds her judgment and spurs her on a mission that may end her career. Army Ranger Alex Anthem soon finds himself side by side with the attractive state patrol trooper. As the pressure mounts, Ell and Alex both have decisions to make that could change the courses of their lives forever.

Ambassador International's mission is to magnify the Lord Jesus Christ and promote His Gospel through the written word.

We believe through the publication of Christian literature, Jesus Christ and His Word will be exalted, believers will be strengthened in their walk with Him, and the lost will be directed to Jesus Christ as the only way of salvation.

For more information about
AMBASSADOR INTERNATIONAL
please visit:

www.ambassador-international.com

Thank you for reading this book. Please consider leaving us a review on your social media, favorite retailer's website, Goodreads or Bookbub, or our website.

Rob Wilkinson finds himself traveling alone on the second anniversary of his wife's untimely death. But through a couple of seeming coincidences, he meets and befriends Gabby, a young woman from Germany dealing with heartaches of her own. As their relationship deepens, Rob must draw on his recently-tested faith to help Gabby overcome her own lapsed faith in God and find a new life beyond her pain.

Nine-year-old Dana Foster will follow her older brother, Luke, wherever he goes. But when tragedy strikes the Foster family, everything that Dana has ever known is suddenly turned upside down. In this coming-of-age story, discover the truths of God's grace in suffering, the blessing of forgiveness, and how to hold on to your faith when all hope seems lost.

David al-Nassery is a man of renown. Hailing from distant Chaldea, he has made a name for himself in the United Kingdom as a philanthropist and an advocate for the political interests of the Middle East. Yet even as he surrounds himself with allies, enemies from his past await him. When confronted by a figure from his past on a cold, dark night, David is forced to reckon with the decisions he made in Chaldea—choices that cost thousands their lives.